Shadow
of the
Storm

Books by Connilyn Cossette

OUT FROM EGYPT

Counted With the Stars

Shadow of the Storm

OUT FROM EGYPT · 2

SHADOW

of the

STORM

CONNILYN COSSETTE

BETHANYHOUSE
a division of Baker Publishing Group
Minneapolis, Minnesota

Published by Bethany House Publishers
11400 Hampshire Avenue South
Bloomington, Minnesota 55438
www.bethanyhouse.com

Bethany House Publishers is a division of
Baker Publishing Group, Grand Rapids, Michigan

Printed in the United States of America

Library of Congress Control Number: 2016938454

ISBN 978-0-7642-1821-7

Cover design by Jennifer Parker

Author is represented by The Steve Laube Agency.

16 17 18 19 20 21 22   7 6 5 4 3 2 1

To my beautiful and faithful mother—

Her wisdom teaches me
Her prayers surround me
Her love embraces me
Her heart hears me
Her friendship encourages me
Her strength inspires me.

Although I may not have been born of her body,
I am grateful to be a child of her heart.

When the people saw that Moses delayed to come down from the mountain, the people gathered themselves together to Aaron and said to him, "Up, make us gods who shall go before us. As for this Moses, the man who brought us up out of the land of Egypt, we do not know what has become of him." . . . So all the people took off the rings of gold that were in their ears and brought them to Aaron. And he received the gold from their hand and fashioned it with a graving tool and made a golden calf. And they said, "These are your gods, O Israel, who brought you out of the land of Egypt!"

Exodus 32:1, 3–4 ESV

1

SHIRA

17 TAMMUZ
4TH MONTH OUT FROM EGYPT

Wild drumbeats rumbled through the ground like distant thunder, pulsing in defiant rhythms and vibrating the hollows of my chest. My fingertips echoed the beat against my knee until a glare from my mother across the tent stilled their dance.

"Shira, finish your work." Her bone needle resumed its skillful motion as she bent her head to peer at her embroidery. The dim oil lamp highlighted the silvery strands that seemed to thread her dark hair more each day—a trend that had begun a few years ago, when my father died against an Egyptian whipping post.

I plucked at the black goat's wool in my lap, picking out thorny burrs, specks, and shards of leaves. The fibers snagged

7

against my thirsty palms. Unable to latch my attention on the tedious chore, I had been cleaning the same batch for most of the afternoon while my mind wandered up the rugged mountain path that Mosheh, our leader, had climbed forty days ago.

I imagined myself standing in his place, leaning on his staff and gazing out over the vast army of tents that flooded the valley floor, surveying the multitude he had led out of Egypt. Countless Hebrews camped here alongside a large number of *gerim*—Egyptians and other foreigners—all reveling in these last three months of freedom since the sea had swallowed Pharaoh's army.

As soon as Mosheh had vanished into the swirling storm that hovered over the summit, rumors began to multiply like flies on a rotting melon. Would he still lead us to Canaan, the land promised to our forefathers? Or had he slipped over the back side of the mountain range to flee south toward Midian? Was the old man even alive? Doubts buzzed around in my own mind, but I swatted them away with a shake of my head. Mosheh would return. He must.

Yet the golden idol standing on a group of boulders near the center of camp argued against my assertion. Aharon, Mosheh's own brother, had been swayed by those who insisted Mosheh was dead and allowed the bull-calf to be lifted up—a blatant disregard for the new laws spoken by Yahweh himself from the center of the fiery Cloud atop the mountain.

From her cross-legged position across the tent, Kiya gestured for my attention with a surreptitious tilt of her head and a darting glance at my mother. My Egyptian friend dared not cross the unspoken order for silence from the woman whose son she would soon marry, but her honey-gold eyes begged me to disobey in her place. The man she loved, my brother Eben, and her own brother, Jumo—both heavily armed—had been gone for hours at the command of the Levite elders.

Compelled by her wordless plea and my own curiosity, I chanced a question. "What is happening out there, *Ima*?"

Although the cadence of her needle faltered, my mother shook her head without looking up. "Nothing good."

"Must we stay inside all day?" I waved a useless hand in front of my overheated face. "Perhaps we could roll up a wall? Let in some air?"

Shoshana and Zayna, my two little sisters, lent their pleas to mine, begging our mother to let them play outside.

"No," said my mother, her tone brooking no argument. "You both will stay inside. The elders said to remain out of sight until this foolishness is over." She gestured for the girls to continue cleaning the mound of wool that sat between them on the rug. My mother's talent for weaving ensured that our temporary home was carpeted with vibrant designs of every hue, a luxury in this dusty wilderness.

Her adamancy piqued my curiosity again. "What will Mosheh do when he discovers Aharon made that idol?"

She scowled at me, her eyes dark as obsidian. "Aharon will regret such a reckless decision."

"Surely he won't let it get out of hand. He said the festival would be for Yahweh—"

"It already is more than out of hand. That abomination should never have been made." She punctuated her words with a resolute jab of her needle into the fabric and a pointed drop of her chin. There would be no more questions.

I flicked an apologetic glance at Kiya, but she had plunged into the distraction of her weaving. Her deft fingers danced across the handloom, lacing together a striking pattern of blue and white, a belt that would be presented to my brother Eben on their wedding day in three weeks' time.

Kiya resembled her mother more every day: the golden eyes, the sheen of her straight black hair, the easy laughter

9

and graceful move of her body. Nailah's legacy to her daughter had been a rare beauty that made her the envy of every woman—including me.

I was plain. Pale for a Hebrew, plagued by freckles, and with a body more like a child's than a woman's. I smoothed my woolen shift over my narrow hips, reminded again of their utter lack of promise. Arching against the dull ache in my lower back, I pressed a disobedient curl into my waist-length braid and my barren future into the back of my mind.

As lurking shadows deepened in the corners and the pile of clean wool grew in the basket at my knee, the revelry took on a different attitude, a more feverish tone. The pitch and sway of the music became more rhythmic and less melodious. By nightfall, shrieks, provocative laughter, and chanting rode on the breezes, sounds eerily reminiscent of the depraved temple worship back in Egypt, sounds that proved my mother had been right—Aharon had lost even the veneer of control.

As Kiya lit another oil lamp, I tugged at the neckline of my sleeveless gray shift. Although our small indoor cookfire had died out, its sharp smell lingered. The walls seemed to press closer with every smoke-laden breath. I longed to toss aside the wool in my lap, burst free of the suffocating tent, and reward my lungs with fresh evening air.

The drums stopped.

Deafening silence whooshed into the empty space, and my scalp prickled. I shivered in spite of the stifling heat. My mother's needle halted. My sisters had long since traded the sweltering boredom of our woolen prison for sleep; their slow breathing was the only intrusion into the menacing stillness.

"What happened?" I whispered to avoid waking the girls.

My mother shrugged, tight-lipped, as if reluctant to breathe.

Still and silent, the three of us focused on the far wall, as if the jutting black peak of the mountain were visible through the tight weave. The ear-splitting bray of a shofar sounded close by, echoed by others that returned the pattern. Although a familiar ring of communication, these calls were urgent, pained. Every hair on the back of my neck rose in response.

A call to arms? Or had I misheard the summons of the ram's horn?

The girls startled awake, their cries of confusion melding with an uproar that began to swell near the foot of the mountain. Something had put a swift end to the celebration.

Had Mosheh returned? What would he do? I struggled against the instinct to dash outside and see for myself. My mother gestured for my sisters to lay their heads on her lap. Her fingers stroked their dark curls, a steady outlet of nervous energy, as her eyes darted to the glint of the common fire through the slit of the door flap again and again.

The woolen wall billowed as someone ran by, the distended silhouette of a drawn sword in his hand. The hasty scuffle of his sandals against the pebbled ground dissipated into the night. I could hear little else over the stuttering pulse in my head as a thousand imagined outcomes flickered through my mind, stretching suffocating minutes into hours.

Would Mosheh leave us after such blatant disobedience against the edict not to bow to a graven image? Would Yahweh? Aharon may have declared the golden bull-calf an intermediary to the God who had rescued us from Egypt, but it resembled the sun-crowned god of fertility and strength that my Egyptian mistress had forced me to polish every day for four years. Apis.

Suddenly, just as on our last night in Egypt—the night all the firstborn sons were sacrificed for our freedom—keening cries lifted over the camp. My mother, Kiya, and I gaped at one another, mute with terror.

The cry of death.

Dreadful wails rang through the enclosed valley, echoing

against the granite cliffs, overlapping one another like endless waves on the shore. Dizzy and disoriented, I clamped my hands over my ears, bent forward like a broken reed. Would we all die tonight? Would the fearsome Cloud of Fire that had led us out from Egypt consume us all?

2

A torch outside soaked our tent wall with light. "Zerah!"
The woman's voice was laced with alarm. "Zerah!"
Pale and stricken, my mother rushed to meet the
source of such a plaintive call. Shoshana and Zayna huddled
together on their sleeping mat, arms tight around each other
and eyes wide. Kiya's frozen hand slithered into mine.

"Here I am, Reva." My mother's silhouette wavered on the
other side of the thin wall.

"I need you!"

"Is it my son?" My mother's voice faltered with concern for
her firstborn.

Kiya and I gasped in tandem. Would she lose Eben before they
even had the chance to begin their life together? Would I lose
my brother? What of Jumo, who had only just been freed from
a lifetime of captivity within a crippled body? Surely Yahweh
would not heal him only to let him be killed!

"No. No. Not Eben. Babies are coming," said Reva.

I stifled the cry of relief that sprang to my lips and squeezed
Kiya's hand to reassure both of us.

"There are not enough midwives. The atrocities have thrown

many women into labor. A few are in distress. I need every experienced hand. You helped me a time or two back in Egypt." The exhaustion in Reva's voice tugged at my empathy.

"Reva, tell me, what is happening? What is all the screaming?"

"Oh, Zerah. So many have died." The weight of Reva's sigh smothered my hope. "Mosheh is furious. When he saw the disgusting things those rebels were doing, he threw two stone tablets from the cliff. Smashed them to pieces."

"What was on the tablets?"

"No one knows. He confronted Aharon in front of everyone and challenged any who would fight on the side of Yahweh to come forward."

"The Levites?"

"Yes. Hundreds of them, perhaps all, obeyed Mosheh."

My heart swelled with pride in my brother and his loyalty to our leader.

"Many have died this night under Levite swords," said Reva. "Some with the meat of idol sacrifices still in their mouths."

Deflated and unable to rein in the bloody image her blunt statement conjured, I swallowed against the bile that stung my throat.

My mother groaned. "No wonder so many have gone into labor."

"I am attending three by myself. We must go, now."

"I cannot leave the girls." Her voice lowered. "What if things get worse?"

"They are safe. Look there. See? There are men stationed all around here, ready to defend the women. Come, I need you." Reva's assurances must have convinced my mother; the torchlight outlining their shadows faded to black as they sped off into the night.

I fidgeted with the end of my braid, wavering in the decision that had formed tentative roots. I had to do something—

anything—to get my mind off my brother's fate. The draw of assisting at a birth pulled at me with both hands until I could no longer resist.

"Stay with the girls," I said to Kiya as I sprang to my feet.

Little Zayna protested with a gap-toothed lisp. "Don't go, Shira!"

"All will be well." I kissed her forehead and then ten-year-old Shoshana's dark curls. "You are safe here. I need to go . . . I must help."

Kiya moved next to my sisters, wrapped her long arms around them, and gave them reassuring smiles. "The three of us will do just fine. You go." She winked with false enthusiasm. "Kiss a baby for me."

Could I find my mother and Reva? Had I hesitated too long? Momentarily engulfed in blackness, I shivered as my eyes adjusted. The glow of the ever-present column of light above the mountain cast deep purple shadows all around the campsite, but clouds veiled the stars. The shouts and cries from earlier had yielded to an eerie silence that spurred my imagination to ghastly conclusions.

I scrubbed at the chilled flesh on my arms and pressed into the dark maze of tents. Moving in the direction I had seen the torch disappear, I hoped someone along the way might guide me. But I was met with an empty path. Everyone around us must have taken seriously the directive to stay hidden inside. Only a few donkeys and goats huddled close to the tents, as if they too were obeying the command. Dimming cookfires glowed in the shadows, their remnants leaving a smoky sting in my nostrils.

Stumbling over an abandoned basket, I fell to one knee. A large hand grabbed my arm and pulled me upright. With startling clarity, my mind lurched back to Egypt. I cried out, seeing only the memory of an overseer's sneer and the ruthless gleam in his kohl-shadowed eyes as he stole everything from me. A hand pressed against my mouth. I struggled hard against its suffocating grip.

My captor rasped my name in my ear, and for a few savage heartbeats it was the overseer's voice and hot breath against my face—until I registered that it was Kiya's brother, Jumo, with an arm wrapped about my waist from behind and his gentle voice urging me to calm down, be still. My chest pounded furiously, but my body wavered with release.

"Shira," he whispered again. "Are you all right?"

I nodded, but cords of latent fear held my voice prisoner.

"Forgive me for startling you." He released me, and I slumped, my knees nearly buckling. He reached out to steady me, but I pulled away, not yet ready to be touched, even by a man I considered a brother.

Assembling my equilibrium, I pulled in one shaky breath after another, until my pulse slowed its breakneck speed.

Partially shrouded in shadow, Jumo stood silent. Only his dark eyes, bright with concern, were illuminated by the blue light from the mountain.

Someone from a neighboring tent called out, "What is going on out there?"

"I am fine." Forcing a laugh, I lifted my voice. "My friend caught me off guard. My apologies."

Jumo bent to pick up his sword. He must have dropped it in his haste to catch me. "I should have announced my presence. But you fell so quickly . . ." He slid the curved bronze *kopesh* into a leather scabbard—one of the many swords scavenged from the bodies of Pharaoh's soldiers at the edge of the sea that had engulfed them.

I waved a dismissive hand, amazed that it had already ceased trembling. "I was so focused on where I was going, I did not hear you approach."

"Where are you going in such a rush?" Jumo tugged at the

black beard that swathed his face. Unlike many of the Egyptians that traveled among us, he allowed his facial hair and his thick curls to grow freely, embracing his new identity as an Israelite. Yet the change since he had been healed a few weeks ago was even more striking—his unruly limbs were now straight and strong, his garbled speech clear and unfettered.

"I am looking for my mother and Reva. There are babies coming tonight. I need to help."

"I just passed them. I will take you there."

I smiled, hoping he would see that I was no longer frightened. But a thought flashed into my mind, erasing my pretense. "Where is Eben?"

His gaze cut to the mountain. "We were separated in the confusion. He has not yet returned?"

Confirmation lodged in my throat.

"He will, Shira. You needn't worry about your brother." He nudged me with his elbow. "Have you not seen that man wield a knife?"

I ignored his obvious attempt to distract me with humor. "What happened tonight, Jumo?"

His long sigh was wrapped in grief. "I'd rather not speak of it just now."

In uneasy silence we wound through camp until we heard the unmistakable cry of a laboring woman. We changed course to follow its summons and discovered my mother standing outside a large black tent with Reva's reassuring arm across her shoulders.

"I am a weaver, Reva, not a midwife." The tremble in my mother's voice surprised me.

Reva's pragmatic tone did not. "This one has given birth before. The baby is coming normally. Her mother and two aunts are here as well, and they will be an enormous help."

She patted my mother's shoulder. "I must go to the other girl.

She is much further along. Just be there to guide her, Zerah.
You've done this four times yourself, you know the process. Let
the body follow its natural course. You'll do fine." Reva nodded
and turned away, giving her no chance to waver. She knew how
to maneuver my mother—a feat not easily managed.

I stepped forward. "I can help as well."

My mother twisted her body around to glare at me. "No.
Shira, you should not be here."

"I want to help."

She regarded me with an utter lack of faith, and I met her
pointed stare with a silent plea. *Please. I cannot sit idle tonight.*

Reva came to my defense, arms firmly crossed and authority
in her voice. "She will be fine, Zerah. She is a strong girl. You
and I both know the extent of her strength."

Fighting the instinct to disagree with her assessment, I held
my breath. A bevy of emotions played across my mother's face—
doubt, anger, panic—but resignation conquered.

"All right, just this one time." My mother lifted a threatening finger. "But you will go with Reva and run any errands she
needs. You will not be in the way. Is that understood?"

"Yes, *Ima*."

A heady thrill stirred my senses as I followed Reva. A life
would be entering our camp tonight, and I would be there to
welcome it! Determined to take advantage of the distraction
from my missing brother, I blinked away the fleeting image of
Jumo walking back to camp, shoulders hunched, tunic soaked
in blood.

3

D isoriented by the black sea of tents, I skittered along to
keep up with Reva's brisk pace. As usual, the midwife's
wiry frame moved with relentless purpose, and two
small eyes above her hawk-beak nose threatened first blood on
anyone who dared cross her.

Reva was much older than my mother and had been a widow
herself most of her life. After my father was killed when I was
eleven, it was Reva who came to our mud-brick home and built
my mother back up after her world crumbled to dust.

"There are two more women in labor," she said over her
shoulder. "One is only in early stages and has given birth before.
I am more concerned about this other girl. The baby is in a
good position, but it is her first and she is a few weeks early."

Near the center of the Levite camp, she stopped and turned
those piercing eyes on me. "Are you ready for this? I told your
mother that I think you can handle it, but childbirth can be a
gory business. I can't have you fainting on me."

Was I ready? Could I endure the sight of a woman agonizing,
writhing in pain? There was only one way to know for sure.

I lifted my chin, ignored the violent flutter in my chest, and forced an even, confident tone. "I am."

The poor girl inside was sickly white, sweat running in great rivulets down her face and into her black hair. Another woman knelt next to her, rubbing the girl's lower back as she moaned and rocked back and forth.

"I cannot do this. I cannot," the girl groaned. She was so young, a few years younger than me—barely into her womanhood. Her eyes wheeled as she gripped the blanket with white knuckles, pain written so clearly on her face that an echo of it panged my heart.

"Now, Hadassah." Reva's usually brusque tone gentled and lowered. "Vereda tells me you have done very well so far. Soon you will hold your child in your arms."

After lighting two more oil lamps to brighten the tent, the midwife washed her hands in a nearby clay bowl. Vereda guided Hadassah to lay with her legs bent—all modesty set aside in relief that the midwife had arrived.

Although I had anticipated being unnerved by the process, I watched Reva with fascination. How many babies had her capable hands ushered into the world? The many lines around her eyes, like ripples in sand, attested to her concentration. She nodded as she examined Hadassah, mouthing a few unintelligible remarks to herself, and then patted the girl's knee.

"Almost there, my dear. Let's have you up and moving around now. The baby will come easier if you are standing and moving. Do whatever feels comfortable—rock, moan, yell if you need to."

I laid a hand on Vereda's shoulder. "May I give you a rest?"

"That would be wonderful. I must find my son, her husband—or find someone to send him word." She tugged at her fingers, voice dropping. "He has been gone since this morning, when the festival began."

Was Hadassah's husband involved in the worship of the

golden idol? I swallowed against the foul taste that coated my tongue. The Levites were at this moment carrying out Mosheh's orders. He may not return at all.

The pinch of Vereda's face told me she, too, was concerned that her son might be gone for good. I gave her the best of my reassuring smiles. "I will assist Hadassah so you can go."

I helped the girl to her feet and onto the two clay bricks designed to lift and support her as she labored. Placing my hands on her back, I rubbed gently.

"No." Hadassah moaned. "Press harder." Then, through clenched teeth, she cried out, "Oh! Another!" She threw her arms around her belly and screamed so loud my ears rang from the violence.

Reva squatted in front of her. "Are you ready to push?"

Hadassah nodded but drew her brows together, her brown eyes murky with fear.

"Breathe, my dear, breathe."

The girl released her air with a painful groan. "It hurts, it hurts!"

"Yes, it does, dear one. Bear down for me now. Lean back against Shira. She is little, but she is strong."

Hadassah leaned against me and squatted down on the birthing bricks. The girl screamed again and then bore down hard. Digging my toes into the sandy floor, I put my hands on her rock-hard belly and gently pushed, hoping it would help.

After a number of hard contractions with little respite, Hadassah's breaths shallowed into a pant. "I can't do this." She shook her head violently. "I am too tired. I need to lie down. Where is my husband?" She whimpered, sounding more like a little girl than a woman. "Where is he? I need my husband."

From her seat on the ground, Reva rubbed the girl's leg. "This is no place for a man. You are stronger than you know, Hadassah. Yahweh has prepared your body for this. Everything is working as it should. I know the pain, dear girl. But we are here: you, me, and Shira. We will bring this baby into the world. You are young, but you are as strong as every woman who has ever given birth."

Hadassah's legs wobbled and I struggled to hold her upright, digging my toes into the dirt floor.

"Stand firm," Reva said, whether to me or the laboring girl, I did not know, but I tightened my grip and tensed my muscles.

After another contraction, Reva declared she could see the head. But Hadassah sobbed, insisting with a piteous cry that she could no longer push.

"You must!" The midwife's brusque tone returned.

"No! No! No!" Hadassah screamed and thrashed about.

What could I do? Reason with her? I could not sympathize, could not even fathom the depths of her pain and fear. My interference would probably cause more harm than good. Yet something deep inside commanded me—*Sing.*

In the wilderness after we had crossed the sea, when my sisters were starving to death and their bodies lay lifeless from thirst, my songs had distracted them, calmed their fears. Perhaps it might do the same for Hadassah. Hope surging, I opened my mouth and sang a wordless tune, the flush of foolishness hot on my cheeks.

Hadassah moaned and bucked against me. I pulled her back, pressed my mouth close to her ear, and sang a lullaby that my mother had sung to me long ago. Within the first verse, Hadassah's shoulders dropped, her breathing slowed and, although she still moaned, she did not try to pull away. I sang through the next contraction, and the next, and somehow the girl summoned strength to push the baby free of her body.

The surge of elation at the sight and sound of a squalling baby boy was staggering. The force of emotion flowed through me like a crashing river. It was more than a miracle, it was the imagination of the Creator wrapped in the skin of a newborn babe. He blinked fresh eyes at the brightness of his new world.

The pure joy of the moment was marred by Hadassah's next question. "Where is Nadir? My husband will want to see our boy."

"He will come." My mind protested the lie, but I composed a smile and brushed sweat-drenched hair from her face.

Reva laid the sweet baby, covered in birth-slime, across Hadassah's chest. The cord that connected the two of them still pulsed with life. All concern for her husband faded into wonder as the young mother gazed into her son's eyes, cooing and stroking his swollen face with a finger. After the cord was severed, Reva gently showed Hadassah how to guide him to his first meal. Hadassah's eyes shone with pride when he latched to her breast with little effort, his downy head moving in eager rhythm as he suckled.

Reva winked. "An eater, this one. He will be strong as a rock."

Eben. Just like my brother.

Hadassah glanced up at me, then back to her precious boy. "Yes, a rock. We will call you Eben, little one."

Had I offered the name out loud? I fluttered my hand, embarrassed at my presumption. "Should you not wait until your husband returns to name him?"

"Without you and your beautiful voice calming me, I could not have endured the pain. Your song blunted my agony. In honor of you, my rock this night, I will name my son Eben since I cannot name him Shira."

Startled by his mother's giggle, little Eben lost his source of food and made sure we all took note of his displeasure. The thought that this sweet child might never meet his abba made my own laughter seem false in my ears. I knew the void of fatherlessness only too well.

My thoughts flew to my brother Eben and the grim, dangerous task given to him by Mosheh. Would I lose the brother who had taken up the mantle of responsibility after our father had been murdered? The brother who would do anything to protect me?

DVORAH

My husband's body was still, dark blood oozing from the gash where a sword had penetrated his side. Every hope I'd ever had lay dead with him.

He had laughed at me this morning when I'd begged him to stay, or to take me along to the festivities—even pushed me out of the way when I threatened and cursed and stood in front of the door flap. "I'll go where I want, when I want, Dvorah," he had said. Now, he lay facedown in the dirt, his impossibly light hair reflecting the last flickers of the common fire, steps away from our tent.

How will we survive now?

Around me, the sounds of mourning rose and fell, the tremulous wails calling attention to the number of the dead all over camp. Ice flooded my limbs. Would they kill us all? Would that crazy, voice-hearing Mosheh murder the families of the fallen as well? My stomach contracted painfully. What of Matti, my little son, who slept nearby, blissfully unaware that his father had been slaughtered like a pig? How had they found Tareq here, on the edge of the camp? So far from the Apis idol near the center of the valley? Only a few more paces and he would have made it inside.

"You there!" a voice shouted.

Startling, I scrambled away from Tareq's body. I sprang to my feet as a tall man carrying a torch strode up to me, dagger outstretched, tunic stained with blood. "Open your mouth," he commanded.

"My mouth?"

He leaned over me, pressing the point of his weapon into my collarbone. "Now."

Disoriented by the strange order, I obeyed. Sheathing his dagger, he gripped my jaw in his large palm, jerked it upward, and squeezed my cheeks together as he lifted the torch higher to inspect my mouth. With a grunt he let go. "You're clean."

"Why would you care about my mouth?" I snapped, rubbing my chin.

"It's not red." He pointed at Tareq's body with the torch, the light illuminating the bright crimson of his lips. "Only looking for the ones who drank the red beer."

Of course. If revelers partook of the sacred ochre-tainted drink to drown their inhibitions, their crimson mouths would be easy to distinguish.

"You know that man?" he said, tipping his head toward Tareq.

The father of my child? "No." I flicked a dismissive hand at my husband's body. "I heard a commotion. Thought I could help."

"Get back inside, then. All of us Levites are scouring camp, cutting down every rebel involved in that disgusting display. Good thing Mosheh came back when he did. Could have been worse." He shook his head and walked away, bloody dagger again at his side and knotted tassels of his garment swinging to the rhythm of his gait.

I cursed the arrogant Levite under my breath. Worse than the murder of the only man who'd ever protected me? Worse than a fatherless boy? What could possibly be worse than being a half-Egyptian widow in a multitude of Hebrews?

Seized with a violent pain in my abdomen, I doubled over, retching on the ground. I had been wrong. It could be much worse.

SHIRA

Closing my eyes, I pulled a deep breath through my nose. The fresh air combated the weariness that had washed over me as soon as I placed my foot outside Hadassah's tent. A little white dog flashed through the deserted campsite, yipping at the sunrise.

"You did well, Shira." Reva wrapped a sturdy arm around my shoulders. "And singing to calm Hadassah—I have never thought of such a thing before. However—" She chuckled. "My singing would make the pain of labor harder, not ease it."

I brushed away her compliment with a flip of my hand. "Music settles my own soul, chases away the shadows. It's my first reaction when others are anxious as well."

"It did the job." She adjusted the leather pouch at her waist that held the tools of her trade. "Have you ever considered midwifery?"

My heart thrilled at the tiny seed her question planted. To experience the miracle of birth, day after day? To know the things Reva knew and guide a new life to its mother? To see hundreds of babes catch their first breath, blink their eyes for the first time?

Marriage, my own children—they were an implausible dream. But was midwifery a possibility? My stomach ached with the wanting, but before I could respond, reality slammed a flat palm over the notion. My mother would never allow such a thing. She had said "just this once" tonight, and she had meant it. I could never bear the disapproval in my mother's eyes if I went against her.

Swallowing the knot in my throat that tangled with the compulsion to say yes, I shook my head. "I have been weaving with my mother since I was smaller than Zayna."

Reva looked down her long nose at me, one wispy silver brow lifted high. "That is not what I asked."

My mother had made it clear, without a word, that I would learn her trade—the trade she'd learned from her own mother, as did her mother before her, the trade that had sustained us after my father was killed. Zerah's talent was the continuation of skills cultivated, stitch by stitch, by each successive generation. I could not break the chain and let my mother down in such a selfish way, even if every part of me yearned to follow another path.

Conflict raged inside me, but I arched a flippant tone into my voice. "It was a wonderful experience, but I love weaving. Thank you, though, for allowing me to help."

Reva was not fooled. "Shira. Look at me."

I faced her with reluctance. Wisps of mottled, silvery-brown hair stuck out at all angles from her loosened braids.

"I watched you with Hadassah." She narrowed her eyes, red-rimmed from lack of sleep and old age. "Your cheerful manner and unflappable demeanor is perfect for working with laboring mothers. You should discuss this with your mother."

She scrutinized me. "Or." She tapped her chin. "Shall I?"

"No!" I put a hand out, then snatched it back, embarrassed at my insolence.

She crossed her arms, determination etched in the many lines of her face.

I pressed my hands together in a plea. "I will . . . I will think it over and talk to my mother and my brother, if need be."

Eben. Urgency slammed into my gut. Jumo's bloody tunic once again stained my vision, and I ran from Reva with quick apologies over my shoulder. With every footfall, dread built inside me like the menacing cloud of sand that had crowded over the horizon. I raced toward camp, desperate to see my brother's face.

But it was Jumo I saw first as I entered the clearing, huddled on the ground near the remains of the cookfire, his black curls against his bent knees. Slithering fear coiled in my stomach as I approached him. I pulled my headscarf tight across my face to avoid the stinging lash of the sand-laden winds. "Where is Eben?"

He peered up at me, his face pale and troubled. "He returned just after sunrise." He tipped his head toward the tent he shared with Eben. "Your mother and Kiya are in there with him, and a healer as well."

Relief rushed out of me in a huff of air. *Only someone still living would need a healer.* "What happened?"

"He will live. The sword only grazed his side, but his hand is wounded. They are unsure whether he will have use of it again."

My brother built musical instruments; his livelihood dependent on the use of those skilled hands. Music was like air to my brother, he would suffocate without it. As heartsick as I was for my brother, I knew Jumo felt the same. Eben had become a brother to him since we left Egypt—and, in some ways, a replacement for the father who died with the other Egyptian firstborn sons.

There was nothing either of us could do for the brother we loved except wait. Without a word, I sat beside Jumo, drew up my own knees, and tucked my head into the gap.

Although I tried to concentrate on lifting prayers to Yahweh for Eben's quick healing, my mind returned again and again to Reva's tempting suggestion that I learn midwifery alongside her. A fleeting image bubbled up—a picture of myself as a midwife, holding a baby in my arms and placing it on a new mother's chest. Trickling though me with the refreshing coolness of a gentle brook, the idea almost seemed to whisper my name. Did I have the courage to approach my mother with such an audacious suggestion?

5

18 TAMMUZ
4TH MONTH OUT FROM EGYPT

Before today, Mosheh had always been a tiny blur against a faraway wall of granite to me. But now only twenty paces separated us from the new stone barrier that divided the mountain from the multitude. The tribe of Levi had been brought close, a reward for faithfulness at great cost. I would finally see our enigmatic leader in person.

My brother stood behind me, wounded side bound and destroyed hand swathed in thick linens—a stark example of the sacrifice the Levites had offered on the altar of loyalty last night. And a horrendous task it had been, for nearly as many Hebrews as *gerim* lay beneath the desert sand. Three thousand men and women joined together in death by folly.

I wondered how Hadassah and her little boy fared. The young mother should be wrapped in joy over her new son, not dressed in sackcloth for her faithless husband. I searched Eben and Jumo's stoic faces, trying not to wonder if one of them had dispatched little Eben's father from this world. Reva had delivered confirmation of his death this morning, along with compensation for my mother's help in the form of a soft kidskin bag.

Although I had hinted at it a few times, my mother had not asked me about last night. I brushed Reva's suggestion aside, again chiding myself for even considering such a selfish thing when my brother's ability to provide for his family was at stake.

A shofar demanded our attention as Mosheh appeared on the rocky promontory above the crowd. With Zayna's hand in mine, I took a few steps forward and stood on my toes to attempt a glimpse at his face.

My mother had once described Mosheh's appearance as a young man, when his wide shoulders bore the royal robes of a prince. She'd said he was handsome, strong, and exuded confidence. But he was past his eightieth year now, forty of which were spent in the unforgiving desert tending sheep. The two epochs of his life could not have been more different. Royal life in the glittering palaces of Pharaoh stood in sharp contrast to the humility of life among livestock.

His bearing, however, was still regal. He stood a head taller than the men gathered around him, and the strong set of his shoulders no doubt resembled his days as commander over the armies of the Two Lands. This was no bent elder. No bedraggled shepherd. This was a soldier standing above us, chin high. He appeared almost ageless, in spite of his silvery hair. The light from the Cloud refracted against it, lending an odd shimmer to his head—as though lit from behind.

Scouring the crowd with a slow, piercing gaze, Mosheh's eyes met mine for the briefest of moments. My breath snagged. A curious feeling, that somehow he could see straight into my weak soul and divine the foolishness and the doubts held within, stole over me.

Mosheh nodded to the man next to him, and a shofar sounded nearby. Then he lifted one hand high into the air until all eyes were on him and every mouth still, as if waiting for a large gathering of children to come to attention.

His lips moved, but the relentless desert wind swallowed his voice. However, Mosheh was not speaking to us, but to someone beside him. Aharon, I assumed. The irony of a man who had commanded Pharaoh's armies of thousands yet lacked the confidence to address his own people was not lost on me.

I knew Aharon to be a man of words, a man of great intelligence, but I was not prepared for the power of his voice and the resonance that rang throughout the valley, as if his words had wings that delivered them to my ears.

"Yahweh has seen your rebellion." The accusation was delivered with precision. Aharon paused, scrutinizing the dumbstruck crowd. "His anger against your disobedience burns hot. He freed you from Pharaoh, by his own hand. Yet you hasten to sell yourselves back into slavery to Egypt's gods."

I stole a look at the Cloud, which hovered above the highest peak. The light emanating from its glow flamed orange and red instead of the gentle blue that normally characterized its presence. I could almost feel the heat against my face.

"Yahweh is *kadosh*. Separate. Holy. There will not be such blatant sin against his Holy Name within this camp," Aharon continued. "You too were called out, to be *kadosh*. You have broken covenant with Adonai. And those who turned their eyes to idols were not spared."

A shiver spiraled in my belly as I watched Aharon speak condemnation of his own behavior. His life had been spared for his part in the building of the idol, but his countenance spoke of heavy grief. Would Mosheh's brother endure a harsher consequence for his disobedience?

"Mosheh returned from the top of the mountain with two tablets containing the Ten Words, inscribed by the very finger of Yahweh himself, laws that now lay shattered in pieces."

Curious murmurs buzzed around me. Reva had said that Mosheh had thrown down two tablets that night. What did it mean, that he had destroyed the very laws that undergirded the covenant with Yahweh? What would be the consequence for breaking such a treaty—a royal suzerain contract made between a king and his subjects—confirmed by our lips and the blood of sacrifice?

With a gesture to the Cloud, Aharon answered my question. "Yahweh is leaving. He has refused to go with you any farther."

I clapped my hand to my mouth. Without Yahweh's protection and provision, we would perish. He fed us with manna, the miracle grain that accumulated on the ground each morning to sustain us. He provided enough fresh water for millions from the heart of a rock. Without Yahweh's help, we had no chance against another vicious attack by the Amalekites, or of standing against the Canaanites, the fierce tribes that inhabited the land promised to us.

Aharon waved his arms until the protest quieted. "However . . . Mosheh will go back to the mountaintop and plead with Yahweh on your behalf."

Again Aharon's voice was overcome by shouts begging him to do whatever Yahweh asked.

"You will take off your ornaments," yelled Aharon over the uproar, "the jewels and the gold given to you by the hands of the Egyptians, and mourn for the wrong done here. Without full repentance, you have no hope of appealing to Yahweh for forgiveness. You will *all* suffer the consequences for your silence in the face of such grievous sin against Yahweh."

Loud murmuring rippled through the crowd and, by the drop of his shoulders, I could tell that Aharon, too, felt the sting of such a harsh statement.

When the furor calmed, Aharon pointed to a few large pots that stood next to the wide stream flowing down the mountain and through camp. Together with the torrent from the rock that Mosheh had split with a strike of his staff, the stream fed a small lake, providing enough water for all of us in this desiccated land.

Aharon motioned to a few young men nearby who began lifting the pots one by one and dumping the contents into the stream.

"Look, Israel," he called out. "Mosheh has burnt up your golden abomination and ground it to a fine powder. Now you will drink the ash of your sins. You will remember the bitterness of Yahweh's anger toward you. You will smell the stench that fills his nostrils when you break his perfect laws."

With the sunlight flagging in the west, I could not see the remains of the Apis idol as it was consumed by the waters, but a bitter, metallic smell assaulted me. Gagging, I covered my nose and pulled Zayna closer. What had they done to the sweet waters that flowed from the heart of the mountain?

Thunder rumbled from the Cloud at the summit, as if in confirmation of Aharon's pronouncement and a reminder of the terrifying sound of Yahweh's pure voice on the day of the Covenant. Screams and shouts ripped through the crowd, overtaking Aharon's words.

"He poisoned the waters!"

"Yahweh! Have mercy!"

"Will we all die this time?"

The once reverently hushed crowd now roiled with fear. Some prostrated themselves in the dirt, begging Yahweh to spare them and their children. Many turned and ran. Swept up in collective panic, the press of bodies pushed Zayna and me forward with a jolt. The sudden chaos reminded me of the long moments on the beach when Pharaoh cornered us with our backs to the sea and people went wild with fear and rebellion.

I considered slinging Zayna onto my hip, but her legs would trail past my knees. Instead, I pulled her close, one arm tight around her shoulders and the other gripping her little hand. Fear brimmed in her eyes, tears threatening to spill down her cheeks. Over the tumult, I assured her that she would be safe, ignoring the echo of her panic in my own chest. I looked around for my family—but others had filled the gap between us. I could not even see Jumo's head above the crowd.

A shofar drowned out my pleas to let us through. The desperate bleat issued an order for calm, but few heeded the call. Instead, the multitude began to flee in all directions. The surge of people forced Zayna and me forward again, further cutting us off from our family and locking us into a cauldron of swirling bodies and blinding dust.

Someone knocked into me, jamming an elbow into my back. I cried out in pain as my leg buckled. I fell forward, pulling Zayna down with me. Someone stepped on my fingers and slammed a knee into my head. I bit my lip against the scream that kindled inside me as I tightened my hold on my precious sister.

Buffeted on all sides and tasting dirt churned up by a million feet, I could do nothing but cling to Zayna and pray we would not be trampled to death in this panicked crush.

A strong hand wrapped around my arm, pulling me to my feet, my sister along with me. "Give me the girl!" commanded a deep voice.

I whipped my head up. A man towered over us, the growing twilight muting his features. Only his short, dark hair, a well-trimmed beard, and the gleam of the Cloud's light in his eyes were discernible.

Shrinking away, I pulled my sobbing sister closer to my body, my pulse racing a jagged beat. Was this man a rescuer? Or fresh danger? Although his concern for our safety seemed genuine, I was not about to hand my sister over to a stranger.

"I am a friend of Eben's," the man hollered over the deafening noise. "You'll both be crushed! Please!"

A woman screamed nearby, making the decision for me. We would not make it back to our tent without help. Swallowing against the terror that clawed my throat, I relinquished my hold on Zayna as the man scooped her up and then wrapped his long fingers around my arm.

Dragging me along behind him, he pressed forward into the swirling chaos of bodies, his tall form protecting me from the onslaught. Zayna's face peeked over his shoulder, her brown eyes wide and full of terror.

The man spoke into Zayna's ear. She regarded him with suspicion for a moment before the promise of a smile ticked in her cheek. She nodded her head and then looked back at me, all fear erased from her countenance. What had he said that tempered her panic?

The crowd thinned the closer we came to the Levite encampment, and the man asked me to lead the way through the narrow paths between tents. A chain of cookfires led me through the dark to our campsite.

"Shira! Zayna!" Shoshana's voice rang out. "They are back!" Ever the lookout, my sister was perched atop a wagon. She shimmied down like a monkey and flew to me, dark brown hair streaming like ribbons behind her. With strength that belied her ten years, she pulled herself to me, her tears soaking my tunic. "What happened? We could not see you. Eben tried and tried to find you and Zayna, but there were so many people—"

I kissed her forehead to halt the hysterical barrage of questions. Although my head ached from the blows I had received, my scuffed fingers stung, and oncoming bruises throbbed in my hip and my shoulder, I reassured her that we were unharmed.

My mother approached, arms folded across her chest and a stern look on her face—an expression I knew well. "You should have stayed closer," she said, her thick brows lowering in censure. "You both could have been killed."

It would profit me nothing to argue with her. Although we were the same height, I shrank beneath her scrutiny. My mother was the strongest woman I knew, her mettle forged by years without a husband and endurance under the heavy hand of the Egyptian overseers. It was by her determination alone that her four children were alive. From my earliest memories, my mother was in motion, her hands always busy at one task or another, as if occupation itself kept her from disintegrating.

Even now she shifted from foot to foot, her eyes roving over me as if to ensure that I was indeed uninjured. I had the feeling she was restraining herself from grabbing me by the shoulders and shaking me senseless.

Kiya's tear-streaked face hovered over my mother's shoulder. "How did you make it through that chaos? More than a few people were trampled to death."

That could have been Zayna and me, bloodied and lifeless on the valley floor. My mother was right to be angry, I should not have stepped away from my family. My poor choice nearly cost my sweet sister her life.

"Eben's friend saved us." I glanced at the tall stranger speaking with my brother across the campsite. He was gesturing to Eben's injury, obviously surprised by the severity. The flickering cookfire highlighted sympathy on his brow. It was clear he'd told the truth about his friendship with my brother, but why had I not met him before now? And how had he recognized Zayna and me in the midst of such upheaval?

He clapped Eben on the back, nodded a swift farewell to me, and then vanished into the dark like a phantom—as if we had been delivered back to the arms of our family by a benevolent spirit of the night.

6

I thought you were coming to help me this morning."

"Ayal!" My brother beckoned the man with a wave of his good hand. "Come, join us. There is plenty."

A surge of gratitude muddled with a disturbing flight of nerves at the sight of my rescuer—who, in the daylight, clearly resembled flesh and blood instead of the apparition of my imaginings for the last seven days.

"I've had my share of manna today." Ayal patted his flat stomach with a grin. "Just heading out to help my brothers."

"I told you I'm not up to helping yet, my friend." Eben gestured to his useless arm.

Ayal peered down at Eben. "What? Too busy staring at the cookfire? It's been a week. At least keep me company while I shear. You can toss fleece into the wagon with your good arm."

Eben scowled up at Ayal. With feet planted and arms across his long torso, Ayal seemed unwilling to take no for an answer, as if he had determined to distract my brother from his grief.

Ayal must be Hebrew, but I suspected there was Egyptian

somewhere in his bloodline. His hair was almost black, his skin a rich copper, undoubtedly burnished from shepherding out in the elements. Against its depths and rimmed by thick lashes, his light brown eyes glowed amber, as if backlit by the sun.

Now that I could see Ayal's face clearly, there was something about him—perhaps I was imagining it—but had I seen him somewhere before? Thousands of men camped around us, just within the Levite tribe, so he simply must have crossed my path, even before he saved my sister and me.

My brother huffed in acquiescence, running a hand through his wavy, shoulder-length hair. "All right. I will come with you as soon as I finish here." He winked at Kiya with the first bit of tease I had seen out of him in days. "Wouldn't want to waste this meal made by my bride."

The humor in his green-gray eyes reminded me of our father. The eye color Eben and I had inherited was the only tangible thing I had of my abba—other than scattered memories of his rich laughter, his stories, and his silvery voice lifted in song.

Kiya nudged Eben with her elbow. "I am not your bride yet. Still time to change my mind."

I laughed out loud, grateful that Eben had been yanked out of his black mood, but slipped my hand over my mouth when he directed a mocking glare my way. Kiya's threat was without teeth; she adored him and would no more break the betrothal than shave her head. Although Kiya was still grieving her beautiful mother, Eben's devotion had seemed to blunt the sharp loss a bit. He never passed by her without a gentle caress to her face, a touch to her hand, or a stolen kiss. They were tethered by a depth of affection that caused a curious ache in the pit of my stomach.

Returning from a trek to the stream, Shoshana and Zayna bounded into the campsite ahead of my mother. The girls were growing fast, their little legs stretching long under their tunics. We would need to make them new clothes soon.

As usual, they both plopped down near Eben, who fit easily into his role as father and brother to the girls. Zayna crawled into his lap and tugged on the end of his beard.

He scrunched his face into an artificial frown. "I need to get up, sister. I must help Ayal with the sheep. He is forcing me."

"I want to go!" She bounced up and down, her unruly dark curls—so like mine—springing to life. "Ayal said I could come see the baby lambs!"

Ah. That must be what had brightened her mood that night when Ayal whispered into her ear. A distraction brought about by a promise to see a lamb. The mischief in Ayal's eyes confirmed my guess.

Eben winced as Zayna jostled his injured hand. "You will only be in the way. And I cannot watch you."

She pressed out her bottom lip and widened her brown eyes into moon-sized pleas.

"No, Zayna, I cannot supervise you during shearing. It is a big job."

"I'll come and watch the girls, Eben, so they won't be under your feet," I offered, eager for a diversion.

A heavy pall of mourning had hung over the camp for days. The metallic bitterness of Mosheh's rebuke had finally run its course, and fresh water flowed in abundance again, but the remembrance of its sickening smell and acerbic taste would linger long in my memory. Perhaps the excursion would also distract me from the nagging desire to beg my mother for permission to accept Reva's offer, if only for a while.

"Yes! Please! Oh, please, brother! We will be good! We promise!" Shoshana joined the chant, and both girls plied Eben with giggles and kisses. Of course he would give in. Our brother was no match for little-girl persuasion.

"You must stay near Shira." He gave his best fatherly glare. They nodded solemnly.

Lifting her eyes from the black and brown fabric she was weaving on a ground loom, my mother gave me a pointed look. "You may go for a while. But we must finish that last tent wall today, and I need your help."

Another reason to join the excursion. My wool-worn palms were parched, and my shoulders ached from hunching over the ground loom, fashioned from acacia poles hammered into the rocky soil. A delay, even a small one, was welcome.

Hand in hand, the girls and I followed Eben and Ayal southward through the camp to where the flock was penned in a wide wadi. An offshoot of the stream from the mountain murmured through the thirsty canyon, sustaining plenty of green for the small flock that Ayal and his brothers maintained. Although the animals enjoyed the manna on the ground each morning, just as we did, they seemed to have a compulsion to nibble at the abundant desert grasses and thorny acacia bushes to bide their time.

These sheep were in desperate need of shearing. Their woolly brown coats hung heavy, tangling in the prickly vegetation that populated the wadis. Ayal's brothers were already at work, the three men laboring in tandem, each holding down a sheep with one arm and using the other to clip the wool. I watched, fascinated at the quick work they made of the task as one fleece after another was tossed into the wagons.

At the sight of a ewe with spotted twin lambs tottering behind, Shoshana wrenched her hand from my grip and surged toward them. Startled, the ewe bounded away, her babies scurrying behind her. Defeated, Shoshana returned with a pout. "I only wanted to pet one." She crossed her arms with a huff.

Eben and I exchanged amused glances. Our ten-year-old sister was notorious for rushing into situations without considering consequences.

"Sheep can be very skittish around people they aren't familiar with," said Eben. "It's how they protect themselves from predators. Why don't we let Ayal find you a lamb to touch instead?"

With a quick wink at Shoshana, Ayal obliged and, after only a few large strides, snatched up a lamb. Kneeling down, he held the lamb in his arms and invited the girls to come closer. Having learned her lesson, Shoshana approached more slowly this time, her hand outstretched. The little animal responded with a pathetic bleat and struggled before submitting to her ministrations.

"These two were born in the last week," said Ayal. "Most came earlier in the season. It's always frustrating when new ones arrive during shearing."

"So very sweet." I scratched the lamb between his ears. "Do you want to pet the lamb, Zayna?" My youngest sister was curled around Eben's leg, her earlier excitement having melted into trepidation.

After some encouragement from Eben, she reached toward the lamb but jerked back her hand as soon as its ear flicked forward, sliding behind our brother again.

"It's all right, Zayna. The lamb won't hurt you," he said.

She curved her face away, expression shuttered.

"It's all right. You don't have to touch him now." He bent down to slip an arm around her shoulders. "We'll just watch the lambs for a while, all right?" He offered his hand, and they walked off toward the herd, Shoshana trotting ahead of them, attempting to corral the other twin lamb against the canyon wall with her outstretched arms as the ewe looked on warily. The baby skittered off to its mother with a pitiful bleat.

"Zayna was bitten a few weeks ago," I told Ayal, "by a neighbor's dog. Since then, she shies away from all animals."

"Ah. Understandable." He scratched the lamb beneath the chin, and the little one closed its eyes to relish the attention.

"The bite didn't break skin, but I fear it may leave a scar just the same. The animal knocked her down and clamped onto her arm so quickly none of us could react. I hate to think what would have happened had she been alone." I scrubbed the shiver from my arms, surprised at the sudden chill that flashed through me. Not all animals walked on four legs.

Looking up at me, Ayal's gaze roamed my face, as if somehow he'd sensed the shadows behind my words.

I lifted sunshine into my smile to avoid the scrutiny of the stranger who had whisked me from danger and then had brushed through my thoughts too many times since. "I must thank you, though, for what you did for Zayna and me. How did you know that I was Eben's—?"

A sharp cry interrupted my question, and Ayal's chin jerked toward the sound. He freed the lamb and, with a quick apology and a beckoning gesture to Eben, strode away, disappearing behind a boulder. Had some wild animal gotten ahold of a sheep?

Eben followed Ayal, and curiosity caused my feet to do the same. The path behind the boulder curved up into the hill. I could hear Eben and Ayal talking nearby, voices overlapped by the sounds of a sheep in distress.

Telling the girls to stay close, I followed the narrow ditch that served as a footpath, keeping watch for snakes as we stepped around prickly bushes and desert primroses.

The men were tending a ewe that lay tangled in the brush, her sides heaving as she panted and thrashed, much like Hadassah had during labor. I'd seen enough animals giving birth to know that the ewe's huffing bleats and the saliva spilling from her mouth indicated a complication.

Ayal cleared the brush and helped her to her feet, then guided her toward a clear patch of ground. A shofar blew back toward camp, its notes bouncing off the granite boulders around us. Eben shielded his eyes against the glare of the morning sun, standing very still, as if straining to discern the echoed patterns against the hills. When the ram's horn sounded again, his frown deepened. A Levite signal, one calling all heads of households to meet.

"There must be something wrong. I should go. Ayal, I am sorry."

"Of course. Go find out what is happening. You can return later." Ayal clapped Eben on his good shoulder. "Such is the burden of a firstborn. Glad I am not the eldest."

"I'll walk you girls back home on my way," Eben said, waving a hand to Zayna and Shoshana. "Shira will stay and help you with the ewe, Ayal."

My stomach clenched, and I stepped back, stammering, "Me? But I—"

"She may look little, but she is surprisingly strong," Eben said with a grin. "Almost beat me at arm-wrestling once. Besides, she'll be more help than me anyhow." He lifted his bandaged hand. I tossed him an anxious glance that I hoped Ayal would not notice.

"I would appreciate your help, Shira. This ewe needs assistance." Ayal scrubbed at his beard. "I'd rather not interrupt my brothers during shearing, especially since Yonah will have to go to the meeting as well. She's fairly small, though, so all you'd have to do is hold her still."

With silent acknowledgment of the reason for my hesitation, Eben reassured me with a look that communicated sincerity. "I know Ayal well, sister. He is a fellow Levite. I would trust him with my life. And yours." He squeezed my shoulder.

My gaze flicked from my brother to Ayal, and confusion reigned in Ayal's light brown eyes. Guilt for my quick judgments warred with my fear, and curiosity conflicted with my instincts to run. Somehow, the fervent desire to experience another birth conquered them all.

I clasped my hands together to hide their trembling and mustered a smile to mask the panic swimming in my chest. "I would be glad to help."

"Good. Ayal will see you safely to camp when you are finished," he said, his tone again promising complete faith in his friend. "I'll see you in a while." He turned and walked away, Shoshana and Zayna hand in hand behind him, leaving me staring at my brother's back, alone with a strange man for the first time since Egypt.

7

My stomach lurched. In spite of my brother's assurances, a tight fist of fear gripped my throat. I retreated a step, muscles tense and ready to flee.

I must have gone pale because Ayal put out a hand to steady me. "Shira?" Confusion swept across his face, followed by concern.

Surely Ayal would not hurt me. My overprotective brother trusted him enough to leave me with him, and Ayal had cared enough about Eben to drag him away from his moping around the campsite. So why would my heart not slow its erratic rhythm?

"Perhaps I should get one of my brothers . . ." Ayal's tone was gentle as he ran his fingers through his fine, dark hair.

I inhaled, hoping he would attribute my trepidation to anxiety about helping with the ewe, instead of being alone with him. "No, I am fine. Let's help this *ima* with her baby."

The ewe was straining heavily against the contractions, her nose in the air. Circling again and again, she bleated, tossing her brown head back and forth.

Arms spread wide, Ayal and I corralled the ewe in the shade of an acacia. She made no move to escape, as if she understood our desire to ease her suffering. With a slow approach, Ayal rubbed the ewe's back and breathed soft assurances. She quieted, but her eyes still wheeled about.

He glanced up at me. "Can you hold her steady? I must see if the lamb is breech."

I wound my arms tightly about the woolly neck, echoing Ayal's gentle words to calm the agonized sheep as she labored. The pleading in her luminous eyes cut into me.

Remembering how my voice had calmed Hadassah, I leaned close to the ewe's ear, rubbed the bridge of her brown nose, and sang a quiet tune. After a few moments, she huffed and stilled. I grazed the back of my fingers against her smooth cheek, and she leaned into the caress.

"Has she not lambed before?" I looked back to find Ayal watching me, a little smirk tugging at his lips. A flush warmed my cheeks.

He smothered his amusement. "No, she is so small, we had hoped she would avoid the ram for another few months. But nature had its way." Ayal's face contorted with concentration as he examined the ewe. "Hmm. The lamb is not breech, but the front legs are bent down. Coming nose first."

"Oh. Poor thing. No wonder she is hurting." I bent to speak into her ear. "Don't worry. Ayal will help you."

He grunted as he pulled. Then he shook his head. "I cannot get the leg to turn. It's twisted at a strange angle." Frustration darkened his face. "I'm not sure I will be able to help her."

"Is there something I can do?"

He kneaded the back of his neck. "Not unless you can get that leg turned around."

Fluttery nerves unfurled inside my stomach, but I assured him I would try.

"Your hands are very small." Apprehension colored his tone.

"They are." I lifted my palms. "But that may be an advantage."

He shifted his stance and scratched at his arm. "I suppose it could not hurt. But prepare yourself, it's gruesome work."

"I'll be fine. I am . . . I will soon be training to become a midwife."

Reva's offer to learn the secrets of midwifery had taken a fierce hold on my imagination. I had considered the idea, tossed it out, picked it up again to examine each facet, hidden it under my pillow at night, and a few times, when alone with Kiya, nearly let it spill out of my mouth. The desire to accept was nearly unbearable. But I knew what my mother's arguments would be.

Too young. Inexperienced. Unmarried.

All true.

All valid.

Ayal arched his brows, but with a shrug of his shoulders, he moved aside.

Eager to show him—and myself—that I was made of heartier material than he assumed, I took up my place behind the ewe as Ayal held her in an iron grip.

Summoning a blank expression to mask any internal reactions, I reached inside to feel for the lamb's nose, then trailed my fingers down to its shoulders. The ewe bucked against me suddenly, and I lost my grip.

"It's all right if you cannot get it," said Ayal. "The leg is very twisted."

I blew stray hair out of my face. "No. I can do this." I closed my eyes as Ayal had done, imagining the position of the shoulders and the legs as I moved my hand deeper. There! A little hoof! Gently, I tugged, then put more pressure against it, wincing at the thought of hurting the lamb, or the ewe.

"They are more flexible than you think. Do what you need to do to turn that leg. Even if you must break it. Otherwise, they both will die."

Determined not to allow that fate, I twisted the leg with more force and guided it toward the head, blinking away the sweat that trickled into my eyes from such exertion.

The leg released with a jolt. I could not restrain the bubble of relieved laughter that burst from my mouth. "I did it! The hoof is outside now."

"Wonderful!" The warmth and pride in his light eyes gave me confidence to work at the second leg with renewed vigor.

The other leg was not twisted as much as the first, and soon both tiny hooves were visible. Ayal exchanged positions with me, unwound a rope from his narrow hips, and looped it around the lamb's ankles. I gripped the ewe with all my strength as he pulled the lamb free.

While I restrained a gleeful shout, he knelt on the ground, brushing aside the sac that covered the baby's nose. After a moment, his face fell, the slump of his shoulders announcing that the lamb was stillborn.

"No." I drew an unsteady breath, knees wavering.

"It happens, Shira, all too often." He gave me a sympathetic smile. "You did so well."

Keeping my eyes averted from the motionless form on the ground, I focused on the mother, still contracting and heaving heavily against me.

"Why is she still in distress?"

"The afterbirth will come and she will calm." He patted the ewe on the hindquarters. "I am so sorry, Ziba."

"Her name is Ziba? You name the sheep?"

He scratched at his bare arm, darting a look back up the trail. "I do. My brothers tease me. But the ewes, especially, become like pets to me. I think I spend more time with them than I do my family." He turned away, obviously a little embarrassed at revealing such a soft spot for his animals.

"I like Ziba. It's a good name for such a sweet mama. You

will breed again, Ziba." I stroked her velvety chin with my palm.

The ewe bleated and yanked her head back, twisting to look behind herself.

"Another one is coming!" Ayal said.

"Twins?"

"Yes, hold her still. This one is in a good position. I see both hooves."

I held my breath, fighting hard against the hope that sprouted. This one may be lifeless as well. Ziba bleated, straining hard. Ayal pulled and groaned, sweat dripping down his face. With a jolt, the lamb came free. Ziba and I both let out a huff of release.

Ayal cleaned the nose of the little one. His triumphant smile sent dizzy relief swirling through me. One lived! I released Ziba, and she turned to examine her baby. She nuzzled him with her brown nose and then licked his head with a low, comforting nicker. He jostled against the pressure of her rough tongue and bleated a tinny noise as she cleaned him, head to hoof.

Ayal and I stood by in silence as she tended the live baby, then left him for a moment to sniff at the stillborn. I dug my nails into my palms as she gently butted the lifeless form with her forehead, but she returned to her living little one just as he was attempting to stand.

The comical movements of the newborn made Ayal and me laugh. The lamb cried out a few times, ears flopping about as he jerked forward. Finally, he pushed his hindquarters up into the air and then, with a quick upward thrust of his knees, triumphed to a standing position. I could not help but clap. The lamb nudged his way around Ziba, looking for his first meal.

"A miracle," I whispered. As I spoke, my flippant declaration—that somehow I would become a midwife—took permanent root.

"That it is." The lift of Ayal's broad smile created deep grooves on either side of his mouth. The emotion of the last hour heightened my senses, and I returned the smile with an awareness that he and I had shared something remarkable—witness to a new life.

Joy danced in his eyes as he watched the lamb nurse. I chided myself that I had feared Ayal, even for a moment. His rescue of Zayna and me during the stampede, as well as his gentleness with Ziba, spoke volumes about his character. Something sparked deep inside me, a pull to stand closer to him—a sensation that I had not felt in a long time.

"You did well. Eben was right, you are strong. I'll remember not to challenge you at arm-wrestling." His lips curved again under his close-cropped beard as he held me in a gaze that curled around me like a warm embrace.

8

DVORAH

It was the empty hole in my gut that pushed me out of the tent after only two weeks, along with the desperate desire to feed my son. At nearly three years old, he would be weaning soon, and although Mosheh had announced that manna would appear every morning on the ground, I didn't believe it. I needed a skill or I would be dependent on my brother-in-law, Hassam, forever.

Midwifery was the only thing I'd learned how to do at the brothel—other than things Mosheh had forbidden on pain of death. Leaving Matti with the two Egyptian fools Hassam called wives was not ideal, but I must find some way of providing for him. As it was, I was surprised Hassam hadn't already washed his hands of me. He'd said we were welcome to stay with his family, perhaps out of loyalty to his dead brother, but then he sold my tent and nearly all my belongings the next day, ensuring my complete dependence on him.

How Hassam had survived the slaughter when the Levites tore through camp, I'd never know. He was wily. Much more shrewd than Tareq, who'd always gotten carried away when beer flowed freely. In the daylight, when the Levites came to carry him away for burial, I'd gathered up the shards of my own body to rise and peek outside. Not only had Tareq's mouth been colored red, his light beard and gray tunic bore extensive stains as well. I wondered how he'd even found his way back to our tent that night while so inebriated.

Following the directions given to me by a neighbor, I walked through camp and searched out the Levite banners that flapped arrogantly near the center of the valley. Out of all the tribal encampments, I had to choose a Levite midwife to learn from? Were the gods mocking me?

I asked the first Levite woman who crossed my path to point the way to a midwife's tent. She glared at me, perhaps confused by my distinctive Egyptian features, but I was skilled at playing up the Hebrew side of my heritage.

"My sister is in labor." The lie slipped off my tongue with ease, in the language of my mother's ancestors. "The Ephraimite midwives are all occupied, so I came to ask one of yours to help us." Swallowing the acrid taste of false camaraderie, I arranged my expression into a watery plea. "Yahweh help us if I don't find someone soon. My sister has lost three babies already."

With the glint of a tear in her eye, the Levite woman pointed the way, indicating I was only a few tents away from my destination.

Most Hebrews lived with their extended families, adding room after room as they expanded. This midwife's tent was a very small one, nondescript except for a broad, multicolored canopy that spread across the front of the tent. Perhaps this midwife was a widow too. Strange to call *myself* such a thing.

I listened at the door without announcing my presence.

There were voices inside, so I waited, ears stretched toward their conversation.

"No. I told you last time, Tarra. I will not give you anything." The voice rang with authority; it must be the midwife.

"Please, Reva, it's still very early. And I have so many." Exasperation stretched Tarra's voice thin.

"Yahweh is the giver of life. You have no right to take his place." Reva's rebuke softened. "Go back home, my friend. Enjoy all your children. Be glad Pharaoh is no longer crouched between your knees like a crocodile, waiting to devour them."

Ice trickled through my limbs, drop by frozen drop. In the dark well of my mind, it wasn't Pharaoh's eager jaws, but Mosheh's, that gaped before me.

Reva dismissed Tarra with an admonition to get some rest. Before the desperate woman could slip past me, I snagged her wrist, pulled her ear close to my mouth, and whispered the ingredients she would need to rid herself of her problem. Her white face turned toward me, and her lips quivered as she thanked me with a silent nod. The empty space in my gut grew larger. *One less Levite brat*, it echoed, pleased with itself.

The woman's face was forgotten by the time I dropped the tent flap behind me and faced Reva, the old midwife. Her frazzled gray braids hung over her shoulders, bringing attention to her long, skinny neck. Somehow, with such a long nose and dark eyes that scrutinized my face with too much intensity, she reminded me of an ostrich.

"Are you pregnant?" she asked.

The void in my abdomen hissed the answer first. *No!*

"No," I echoed. "I want to be a midwife."

"And what are your reasons?" Reva cocked her head to the side, her lips pursed, completing my picture of her as an overstretched, beady-eyed bird. "Midwifery is not easy. It is demanding, bloody, and exhausting."

The truth was as good as anything for my purposes. "My husband died, and I must take care of my son. I need a trade so we can survive in the new land."

Reva searched my face far too long for comfort. I resisted the urge to shift my stance and kept my expression benign. Her long gaze traveled from my kohl-rimmed eyes, to the gold ring in my nose, to my coarse widow's tunic, and down to the silver-belled anklet Tareq had given me when we'd married. I didn't care what Mosheh commanded. I was not taking it off.

"You look Egyptian," she said.

"My father was. My mother was a Levite." The lie tasted worse than the gold-powdered water Mosheh had made us drink for days. I'd never been proud of my heritage as the daughter of a Danite whore, but I could nearly hear my mother's curses howling from the grave.

"And your husband?"

Somehow revealing Tareq as a Hittite, traveling among the Hebrews only to relieve them of their abundant gold, seemed unwise. "Egyptian as well. We live . . . I live in the foreign camp."

"What do you know of midwifery?"

"My mother was a midwife. She taught me many things as a girl." *How to get what I want. How to survive. How to tread the dark path she walked.* "Had she not died, I would have followed in her footsteps. I want to honor her and feed my son at the same time." I followed my half-truths with a pathetic drop of my shoulders.

"Where is he?"

"My son? A neighbor is willing to watch him while I work."

"He is weaned?"

"Nearly."

She began to test my knowledge, asking how many births I had witnessed, what techniques were best, the signs of an expectant mother. Although I was thrilled that she was considering taking me on, the questions prodded my memory with a sharp stick.

I let her imagine the births I'd seen were those of nice Hebrew women, slaving away at their looms or weaving baskets, grateful for every life that defied Pharaoh's bloody edicts; not hardened prostitutes who more often than not left the squalling infants out in the elements until their cries were swallowed up by the harsh cold. Except a few of the girls—females were worth something in a brothel.

If only I'd been born male.

"I'll teach you," said Reva, her keen eyes pinning me. "There are only six other midwives among the Levites, and we are in desperate need of help. I don't have the luxury of months to train you, but without the threat of Pharaoh, we will multiply quickly. I barely sleep as it is." Her bloodshot eyes testified to the truth of the statement.

"However, you will stay with me until I feel you are ready to have a partner, one whose strengths will balance your weaknesses, and the same for her. A partner of *my* choice." She raised her wispy brows, challenging me to refuse.

I concentrated on keeping my expression pleasant. "Of course. Thank you." I raised my palms, painting on gratitude with a thick brush and even feeling a bit of the excess near my heart. Matti would be safe. There was nothing more important than Matti. He was the only thing the blackness hadn't yet touched. And I meant to keep it that way.

9

SHIRA

10 Av
5th Month Out from Egypt

My brother had come for his bride under cover of night. They would enter his tent together, ending the betrothal and confirming their *ketuvah*, the covenant that bound them in marriage. The commotion, and the promise of a wedding feast, had attracted many unfamiliar guests.

Was Ayal here? I had not seen him since Ziba's lamb was born two weeks ago, but the music of his laughter lingered in my mind. As I scanned the crowd for his tall form, voices from the far edge of our campsite snatched my attention.

"How can they allow it? An Egyptian marrying a Hebrew?" said a woman.

"Mosheh should never have let any of them come with us. They could turn on us anytime," sneered another.

A man's voice joined the attack. "A seductress, like every other Egyptian woman."

"Perhaps even a spy—I have heard there are still many among us." The first woman spoke louder this time, unrepentant in her disruption of our celebration.

On my right, my mother hissed in a breath and drew Shoshana and Zayna closer to her sides but, with a glance and a quick shake of her head, warned me to keep my eyes forward. If she could ignore the interlopers, so could I.

Kiya was dressed in one of her mother's pure-white linen gowns, a bittersweet reminder that Nailah was not here to witness this day, and—with her golden skin and sleek black hair hidden beneath a veil—perhaps an unfortunate indication that Kiya was thoroughly Egyptian. The instinct to place my body between my friend and the poisonous words nearly propelled me forward. Could they not leave her alone just for one day? Kiya could go nowhere in camp without a few jabs aimed her way. From both Hebrews and *gerim*.

On my other side, Jumo stood rigid, jaw working and nostrils betraying heavy breaths. He no longer looked as distinctly Egyptian as his sister did, the thick beard and woolen clothing masking his heritage. But it was obvious he felt the barbed attacks against his people and his younger sister as deeply as ever. From the corner of my eye, I saw his hand twitch at the hilt of his ever-present *kopesh*.

Eben, as well, always carried the ivory-handled knife our father had given him a lifetime ago, however useless it was to him with an injured hand. But with his eyes on his bride, he was oblivious to everything but the subject of his affections and the well-wishes from family and friends gathered around the couple.

It was enough for him that Kiya and Jumo had taken part in the sacred Covenant with Yahweh at the foot of the mountain two months ago. He had not hesitated to petition the elders for permission to marry Kiya, and even to shorten the betrothal period. The elders had given their blessing, after some debate, ultimately agreeing that my friend and her brother had indeed thrown off their Egyptian lifestyle, and gods, to follow after Yahweh. But that did not mean they were accepted by everyone.

Tensions were still stretched taut from the incident with the idol. Such pointed words could shear the fragile cords that bound all of us, Hebrew and foreigner, as easily as sharp-tipped arrows slicing through fine linen threads.

Just as Eben turned to lead his bride into their marriage tent, the intruders took aim and fired.

"Go back to Egypt, *zonah*!" cried one man.

"And take your traitorous lover with you!" joined another.

With an uncharacteristic growl, Jumo swung his body around, pushing me aside in his haste—but Ayal was faster.

He had appeared from behind me and now stood with a firm hand against Jumo's chest, his eyes darkened in warning. "No. This is what they want. Do not give them an excuse to stir up a conflict. There cannot be any more bloodshed here among us."

"Let me go, Ayal." Jumo ground the words through his teeth. "I've had enough."

A shadow passed over Ayal's face, but he did not flinch. He gripped Jumo's tunic, knuckles white, as Kiya's brother surged forward. The two men stood locked in a battle of wills for what seemed an eternity as the uninvited guests continued their haranguing calls.

With a shake of his head, Jumo took a step backward, hands raised in reluctant defeat. Ayal gripped his shoulder and leaned forward to whisper something, then slipped away through the crowd.

Eben's protective arm around his bride's shoulders tightened. He spoke quietly into her ear and then kissed her veiled cheek. My heart fluttered at the tender gesture between my brother and my dearest friend. Although the shouts from the rabble grew louder, Eben escorted his new bride inside the covering of their marriage tent, a signal to everyone that Kiya was now flesh of his flesh, no matter her heritage.

Although the smell of freshly roasted venison tempted me, my stomach was uneasy during the wedding feast, and I offered my portion to Jumo. Ayal had returned with a small contingent of Levites, and the rest of the uninvited guests had slithered into the sea of tents around us, taking their venom with them—but their insults lingered in my mind.

Ayal's presence across the fire from me squelched my appetite even more. When we had been in the field, helping Ziba, I had purposely avoided staring at him. But now, whenever he turned to speak to the men seated near him, I drank my fill of his face, the strong line of his jaw, and the humor in his amber eyes.

After the confrontation with the hecklers, I was able to add strength and courage to his attributes, along with the gentleness he displayed with the ewe. I had thought, a number of times, to ask my brother more about Ayal, but it would make obvious my interest. I must form my own conclusions.

Something in his manner reminded me of my father—the calm authority in his voice and the concern that had flared in his expression when I reacted to being left alone with him. My father had exuded the same quiet strength. A sudden yearning to lean against my father's broad chest spasmed in my throat.

Eben, although the best of brothers, was no replacement for my father's deep wisdom and paternal guidance. Something told me Ayal would be the same type of father, his long arms wrapping his family in kindness and fierce loyalty.

Although he joked and laughed throughout the meal, he scratched at his beard often, a gesture I had already learned meant he was on edge. The desire to draw closer, to sit beside him and uncover his concerns, was almost overwhelming. A lyre strummed and I startled, hoping no one had noticed the direction of my curiosity. I glanced around, thankful everyone seemed occupied in conversation.

Eben's musician friends had brought their instruments, and Jumo led them, pounding out a complicated rhythm on his drum with skilled hands. As the joyful melody spun faster and faster, dancers filled the empty space around the fire—anklets jingling in rhythm, headscarves swirling, and loud trills spinning upward with the flames. I clapped along, unable to resist the lift of my spirits and my own laughter.

Zayna tugged my hand, begging me to join the dance. Although I hesitated, for the first time feeling self-conscious about taking part, her sweet pleas and excitement convinced me. Hands clasped, we whirled into the dance together until the beat of the drums, Zayna's delighted laughter, and a rush of dizzy pleasure conquered every other concern.

When the music slowed and softened and dancers rested tender feet, Jumo began to sing a song dedicated to Yahweh. Although his voice was not as rich as my brother's, Jumo's words were steeped in awe for the God who had healed him from a lifetime of crippling pain and entrapment within his own body.

Inspired by his emotion, I lent my own voice in harmony and quickly lost myself in the thrill of weaving into the melody. My eyes slid closed, and I concentrated on savoring each note, each word of praise to the Creator who had freed us from Pharaoh's strangling grip. By the time the last strain ended, a hush had fallen over the gathering. Everyone seemed just as lost in bittersweet memories as I had been. I blinked to clear the haze that had enveloped me and, without meaning to, connected gazes with Ayal across the fire. There was such stark devastation on his face that I flinched and looked away. He must also be contemplating the suffering our people had endured. What had life been like for his family? Had they been spared the worst of the overseers' lashes out among the sheep, where Egyptians refused to go? The thought raised the vision of an overseer's face in my mind, along with the too-familiar echo of his words—*worthless Hebrew.*

Dancers migrated back to the center of the gathering as the drums began again. Suddenly feeling depleted, I told Zayna I was thirsty and would return shortly. Slipping out of the circle, I edged toward the shadows and found an empty wooden handcart to perch on. After re-braiding the wayward curls that had escaped during the dance, I leaned back on my palms and gazed into the sky, peering at the stars spilling out above me like myriad diamonds against a black cloth.

There were so many tiny lights up there, blinking rhythms against the night sky. The Creator who had formed my body had spoken them into existence as well. The same stars that danced through the endless spiral of time were the ones looked upon by HaAdam and Chavah in the Garden of Eden.

Flesh of my flesh. Would I ever know such a thing? Would I ever be the helpmate of one who loved me, as Kiya was now? Who would want a barren woman, other than some old widower desperate for a caretaker for his brood? But a young man, strong and handsome, someone like—

I shook my head. There was no use allowing the desire to take root. Closing my eyes, I focused on the swirl of music instead of the unwelcome dart of grief that seemed to find its mark all too often lately. A warm breeze swept from the wadi, lifting my headscarf and curling it around my neck. I hummed along with the tune Jumo was singing. The ancient words were a balm to my lacerated heart, and I sang in quiet tones until the ache began to dull.

"Too tired to dance anymore?"

The soft voice startled me and I sat up, the sudden movement unbalancing the handcart—and my pulse. Ayal stood in front of me as if conjured by my thoughts, amusement on his face as he gripped the wooden handle to prevent it from toppling forward.

"Thank you . . . No . . . I mean . . . Yes, I am a bit tired," I stammered.

He lifted a brow. "Is something wrong? You disappeared."

Frantically, I searched my mind for a way to deflect his curiosity. "Those . . . those women, do you think they will be back? To harass Kiya?"

He pressed his lips together, studying my face as if he suspected something else plagued my thoughts. "Perhaps. There are quite a few among us who think Egyptians have no place here."

"But Kiya is part of the Covenant. And married now to a Hebrew."

"To some that makes no difference."

"And you? Does it bother you that my brother loves an Egyptian?"

Ayal cocked his head. "No. Why should it?" He looked toward the shadowed mountains, his expression shuttered. "He is blessed to be able to choose a wife he loves."

He sighed and met my curious gaze. Silence flooded the empty space between us as the flicker of firelight danced in his eyes. I found myself holding my breath, relieved that the evening shadows would disguise the blaze of my cheeks. The muscles in his bare arms tensed and flexed, as if barely in control. But suddenly weariness, or something like it, seemed to wash over his face and he shifted his weight backward. A loud laugh somewhere behind us seemed to break the spell, and he began to turn away.

Don't go. Desperation seized me, causing words to tumble out of my mouth. "Thank you . . . again, for rescuing me and Zayna. And for earlier. Stopping Jumo, and bringing those men."

He shrugged. "I could not let the wedding feast be ruined."

"I appreciate it. I certainly could not have stopped Jumo."

"No." Humor twitched his lips. "Although for such a small person, you are quite strong. You amazed me with Ziba."

"I told you I was sturdier than I look."

"Yes." He crossed his arms over his chest, a smirk on his face. "And you have much courage for one so young. I'll never forget your expression when you put your hand inside that ewe."

The comment stung. *He thinks I am a child. I am nothing to him.*

Suddenly uncomfortable with him looking down at me, I stood and straightened my shoulders. "It is something I must get used to, as a midwife." *When, and if, I gather the nerve to petition my mother.* Forcing a bright smile, I dipped my chin in farewell. "Excuse me, I must return to my family. Enjoy the festivities."

I walked away, shrugging off the disappointment that clung to me and reminded me with every step that I was worth little to a man like Ayal. To any man.

10

B lack threads tangled into a coiled knot between my fingers. The wool snagged on my skin, dry from endless work with the fibers and the scorching desert air. I dropped the spindle into my lap with a moan. Dipping my finger in a pot of animal fat, I worked it into my parched palms. Although the canopy above Kiya and me filtered the brunt of the sun's angry glare, sweltering heat enveloped us, pressing in on all sides. I lifted my sweat-soaked braid and kneaded my sore neck.

As Kiya's tapered fingers forced a small shuttle back and forth across the handloom, an intricate pattern of black and brown emerged. Since we had left Egypt, she had become a surprisingly advanced apprentice to my mother.

I tipped my head to the side, envying her dexterous motions. "You truly enjoy weaving, don't you?"

She skimmed her hand across the half-finished project with a satisfied smile. "I do."

"Why?"

She smirked at my abrupt question, then laid the hand-frame

in her lap and twined her fingers together. "I have always been fascinated by the skill it takes to create beautiful fabrics." She gave a rueful smile. "Salima, my handmaid, was always so patient with me in the market. My favorite stall sold fabrics imported from all over the world, and I would study the intricate designs for hours, trying to decipher how they were created."

She lifted her eyes in faraway thought. "In fact, the day I discovered my father sold me to Shefu and Tekurah, I had just purchased a beautiful scarf. I have never seen its equal; the embroidery was exquisite. I wish I could emulate its design somehow. I actually gave it to Salima before I was taken away . . ." She shook her head as if to clear her mind of the bittersweet memory. "But, to answer your question, I enjoy weaving because each piece is like a work of art. As if I am creating something as beautiful and precious as Jumo's paintings." Her hopeful expression pleaded for my understanding. Jumo was a master artist, every painted piece characterized by impossible detail that defied his self-taught skill and the affliction that had plagued his limbs since birth.

I patted her hand. "The patterns you've been designing lately are every bit as extraordinary as any of Jumo's paintings."

"But somehow"—she rubbed her brow with two fingers, a habit that reminded me of her father—"even when we are working on the tents, using just the rough black threads from goat's wool, that task seems to be almost . . . worship."

I blinked at her, confused by such a strange statement. "How so?"

"When I work the looms, making tents to protect my family and friends, blankets to keep them warm, and clothing to adorn their bodies, it feels like love. Love for my family, and love for Yahweh." She glanced up through her long lashes. "Does that make any sense?"

Weaving was love to Kiya? I enjoyed watching my mother

work—the whir of her unheeded spindle in the air, the flick of her wrist as she twirled the distaff against her left shoulder, the rhythmic back and forth of the shuttle—it was an entrancing process to observe, but one that I struggled to master, or even tolerate.

And now, after deciding that I would train as a midwife, it had become even more difficult to endure, nearly torturous. Yet ten days had passed since Kiya and Eben had been married, and still I could not summon the courage to speak my mind.

"You are welcome to do my share." I waved a hand at the overflowing basket next to me.

Kiya laughed, again occupied with the dance of the wool strands across the warp threads. "Do you not enjoy weaving?"

Shrugging, I twirled the end of my braid around my finger. "I wish I did."

Kiya's brow furrowed. "I thought you were upset when you had to leave the weavers, after . . ." Her voice trailed off, ushering me into an unwelcome memory.

Akharem's dark eyes, kohl-rimmed and full of mischief, had called to me from across the weaving room that day, causing a warm blush to sneak its way up my neck. The chatter of women filled the stifling room to overflowing as shuttles flew back and forth in the never-ending dance of linen-making. Combing the flax threads through a long-toothed hatchel had been my job from the time I had been Shoshana's age, but that very morning I had finally been allowed to work the standing loom. Akharem's covert attention heightened the pride of leaving childhood behind. If only that had not been the only day I worked the loom . . . perhaps I would be more adept at it now.

I squirmed, blinking my eyes until they were dry.

"I'm sorry, Shira." She grabbed my hand and squeezed. "I did not mean to upset you. I should not have—"

"Oh now, I am fine. It's all in the past. Let's leave it there.

Instead . . ." I forced a merry laugh to deflect her attention. "Instead, let's talk about how you've survived being married to my exasperating brother. Regretting it yet?" I lifted a brow in tease. "Or too smitten to notice how annoying he can be?"

She swallowed the bait. "Oh, no. Don't you remember that he frustrated me from the start?" She giggled. "Only now I kiss the smugness from his face instead of wanting to slap it off."

This time my laugh flowed easily. "I am sure he does nothing to protest such punishment."

"I fear he has taken to doing it on purpose now, just to see how far I will go to change his moods." She blushed at the suggestion of their intimacies, her eyes going wide and fingers pressed to her lips, cheeks dark with embarrassment.

I held my hands to my chest, brows high. "Really, Kiya, how shocking! You wanton!"

We laughed until tears rolled down our faces, hands pressed to mouths to avoid waking my napping aunt with our foolishness. Such easy camaraderie with Kiya reminded me of our first tentative days of friendship, meeting among the rushes along the Nile to evade our cruel mistress. What a long road we had traveled to become sisters.

Kiya returned to her weaving, although humor still twitched at her lips. Considering the strength of our friendship, and desperate for encouragement, I decided to test my revelation about midwifery on her, to gauge her support before unleashing it on my mother.

The urge to speak to my mother, to tell her of my desires, was boring a hole in my stomach. The words begged to be said a thousand times a day. They sprouted on my tongue constantly, pleading to be set free, but anticipation of her disappointment made me swallow them instead. Yet every day since I had helped Ayal with the sheep, my mind would adhere to little else.

Without preamble, I spoke out. "I want to become a midwife."

The release of saying the words aloud rushed like a cool stream through my veins, even as indecision swelled in my gut.

Kiya dropped her hands into her lap, both weaving and amusement forgotten. "Truly?"

"Since that night when I assisted Reva—and then after helping Ayal with that lamb—I have felt almost . . . as if I was *made* to be a midwife." I searched Kiya's face for affirmation.

Instead, apprehension curved across her forehead. "What will your mother say?"

I exhaled a sigh. "She will be upset, I am sure." I pressed my fingers to my eyes, trying to rub away the guilt. "Perhaps I should say nothing."

"And why shouldn't you?"

I shrugged. "I don't want to hurt her."

"But if midwifery is what you feel you were created to do, then you must do it." She reached over and gave my shoulder a little shake. "Why is it that you are so willing to stand up for everyone but yourself? You were fearless when it came to Tekurah back in Egypt. You took my place, twice, in the face of her wrath. Use some of that courage to speak with your mother."

I tugged at my fingers. "I would not know how to start. . . ." Explaining to Kiya that my mother made me feel even younger than Zayna at times seemed disloyal. I covered my face with a groan. "But I really do hate weaving. I hate everything about it. Always have."

"Then why did you not tell me sooner?" My mother's voice came from behind us, hard as flint.

I whipped my hands away from my face and looked over my shoulder, stomach dropping like an anchor stone. There was no turning back now. I must float on the tide I had pushed so hard against for these past weeks.

"I want to be a midwife, *Ima*. Reva has offered to train me." My eyes stung at the admission.

A dark expression pinched my mother's face. "I told her no."

I sprang to my feet, dropping the untwisted wool in the dirt. "You spoke with her?"

"Yes. I made it clear you were not cut out for such a thing."

"Why would you . . . ? That is not true." How long had she known and said nothing? How could she make such a decision without consulting me? I was old enough to be married, to have children of my own, yet she saw me as a child—just like Ayal did.

"You and I both know that midwifery is not a . . . a healthy thing for you."

"Because I am unmarried?"

Her lips twitched. "No, Shira, because you are barren."

I jolted backward at the verbal slap. She had never put it into such stark terms before. I barely registered Kiya's pale face and dropped jaw. I had never told her of my affliction. But now was not the time to explain. I pulled the fragile threads of my resolve back together.

"That means nothing, *Ima*. Just because I cannot have children of my own does not mean I cannot help others bring theirs into the world."

My mother's mouth gaped. "You can't . . ."

"I will never have a family or children"—my chest squeezed at the reminder—"and I know that I brought shame to our family. I may not be worth anything to a man, or as a daughter, but I cannot do this anymore."

My hands and knees trembled violently, but I turned and walked toward Reva's tent, all the while battling the overwhelming desire to run back, kneel at my mother's feet, and beg her forgiveness.

Without a question as to why I had defied my mother, Reva simply nodded at my acceptance of her offer and gestured for me to follow along. The image of my mother's shocked expression continued to plague me. Would I have the strength to stand strong if she forbade me to continue? Would Eben, as the head of our family, back her prohibition?

Reva led me to a campsite not far from where my own family lived. Women were gathered in groups on the ground, many industrious hands employed with various tasks: basket-weaving, grinding manna with mortar and pestle, flattening dough between their palms. A number of children threaded through their animated chatter, playing chase.

A few of the women greeted the midwife, but they continued their circles of conversation, seemingly unconcerned about the laboring going on inside the tent. They seemed to know Reva well. How many of their children had been guided to birth by Reva's capable hands?

There were almost as many women inside the enormous, multi-roomed tent as out. It took some maneuvering to get to the mother. Splayed across cushions on the floor, and unabashedly naked, the laboring woman was chatting amiably with a woman in dark widow's garments.

Reva knelt, laying her leather pouch on the ground beside her. "Are the pains coming at regular intervals, Bithya?"

Bithya's face contorted in response. She drew in a long breath and then puffed it out in bursts until the pain released its grip and she was able to reply. "They have been, all afternoon."

Reva examined her belly, pushing and measuring with her fingertips and palms, eyes closed as she concentrated. "Yes, baby is in the correct position." She looked over her shoulder at me. "Come, Shira, feel."

My pulse raced. I had not expected Reva would start teaching me here and now, in front of this large audience. What must they think of me? An unmarried girl, supposing I had the right to examine this woman?

But I knelt down beside Reva and she took my hands, placing them at the top of Bithya's belly. I refused to meet the mother's eyes as Reva explained how to feel for the position of the baby.

"Baby must be faced head down, backside up. Here"—she pressed my fingers deeper into Bithya's flesh—"can you feel the outline of the body?"

I winced at the unexpected force of pressure Reva used, but with utter indifference Bithya continued her conversation with a woman sitting on the floor next to her—until another contraction seized her body. I tried to slip my hand away, but Reva kept my fingers where they were. "There now, do you feel how the abdomen becomes hard? Her body is working to push the baby out."

Bithya's belly was tight, and she groaned, gripping the hands of the two women who knelt on either side of her.

"It is almost time to push." Reva patted Bithya's thigh. "Shira, open my satchel. There is a jar of oil there. Take it out to the fire and place it among the coals, it must warm for a few minutes. Not too hot, though."

Keeping my eyes on the ground, I wound my way through the crowd outside to tuck the alabaster jar among the embers of the campfire. A spicy-sweet fragrance curled around me as the oil warmed. What ingredients had Reva used? What use did the ointment have? How long before I could carry a midwife's pack of my own? I could not wait to ask the bevy of questions scurrying through my head.

"Is my baby brother or sister born yet?" a little voice asked behind me.

I turned to find a girl, close to Zayna's age, gripping the hand of a small boy with a dirt-smudged face.

"Not yet," I said. "Your *ima* is doing fine, though. It should not be long. What is your name?"

"I am Lenaya, and this is Shemi." Fear swam in the girl's big brown eyes. "Is the baby all right?"

72

"Why, yes, Lenaya, as far as I know everything is going smoothly."

"The last one died," she said without a change in her voice.

"Oh, I am sorry."

She shuffled her grimy toes in the dirt. "There are already eight of us."

No wonder Bithya seemed so unconcerned; she had done this many times. Perhaps if this one lived or died mattered little to a mother with such a full brood.

I knelt down to look Shemi in the eye, smiling to reassure him. "Are you excited? For a new baby?"

He stuck out his bottom lip. "Babies cry."

"Yes." I laughed. "They certainly do. But you will be a good big brother, won't you? And help your *ima*?"

Shemi nodded his head solemnly.

"Good." I ruffled his thick, black curls. "Now I must go help. I will come tell you when the baby is here."

I expected Bithya to cry out like Hadassah, but she gritted her teeth each time a pain struck her, breathing in concentrated rhythm. The women on either side helped her balance on two birthing bricks that must have been designed specifically for Bithya. Her feet fit perfectly into the molded footprint on top of each mud-brick. Thankfully, they lacked the vibrant designs of fertility goddesses I had seen on birthing bricks in Egypt.

Bithya pushed for only a few minutes, with little more than a few loud grunts, and delivered a baby girl, thatched with thick, black hair that I guessed would turn to curls like Shemi's. At the sound of the baby's lusty cry, Bithya's attitude changed. She commanded Reva to hand over the baby, and her eyes glistened as she cradled the squirming bundle, cooing and guiding her to the breast.

Reva's low voice came from behind me as I watched the scene of mother and babe wrapped in each other's newness. "She was guarding herself. Bithya has given birth to three stillborns, so she has learned to keep her expectations low until the precious one is born breathing. It's the only way to keep the agonizing fear at bay."

Bithya's fingers traveled over the tiny girl's body, counting fingers and toes, tracing the curves of her little face, still red and swollen from her difficult journey to her mother's arms. Tears trickled down Bithya's face and neck. Even this ninth child came into the world with tears of joy. How full of love her heart must be, stretched to greater capacity with such a blessing.

An emotion slammed into me, shocking me with its force. Only Reva's strong hands on my shoulders kept me from running from the tent to nurse the jealousy that reared its poisonous head. What was I thinking? What was Reva thinking? My mother had been right, I could not do this. My head shook of its own accord as I braced against the instinct to flee. Reva must have felt the tremors vibrating though me, for she pulled me around by the shoulders to look into my eyes.

"You have been given a gift, Shira." Her voice rasped low, so Bithya would not hear. "I could see it from the moment you walked into Hadassah's tent that night. You were so calm. Like an unwavering flame in a whirlwind. Your hands were steady, not a twitch. And the strength with which you held that girl up was supernatural."

I blinked at her, astounded by her observations. It was true that, when Hadassah screamed, I had somehow willed my breathing to decelerate and my pulse to lengthen its pace—as if my rhythms could influence hers. "But I cannot understand the pain. I will never . . ."

"No, you cannot. And that will be a drawback for you. I will not lie. But you have a gift, a gift of compassion. I have seen it in you since you were a young child."

I questioned her with a raised brow.

"You were always bringing home other children or animals that needed special care, Shira. Even before you could speak words, your singing soothed others around you. You have maternal instincts, even though you have no children of your own." Compassion was etched into every line of her wrinkled face. "And I will teach you, just as Miryam herself taught me many years ago."

"Mosheh's sister taught you midwifery?"

Reva nodded even as a shadow of pain crossed her face. "And now I will pass on the same wisdom Miryam gave me when I first became her apprentice." She leaned close, her eyes steady on mine. "Stay here. Force yourself to watch. Focus, not on your own loss, but on the joy in Bithya's eyes."

"But—"

"No excuses. This is the only way, Shira. You were made to do this. And you *will* grieve. Every time you help a baby come into this world, you will mourn a little. But instead of letting the grief overcome you, allow the miracle to overcome the hurt."

Gently, she turned me back around to watch the new mother. Her reassuring grip on my arms tightened as she whispered into my ear. "Each life is a gift from Yahweh. And your gift is to help bring those miracles into the world. You may not have any children of your own body, Shira, but every baby guided to birth by your hands will be a child of your heart."

11

Dvorah, this is Shira." Reva pressed me forward. "She will be observing your examination of Leisha today. I must tend to a stillborn. I will leave her here with you."

Dvorah looked me over, head to toe, obvious skepticism in her almond-shaped eyes. Her dark hair was hidden beneath a severe turban that matched her ankle-length widow's tunic, fashioned from rough, black goat's wool.

Her olive complexion and the slight hook of her slender nose marked her as Hebrew, yet Egypt announced itself in the haughty tilt of her kohl-lined brown eyes. A gold ring sparkled in one nostril. She waved a flippant gesture for me to sit next to her on the ground near the mother's feet. A silver anklet on her leg, lined with tiny bells, jangled as she scooted a few inches away.

I had observed Reva for two weeks now, trailing behind her at every waking moment, drinking deeply of her expertise like a thirsty seedling in a downpour. Being left in the hands of another apprentice midwife frustrated me, but Reva must have confidence in Dvorah's skills to do so. Besides, I was not eager to watch another tiny, still body being swaddled for the grave.

My mother had not explicitly forbidden me to learn midwifery—however much she frowned and huffed whenever I left to follow Reva. I attributed her reluctant acceptance solely to Kiya and her influence over my brother.

Leisha lay on a narrow pallet with her rounded stomach bared and thick, gleaming black hair fanned around her. Only Kiya's late mother, Nailah, could compete with this woman for beauty. Although she was Hebrew, I guessed that many an Egyptian had been envious of her high cheekbones and thick eyelashes. Her eyes were so light—an unusual shade of hazel rimmed with dark brown. They seemed to glow in the late-morning sun streaming through the tent flap.

"How many have you given birth to?" Dvorah asked Leisha as she pressed on her belly.

"Just my boys. Twins."

Her gesture, toward the other small pallet in the tent, piqued my interest. Assuming the boys slept there, I glanced about for evidence of her husband. The tent was sparse. Besides the two pallets, only a few baskets, a small cookfire with a few scattered utensils, and a thick sheepskin rug that reminded me of Ziba and her lamb furnished the space. There were no other sleeping arrangements, no male clothing, nothing to indicate a man lived here. Curious—Leisha did not wear widow's garments like Dvorah.

Dvorah placed her ear on Leisha's stomach, one hand raised in a gesture for silence as she listened. "Have you felt much movement?"

Leisha nodded, but her eyes drifted toward the back wall, as if avoiding closer inspection.

A silvery shiver of intuition jangled in my head. Without thinking, I asked, "Were your twins born without complications?"

Both women turned toward me, sour-faced, as if my question

were an irritation. Dvorah lifted a thick brow. "I believe I can handle this. You are here to learn. Not interrupt."

Chastened, I looked down at my hands and mumbled an apology.

Dvorah gestured for Leisha to pull her dress back down. "Everything seems normal to me." Standing, she slung a leather satchel over her head and shoulder, similar to the one Reva carried containing her oils, herbs, and tools. I sprang up and retreated to the doorway.

"There were . . . complications," Leisha said to Dvorah, as though she were the one who had asked the question in the first place. "With the twins. They were born early. Of course they survived, but . . . I worry."

"I'm sure you will be fine. You seem healthy enough." Dvorah swept Leisha's concerns away with a flip of a hand.

I wanted to press more, ask exactly what the woman had experienced, but as my curiosity was obviously an uninvited guest, I kept silent.

Leisha sat up and smoothed her dress over her hips. "Back in Egypt, the midwife gave me . . . something . . . to ensure the baby would be healthy." Her hazel eyes flicked to mine and then back to Dvorah. "I was told that you were not opposed to such things." She lowered her voice, but the covert meaning of her statement was as loud as a shofar call. "It's why I asked for you to examine me."

Dvorah, too, looked over her shoulder at me, eyes narrowed as if in warning. Then she reached into the satchel at her hip. "Here." She handed Leisha something—a necklace perhaps? "Wear this inside your dress. It should protect you both."

Had Dvorah given Leisha some type of charm? An amulet of Tawaret or Hathor like the pregnant women in Egypt used to ward off evil spirits? She had to know better. One of the first directives Yahweh had spoken from the mountain specifically forbade idols. How could she risk such a thing, especially after the incident with the golden Apis?

My mind raced. I feigned interest in the woven mat at my feet as Dvorah recommended herbs to prepare Leisha's body for labor. Should I tell Reva what I had seen? She always spoke against such things. But after the dark looks Dvorah had given me today, it might be best to keep quiet. Perhaps Reva would find out on her own that one of her midwives was dispensing idols along with pregnancy advice.

I followed Dvorah into the open air, but before we left the campsite, she stopped, spinning around to face me. Hands on her hips, she jerked her chin at the tent. "Go back and get my bracelet. I left it on the ground."

Dvorah was obviously set on putting me in my place as the new apprentice. Obediently, I returned to the tent, apologizing when Leisha startled as I came back inside.

"Dvorah forgot something." I pointed to the discarded bangle on the floor.

Leisha scowled at me. "You are too young to be a midwife."

Surprised by her pointed tone, I stumbled over my words. "I am . . . I am nearly eighteen."

She scoffed. "Well, you've never had a baby." She pointed at my midsection. "Nothing could come out of those tiny hips. How could you possibly understand what it feels like?"

Although I had learned that small hips made little difference during delivery, her sharp words met their mark. If only she knew how true they were.

I took in a deliberate breath and met her haughty stare. "That is true. I've never had a child. But one does not need to bear a child to understand pain, or to be of service to a laboring mother."

Surprise widened her hazel eyes, and the set of her shoulders softened.

"I only want to be of help." My confidence sprouted a bit, and I stood straighter as I recited Reva's words. "That is what a midwife does—helps the mother be comfortable so the body can do its job."

All hostility abruptly drained from her expression. "I am frightened." Her eyes glistened with tears. "Last time was so painful . . . I can't do it again."

"You can." I summoned enough courage to step closer and place a hand on her wrist. "Yahweh will give you the strength. And we will be here, along with your family."

Her beautiful face contorted into an ugly sneer, and she jerked away. "I have no family."

I mumbled an apology for my careless words, but my mind buzzed with confusion. Why would she not have a family? She must have a husband, and she had spoken of other children. Had they not traveled with her husband's family?

Leisha peered at me, her peculiar eyes locked on mine. She still held the necklace Dvorah had given her in her palm, but she worried the blue and green beads between her long fingers. It slipped from her grasp and fell to the floor. The distinctive golden horns of Hathor lay exposed on the reed mat.

"Leave." Leisha's body stiffened in defense. "Now."

Snatching up the turquoise bracelet Dvorah had left on the ground, I fled the tent, avoiding Leisha's penetrating stare as I did so. I hoped that when the time came for her to give birth, I would be well occupied somewhere else. The woman's changeable moods shifted directions faster than a shuttle across a loom.

12

My arms ached from stirring the simmering pot of heavy wool. Wisps of steam rose from the surface of the water, mingling with the sweat that soaked my tunic. Tendrils of wet hair clung to my skin, and I brushed them off my neck, wishing I could tighten my fraying braid. The acrid smell of the wool marinating in the blood-red dye made me ill. I was forced to breathe through my nose as I pushed the enormous wooden paddle around and around for what seemed like hours.

"Do not stop stirring, Shira, or the dye will not take evenly." My mother's terse command made me bristle as she passed by with a bundle of fresh wool in her hands.

I had hoped that offering to help today might soften the thorny demeanor she'd had toward me since I stood up to her. Instead, it only proved to emphasize the depth of my ineptitude with her trade. The enormous task of dyeing the wool that would be woven into fabrics for the new Tent of Meeting would drag on for weeks. I'd made it clear I could only help this one day since Reva insisted I needed a break from midwifery. But I was anxious to know everything, and taking even one day off might cause me to miss some important knowledge.

Mosheh had descended from the summit of the mountain a few days ago, his face glowing with an eerie, terrifying incandescence. So with a veil to cover the strange radiance and new Covenant tablets in hand, he relayed clear instructions to design a grand dwelling place—a Mishkan—where Yahweh had mercifully declared his presence would reside. As one of the most talented master weavers in the camp, my mother was commissioned to create one of the ten-cubit-long panels that would hang at the entrance to the expansive courtyard.

This morning, a caravan from Midian had arrived with another wagonload of madder root and crimson *shani* powder—made from the crushed remains of the *kermes* worm. The red wool would be woven together with brilliant indigo blues, Tyrian purples, and fine white linen into an intricate design fit for royalty.

Soon after Mosheh's return, the elders had outlined the reorganization of the tribes around a large rectangular clearing at the center of the valley. The chaos of moving thousands of tents was reminiscent of our first assembly beneath tribal banners, the night the Cloud appeared to lead us out of Egypt. It took days for the shuffle of animals, belongings, wagons, and dwellings to settle. Our new campsite lay along the western boundary of the clearing, closer to the mountain. We now lived with the other Gershonites, since my father was descended from the firstborn son of Levi.

Ensuring that my mother's back was turned, I hunched my shoulders to stretch and then brushed the perspiration from my forehead. I rocked forward on my toes, trying to catch a glimpse of the Levites who were working to clear and flatten the place designated for the Mishkan, wondering if Ayal was among them and where his campsite was located among the rearranged sea of tents.

Regret for the way I had walked away from him that night nagged at me. If only I could see him again, apologize for my rudeness. His face, the sheen of his amber eyes in the firelight, even the low rumble of his voice, appeared in my mind without warning at all times of the day and night. Had he even thought of me since Kiya's wedding?

My new sister came up beside me, carrying a basket of hairy madder root against her hip. "Don't let her catch you idling."

Flushing as if my friend could see the path of my thoughts and the tall man at the end of them, I gripped the paddle and swirled the musty stew with a groan. "Even working with Dvorah is better than this."

Kiya dumped the contents of her basket into another dye-pot hanging suspended over a fire. She added more kindling to bring the water to a boil. "What does that woman have against you?"

"To tell you the truth, I have no idea. She is so cold. Indifferent. As if simply speaking to me is an affront to her. She hated me the first moment we met."

Kiya wrinkled her brow. "How could anyone hate you? It's not possible."

I smirked. "You did, when you first came to Tekurah's home."

Her expression turned somber. "That is not true. I did not understand you, and—" Her sun-darkened skin flushed. "In all honesty, I felt superior to you. You were Hebrew, I was Egyptian. Everything I knew back then told me that Hebrews were created by the gods to be our slaves." She nudged at a large stone with the toe of her papyrus sandal. "It galls me to think that I ever considered myself so far above you."

"Well." I bowed with a flourish. "Mind that it doesn't happen again, My Queen."

Kiya's bright laughter made my heart sing. Although the shroud of mourning that had hovered over camp for weeks had given way to an air of jubilant relief since Mosheh's return, Kiya

83

still could not walk through our camp without harassment, and very few women outside our family spoke to her with kindness. I could tell that it stung her to be cast out by the other Hebrew women, and I had apologized on their behalf. But she insisted that nothing anyone could say was worse than the daily verbal assault she had endured from Tekurah.

"Are you here to giggle? Or help?" My mother's chastisement lashed like a whip across my back.

I stiffened but presented my mother with a smile. "I am glad to help you, *Ima*. Reva does not need me today."

She scowled. "Are there no babies being born?"

"I am certain there are. I think half the women in this camp are expecting." I winked at Kiya. "Perhaps the men have too much time on their hands since leaving Egypt."

Kiya flushed to her hairline at my blatant tease. I doubted it would be long before she would search out Reva's services as well. Although the thought caused a small pang of jealousy beneath my ribs, I knew the healing a child would bring to Kiya after the loss of her mother.

With a shake of her head, my mother nudged me aside. Using the broad paddle, she lifted the saturated wool from the pot. She compared the oozing lump with a sample tied to her wrist and nodded to herself, apparently satisfied with the depth of its color.

"Squeeze the water from that batch now, before it darkens any more. Then hang it to dry." She pointed behind me, where crimson loops dripped from ropes strung between our tent poles.

With an inward grimace, I reached for the mass, catching my breath as the sour smell wafted upward.

"If this disgusts you so much, you are welcome to leave." My mother frowned, her fists at her narrow hips. "I don't understand how it could, after what you insist on doing with Reva."

We had danced around this issue for weeks now, my mother needling me with subtle comments that I pretended to ignore. Perhaps it was time to bring an end to the pretense.

"I love what I am learning, *Ima*. I know you do not approve, but I wish you would at least try to understand—"

My mother cut me off with a palm in the air. "I have indulged this foolishness only because your brother insisted. But mark my words, daughter." She raised a finger. "No good will come of this. You will end up with your heart trampled on the ground."

"But *Ima*—"

"That batch will be ruined soon. Do not waste wool." Turning, she walked away from us, leaving me wounded by her dismissal and my hands stained a bloody red.

13

29 Elul
6TH MONTH OUT FROM EGYPT

Y ou are ready." Reva's strong fingers gripped my shoulders. "And I am here beside you. There is nothing to fear."

I glanced at the laboring woman whose loud moans overtook our whispered conversation in the corner of the tent. "It has only been a handful of weeks. You cannot expect me to be prepared."

"You are prepared. You have attended many births. And your intuition is just as I guessed it would be."

"But if there are complications—"

My gaze flicked to Dvorah near the far wall of the tent. She turned away with a bored expression, but not before a hint of jealousy flashed in her eyes. Surely she had performed a birth on her own? She'd been working with Reva for weeks longer than I and seemed to have previous experience as well. What possible reason would she have to envy me?

Reva tipped her head toward the mother without loosening her reassuring hold on me. "I have examined this one, dear girl. Everything is normal. She is healthy and nearing the time to push. All you need to do is comfort her, encourage her, and catch the baby."

"Are you certain?"

"I am." Pride burned in Reva's eyes, flaming as bright as if she were a fresh young girl instead of a woman haunted by a lifetime of slavery and loss in Egypt.

Would that pride ever gleam in my own mother's eyes? Why could she not see that becoming a midwife made me feel more like a resilient sapling and less like a hollow reed?

I wiped every stray wisp of apprehension off my face, constructed a smile in its place, and knelt in front of Tova, the laboring woman.

Her eyes went wide when she realized that it was me, and not Reva, in that position. "What are you doing?"

"I have attended many births." I repeated Reva's words, concentrating on keeping my tone smooth and steady. "And Reva is right here."

"But you are not experienced enough to deliver—" A pain seized Tova, cutting off her complaint.

When the contraction lessened, I looked up at her, ignoring the glares of her mother, who loomed next to Tova like a lioness with her cub. Instead, I focused on holding together a look of peace and confidence, in spite of the shaking hands that gripped each other in my lap.

"It is not I who will deliver this baby, Tova."

Her brows arched.

"It is you; your body is doing all the work. I am simply here to catch your little one and be your servant. You keep doing what you are doing. Breathe deeply, concentrate on pushing this precious one into the world, and I will simply make sure he or she does not fall. All right?"

Obviously still skeptical, Tova and her mother continued

glaring, but when another wave of pain hit Tova, all arguments ceased, and my training, young as it was, slipped into place.

"Push into it, and let your body do its work. There, that's right. Baby is already showing the top of its head. You are doing well." I had seen every part of labor, from the early pangs to the bloody, triumphant end, but as I talked Tova through the process, something instinctive came over me, and I heard myself saying things that I did not realize I knew. As if outside of myself, I heard my voice, calm and collected, reassuring that she was doing well and that it would not be long before she held her child in her arms.

"There now, the head is out." I ensured the cord was not wrapped around the little one's neck and breathed thanks to Yahweh. "Good. Tova, we need an enormous push here. Bear down hard and yell all you want. This will hurt."

I repeated the words I'd heard Reva say so many times, though I had no real understanding of the pain any mother endured. An irrational thought—that I would never know such pain and wished that I could—floated to the top of my mind. I batted the foolish desire away with an internal swipe of my hand. What a ridiculous notion—jealousy of Tova's pain.

With one last scream from Tova, the baby made her way free from the cocoon of her mother. As I held the tiny body in my hands, watching her take her first breath, wonder swept through me. It was as if a new light had burst into flame inside the tent, a tiny offshoot of glory borrowed from the Cloud atop the mountain.

I laid the baby on Tova's chest, and she caressed her daughter's face, still covered with the slime from birth and swollen from the traumatic journey.

"So beautiful. So beautiful." Her whispered chant held pure adoration.

Sparked from the union of mother and father, this little life had been pieced together by Yahweh himself. Understanding, like a new bud, sprang up inside me. *This* was why Reva had been so adamant that I learn midwifery. She knew me well enough, from youngest childhood, to know that I would cherish such an honor.

With sudden lucidity, I could see my path stretched out in front of me. I would never marry. My fulfillment would not be in birthing my own children, but in having a hand in birthing many, perhaps hundreds or thousands of children. And when my hair was silver and my fingers gnarled and pained, I would pass the knowledge to the next generation—not my own child, of course, but someone like me, a girl I would intuitively know would follow in my footsteps. Perhaps it would even be this sweet baby who cooed now at her mother's breast, fingers stretching and kneading the air.

A movement at the edge of my sightline caught my attention, and brief as it was, I could have sworn I saw Dvorah's hand slip from a basket and slide something into her satchel. The movement was so quick that I brushed it off as my imagination in the next instant. Surely Dvorah would not take something from a Hebrew family, especially in plain sight.

Indecision flipped over and over in my mind. Reva should know if Dvorah truly had stolen something, but I had seen only a hint of movement. What would be the good of saying something if I was wrong? I could not risk accusing her falsely. Dvorah's hatred of me burned bright enough now; I had no interest in adding fuel to the flames.

14

6 TISHRI
7TH MONTH OUT FROM EGYPT

Ziba and her baby are doing well, thanks to you."

Ayal! I gasped, and my foot slipped from the wide rock I'd been balanced upon, staring into the burbling water under the dappled shade of a juniper. Crumpling, I pitched forward off the rock. With swift dexterity, Ayal grabbed my arm to prevent me from tumbling into the stream.

"Thank you. How clumsy." A blush heated my cheeks as he righted me. The subject of the daydream I'd been swept away with was here, touching me.

"My fault. I surprised you." His grip tightened, and his thumb traced a quick path across my skin. He blinked a few times before letting go and stepping away.

Steady on my feet but still reeling from his touch, I looked around for Dvorah. She must have migrated farther downstream, out of sight. No matter my protest, Reva demanded that Dvorah and I work together, insisting that we were well suited. What made her think so, I could not begin to fathom. Even after the excitement of a twin birth this morning, Dvorah had merely informed me she needed to wash the blood from her garments and stalked off without another word. Ayal and I were alone next to the stream that twisted out of the wadi, not far from where his sheep were penned.

Collecting my nerve, I tried to mask my wobbly voice with curiosity. "How is the rest of your flock?"

He stood taller, and a warm smile spread across his face. His hair was longer now. It tousled about in the breeze like fine strands of richly dyed linen, inviting my fingers to tame its dance. "Doing well. We just finished the last of the shearing, so that should keep you and your mother busy."

"Well, my mother and Kiya at least. And my sisters are learning to take my place."

"You are no longer weaving?"

A leaf rushed by on the current. I focused on its dips and swirls to distract myself from his nearness and the effect of his low timbre on my pulse. "No, I am learning to be a midwife under Reva."

"I am glad to hear it. You were so steady with my ewe. So calm. I can only imagine what a wonderful midwife you will be."

"My mother might disagree." I toed the pebbled ground.

"Your mother was not there when you calmed Ziba with your lovely voice, or when you freed that lamb's hoof with impossible serenity."

I tugged at my braid, flattered by the unexpected compliments. "Thank you for allowing me to take part. It gave me the confidence to fully embrace the idea of midwifery."

"I do not doubt you were made for it. To bring life into the world," he said, his smile affirming the sincerity of his praise.

He understands. He sees me. Sweet warmth curled in my stomach at the realization, and at the honest encouragement in his kind eyes. Eyes I had no business searching as deeply as I was. Would someone see us here, alone, and misinterpret?

A flutter of wings in the juniper above us drew my attention upward. A small, brown sparrow had alighted on a twisted branch, tilting her head back and forth as she studied me from her high perch.

"What a curious little bird!" I said.

The sparrow chirruped and then warbled out a call, speckled breast vibrating to the rhythm of her high-pitched song.

"I wonder if her mate is nearby." I smiled at the thought of the sparrow calling to her love.

"If so, he will no doubt be drawn to her." Ayal peered into the foliage with an enigmatic expression. "No male could resist such a beautiful voice."

"She needs such a voice, as drab as she is, or he would never find her hidden there among the leaves." The tiny bird preened her feathers as if preparing for her mate's arrival, then repeated her lilting twitter. I sighed. "I wonder if little brown sparrows long for their colors to match the brightness of their songs."

"Perhaps it was the voice that drew him in at first." Ayal's cheek quirked and he paused, his gaze traveling from the sparrow to me before he continued in a gentle tone. "But I think that although others may see a quiet, unremarkable brown, he discovered a depth of beauty and strength that fascinated him—made him long to see her again. Made him ache for just one more note of his songbird's sweet music."

Warmth rushed to my limbs at his words—words I suspected had little to do with the tiny bird nestling in the juniper.

A cool breeze swept through the wadi, bringing with it the scent of wild jasmine and pushing back my headscarf. Grateful for the distraction, I lifted my chin, closing my eyes to enjoy its sweet caress. When I opened them, Ayal was watching me. Not with a glance of curiosity or a brief perusal, but with a desperation that slowed time. He took a step toward me, then two, before stopping as if by force. The gentle breeze shifted and swelled into a wind. A few rebellious curls slipped from my braid and whipped about, lashing my face.

"I cannot stop thinking about you," he rasped. "I've never known anyone like you, Shira—bravery in perfect balance with sweetness." He reached out and brushed an errant lock of hair from my cheek and tucked it behind my ear. His hand lingered against the side of my neck, his touch burning like fire on my skin. "I wish . . ."

My knees trembled. He was so close, yet somehow still too far away. Indecision tugged at me. *You have been here before,* said one side of my heart. *He is not the Egyptian,* whispered the other.

"I have no right . . ." His manna-sweet breath washed across my face, causing me to lift my chin as the two sides melded into one question—why had Ayal not been the first to kiss me?

As if in response to my silent wish, he bent his head, whispering my name with aching tenderness. He drew a quick breath that resembled a sigh and touched his lips to mine. A haze of blissful disorientation washed over me, and I clung to his tunic with trembling hands as he pulled me closer. I'd wanted nothing more than to be in this man's arms since he'd said he called his sheep by name, but the sudden image of Akharem's accusing eyes floated across my vision. I stiffened.

Ayal released me—the move so swift that I stumbled backward, breathless and dazed. He dug his hands into his hair with a tortured groan.

"Shira. Oh, Shira. I am sorry." He backed up a few steps, clawing at his beard with one hand. His eyes were like twin caverns, wild and bottomless, before he turned and strode away, head bowed and shoulders slumped, leaving me standing by the stream in a cloud of confusion.

DVORAH

Shira walked right past me, so caught up in thoughts of her lover she did not see me behind the thorny acacia bush. I hadn't meant to spy on them and had only been washing the mess out of my tunic when I noticed them standing next to the stream.

By the way the man looked at her, I could see it was not just a friendly conversation. The fervor in his gaze reminded me of how Tareq's sapphire-blue eyes held me prisoner the day I met him in the marketplace in Thebes.

Yet the man who stood with Shira did not have the confident set of my husband's shoulders or the entrancing brashness that had pulled me toward him like the tide to the shore. Instead, he spoke quietly, watching her as a man studies a rare jewel. I was shocked that he kissed her, but even more surprised that he slithered away so quickly.

The ethereal expression on Shira's face as she floated by told me that she had not seen what I had. Regret hung like a death shroud around that man. I knew the feeling well, it was the mantle I had worn far too long. Only one familiar with its folds and valleys would recognize its depths.

In contrast, Shira's constant optimism was grating. Like a little girl, she was giddy with excitement over every little thing—blood, fluids, screeching mothers—none of it bothered her. She worshipped at Reva's feet like a dog and beamed at every baby like it was her own. She would have her own children someday, so why did she act ridiculous over everyone else's?

And the singing! The girl hummed all day long, as if by compulsion. Every single task was accompanied by music. Her voice was not awful, but I was well past tired of hearing it.

When she'd seen me give that amulet to Leisha, revulsion

had been plain on her face. If she revealed what she had seen, I would no doubt be dismissed, since Reva prohibited such things with some nonsense about being offensive to Yahweh. But how else could a woman ensure protection from the demons that snatched a baby's breath at birth and weakened a mother during her travails? Besides, Yahweh cared nothing for me or my son, or he would not have killed my husband.

Just this morning, I had again begged Reva to let me work with someone else. But like always, she refused, insisting that Shira and I would learn to work well together and reminding me that I had agreed to the stipulation. The old midwife must be going senile to pair the two of us, but I did not have the luxury of walking away. Working with this strange girl was a necessary evil—for now. I hoped it would not be too long. By all the gods, I did not know how much more I could endure.

15

SHIRA

Weynat are you smiling about, Shira?" Reva's hawkeyes
were on me as I slathered oil and salts on the newborn's flailing little body, giving the distinct impression she could discern my thoughts in detail. My heart quailed
at the suggestion. Reva was much too observant for my comfort.

"Just enjoying this sweet one." I kissed his tiny nose, glad
I had a good excuse for the ridiculous grin that had insisted
upon revisiting my lips all day.

Has Ayal approached Eben yet? I should have spoken out
before his hasty retreat yesterday, but surely Eben would not be
angry that Ayal had stolen a kiss before securing a betrothal. I
knew from Kiya's own mouth that Eben had done the same. Such
an honorable man Ayal was, to feel such guilt even after such an
innocent, and welcome, kiss—so different from the Egyptian.

Was there truly a chance I might not be alone for the rest of my life? Hope hovered around me like a dove taking flight as I indulged the tender memory of Ayal's strong arms around me.

I did not miss Dvorah's glowering presence today as I hummed to myself, wrapping the infant in long strips of cloth and pulling them taut. The baby immediately stilled, comforted by the swaddling.

Placing a babe in his mother's arms was always a joy. I did so with relish, tucking the precious bundle into the crook of her arm. She looked up at me with tears of gratitude in her eyes, a stark contrast from the curses she had thrown at me less than an hour before. I hoped she would not remember such words and be ashamed of them later. I could not imagine the searing pain that would cause such venom to be spewed at a midwife.

I shifted back on my heels to enjoy the interaction between mother and baby, but something cut into my bare sole. I lifted my foot, not at all surprised to see a small stone etched with a hippopotamus head painted in vibrant red.

Another charm. In the many tents I had visited over the past few weeks, I had seen many such items. Amulets, small statues, even shrines with household gods at the center. Anger buzzed through me. Why would this young mother resort to calling on the gods of Egypt to protect herself and her baby, with Yahweh watching over us day and night?

Reva always lectured the women when she saw such items in their tents and refused to come back unless they were gone. What would be the use in drawing attention to the charm as the new mother cradled her newborn? I moved to pack my oils, trying to brush away the unease that now tainted the beauty of this birth.

Unaware of my discovery, Reva was admonishing the young mother to rest as much as possible over the next few days, to enjoy the gift of her time of cleansing. How kind of Yahweh to bless a new mother with a command to be alone and at peace with her new child for a few days.

An elderly woman who had stood silent in the corner throughout the delivery now caught my eye. Assuming she was one of the new mother's relatives, I gave her a congratulatory nod before I left the tent.

I sat cross-legged near the cookfire, re-braiding my rebellious hair and waiting for Reva to finish. The old woman from the tent appeared at my side and folded herself down to sit on the ground beside me.

"I watched you today, *almah*." She tilted her head to one side and looked at me from the corner of her eye. Her thick, white hair was braided, like Reva's, in two long braids, and she wore no jewelry except a worn copper bangle around her wrist.

Almah. Unmarried and childless. This woman did not know me, yet the epithet stung.

"You did a fine job assisting that mother. But you will not make a good midwife."

My jaw dropped. A dull pain lodged in the middle of my chest, cutting off any reply.

"Being a good midwife is more than knowing how to birth a baby, it is being willing to deal in truths." She patted her weathered palms together in emphasis. "Babies die. Mothers die. These are truths. And if you cannot say what needs to be said, no matter how painful, insulting, or embarrassing, then you cannot be the midwife you should."

Echoes of my mother's words rose up in my mind. What did I know of being a midwife? Or of the depths of pain a laboring woman would endure?

"Now . . ." She curled a finger beneath my chin. "Do not misunderstand me. Yahweh gave you a special gift, I can see it in you. But you will waste it if you are not careful. You cannot be afraid of the truth, no matter the risk."

"I do not know what you mean."

"Yes, you do."

The charm? Did she mean I should say something about the image of Tawaret?

"Let me tell you about my brother." She folded her arms and lifted her eyes to the mountain. "Never have you known a quieter man. When he was a child, it took an enormous amount of coaxing for him to even speak. But when it was time for him to stand strong, even in the face of complete destruction, he did it. It cost him everything, but he spoke the truth, even though it pained him to do so." She pointed a knobby-jointed finger in my face. "And you, dear one, do not have that courage yet."

My mouth was a desert, my mind a blank wall. Tears formed at the corners of my eyes, and my face burned.

She patted my hand. "Now, do not cry—it may come." She unfolded her legs and stood with a graceful move that contradicted the myriad wrinkles on her face. "I just hope it does not take you forty years in the wilderness to find it, like it did for Mosheh."

She winked and left me sitting by the fire, attempting to hold together the shattered pieces of my heart and stunned that I had been unaware I was speaking to Miryam, Mosheh's sister—the same woman who had ensured her brother's safety in the little basket on the Nile, and who stood with courage before Pharaoh's daughter as a young girl, and the woman who had taught Reva to be a midwife decades ago.

Reva had always spoken truth to me. Even after that horrible day—the day I lost my childhood and my future all in the same afternoon.

Reva spoke to me without condescension even as I lay curled in bed, burning with fever, broken to pieces, and abdomen still throbbing from the assault the Egyptian had unleashed on me many days before. She plied me with questions a thirteen-year-old girl should never have to be asked. The bruises he left on my body were nothing compared to the bleeding wounds in my heart. Although the heat of shame flamed time and time again, I answered every one with frankness. I trusted Reva and was grateful that it was from her lips such unsettling things were asked.

She gently examined me and applied an herbal poultice to lessen the effects of the raging infection. Her dark eyes were full of wisdom gleaned by guiding countless women through the cycles of life, from birth to death.

"Will I die?" I asked, peering at her through swollen eyes and tasting blood as the scab on my lip split anew.

"No, my dear. You will survive." She patted my shoulder, but her glance darted away. She was hiding something.

"What is it? Tell me. Please, Reva. I want to know."

She studied me for a moment, as if gauging my resolve. "I will not dip my words in honey to nurture false hope in you. Your cuts and bruises will heal. But the infection you are suffering from . . . I have seen far too many women with the same symptoms—" A flash of pain crossed her face. "I cannot declare it with absolute certainty, Shira, but it is most likely that you will never have children."

Would I ever have Reva's courage? Would I ever be able to deliver truth, no matter the cost, with such unflinching, brutal honesty? And would Ayal even want to marry someone whose body could never bear him a child?

DVORAH

22 TISHRI
7TH MONTH OUT FROM EGYPT

Wailing was futile. Pointless.

I turned away from the shrieking woman and wrapped the

bundle in a cloth, avoiding the still face and the too-tiny fingers and toes. Undeterred by my assurances that there was no way to save such an underdeveloped infant—that it was dead long before we even came to her tent—the woman shrieked for me to return it to her.

Shira put her hand on my arm. "Please, can she not hold the baby? Only for a few minutes?"

Death was reality. Almost as many women lost their babies as saw them weaned. Did she think she was more special than any another?

Irritated by Shira's pandering, I huffed out a sharp breath. "It won't do any good."

"I think it would help her to see that he is really gone." Although she spoke gently, the set of her hands on her hips told me she would not be dissuaded.

Stupid girl. Shoving the bundle into her arms, I gathered my things, resisting the urge to flee. It was suffocating in here, and too dark. My chest constricted. Adjusting my neckline, I squeezed my eyes shut.

A hand on my shoulder startled me. "Dvorah, are you well?"

Shira's curious expression flared my anger. I shrugged her away. "Is she done now? Go bury that thing."

She flinched, a sheen in her green-gray eyes.

Good. Shira, too, must face reality as much as the woman who lay there, clutching a dead infant to her breast, talking to it as if it would come back to life at the sound of her voice. I had the urge to shake the stupid woman and scream, *It is dead! Nothing will bring it back!*

Shira would likely have her own share of miscarriages. She'd be lucky if she even made it through labor with such a fragile build.

Besides, she was one of those haughty Levites who had succumbed to the worship of only Yahweh—walking around with their noses grazing the clouds as if they were so far above the rest of the tribes—and all the while shamelessly murdering their own brothers. Disgust, like bile, coated my tongue.

A male deity would have nothing to do with something so mundane as childbirth. It was the goddesses—Tawaret, Hathor, and Meskhanet—who guided a child along the journey to life, and Isis who guarded against evil spirits during labor. Yahweh was a god of war. A god of judgment. A thief. He may be the god of my forefathers, but he was certainly not mine.

He and the Levites had stolen everything. The image of Tareq splayed blank-eyed in front of our tent jeered at me. I cinched my mouth tight against the inexplicable urge to call his name, just as I had the night he was murdered. I had moaned his name into my pillow, over and over, until my throat burned like fire—until everything inside me was a charred ruin, fit only to be cast out and placed in a shallow grave.

I glanced around the tent again. There were no household gods here. No altars. No offerings. Foolish woman. No wonder she lost the child today. A set of large sandals lay on the ground next to me. I shoved them away with my foot, my anklet jingling.

At least this woman had a man. She'd be with child again soon enough.

16

SHIRA

Dvorah and I snaked through camp, following a tall, ebony-haired woman named Aiyasha who had summoned us to a birth. We had both delivered babies under Reva's guidance over the past couple of months, but neither of us was yet prepared to stand on our own, and none of the other Levite midwives were available. Reva had assured me she would join us after dealing with a frantic woman whose new infant refused to nurse.

The woman led us to the very end of a row. The location, along the southwestern boundary of the Mishkan courtyard, signaled that the laboring woman's family was directly related to Aharon. Ayal wandered through my thoughts, and I wondered for the hundredth time why I had not seen him for almost three weeks. Embarrassed to ask my brother about such a thing, I consoled myself—again—with the reminder that all the Levites were busy building the huge meeting tent at the center of camp and had time for little else.

With a dismissive flash of her blue-green eyes, Aiyasha left us with no more than a silent gesture toward a tent as she ducked inside her own, escaping the torrent that had just released from the black sky.

As we entered the dim room, I took in the ashes of a small cookfire, a thick sheepskin rug, and two narrow pallets, then groaned internally. I had been in this tent before, the day I met Dvorah. I had hoped my first encounter with Leisha would be my last.

Aside from the unpredictable mother writhing on her pallet, there was only one woman present. Dvorah introduced herself, ignoring me completely. Replying that her name was Marah, the woman said nothing of her relation to Leisha. The fading brown hair tucked beneath a gray turban indicated she was quite a bit older than Leisha. Her mother perhaps? Her husband's mother? Yet Marah's pursed mouth and the arms crossed over her ample chest gave the distinct impression that she was not thrilled about being by Leisha's side.

Dvorah swept her leather bag off her shoulder and handed it to me, as if my sole purpose was to hold it for her. "How long has she been having pains?"

"Not long," said Marah. "But her waters came at the same time, and her pains are one on top of the other." With a none-too-gentle hand, she swiped a wet cloth across Leisha's forehead. Leisha moaned and squirmed, shrinking from the touch.

Dvorah examined Leisha, her movements brisk but efficient. Regardless of her disdain for me, Dvorah was skilled in mid-wifery. What she lacked in tact she made up for in knowledge and physical strength. She seemed to absorb Reva's lessons like a sea sponge and could repeat any information word for word later. She reminded me of a scroll that could be opened at any point to deliver the correct answer on the spot. Should she ever stop seething at the very sight of me, perhaps Dvorah and I would complement each other well.

"Are you experienced with childbirth?" I asked Marah.

She shook her head and frowned toward the door of the tent. "Only that of my own children." Her face contorted with frustration. "I tried to get the other women to help. But they refused." I sensed she wished she could have refused as well. Why would anyone be so cruel as to abandon a laboring mother?

Leisha gripped her belly as another contraction seized her. I rubbed her lower back in small circles. She moaned as Dvorah instructed her to start pushing. The baby's head was already crowning.

"No. No. I can't." Leisha cried out. "It hurts! It hurts!"

Dvorah scowled. "Of course it hurts. Go ahead and yell. But push too. This baby needs to be delivered."

"I can't do this again," Leisha whimpered. "It took everything the first time."

I looked up in curiosity at Marah, but she turned away with a scowl. What a strange tension existed between these two women.

I could not heal the rift in this family, but I could do my job. I put my mouth to Leisha's ear. "Whatever happened last time, this sweet baby is ready to meet its mother. You must push now, bear down hard."

Leisha's wild-eyed stare reminded me of Ziba, but she surprised me by nodding.

"Here." I grabbed her hand and gestured for Marah to grab the other. "We are with you. Use our strength to push."

She did. Leisha pushed and groaned and panted, but instead of emerging, the baby's head slipped back. Dvorah commanded Leisha to stop and applied more warm oils. But even after a few more tries, the baby was nowhere near coming free.

"The shoulder must be jammed up against the bone. I cannot even get a grasp on the head." Dvorah sat back on her heels.

I attempted to keep my voice even, hoping to avoid alarming Leisha. "Can you turn the baby?"

Dvorah's kohl-rimmed eyes widened. "I have never done such a thing. Reva has always handled any complications."

Again, Ziba flashed through my mind, along with the fleeting image of Ayal's appreciative smile. "I have. I can do it." It could not be so different, could it? And unless one of us did something quickly, the baby would die. It was worth a try.

After a first unsuccessful attempt on the birthing bricks, I asked Leisha to get down on the floor, on hands and knees, hoping that the change in position might help my efforts. She did so, but only after many soothing words and reassurances that it would not hurt her or the baby.

From the new angle, I was able to push the baby's shoulder down. With much thanks to Yahweh for my small fingers, and with one final moaning push from Leisha, the infant came free and slid into my waiting hands.

A baby girl squalled lustily from the first moment her skin hit the cool air. Once again, the rush of delight and joy knocked the breath out of me. A sob built in my throat, but for Leisha's sake, I held it back.

Black hair was thick on the baby girl's head. I did not know what the father looked like, but she would emulate her mother, it was certain.

After Marah and Dvorah helped Leisha settle onto her back, I laid the baby on her chest and watched as the two made their first acquaintance. It never failed to thrill me, watching a mother fall in love with her baby, even as a tiny sliver of jealousy vied for attention. But with as many births as I had witnessed now, I was much more skilled at pushing it aside and instead, as Reva had so wisely taught me, to revel in the wonder of new life.

Leisha kissed the baby's head as the infant suckled, but her body jerked when an afterbirth contraction startled her.

"It's all right, Leisha, it's just the placenta coming free. It is natural." I patted her thigh and gave her a reassuring smile.

Leisha's face went white as a linen sheet as the afterbirth came. Blood gushed from her body—an unnatural amount of blood. Her arms went slack. Marah grabbed the baby before the little girl tumbled to the floor.

"What is happening?" Dvorah screeched. "What did you do?"

I tried to apply pressure. Tried to sop up the blood with the bedclothes. Nothing staunched the crimson flow. My mind tried flipping through anything Reva had ever said about excessive bleeding but came up with only blank spaces.

In response to the prayer that had not even made its way to my lips, hands pushed me aside. Reva was suddenly there, pressing down on Leisha's abdomen, concentrated wisdom heavy on her brow.

Marah was holding the baby, horror written into every line of her face, and Dvorah was calling Leisha's name, shaking her shoulder and trying to revive her.

Kneeling down beside Leisha, I placed my hands on either side of her face. "Leisha. Come back to us. Your daughter needs you."

Her eyelids flickered.

I kissed her forehead, then spoke right into her ear. "Your baby needs her mother."

Leisha's hazel eyes popped open and stared at me, looking for all the world as if she was seeing right through me. "You care for her."

"You will be fine," I said, willing myself to believe it.

"No!" With a sudden burst of strength, Leisha pulled herself upward. "Promise me! *You* will watch over my daughter."

I slid my arm around her back to support her. "But your family—"

"They hate me, and they will be glad when I am dead." The rancorous words spat from Leisha's lips.

I glanced at Marah, but she avoided my eyes.

"Give me your word," Leisha rasped. "Vow it."

I nodded my head, unable to say no to this woman whose life was slipping away by the second. Lying back, she sighed and turned her head toward the baby. Her eyes fluttered shut and did not open again.

Reva did everything she could, pressing down on Leisha's abdomen, massaging, but nothing stopped the bleeding. Although I did not know when Leisha breathed her last, emptiness suddenly filled the tent. The only sound was the fussing baby as she squirmed in Marah's arms.

I am covered in blood was my only thought. I must get clean. I stood, swaying slightly from the lightness of my head. Remembering a jug of water outside the entrance to the tent, I stumbled into the hazy drizzle.

My dress was ruined. Nothing would remove the deep crimson that covered me, chest to knee. I pulled at the saturated fabric, plucking it away from my body, reminded of the red dye-pots and the bloody stains that had colored my hands for days. Tilting my head back, I let the rain run down my face, welcoming the numbing cold.

A man's quiet voice came from behind. "Is the baby born?"

I stiffened, afraid to face him. "Yes, you have a daughter."

"And my wife?"

My feet were like lead weights. Must I tell this man his wife's fate? How could I even form the words? I looked down at my crimson palms. It was my fault. I could only face the guilt head-on.

He cleared his throat. "Shira?"

Terror seized me, gripping my chest with sharp talons. Against my will I turned, desperate for the face to not match the voice

I now recognized as all too familiar. The voice that had spoken hope into my dreams for weeks. The voice that had whispered my name by a stream.

Ayal stood before me, eyes locked on the blood that stained my clothes.

The necessary words refused to release their hold on my tongue. This man had betrayed me. Had betrayed the woman who had just died in my arms.

Nevertheless, I could not deliver the striking blow. Miryam had spoken truth—I was a coward.

I ran.

17

My mother's eyes traveled over the blood on my tunic and the devastation on my face. A brief flicker of compassion crossed her own face but was quickly replaced by a knowing shake of her head.

She had been right. She had known how this would end, and although loath to acknowledge that her prophecy had been correct, I bowed my head.

"I told you no good would come of this," she said.

"I know, *Ima*." I swallowed hard against the salty rush that threatened to overflow.

"And yet you defied me." When I did not respond, she huffed a sigh. "Let me help you wash."

Without a word, she fetched a pot of water. She washed my hands, arms, and face, then stripped me of my blood-soaked tunic and replaced it with a soft, gray woolen shift. Although her expression was stone, the gentleness of her hands drew forth the tears I had been so hesitant to shed in front of her. She drew me to her chest and let me sob until the well ran dry.

"Now." She wiped my face with the edge of her headscarf. "Tell me."

"Ayal's wife died tonight. And it was my fault." The revelation that Ayal was married only added to the whirlwind of guilt and grief that had taken up residence beneath my ribs. *How did I not know?*

Her breath quickened. "Did Reva say that? That it was your doing?"

"No. Reva wasn't there. Until . . . until it was too late."

"You dealt with the delivery on your own?"

"Dvorah was there, but she wasn't sure what to do . . . so I tried . . . but I must have done something wrong—there was so much blood—" My stuttering explanation came to a halt.

"And the child?"

"She lives."

"Well." My mother patted my hand. "Then some good has come of this sad night."

I sniffed and closed my eyes, but Leisha's pale face was painted there in stark detail. My eyelids flew open. "I cannot go back."

"Why would you go back?"

"She made me promise."

"Who?"

"Leisha made me promise that I would help with the baby, make sure she was cared for."

"Why wouldn't her family take care of the child?"

I tugged at the braid that hung over my shoulder. "There was something . . . wrong, between Ayal's family and Leisha . . . She was so adamant . . . said that they would refuse."

"Hmm. Strange." My mother pulled at her chin, her tone pensive. "Ayal will need help if his family refuses to accept the child." She was silent for a long moment, then a curious expression lifted her brow. "You must go back."

"What? No, *Ima*, please don't make me—" I took two quick steps backward.

She pursued me, determination on her face. "You will go. Ensure the baby is cared for. You made a vow to that woman.

You must honor her final request." She lifted my chin with a finger, censure giving weight to her words. "You made the decision to go against my wishes, Shira. Now you will do as I say and face the consequences of the choice you made. You will harvest what you have sown."

I searched her face for any sign of yielding, but it was plain that her decision was wrought in iron. I had no choice but to obey. No matter what had been Ayal's intentions by the stream that day, or how loud my pulse thundered at the prospect of seeing him again, I must face the man whose wife I had killed with my incompetence.

If it took the rest of my days, I would atone for what had happened today. My mother was right. There was no option but to pay for Leisha's life with my own. *A life for a life.*

⁓

Ayal was sitting cross-legged in front of the tent, long fingers splayed in the dirt. His head was down, his face concealed in shadow.

I approached, the soles of my hesitant feet scraping against the rough ground. Bracing for his anger, I cleared my throat. "How is the child?"

He did not look up but stared at his fingers as they traced circles in the rain-soaked sand. "Dvorah is with the baby." His voice was gentle, as if he was afraid I would run again.

"I came to help. I . . . I promised your wife I would." I straightened my shoulders. "I will stay as long as you want me to."

His fingers stopped moving.

Will he send me away now? Silently, I pleaded with him to do just that, but without lifting his head, he gestured for me to enter the tent. Stomach swirling with dread, I complied, half expecting to see Leisha's body laid out. But during the couple of hours I had been gone, someone had taken her away.

"It's about time you came back. I have to go." Dvorah pressed the baby into my arms.

Staggering backward, I nearly collided with Ayal, who had followed me inside.

"Will you come back? She needs to be fed again soon," he asked Dvorah.

She huffed. "I have my own son to nurse. He isn't fully weaned."

Dvorah has a son? How had I not known this?

"Please. I have no one to nurse her. None of my brothers' wives have infants—even if they were willing to help."

Dvorah lowered her thick brows, her stance unyielding.

"I will pay you. In wool and in milk," said Ayal.

Her shoulders softened, and her brows lifted. She cocked her head, dark eyes pensive and latched onto the sleeping baby in my arms. "I will ask my—" A look of indecision brushed across her face. "I will try to come twice a day. But that is all I can do. I still have my duties as a midwife."

"I will do all I can to help when you are not here," I said.

She peered at me. "Reva will want to know where you are."

"Please tell her I am needed here for now." I gestured to the newborn. "My mother gave permission for me to stay."

Dvorah looked at Ayal, then back to me, as if searching our faces for something. Her eyes narrowed slightly, and the corners of her mouth quirked. "You'll have to find some goat's milk to supplement. I cannot be here every two hours," she said. "It's a good thing the others are weaned."

Ayal had other children? I stifled a groan, remembering that Leisha had spoken of twins. Two more motherless children added to my account.

Dvorah turned to me but spoke to Ayal. "I don't have time to watch the boys. Shira will have to keep an eye on them."

Ayal had moved to the far side of the tent, as if ensuring a wide space between us. With his mouth turned down and his shoulders slumped, he seemed to have aged ten years since that day by the stream. Shaking off the now-tainted memory of his lips on mine, I cleared my throat. "Unless your mother wants to be the one to care for them?"

His brow furrowed. "My mother is dead."

"Oh, I thought Marah was . . ."

"No, Marah is my brother's wife. She has no interest in helping me. She only agreed to watch them until Leisha was . . . until I buried her."

What was between Leisha and these women that they refused to even care for her children? Surely not everyone in Ayal's family held such disdain for her. And even if they did hate her, now that she was dead, why would they not step in to support Ayal?

The baby in my arms shifted in her sleep. She had been so quiet I'd nearly forgotten I was holding her. I'd held many new infants in the past few months, but after cleaning and wrapping them in salts and oil, I always handed them to their mothers for nursing. I had never had the chance to hold one close and watch it sleep.

Her face captivated me. Her rosy lips puckered, as if nursing in her dreams, and then she sighed. Her contentedness pierced me, causing anguish to well in my throat. Her mother was dead, at my hand. She would never know her touch, never feel her kiss, never hear her voice. *Oh, little one, forgive me.*

I braved a look at Ayal, expecting to see grief in his expression, but when his gaze clashed with mine, something flashed in those amber eyes that I did not understand, something that reminded me of that day by the stream. Instinctively, I stepped backward, fear curling in my stomach. My resolve to help with the baby for Leisha's sake withered. Ayal was not trustworthy. What was I doing in a tent alone with a man who had made advances toward me? A married man who had tossed aside his vows?

As if he sensed that I was near to bolting back to the safety of my family, he retreated to the door. His voice came out rough and harsh. "I will keep the boys with me tonight. You can sleep here with the baby. I do not anticipate she will sleep well."

I nodded, but my stomach continued to roil. My impulsive vow to a dying woman, and my mother's insistence that I fulfill it, had put me directly in the path of her wandering husband.

"I will go find some goat's milk," he said before sweeping out of the tent.

I sank to the ground in relief, cradling the baby, and soon I was entranced all over again by her tiny features. The sounds of evening surrounded us—the crackle of campfires, hushed tones of mothers putting restless children to bed and whispering prayers of safety over their heads, the laughter of young men, probably huddled near a fire joking together like Eben and Jumo always did in the evenings. A yearning to be among my own family tugged at me.

The baby twitched and murmured in her sleep, eyelashes fluttering. I paced the floor, rocking her gently, humming a wordless tune until she relaxed in my arms.

"Who will you be now? With your *ima* gone? Who will you look to?" I kissed her forehead and breathed deep of her fresh scent. "Mmm. You smell like *talia*, morning dew. That would be a good name for you."

"You can call her whatever you wish." Ayal's intrusion, and his emotionless statement, caused me to flinch.

Unnerved, I lifted the baby toward him. "Are you ready to hold her?"

He shook his head. "I am unclean. I just buried a body. Mosheh gave us instructions that we cannot work at the Mishkan for seven days after handling the dead. We must wash our bodies and begin the purification ritual." His words were clipped, as if delivered from a place of rote memorization instead of regret for their meaning.

Why would he speak of his wife in such stark terms? As if she were no more than a stranger to be tossed into a shallow grave? His refusal to even touch his new daughter provoked me. How could I have misread this man so completely?

My response was razor-edged. "Then I am unclean as well. As well as anyone who was in this tent when your wife died." His gaze darted to the back wall, his jaw tight. Regretting my harshness, I softened my tone. "You could begin purification tomorrow."

Ignoring my suggestion, he handed me a sloshing skin-bag, a small pitcher, and a narrow strip of linen cloth. "I brought milk. My brother's wife gave me this pitcher. It's meant for feeding an infant. I do not know if the child will take to it, but you can try."

I sat cross-legged on the pallet where Leisha had died, trying to disregard the images it conjured in my mind. Someone had removed the soiled linens and replaced them with fresh ones. Every remnant of the woman who had passed from life to death here was already wiped away, except for the little bundle I held in my arms.

A tiny spout carved into the side of the alabaster pitcher offered a small trickle of milk. I wrapped the linen cloth around the end to protect her tender mouth. After a few messy tries, she began to suckle the fabric, taking the goat's milk. Relieved, I released a sigh and gently rocked her. When an ancient lullaby sprang to mind, I gave it voice.

After a few moments, my attention suddenly flew back to Ayal. I'd nearly forgotten he was there, watching us with hooded eyes. He startled and turned away. "Call out if you need me. I will sleep next to the fire tonight with the boys. We will discuss arrangements tomorrow."

I watched his back as he escaped the tent, and then I began to sing again. I was glad to see him go.

18

Dvorah strode in after sunrise, an unwelcome interference after a wakeful night of feedings, changing soiled wrappings, and pacing the floor with a restless infant. I was not sure who was more annoyed by the woman's noisy entrance, the baby or myself. Talia announced her displeasure with a loud yowl.

"Not as easy as you thought, is it?" Dvorah smirked, thick brows aloft.

My first instinct was to disagree and feign cheerful confidence, but instead, I sighed and dropped my head back to the pillow. "No, I am exhausted."

Dvorah lifted the baby from my side, which provoked an even louder squall. But as soon as she dropped the tunic from her shoulder, delicious silence filled the tent. I stretched, hands over my head and as far as my toes would reach. A night of curling around the baby, terrified I might roll over on her, had tied my back into a thousand knots.

"There is an *omer* basket on the floor. Go collect manna

117

before it melts in the sun," Dvorah said with less concern than I thought possible.

My stomach complained. How long had it been since I had eaten?

Although Talia was not mine, somehow anxiety tugged at me. "Will you be all right?"

Dvorah lifted her brows with a condescending twist of her lips, as if offended I should question her competence. As well she should. She had at least one child, possibly more, and all I knew of mothering was with my sisters.

I passed through the door into the weak morning light and stretched again. Cold air slapped at my face, and my breath trailed away in a white cloud. The stifling heat had finally given way to the season of rain. The campsite was deserted, except for Ayal, who sat near the fire with his long legs pulled up to his chest, and two little boys playing swords with sticks—his twins. Looking up from his blank-eyed gaze at the flames, Ayal acknowledged my presence with a nod, then glanced off toward the mountain as if it were painful to look at me.

The sounds of the boys' carefree play dredged up fresh grief, but I pasted on a smile and approached them. "Shalom."

"Shalom!" said the dark-haired boy. "Want to play swords with us? Dov is Pharaoh, and I am Mosheh!"

"Oh. Well now, who would I be in this game?"

Dov, the bronze-haired boy, waggled his sword-stick at me. "You are a bandit."

I raised a brow. "A bandit? What have I come to steal?"

Dov scanned the campsite, contemplating, and then pointed at Ayal. "Abba. You've come to kidnap Abba."

Before I could respond, Ayal stood. "Dov, Ari, no more." The censure in his voice gave the boys immediate pause and shocked me. A couple of silent moments passed before he released the tight set of his shoulders and the draw of his mouth. He took a quick breath and then spoke gently. "Shira has only just awakened. She is tired from tending your new sister."

Dov's eyes widened in excitement. "Can I see the baby?"

Ari added, "Please, Abba?" on top of his brother's plea.

Ayal's lips twitched. The boys' sweet voices had blunted his sharp edge. "Not now, she is nursing. But perhaps we can help Shira gather manna?"

Dov and Ari applauded the suggestion, and I found both my hands grasped in their small ones. My heart squeezed as if trapped in one of the vises Eben used to train wood for his instruments.

My fault, my fault, the guilt jeered at me. Without my failure, these boys would be holding their mother's hand this morning and not that of an unwelcome substitute.

Obviously Ayal had not yet told them of their loss, for they chattered with abandon, asking what their sister's name was and when she would be able to play with them. When Ari asked when he could see his *ima,* Ayal deflected by handing the boys my basket with a gentle command. "Go. Fill it to the top now, Shira is hungry."

Unaffected, the boys each gripped one side of the handle. They trudged off, pulling against each other and arguing over where to find more of the white grains.

I looked everywhere but at Ayal, who stood equally stoic beside me. If there were not thousands of people milling about this morning, gathering their own morning rations, I would not have suffered another moment beside this man who had lured me like a bee to honeysuckle. His silence—about his actions toward me, about Leisha, about his coolness toward his daughter—condemned him.

Ayal's kind words, his warm smiles, the rich melody of his laughter—those memories were false. All of them should have been given to Leisha before she died. I focused on the boys and their antics among the desert brush where they dipped their little hands deep into the white manna and filled the basket to overflowing. For their sake, and for their innocent sister, I would endure this time near their father, but not one moment more.

~

Dvorah met us near the campfire, Talia cradled against her shoulder and annoyance on her face. "I told you that I cannot stay here all day. I have my own child to tend and a job to do. And if she"—Dvorah pointed her chin at me—"refuses to help midwife today, I will have twice the work to do."

My eyes darted to the basket in my hands. I had not even voiced the conflict raging inside me, but Dvorah had lifted it from my mind. How could I tend a laboring mother with Leisha barely cold in her grave?

"Can you return this evening before the baby goes to sleep?" Ayal asked.

Dvorah shrugged a halfhearted indication that she would.

"Thank you," he said. "I have some fresh milk for you."

Dvorah handed me Talia, but before leaving the campsite with the small pot of milk on her hip, she glanced back, frowning at me, as if loath to leave the infant with such a novice. Perhaps she was right.

Talia stretched in her sleep, one arm above her head. Dov stood on tiptoe, so I crouched down to allow the twins a look at her face, so peaceful in contented sleep.

"She's all smashed," said Dov, wrinkling his nose.

"And red," said Ari.

I laughed. "She is, but it won't be long until she is the most beautiful girl in the world."

Ari petted her face with a gentle finger. "I think she is very beautiful."

"She is." Tears welled in my eyes. "And you boys will be the best brothers anyone has ever known. Do you know what the job of a brother is?"

They both shook their heads, their eyes wide. Dov's were brilliant amber like Ayal's, and Ari's were changeable hazel like Leisha's.

"Shall I tell you what my mother told *my* brother when he was about your age and I was born?"

They nodded little chins.

"A brother is to be a tall fence for his siblings, a strong wall to protect and to comfort."

Ari puffed his chest. "I am strong."

Dov elbowed him. "I am stronger. Look at my muscles!" He flexed his spindly arms to show me.

With mock seriousness, I told them they were equally brawny and Talia would have no worries with such powerful ramparts protecting her—especially when Ari was named for a lion and Dov for a bear.

Out of the corner of my eye, I noticed the faintest trace of a smile on Ayal's face before he beckoned the boys to help him gather sticks for kindling. He gestured to the two women who squatted near the fire, making bread, assuring me that I was safe with them nearby.

I recognized Aiyasha, the tall, ebony-haired woman who had fetched Dvorah and me for the birth, but the other woman, with tight brown curls framing her round face, seemed closer to Marah's age. Marah was not with them, but I assumed these were Ayal's brothers' wives. Ayal made no move to introduce them.

After he left, the women darted a few glances my way but continued to ignore me. Feeling like an interloper, I went inside Ayal's tent, found a soft blanket, and swaddled Talia. She quickly dropped off to sleep.

With nothing else to do, I lay watching her suckle in her

dreams, tiny eyelashes fluttering against her cheeks, and thought of Ayal. His gentleness with his sons, seeming rejection of the baby, and unacceptable actions with me by the stream wove a tangled mass of questions through my thoughts. I could not reconcile any one with the others.

Lulled by Talia's soft breaths and unable to keep my eyes from drifting shut, I fell asleep, but the steady thrum of accusation whispered through my dreams. *My fault. My fault.*

19

A shadow beckoned me from sleep. Threads of blurred images clung to me for a few moments—a face by a stream, a brown sparrow, a voice calling my name again and again . . .

With reluctance, I opened my eyes. A ring of afternoon light surrounded a form in the doorway, blinding me. I blinked, trying to clear the sleep from my mind.

"I'm sorry to wake you."

Ayal. My pulse thrummed as a barrage of memories further clouded my vision, spurred by his soft words reaching to me from the shadows—his smile framed by deep grooves as we worked side by side with the sheep, his amber eyes holding me captive by the river, his lips beckoning mine. A spike of anger rushed to my heart's defense. Ayal had taken advantage of my girlish fantasies—just like the Egyptian. He had betrayed me.

How long had I slept? I sat up, instantly struck by a headache from the piercing sunlight through the tent flap. Jostled by my quick movement, Talia awoke. Her little arms had slipped free of her swaddling and now grasped the air in displeasure. Clucking reassurances, I pulled her onto my lap.

With an apologetic look, Ayal dropped the tent flap behind

himself, shutting out the intrusive light. He stepped forward, and instinctively I shrank back.

He put out a hand, concern creasing his brow. "I won't—" He closed his eyes for a moment and took a breath. "I won't touch you again. I promise."

I clutched Talia closer to my body, afraid that his words did not match his intentions. Voices murmured outside the tent. If he moved any closer, I could yell. I sucked in a surreptitious breath.

"But I must ask—" His tone was hesitant, almost pleading. "I need your help, since Dvorah can only come a couple of times a day." He dropped a brief glance to Talia. "Until I figure out what to do with—" He swallowed. "With the baby."

Exhaling, I dropped my eyes to the small bundle in my arms. "But surely your family—"

"No." He rubbed his forehead with the heel of his palm. "They won't have anything to do with Leisha's child."

He spoke of the little one as if she was not connected to him at all. A rush of pity for the infant conquered my apprehension. I could not walk away, leaving her alone with a father who wanted nothing to do with her. What would happen to her if I refused?

"I promised your wife that I would help," I said without taking my eyes off the object of my vow.

He blew out a short breath. "Thank you."

"And what of the boys?"

He scratched at his beard. "They can go with me to tend the sheep."

"Two little boys under your feet while you work? And what about building the Mishkan?" I shook my head, remembering their antics from earlier. At some point they would need to learn from their father, but as young as they were, for now they would be more of a distraction than a help. "I will take them with me during the day. I am sure Kiya would be happy to help entertain them."

"Don't you have your duties as a midwife?"

"No." My response was terse. "I am needed here."

"They will not be a bother to you?"

I attempted a tight smile. "They are sweet boys. We will be fine."

Relief dripped from his features. "I cannot thank you enough. I assure you it will only be a temporary arrangement."

I nodded. *Temporary.*

"As for that day . . ." He cleared his throat. "Shira . . ."

The look in his eyes and the desperate way he spoke my name whisked me back to the stream and the brush of his lips against mine. I recoiled with alarm, reminded of his deception.

He held out a hand. "Please, I must tell you—"

"What is going on in here?" Marah stood in the doorway of the tent, naked suspicion in the caustic look she divided between us. Like a mouse trapped in a corner, guilt held me captive.

Ayal sighed. "We are discussing plans for the children."

She squinted at him. "You should not be alone with this girl."

Although I had been suspicious of Ayal before, somehow Marah's insinuations made my hackles rise. He had seemed almost apologetic before she interrupted.

"What kind of a man do you think I am—?"

"I know *just* what sort of man you are." Her accusation was a well-honed blade.

He flinched as though stung, and his fists clenched at his sides. "Shira will be taking the baby with her for now, and watching Dov and Ari during the day. I will supply her family with extra wool and milk in exchange for her help." He glanced at me, all hint of repentance wiped away. "Is that acceptable to you?"

Although tempted to refuse the offer and escape this uncomfortable situation, for the sake of Talia and the boys I agreed. But for my own sake, I would remember—I *must* remember—*this is temporary.*

20

DVORAH

19 CHESHVAN
8TH MONTH OUT FROM EGYPT

Matti clung to me, his little face pressed against my shoulder. Liquid brown eyes gazed up at me as I prepared bread from the day's manna. The shadows behind those dark pools made me grind my teeth.

"*Ima* stay?"

I tried to reassure him, yet skirted around any promises. The truth was, if Reva summoned me, I had to go. Babies were born at all hours of the day and night; they were no respecters of my brief time with my son.

Some days I wished I had never agreed to apprentice as a midwife. At the time it had seemed a way to escape the oppression of an overfull tent, and an occupation for my mind. Crammed into one room with my brother-in-law's two Egyptian wives, their five brats, and Matti—while Hassam enjoyed the other room to himself—was pure torture. But being forced to leave my son *with* them each day was even more excruciating. Whenever I returned from a delivery or from checking on mothers with Shira, Matti was starving, both for attention and for food. The two witches wouldn't lower themselves to doing more than ensuring he stayed out of the fire and their belongings.

"What do you have for me today?" Hassam's voice grated like flint against metal.

"Only some milk." I gestured toward the jug Ayal had provided.

Hassam's nostrils flared. "That's it? You've been in quite a few tents these past few days."

I steadied my breathing, willing myself not to twitch. "No. Either the last ones have their gold hidden well or they've given it all away to build the Mishkan."

He snorted. "Fools. Mosheh and his greedy brother must be laughing their heads off at these halfwits filling baskets with gold and jewelry. No one needs that many materials to build a big tent. Those two are sleeping on finer linens than Pharaoh, I don't doubt."

I shrugged a shoulder. I didn't care if they slept on diamonds and rubies, those sorcerers terrified me with their glowing clouds and their dark magic. I wanted nothing to do with them. When Reva had brought Miryam to witness a birth, the old priestess had slanted condemning glances at me the whole day, as if she could see everything—the cow.

Hassam crouched down next to me at eye level, his cutting gaze slicing straight to my core. "You'd better be telling the truth."

"Of course I am." One wing of the golden Isis amulet pilfered from Leisha's belongings after she died pressed into my abdomen. The safest place for the charm was in my belt, tied about my waist. My goddess would protect me.

Hassam's arrogant smile reminded me of the open-mouthed

gape of a skull. "Bring me something better next time. Much better."

He reached out and I flinched, thinking he would hit me again. But instead he caressed Matti's golden-brown hair. "Hmm. So soft. So like my brother's hair."

Matti pressed closer to me, trembling. Fury thrummed in my temples.

Hassam stood, hooked the jug handle with two fingers, and disappeared into the tent—taking with him my payment for my own milk and the extra hours away from Matti.

Isis. Without moving, I conjured up the golden statue's fair face in my mind's eye. *I've offered years of service to you, body and soul. Please repay me. Give me some way to get away from this man.* I'd rather be working with that simpering little Levite, or nursing Ayal's baby, or even putting up with his out-of-control sons.

The realization that Shira's mysterious lover was Leisha's husband was a gift from the gods and valuable information should Shira ever threaten to cry to Reva. Yet even if she kept her mouth closed, pilfering valuables from tents was a dangerous game and my position as a midwife tenuous at best. It wouldn't be long before Ayal gave in to his leering at Shira and took her as a wife anyhow. And then where would Matti and I be?

An idea whispered in my mind. Perhaps there was a way to ensure that wouldn't happen. A way to get back what I had lost. All of it. Talia was a quiet baby. I didn't mind nursing her, and the boys could be kept in hand. I could start by making friends with Ayal's sisters-in-law. They seemed to have despised Leisha, and I certainly could work that to my advantage—sympathize with their disdain, find ways to get into their good graces, indulge their vanities. If I could convince Marah at least, Aiyasha and Yael would follow. It would take cunning, and the right words, to convince them of just what a wonderful match Ayal and I would be. *Yes, perhaps—*

I dared to slip my finger inside my belt and caress the amulet. *Thank you, Isis. You have given me the answer.*

I kissed Matti's light hair. "*Ima* will stay, my son. One way or the other, *Ima* will stay for good."

21

SHIRA

Every part of me was exhausted this morning. Any hum or sigh or tiny smack of Talia's rosebud lips was enough to jolt me awake, fearing I had rolled over on her in the night, or that she might wake my mother, Kiya, or the girls. But as she drank from the milk-spout in the night, she pulled in close, as if she could melt into my skin, making every sleepless minute of the last week worth the sacrifice.

Bleary-eyed, I entered Ayal's family campsite to fetch the boys and meet Dvorah so Talia could nurse—my peculiar new twice-daily ritual. A flurry of activity in the small area greeted me. A number of children, young and old, tossed a rag ball between them.

Dov and Ari were off by themselves as usual, squatting in the dirt and digging with sticks. My defenses sprang to life as I watched them. What did this family have against Leisha that

130

they would ignore the twins, even after her death? What gave them license to cast out such innocents on account of their parents?

Across the campsite, four women stood in a circle—Dvorah and Ayal's brothers' wives. Marah, Aiyasha, and Yael had seemed determined to make me feel like an interloper. They pointedly ignored me whenever I came for the boys, as if their hatred for Leisha had somehow spilled its black stain onto me.

Had Dvorah found a way to slip into their good graces? Engaged in the conversation, she smiled, something I had never seen before. The change transformed her face, softening the harsh lines that normally framed her mouth. But when she noticed me, her usual scowl slipped back into place. The other three women turned to stare as well, with an abrupt halt to their chatter.

Dvorah had already made friends with these strangers after weeks of rebuffing my attempts at friendship? Why did she hate me so much? And what had she told them, that they all regarded me with such disdain?

Talia sighed against my chest, and my soul echoed the sentiment. This would be painful indeed. Even slavery under a cruel mistress in Egypt had not prepared me for this ring of lionesses.

I arranged a smile on my face and approached. "Shalom." I tipped my head in greeting.

They responded with silence. Aiyasha smirked and sized me up with a glance. Dvorah huffed an exasperated breath and gestured with her hand. "Give me the baby."

I disentangled Talia from the linen wrap that secured her to my chest and instantly missed the weight and warmth of her. Dvorah snatched the baby away as if I'd been holding her for ransom.

Jarred and off-balance, I muttered a quick excuse to the impenetrable female wall and sat down nearby to watch Dov and Ari play. Although I tried to concentrate on the boys' animated questions and the treasures they brought me from their excavations in the dirt, my attention was continually snagged by the conversation behind me.

"She is Danite," said Marah after Dvorah had ducked into the tent to nurse the baby. "But she will make a good wife for Ayal. Yonah insisted he not take too long to remarry."

I could almost feel Aiyasha's haughty blue-green eyes on my back. "Yes. I believe she will. Arrangements should be made soon, for the sake of the children. It's not as if anyone is mourning Leisha anyhow."

The callousness of her statement shocked me, as did the disconcerting spike of envy in my veins. Ayal was considering marriage to Dvorah?

Marah cleared her throat, interrupting my divided thoughts. "Perhaps she can take those twins in hand. Leisha did nothing but let them run wild."

They lowered their voices, most likely speculating about me. When I could bear the tension no longer, I told the boys it was time to go back to my family's campsite, then went to see if Dvorah had finished nursing the baby. She insisted on nursing in private, which was strange, but I'd learned early on to not ask personal questions of the woman. I'd been told to mind my own affairs more than once.

I peeked through the door flap. Dvorah was stroking the baby's face and humming, rocking back and forth as Talia suckled. A narrow ray of sunlight illuminated a tear on Dvorah's cheek. Startled by the realization that I had trespassed on a tender moment, I flinched.

My sudden movement caused a shadow to fall across the pair, and in an instant Dvorah's face transformed from softness to fury. "Why are you spying on me?"

I stepped inside. "I did not mean to intrude."

Her nostrils flared. "She's not yours, you know."

"Of course not. I—"

"You won't get what you want."

I blinked a few times. "What do I want?"

She jerked her chin toward the tent door. "Him."

"What do you mean?"

"Ayal. I know you want him."

"I . . . I only want to help with the children."

Smugness hovered on her lips and condescension on her brow. "I see the way you pant after him."

Stuttering, I tried to contradict her, but she cut me off.

Her almond eyes became slits. "Did you kill her on purpose? So you could have him?"

"No!" The full impact of her accusation pierced me, and my voice rasped against its fiery assault. "I tried to save her. You know I did."

"How do you expect to be a midwife, then, if you are so incompetent?"

My mouth went slack. It was the same question I had asked myself over and over.

She twitched a shoulder. "I could not care less. Either way, you won't get him." She patted Talia's back, pressing the baby closer to her chest. Her false smile oozed malice. "Or this little one."

22

I would have removed my sandals, had I been wearing any. The ground beneath my bare feet already seemed to hum with holiness as Kiya and I entered the wide space that had been cleared for the Mishkan.

"Has Eben described what it will look like?" I asked her.

"He said there will be tall posts all around." She gestured in a wide circle. "And of course the white linen panels we are making with all the other weavers will be strung between, to form an outer courtyard."

I restrained a groan at the reminder. Three weeks ago I had asked my mother to inform Reva that I would not be returning to midwifery and would instead be helping with the long linen panels. I determined to be satisfied with being part of such a valuable service but hoped no one would too closely inspect the weave on the sections my clumsy fingers produced.

I swept my gaze over the heads of the crowd to where Levites worked at shaping and sanding beams hauled from some northern forest—just the first of the expensive materials needed

134

to fashion such a unique sanctuary in the wilderness, one that could be broken down and moved as we followed the Cloud. But the Egyptians had paid us well for hundreds of years of slavery, pushing riches into our hands as we escaped. It was their gold that would line the Mishkan walls, their silver that would fund every imported bundle of flax, their jewels that paid for every precious jar of incense and oil.

Hundreds of people stood in long lines, the atmosphere reminding me of my hometown of Iunu on a celebration day. Excited chatter and loud speculations about the Mishkan murmured all around us. Children perched on fathers' shoulders, and little ones sat astride mothers' hips—some with gold and silver trinkets gripped in pudgy hands, ready to drop in the donation baskets. I nearly expected a parade to march through, with leopard-skin-clad priests, plumed dancers, and golden gods on litters.

Mosheh had announced that his brother and nephews were to be our very own priests. The only ones who could, outside of Mosheh, approach the Most High. Surely the worship of Yahweh would be different than in the Egyptian temple, with its endless chanting and offerings to mute idols. What would worshipping the Living God be like?

Talia slept through the loud cacophony, content in her soft cocoon of linen against my chest. Her tiny, warm body fit against me like an extension of my own—I envied the peaceful sleep of this newborn who did not comprehend the dark clouds she'd been born under, and that the temporary replacement for her mother was so undeserving.

Kiya and I shuffled along with the crowd as we moved toward the collection baskets. I was grateful my mother had been willing to watch Dov and Ari today; it would have been too easy for them to slip away in the confusion.

The leather pouch around my waist missed the weight of

my midwifery oils. Its current burden, a gold and turquoise necklace, might be more costly, but it was the smell of myrrh and frankincense and the earthy tang of herbs that were priceless in my estimation. I should return the supplies to Reva, but I feared the disappointment in her eyes.

The donation baskets were nearly overflowing with gold, silver, copper mirrors, linens, rich cloth, jars of spices, and various other offerings. As I slipped my hand into my pouch to retrieve the necklace—a gift that really was from my mother—Kiya held a gift of her own over the basket.

"What are you doing?" I snatched her wrist. Dangling from her hand was her mother's necklace, given to her by Kiya's father—a token of young love carved from brilliant lapis lazuli into Hathor's image.

"It is all right." She dropped the treasure into the basket. "The memories of my mother are carved in my mind. I have no need of a false god in my tent. Perhaps the Levites might melt down the gold to use in the Mishkan."

"Are you sure?"

Tears brimmed in her honey-gold eyes. "I am. In a way it is my mother's contribution to Yahweh. I know it is what she would have done, had she the chance."

I set my own mother's gift on top of the pile of treasures, wishing I had something to give. I owned nothing, and the only thing I had to offer—my work as a midwife—had been ripped away. Talia snuggled closer, nestling her cheek against my chest. Even if it was a temporary arrangement, having this baby against my skin was like a balm.

Kiya reached over and stroked Talia's hair. "She is so content here, close to you."

Without betraying how much pain that simple statement inflicted, I could do nothing but force a smile.

Kiya dropped her hand to her stomach with a caress so fleeting I almost missed it. I had seen enough pregnant women in the last few months. Reva had told me I had a knack for divining which women were actually expecting and which were merely hopeful.

Kiya was expecting.

"It has been three weeks. Time to come back." Reva's blunt command startled me but, truth be told, only surprised me in that it had taken so long for her to deliver it.

I continued gathering tiny white pearls of manna from the shin-deep patch I stood in. Usually Reva's demands were enough to make me tremble and capitulate, but the image of Leisha's blood on my hands colored my vision red. "I'm not ready yet, Reva. I don't know that I ever will be."

"Shira. Look at me."

I straightened, tugging my wool mantle closer around my body and inhaling deeply of the sweet scent of manna to steady my resolve. The pink sky at Reva's back had already begun to retreat, giving way to a cold morning sun.

Her wrinkled face softened. "I know it hurts, my dear. I have been present for many hundreds of births and almost as many deaths. Childbirth is dangerous. As much as we hope every infant will be born safely, you will lose some. And you *will* lose mothers. Such is a product of the curse."

"I thought I was strong enough. *You* convinced me I was strong enough." The sharp accusation escaped my mouth before I was able to temper my tone. I inhaled and exhaled until I was able to compose gentle words. "But my mother was right, and Miryam was right, I am unable to handle the emotional toll of what you do, in more ways than one." I clutched the handle of my basket with two hands.

"What did Miryam say to you?" Reva leaned forward.

"The truth. That I was not strong enough to deal with the realities of midwifery."

"That is not true—"

"Like my mother says, I have always had my head in the stars. I talked myself into believing that Yahweh made me to be a midwife—"

"So you will throw away the gifts you were given? Turn away from the path you were only beginning to travel?"

"It does not matter what you say, Reva. I will weave with Kiya and my mother and care for Ayal's children until he marries again. It was selfish of me to walk away from my duty. Selfish and thoughtless. I hurt my mother, I hurt myself, and Leisha might have lived had I not interfered."

"That is not true, Shira. Laboring mothers bleed to death sometimes. It's an unfortunate risk to giving birth."

I shook my head again. "No. I don't believe you. Something happened. Perhaps if I had not shifted her—"

"You saved that baby. Leisha would have died either way. Even the Egyptian surgeons, with all their knowledge, would not have been able to prevent her death. I could not have saved her either, the blood came too fast. There are only rare exceptions where the woman's body compensates and the flow ceases. I cannot explain it, other than Yahweh wills it so. Only the giver of life has sovereignty over death."

"Perhaps that is true, but I won't chance hurting another woman like that. Besides, Yahweh did not make me to be a midwife or he would have given me the ability to block out my emotions like you."

Anguish passed across her face, disproving my accusation and causing a swift dagger of guilt to wedge between my ribs. My words had wounded her. But she lifted her chin in defiance. "You may think that I am without feeling, my dear, but I have endured more grief than you can even comprehend. My husband died in the mud pits, suffocated in the muck after being caught under a wagon wheel."

She pressed a gnarled hand to her chest. "Within a month my two baby boys were thrown into the river by the Egyptians. My beautiful sons, two years old and six months, tossed to the crocodiles—" Her voice choked to a halt. But she recovered quickly, her spine straightening. "If I had given up, allowed the devastation to break me, Pharaoh would have won. Instead, it made me stronger, able to carry others' burdens more easily on my own shoulders. And yet, it wasn't until Miryam taught me midwifery that I fully comprehended just how strong I was."

Reva's fine, silver hair floated on the morning breeze, making her appear almost as otherworldly as Mosheh. "There will always be storms, Shira. There will be loss in your life, sometimes devastating loss. But if you let the wind and the rain overcome you, then you will never fulfill the purpose for which you were born, the reason Yahweh gave you breath and brought you to this time, to this place. There will be times when there is nothing you can do but survive, to place one foot after the other into the driving rain."

Her thin lips flattened. "You can tuck your head under your wing for a while, Shira, and wait out this storm. But you will fly again."

23

16 SHEVAT
11TH MONTH OUT FROM EGYPT

Side by side, Kiya and I worked the standing linen loom that Eben and Jumo had built from acacia wood. My mother usually worked it herself, her nimble hands fluttering across the warp threads like butterflies, but today her important task, weaving a long, intricate panel for the Mishkan gates, took precedence.

My fingers ached. I stretched them wide, imagining how gnarled and pained they would be after a lifetime of separating fine flax threads to slide the shuttle through the gap, over and over again. The monotony of white on white seared my vision. I rubbed my knuckles against my bleary eyes and sighed. If only my fingers were more deft. Missed warp threads caused haphazard patterns, and I was forced to undo my stitches too many times, slowing our progress.

"Do you need a stool?" Kiya's patience with me was almost frustrating. I did not deserve it, especially when it was her body that was doing the work of creating new life.

Shaking my head, I adjusted Talia on my back. At almost

three months old, she was heavier by the day, and the sling dug into my collarbone. But determination was all I had to cling to today—I worked to absorb the pain instead of focusing on the burn and the jumble of questions that had followed me back from Ayal's campsite.

When I had gone to meet Dvorah this morning, I'd seen the two of them standing together, backs toward me, watching the boys play with a stick and a hoop. Dvorah placed a hand on his forearm, laughing over something Avi said. The movement seemed like a natural gesture, as if from a wife to her husband. Ayal did not flinch, but responded with a smile and a nod.

I'd been trying to avoid my simmering resentment—and Ayal—since I had overheard Marah and Aiyasha discussing their marriage, but Dvorah's gesture was like flint on stone, and my jealousy flared high.

Ayal should not have even considered approaching me that day by the stream. Yet he had seemed so sincere in his esteem for me then, speaking of my bravery and his belief in my calling as a midwife. Had his words been true? Or simply the words of a man trying to seduce a stupid girl? A stupid girl still foolish enough to be jealous over a man who had betrayed her, a man who, according to his brothers' wives, would soon be marrying another.

If only I could end this fruitless fascination with the man whose low, gentle voice dredged up the memory of his kiss, along with fresh guilt, whenever I was in his presence.

With a start, I realized Kiya was scrutinizing me, the corners of her mouth pulled down. Sometime during my musings over Ayal, my hands had ceased their motion. I mumbled an apology and pulled the weft thread taut.

She placed a palm over the fabric, halting my progress. "Why are you here?"

I cocked my head, startled by her abrupt question and still disoriented by the meandering path my thoughts had taken. She lifted an insistent brow.

"I . . . I am where I am needed," I stuttered.

"We don't need you to weave."

Stung, I flinched and dropped the shuttle. It rolled down my leg, unraveling into a tangle at my feet. "I want to help."

"Sweet sister, there are thousands of weavers in this camp." Kiya's hand swept a circle in the air. "Your hands are not made for this. They were made for delivering babies. You know it, and I know it. You are miserable."

"I will be fine." I rubbed a thumb into my palm, wincing at the roughness of my skin. Reva had insisted that I massage oils into my hands every day. A midwife with rough hands was useless. Now they were cracked and dry from the flax, the goat hair, and the hot water in the dye-pots, no matter how much animal fat I administered. I missed my soft hands. My clean hands. Somehow, no matter how many times I scrubbed them, they still seemed covered in blood.

With a graceless crouch so as not to upset Talia, I retrieved the shuttle from the ground and brushed off the dust. Untangling the weft, I wedged the wood between the threads again. "This is my place. I may not have your talent for weaving, but this is where I belong."

"But—"

I shook my head, ending the conversation. "Let's finish this section before Talia wakes. She will want to stretch her legs soon, and we must prepare for Shabbat."

She turned back to her work with a shake of her head, but it was not the last I would hear of her thoughts. Kiya was not one to keep her opinions to herself. But untangling my emotions was more of a task than weaving, and I had strength for only one endeavor this afternoon. We worked in silence, our movements slipping into familiar tandem as the white cloth slowly took form, top to bottom.

Talia awakened and, after devouring the manna gruel I made for her, was content to lie on her back near the loom and gaze at the sky. She kicked at her wool blanket, grinning at the clouds. A surge of pure love welled in me—a foolish pride in a child that was not, and would never be, mine. She was a universe of beauty wrapped in a tiny package. Her black hair stuck straight up on her little head. Her eyes were gray, a bit like my own, but I suspected they would transform into that peculiar hazel like her mother's.

Ari and Dov flew into the campsite, startling Talia to tears with their loud chatter. I comforted her, thinking to chide them for their thoughtlessness, but with tender kisses they soothed her upset, and soon her toothless smile stretched wide for her brothers. They had seemed to take my admonition to protect their sister seriously and doted on her.

"Abba let us come with him to the Mishkan!" Dov tugged at my sleeve. "We helped him dig holes."

"Oh, did you now? That sounds interesting." I brushed his wild bronze curls back from his face.

He nodded solemnly. "It was. I helped lift a big pole and put it in the ground."

"Is that so?"

"Yes. And pretty soon Yahweh is going to smash down and hide inside the big tent."

I suppressed a giggle at his simplistic description of the Cloud, although none of us knew exactly what Mosheh meant by the statement that Yahweh would live among us.

I tweaked his nose. "When you are an old grandfather, all wrinkled and gray, you can tell your great-grandchildren how you once dug a hole for the Mishkan and what a great responsibility that was."

Ari elbowed his brother with a glare. "I helped too."

I laughed and kissed Ari's forehead. "And did you use those enormous muscles you showed me before?"

Ari's face brightened, and he grinned. "They are even bigger now!"

"I do not doubt that one bit."

"Boys, why don't you go wash your hands? Eben has invited us to stay tonight and take our Shabbat meal together." Ayal spoke from close behind me, his low voice sending uninvited flutters through my stomach. Tension tightened my shoulders.

The twins cheered and ran to join Shoshana and Zayna at the washing pot. I followed without looking back, grateful for the escape.

Although visibly fatigued from weeks of working on the Mishkan, Eben, Jumo, and Ayal were relaxed and in high spirits before the meal. The three of them joked liked brothers, teasing and making light of one another, the promise of our weekly day of rest seeming to lift the cares from their strong shoulders. For slaves who had never enjoyed a moment of freedom in hundreds of years, the Shabbat was an invaluable gift, a beautiful reminder that the Creator cared for us.

"I hope you didn't hurt yourself again, stringing those harps," Ayal teased Eben. "I know how grueling it must be. Those of us hefting logs and clearing boulders have little idea."

"And where do you think the wood comes from for those harps, lyres, and drums? I hefted just as many logs as you, my friend—*with* an injured hand." Eben tapped a finger on his scarred palm for emphasis.

"Perhaps." Ayal scratched his chin, humor glistening in his light eyes. "But Jumo here—he truly endures the most backbreaking labor. All that painting and preparing dyes for the women . . ."

Jumo stood behind Eben and Ayal, arms folded across his chest, which had grown in width substantially in the months since his healing. "I'll have you know that I have a deep splinter from my paintbrush that refuses to come out, and my skin is permanently stained from the *tekhelet* dye." He lifted his hands to reveal lavender palms.

Ayal and Eben snickered, which provoked Jumo to slip his arms about their throats with a threat to throttle them both at the same time. Ari and Dov jumped into the fray, delighted that the men were tussling like little boys.

My mother appeared, hands on hips and black eyes flashing in mock anger. "If the three of you do not go wash and quit acting like children, there will be no meal for you tonight." She shooed them with fluttering hands.

With the look of a chastened flock of sheep, they obeyed, but not without a few wayward elbows and insults.

Ari and Dov, thinking my mother was serious in her rebuke, sidled close to me. Although I should have explained the joke and eased their concerns right away, I held them close to my sides for a few moments before doing so, memorizing the feel of their little bodies tucked under my arms, like a mother bird gathering her chicks close.

How had I fallen so deeply in love with these boys? They were not my flesh and bone, yet it was as if they had been born from my own body. Cutting off my own hand would be a lesser pain than watching them call Dvorah *ima*.

I was torturing myself by continuing this arrangement, and possibly hurting the boys.

For weeks after Leisha's death, the boys had asked me where she was, as if not truly understanding what death meant. But even then the questions were strangely detached, as if Leisha was not a beloved mother, but simply a missing relative. As time passed, my suspicions about Leisha had grown. From her strange, contradictory manner during our first meeting, to the way Ayal's family had outcasted her, to the apparent lack of mourning her children and her husband manifested—I wondered whether there had truly been something wrong with the woman.

Regardless of the tight clench the boys and Talia had on my heart, they needed a mother. And if Dvorah was to fill that void, I must step aside. I had fulfilled my vow to Leisha and made sure that Talia was cared for. Dvorah was more than capable, even if she despised me. I would approach Ayal after the meal and tell him—tonight. The violent lurch of my stomach fought against my decision, even as the rightness of it settled into my bones. I was being selfish by not disentangling myself. *I must snip the cords—now.*

Talia squawked from her blanket in the tent, awake after a short nap, no doubt demanding a change of swaddling. I rolled up the side wall and secured it, letting the afternoon sun spill inside. As soon as she was unwrapped, Talia waved her chubby legs and arms in the air, thrilled to be free. After wiping her clean, I left her unrestrained, content to watch her squirm and burble. Leisha was there in the shape of her eyes, the color of her hair, her creamy almond skin, the slope of her nose. I found myself searching for traces of Ayal and came up short. Strange to find no echo of her father in her features. Nevertheless, I hoped that he would see the beauty in this sweet baby and come to embrace her. Dvorah, brusque as she was with me, seemed to care for Talia. More than once I'd heard her whispering to the baby as she nursed, and I prayed she would love her, even if Ayal did not.

Soon it would be Dvorah tending to Talia's needs and finding joy in every subtle change of her face. I trailed a finger down that sweet face, singing a soft tune to distract myself from the thought. Talia rewarded me with a brilliant smile that twisted my decision into uncertainty. Another few days could not matter so much, could they?

A high-pitched scream jarred me to awareness. The piercing sound traveled all through my body and down to the soles of my feet. Looking up, I crossed shocked gazes with Ayal, who stood just outside the tent as if he had been watching me with the baby.

Dov. Ari.

One of the boys had made that horrific sound. I snatched up Talia and followed Ayal as he ran toward the commotion. My mother, Jumo, Kiya, and Eben stood in a tight group around Dov, who had fallen into the fire. His blistered palms trembled, and his face was bereft of color. Handing off the baby to Kiya, I reached for him. His body shuddered in my arms as my mother tended his burns with cool water, honey mixed with herbs, and soft words. Shoshana and Zayna were off to the side, clinging to each other and weeping for the little boy.

From behind, Ari's arms slipped around my neck. He pressed his face to my back, sobbing. Ayal crouched beside us, one hand on Ari's neck and the other on poor Dov's head, whispering reassurances to them with his lips—and to me with his eyes.

24

S it still for me, Dov. I promise to be careful." I slathered the honey-herb mixture onto his blistered palm with the least pressure possible, but he twisted from the pain, whimpering, luminous eyes pleading with me for relief.

I wrapped that hand in loose linen and, with much gentle coaxing and promises of one of the succulent dates that Kiya had bartered from a Moabite trader, succeeded in tending to the other hand.

Wiping the tear streaks from his face with a cloth, I urged him to lie down and rest for a while. He lay with arms outstretched, his small body shuddering in agony.

"Try to close your eyes, sweet boy. Ari and I will be just outside."

He nodded, but his eyes followed me all the way to the tent door. "Shira?"

"Yes, my brave bear?"

His cheek quirked with a hint of a smile at my reference to his namesake. "Can we go visit Abba? At the Mishkan?"

I had not spent more than a few brief moments with Ayal since Dov had been injured a few days ago. The traumatic ordeal had wiped the necessary conversation from my mind that night, and the compulsion to help tend this sweet boy had kept me from saying anything since then. I would extricate myself after Dov's hands had healed more.

I winked at him. "Yes, little bear, we will go in a while. We can take your abba something to eat. How does that sound?"

His eyes sparkled. I wasn't sure whether it was visiting his father or catching another glimpse of the mysterious Mishkan he was most excited about. My own curiosity was piqued by the idea of seeing the construction up close.

"Shira?"

"Yes, sweet boy?"

"Don't forget my date."

Laughing, I stepped into the sunshine, dropped the tent flap behind me, and then instantly wished I had not done so. Four sets of eyes, none of them friendly, turned my way. Dvorah and the other wives had stopped their conversation to stare at me—again. No matter how many times I told myself that their disapproval meant nothing, that my time here was coming to an end, the rejection stung like the lash of a scorpion.

I sighed inwardly. It was just as well. When Dvorah and Ayal married, it would be better for the children if the other wives accepted their new mother—perhaps the remaining bad blood would be washed away by the union. Dvorah was not unkind to the children. I believed the concern on her face when she discovered Dov was injured was nothing if not sincere.

Talia squealed from the blanket where she lay near the women, flailing arms reaching toward the canopy above her and smiling at the shadows that played across the fabric and the glints of sunshine that penetrated the weave. Although her eyes were still a light gray, she was the image of her *ima*. My heart cinched, both at the remembrance of the woman's death and with the love I held for her child.

Dvorah's scowl deepened. "It's about time."

I ignored the demand behind her remark and smiled. "Dov has asked to go see his father at the Mishkan. I think we will take Ayal a meal. It will be a good distraction from his hands."

"Why don't you go with them, Dvorah? I will watch the baby for you." Marah pointed a barbed glare in my direction. "Ayal will be glad of it."

Dvorah's smug smile spoke volumes. Marah did not want me anywhere near Ayal alone. Did she suspect my divided thoughts toward him? Surely not, for I worked hard to keep my distance from him. But the fact that I was bothered by the slight disturbed me much more than it should.

⟨⟩

The sheer scale of the construction overwhelmed me. What would the Mishkan look like when it was finished? Would the grand tent stand even taller than the posts that stood like giant sentinels all around the courtyard?

Would the Mishkan echo the soaring Sun Temple in Iunu? Grand pylons, intricate lotus columns, and lofty ceilings? I blinked my eyes to clear the failed imaginings out of my head. I would leave the designs to the men selected by Mosheh, some rumored to have been employed by Pharaoh himself.

Dvorah led the way through the hundreds of men raising the last of the tall timbers, a confident set to her shoulders, as if she knew exactly where to go. She had probably visited Ayal here before, taking him a meal like we did now. Again the image of them married hollowed me. I sucked in a deep breath to fill the empty space and gripped Ari's hand tighter. I had ordered Dov to stay between Dvorah and me, so he walked in front of me, his wrapped hands crossed over his chest.

"Shira!" My name rose above the din of tools against metal and wood and the shouts of the men at their various tasks. Ayal waved, laid down the adze he had been using to shape a post on the ground, and strode toward our little band.

"Abba!" Dov and Ari called out together, and Dov waved one linen-wrapped hand, then winced at the pain the enthusiastic gesture cost him.

Wearing only a roughly woven work kilt and dripping with sweat, Ayal approached us. Annoyed by my reaction to the strength of his lean body, I fixed my attention on Ari instead.

"Abba! We came to bring you a meal and some water!" My heart fluttered at the brightness in Ari's greeting. He had been so sullen since Dov had been injured. This trip to see their father had lifted his countenance as well.

"Did you hear my stomach roaring all the way from camp?"

The boys laughed, and the music of it chased away my melancholy. I handed Ayal the skin-bag filled with fresh water. With a nod of thanks he tipped it to his lips and drank deeply, emptying it with haste. With a groan of pleasure he wiped his mouth with the back of his hand, an easy smile turned toward me. I glanced at Dvorah, who hung off to the side, trouble in her expression.

"Dvorah has brought you some food." I motioned toward her, hoping she would see it as a gesture of goodwill.

"There are manna cakes and some dried gazelle meat." Dvorah handed Ayal the basket with a broad smile. The expression lit her face and highlighted the beauty of her dark eyes, her straight nose, and her olive skin. "And also a few dates, since I know you are partial to those."

"Thank you, Dvorah." Ayal took the basket and then turned to me. "Are you all staying to eat with me?"

His lack of acknowledgment of the woman he was to marry caught me off guard. "Oh . . . no. The boys just wanted to see you. Especially Dov." I darted a sad glance at the little boy.

"He is having a difficult time this morning, not being able to run and play."

Ayal's smile faltered for a brief moment, but then his eyes crinkled. "Why don't you two show Shira the hole you helped me dig? I'm sure she would enjoy seeing the fruits of your hard labor."

"Which was it, Abba?" Dov's voice pitched high with excitement.

Ayal pointed to one of the many identical pillars that were spaced evenly along the perimeter of the courtyard. Even with his injured hands still crossed over his chest, Dov beat Ari to the spot, but only because Ari insisted on pulling me along by the hand.

Dov tipped back his dark little head to take in the height of the pillar. "Abba, it's even taller than you!"

Ayal laughed, shielding his eyes against the bright sun. "Yes, son, that it is, and you helped dig the hole it sits in."

Both boys grinned with pride.

"However." Ayal pointed to the western end of the courtyard where a small army of men were working. "The Mishkan will be even taller. Twice as tall, in fact. We will be able to see it from all over the valley."

Ari slipped his hand into Ayal's large one. "What will it look like, Abba?"

"I can only tell you what I have been told, but you see those men there?" He pointed west again. "Those men are hewing logs to build the wooden walls that will make the frame of the tent."

He knelt on one knee and drew a rectangle in the sand, then divided it into a large portion and a smaller one. "There will be a sanctuary here, separated by tall curtains." He pointed to the small area. "And only the High Priest will be allowed inside. The walls, which will be plated in gold, will be able to be taken down and loaded on wagons for our journey to Canaan."

"When will that be, Abba?" asked Dov.

Ayal lifted his face toward the boy. "I do not know. But I would guess from all the construction that we are undertaking, it may be months."

"Won't it rain inside the walls?" Ari pressed a finger into the center of Ayal's drawing. "It needs a roof."

Ayal laughed. "That it does. Hundreds of weavers have been working on two layers of coverings that will span the gap, making a tent over the frame of the walls. And this afternoon many of us will be leaving to go back to the sea to hunt animals whose hides will provide the last layer, a waterproof covering."

"Are you going hunting too, Abba?" Dov's brow furrowed deeply.

Ayal ran a gentle hand across the boy's unruly curls. "Yes, son, I am going too. But I will not be gone long. I will miss you too much." His eyes lifted and met mine with inexplicable intensity. "Perhaps we will have a celebration as soon as I return."

"We will?" Ari clapped his hands. "A feast?"

Even Dov perked up at the idea. "Will you bring back some meat, Abba?"

"That I will." He knelt down and brushed the bronze curls from Dov's face. "And I have a secret—" He leaned forward to whisper in the boy's ear, and Dov's mouth rounded in surprise. "If your hands feel better when I return, we will go. All right?"

Dov nodded and leaned his head on his father's shoulder. "I will miss you, Abba."

Ayal brushed his fingers through the boy's hair. "You and Ari will take good care of the women while I am gone?"

Dov sneaked a furtive peek at me. "Even Shira?"

"Yes," said Ayal with a glance of his own as he placed his hand on his son's cheek. "Especially Shira."

A thread of unbidden emotion snagged against the memory

of his hand on my own face, as if I could still feel the warmth of his work-worn skin. My lungs refused to expand.

"We must go." Dvorah's sharp interruption commandeered my attention.

"Yes . . ." I held out a hand to Ari. "Your father has much to do. Shall we see if my *ima* has any treats for you?" I wiggled my brows. "Jumo discovered a beehive in a cave yesterday."

Ari licked his lips, and Dov's eyes could have engulfed the moon.

"Shira," said Ayal, "I need to speak with you." His solemn tone sliced through my mirth, hinting at the gravity of the forthcoming conversation.

It is over. He is announcing his betrothal. I nodded my head but did not answer for fear that my lips would tremble. I had known it would be coming for so long now, I had justified in my mind every reason why this man should marry Dvorah, but for some inexplicable reason, my heart refused to listen to rationality.

"We are leaving for the hunt in an hour, but perhaps before I leave?"

"Of course—"

A pained cry halted my response, and I swung around. Dvorah was on the ground, one leg twisted beneath her. I dropped Ari's hand and rushed back. "Are you injured?"

She rebuffed my concern with a brusque flip of her hand, but when Ayal approached with the same question, she lifted her head, a guileless expression softening her features.

"I've twisted my foot on a rock," she said with a grimace.

"Can you walk?" Ayal put out a hand to aid her.

Dvorah attempted to stand but cried out when her foot met the ground, a reaction that seemed a bit contrived, considering the small stone she had slipped on. She slumped back to the ground, looking as helpless as a child.

154

"I will take you back to your campsite," Ayal said. He offered a quick explanation over his shoulder to his fellow workers, slipped his tunic over his head, and then scooped Dvorah off the ground with perfect ease, as if she were as light as one of his boys.

"Will you be all right to take the children back to your family, Shira?"

His lack of confidence in me flared irrational annoyance. "We will be fine."

Ayal walked away, cradling Dvorah. She snaked her arm around his neck, looking up at him and smiling as if the sun had newly risen in his eyes. She said something I could not hear, and Ayal's laughter floated back to me. Clutching Ari's hand, perhaps a little too tightly, I walked back to the campsite with the children, firm in the knowledge that my time with them was all but over.

DVORAH

Ayal was lean but strong. He carried me as if I weighed nothing. The job of a shepherd must be more strenuous than I'd guessed.

"How is your ankle?" he asked, polite concern in his voice.

I moved my foot, causing the silver anklet to jingle and hoping to bring attention to the curve of my exposed calf. I feigned a wince, sucked a breath through my teeth, and summoned a sheen of tears.

"That bad?"

I sniffed. "Next time I will spend more time watching where I am going instead of gawking at the construction."

He laughed. "A good plan."

I could not help but compare Ayal's eyes to my husband's again. They were nice—warm even—but could not match the fire of Tareq's sapphire ones and the look of them as he promised to rescue me from my chains. *Come with me, Dvorah. I'll take you away from here. You'll never have to sell your body again.* And he had been true to his word. He snatched me out of my misery, only to lose interest as soon as my belly began to grow with his child.

Shaking off the memory, I determined that its echoes would not interfere with my goal. My ruse must be convincing. Even so, I could not forget that Ayal was one of the Levites. One of those who speared my husband without compunction. I drew a steadying breath through my nose, girding myself for what I must do—make Ayal forget all about that little Levite girl.

Shira had walked away, one boy on each side. Silent. Obedient. It was almost laughable how subservient she was. *This won't be difficult at all.*

Since Leisha died, Shira had been extra careful to not be alone with Ayal, or even within his vicinity. She met me at his campsite every morning with Talia, sat quietly as I nursed her, and then herded the boys back to her own campsite while Ayal went off to the fields. In the evening, the process was reversed, since the boys slept with their father.

She rarely spoke more than a few words to him. In fact, today was the most I had seen them interact. And as usual, Ayal had eyes for nothing but her. Ridiculous.

But I knew how to get what I wanted. I was my mother's daughter. I had spent the last couple of months convincing Marah, Aiyasha, and Yael that I was the perfect wife for Ayal. Now all I had to do was convince him.

"I so appreciate you helping me." I curved my body in closer and, dredging up what little charm I had left beneath the ash, turned up an innocent smile. "I feel quite foolish."

He looked away, shoulders tensing as if to brace against the effect of my body against his. "And I appreciate how much you have helped with the baby."

Curious. In the past few weeks that I had been nursing Talia, I had never heard Ayal say her name. Not once. It was always *the child* or *the baby*. Strange that he would reject the little one. Was it grief that made him do so? *No.* He looked at Shira as if she were the only star in the sky. Ayal was not pining after his dead wife.

He seemed to genuinely care for the boys. He doted on them, taking them with him into the field, playing games and wrestling with them. An ache for my own son and the empty place his father had left began to throb. Would Ayal do the same for my boy? Or would he reject him like he did Talia? I flicked away the thought. It did not matter—anyone, anything, was better than Hassam.

I adjusted my body in his arms, tightening my grip around his neck, my fingers slipping into his dark hair. His muscles stiffened, and he flinched—not a reaction I was used to from men. Perhaps a different tactic?

"Dov's hand is healing well. The swelling is down, and it's beginning to scar over." Of course the boy would let no one but Shira touch him, so I hoped my guess was accurate.

He sighed. "I am glad to hear that. He is being quite brave, isn't he?"

"He is. He is a strong boy."

Pride lit his face. Victory! The way to Ayal's heart was through his boys. Pushing my discovery further, I continued. "And Ari seems to be very intelligent, for one so young."

"I agree. He helps me count the sheep and asks so many questions." Ayal's chest seemed to expand. "It amazes me how fast they learn and change."

"It is true. My Matti is younger than your boys, but every

time I return to camp it seems he has grown a little—" I stopped, shocked at myself for revealing so much. *Keep to your plan, Dvorah.*

"Perhaps you can bring Matti to play with Ari and Dov one of these days. They certainly could use some playmates."

Panic slipped between my ribs. Matti's light hair and fair skin would give away his Hittite lineage in a moment. I could not chance it for now. "My sisters-in-law watch him while I am gone. It's best that way."

A shadow of curiosity crossed his face at my too-harsh words. Frantic to recover, I looked up from under my lashes, smiling and pressing down the repulsion that came with offering up myself, and my son, to a Levite. "But I do think they would get along very well. Matti would adore Dov and Ari."

He returned my smile. Perhaps turning his head from Shira would not be as difficult as I'd thought. Obviously he was unfaithful to Leisha, why would Shira be any different? Before much longer, Talia would be mine. And my son and I would make a permanent move into Ayal's tent.

25

SHIRA

Tears streamed down Dov's face, dripping off his quivering chin in quick succession. My own vision blurred and swam as I held his trembling body in my lap.

Even Reva's unflappable demeanor was affected by the painful cries of the little boy as she unfolded his fingers with her own. Applying a firm-yet-gentle grip on his wrist with one hand, she used the other to slowly stretch the scarred skin on his palms. She winced as he screamed again. My mother had asked Reva to check Dov's progress, and she had declared it was already time to begin such ministrations. Although it physically hurt me to agree, I trusted Reva's knowledge. She had trained with a knowledgeable Egyptian healer in Avaris many years ago.

I kissed Dov's salty face and swallowed my own sob before I spoke. "I am sorry, sweet boy." I gripped him tighter as he squirmed and tried to yank his wounded hand from Reva's grasp. "We must help your hands to heal correctly."

His eyes begged me to end the torture.

"We have to stretch your fingers now, little bear, or you won't be able to stretch them out later. You want to be able to throw rocks and play with your wooden sword, don't you?"

His lip quavered as he nodded.

"Eben also injured his hand, remember?"

He blinked confirmation.

"The healers told him to stretch his hand and apply oils as well, and he is able to move it more and more each day. Eben is very brave, isn't he?"

Dov's eyes grew wide. Eben was a favorite of his, and a kinship had formed between them due to their similar wounds.

"Then can you be brave again? And let Reva help you?"

He sniffed, every muscle in his body stiffening, but he lifted his chin. "Yes."

"Good. I knew you would. Maybe someday you will be as quick with a knife as Eben."

He sat up taller, as if considering that possibility. With a deep inhale, he lifted his arm, hesitated, then placed his hand back in Reva's palm.

"Now." I forced my voice to lift. "Why don't we sing while Reva rubs some oil into your palm?"

Dov always responded to my little songs, and the corners of his mouth turned up, even as Reva poured the oil. The spicy scent of frankincense filled the tent, and I wondered where she had procured the highly concentrated and expensive oil. Perhaps it was a payment for a delivery?

Although Dov jerked back a time or two as Reva worked the fragrant mixture into the thick scar that had begun to form across his hand, he sang with me. The song about chasing a wild desert cat was one I had learned as a little girl, and it got progressively louder and louder with each verse. By the time Reva was done with her ministrations, Dov was smiling and laughing at the outcome of the song and the ensnaring of the wildcat.

"I'd like to have a cat. Have you ever had one, Shira?" He leaned against my shoulder and looked up, admiration in his gaze.

"No, little bear. I have not had a cat of my own, although my mistress back in Iunu had many, and I enjoyed petting them when I had the chance."

"She did?"

"Yes. She had gray ones and black ones and even a golden-colored one with only one eye."

His brows lifted. "Truly?"

"He was an ornery old cat, and I suspect he lost that eye in a fight. I called him Pharaoh when my mistress was not around."

Dov's laughter was a song in and of itself. Fleetingly, I wondered what it would sound like when he was a man, when the timbre of it stretched long. Would it be a low, soothing tone like his father's? A wave of longing pulled at me. The silken rumble of Ayal's laughter still visited my daydreams far too often, especially in the past two weeks since he had been away on the hunt. I'd been almost relieved that he'd been unable to speak to me before he left; it had given me the opportunity to pretend his announcement would not split me in two, and to instead enjoy my fleeting time with the children.

With a kiss to his forehead, I sent Dov off to play. Ari had been sitting near the entrance of the tent, waiting for his brother to endure Reva's oil treatment. A cursory glance at his face before the boys walked off together to find Shoshana and Zayna told me that he was disturbed by the sounds of his twin's distress.

Since the incident with the campfire, Dov had awoken screaming a number of times, terror running in rivulets down his face, calling out for someone to take away the flames. Each time, Ari's stricken expression beckoned me to comfort him as well. Although he said nothing, his dark eyes spoke of a burden that no little boy should have to carry. He blamed himself, I was sure of it. In the dark of the tent, I cuddled him and whispered again and again that it was only an accident, that it was not Ari's fault Dov had fallen into the fire. Though he nodded his head, it was obvious that he could not absolve himself of his brother's wounds.

Jumo had informed me that Ari had indeed pushed Dov as they'd played a game of chase. It had not been malicious, only a sad fact of chance that Dov had backed over a log and wheeled directly into the embers.

A four-year-old boy could have little understanding of such unfortunate and random accidents. His formerly carefree perceptions of life and the realities of a broken world had collided in his immature mind. A realization I remembered all too well from when my father died.

"When can I expect you to resume your duties?" Reva's direct query shattered my contemplation.

"You know I have given it up." I darted a glance away to break the intense stare she unleashed on me, but then, with a strange surge of courage, I met her eyes again. I had made my decision—no matter the yearnings that continued to haunt me.

She frowned, the wrinkles around her mouth converging into a bow of displeasure. "No. You were discouraged, but you miss it."

"I do not." The ripping ache inside my chest battled the falsehood. My heart still bled from the loss. Every pregnant woman I saw, every insistent newborn cry, every shadow that passed by our tent in the still night poured salt on the lacerations. But my desires were worth nothing. I deserved the pain Leisha could no longer feel. Although my insides curled at Reva's perusal, I pulled my arms tight about my middle to hold my resolve together.

"You cannot still be blaming yourself for that woman's death," she snapped.

I busied my hands with brushing sand off the rug beneath me.

"Shira, I told you that had nothing to do with you. She would have died whether I was there or not."

"You cannot know that."

"Yes. I do. Because it is not you or I who hold life in our hands. We are not Yahweh. We are only vessels to be used for his purposes." Her tone softened, and she laid her hand on my arm.

I tensed but held still. *A broken vessel.*

"You have scars, Shira. Deep scars. You forget that I know you. I was there that day. I saw the depths of the wounds you received from that Egyptian. And I know that you blame yourself for what he did. You were thirteen, my dear girl. He saw you as a wolf sees a lamb."

Akharem's eyes, warm and teasing, sparked in my memory, then transformed to black and predatory as the scene in our dark and empty home came at me like an avalanche, suffocating me with the force of its intrusion, drawing hot tears from the fountain of pain that erupted to the surface.

Reva's soft hands were suddenly on my face, steadying me, drawing me back into the present with their firm pressure. "You see, precious girl? Leisha's death deepened those scars, thickened them. I know you feel like that attack was your fault. I know you feel that Leisha's death was your fault, but it's not the truth."

I sniffed and tried to shake my head, eyes squeezed shut.

"You are telling yourself lies and believing them. Instead of putting the oil of truth on those scars, you are allowing them to grow thicker. If you do not stretch those scars, tug at them, force movement into them, then they will continue to have a hold over you."

She brushed my cheekbones with her thumbs. "Open your eyes, Shira."

With reluctance I obeyed.

"I believe—" Her penetrating gaze demanded my attention. "I believe that you will be a midwife whose skills far outweigh mine one day."

Disagreement formed on my lips.

"But—" She interrupted before my argument could escape. "But until you accept the storms, and stop blaming yourself for them, you will not see how Yahweh has blessed you with them."

Blessed with storms?

"Yahweh told Avraham hundreds of years ago that we would endure slavery under Pharaoh. Did you ever stop to ask yourself why he would do such a thing?" She raised a silvered brow.

I shrugged. "To punish unbelief?"

She pushed out her bottom lip and pulled her spindly knees up to her chest. "Perhaps it was a consequence for disobedience. Or for the egregious sin committed by the brothers of Yosef when they sold their own flesh and blood to Egypt for twenty pieces of silver. But I think that although Yaakov's sons meant to destroy their brother, Yahweh meant to show his goodness."

"Goodness?"

"Without witnessing the mercilessness of an evil king, we would not appreciate the kindness of our own. Without the bitterness of slavery, we wouldn't know the sweetness of freedom. Without the blackness of the night sky, there would be no stars."

My attention was drawn to the summit of the mountain by her words. She was right. If I had not seen the miraculous, incomprehensible way Yahweh saved us from Pharaoh with my own eyes, I would not truly understand the heights of his power.

"We have to endure the storms, dear one, so we know how deep our roots go. So we can appreciate the depths of our strength and the freshness of the gentle breezes afterward."

The things she said made sense. Had I been holding on to my wounds? Not allowing them to heal? Closing up my fist until I could not move? I inhaled, her wisdom spinning around inside my head, clashing against the broken pieces and flipping them upside down. Did my roots go deeper than I realized?

26

27 SHEVAT
11TH MONTH OUT FROM EGYPT

Southeast of camp, a group of traders had formed their
wagons into a makeshift market, hoisting colorful awnings
over their wares—one of the steady stream of caravans that
saw opportunity in our numbers. The crush of people pressing
toward the collection of goods was astounding; even the bone-
chilling cold this morning could not dampen the atmosphere
of anticipation.

My mother had agreed to watch Ayal's children so I could
accompany Kiya to look for Tyrian purple dye. It came at a
steep price, but Kiya had one of the last of her mother's jewels,
a gold bracelet studded with turquoise, which should be worth
a decent amount.

My satchel held one of my mother's beautifully embroidered
belts to trade. I hoped to find some trinket to distract Dov from
his still-healing hands, and Ari from the gray cloud that seemed
to hang lower over his head each day.

How unfair it must seem to such a small boy that his only
playmate could do nothing more than sit about the campsite

or sleep. And with Ayal gone to hunt, there was little to spark excitement in either of them.

My divided heart wished for Ayal's hasty return at the same time as it cried out against it. Although Dvorah still met me at Ayal's campsite to nurse Talia, having all three children close to me night and day seemed like a paradise. A delight that would soon be passed on to Dvorah. I would savor these last beautiful days with them.

"Do you see any dyes?" Kiya stood on tiptoe, eyeing the adjoining wagons, her breath hanging in midair from the cold. We had arrived early. The sun was barely peeking over the eastern ridge between heavy gray clouds, yet we were still trapped in the center of the jostling crowd.

I decided to needle her a bit, test my suspicions about her pregnancy. "What exactly do you need this dye for?"

A smile formed in her eyes before it spread to her lips. "A special garment."

"Oh?" I teased. "For whom?"

She pressed a hand to her abdomen. "You know, don't you?"

"About the baby?" I leaned close. "Of course. I have known for weeks. You do not hide your feelings well, my friend."

She elbowed me. "Why did you not say anything?"

"I figured that you would tell me when you were ready."

Regret flickered in her eyes. "I did not want to hurt you . . . after what your mother said . . . and then after Ayal's wife died, there did not seem to be a good time to share this sort of news with you."

"Kiya." I slipped my hand into hers. "You are the sister of my heart. Regardless of my inability to have children, I am overjoyed that you and my brother will soon have your own."

"Will you—" She curled a lip between her teeth. "I know you have been struggling with the decision to return to midwifery. But I want you to deliver my child."

My knees wobbled, and my head shook of its own accord. "No, Kiya. I cannot."

"But Reva says you are a natural midwife. How can you turn away from the gift you've been given?"

When Ayal and Dvorah married, there would be nothing left for me but weaving. And Reva had caused me to question how tightly I was clinging to my fears. I could not deny that I missed midwifery, sometimes to the point of distress. I missed the rush of excitement that accompanied each labor. I missed breathing in rhythm with the women, assuring them of their own strength as they pushed, the collective release inside the tent when the babe let loose its first cry—even the honor of mourning with the mothers whose little ones arrived without breath. Most of all, I missed the feeling of satisfaction after I walked away from a family with one new member whose entrance into the world I had witnessed.

But still, Leisha haunted me. I could never put Kiya or her child in such danger. No. Only a true midwife—one not paralyzed by doubts—should deliver Kiya's baby.

By the time we reached the wagons, supplies had dwindled considerably. The stall in front of us held only bronze daggers, a few clay pots, and a variety of stone and wooden idols and amulets. More than a few of the carvings were quietly being purchased as I looked on.

Hadn't these people learned anything from the incident with the golden bull-calf? Why could they not leave the gods of Egypt behind them, like Kiya and Jumo had done? Why did they insist on clinging to their chains?

The memory of Miryam's rebuke—that I stand up against such foolishness—rang in my ears. A sudden urge to fly at the traders and knock over their stalls surged inside me. I tamped it down with internal rebuke for even entertaining such a strange notion. Who was I to say anything? I was not a prophetess like

167

Miryam, or a leader like Mosheh. To distract myself from my silly imaginings, I focused on scanning the stalls.

"There!" I pointed at a wagon to our left. "I see bright colors and dried flowers in those pots."

Kiya grabbed my hand and snaked her way unapologetically through the mass of bodies. I received almost as many glares as she did, but she ignored them all. If only I could be so assertive; my insides curled into knots at the pointed malice in many expressions.

"Do you have any purple?" Kiya asked the Midianite trader as we reached his improvised market stall.

His bushy brows peaked momentarily, perhaps surprised at the sight of an Egyptian among a throng of Hebrews. But surprise gave way to a practiced expression of casual indifference. This man was ready to haggle.

"Perhaps." He shrugged a shoulder and scratched at his grizzled beard.

"And how much do you want for just a cupful?"

He named a steep price.

Kiya shook her head.

The trader glowered. "Even just a bit is precious. The dye I have is from the far north, made by the only ones who know how to harvest it from the snails."

Kiya was her mother's daughter, and Nailah had been well known as an expert at finagling the best price. Kiya narrowed her eyes at the Midianite. "And how do I know you have the best? Just last week some traders came from the north and claimed just the same. You came up through Egypt." She patted the leather pouch at her waist with a little sigh. "No, I think I will save my gold."

His eyes widened infinitesimally, and Kiya seized on the hesitation. With a dismissive wave of her hand, she turned away.

"Wait!" The trader grabbed her sleeve.

Kiya winked at me. I nearly jeopardized the deal by giggling but held my composure. My friend arranged a disinterested look on her beautiful face before turning back around.

"Truly, this dye is from Tyre itself. Although we came by way of Egypt, we first came down through Edom, where we heard of this nation out here in the wilderness." He stretched a gap-toothed smile across his weathered face. "And this many people in the wilderness . . . well, you can imagine we saw the potential."

"I'm sure you did. But, my friend, my mother was the best of the merchants in the market of Iunu. You will not find me as full of *potential* as many of these others." She shifted her stance and lowered her eyelids. "How do I know you tell the truth?"

"I tell you, this is direct from the shores of Tyre. The whole city reeks of rot during the process." He blew air through pursed lips and waved a dirty hand under his nose. "I've never smelled such a stink. No wonder it's so costly."

Kiya waited, assessing him for a moment, and then named her own price, one much lower than the worth of the bracelet and to include a basket of dried indigo flowers with the purple dye. He countered, accepted the gold bracelet in payment, and handed over the goods.

Spying on the table a couple of magnificently carved horses with heads reared back and tails flying, I nudged Kiya and handed her the embroidered belt. "See if you can buy those as well, for the boys."

Defeated by Kiya's superior trading skills, the merchant handed the two carvings over without any fuss, and we pushed our way back through the crowd. I held onto the back of Kiya's dark green tunic with one hand so we would not get separated, gripping the handle of the basket of flowers, with the horses tucked in among them, tight in my other.

When we were almost clear of the crowd, I shouted to her

over the noise. "Remind me never to barter for anything unless you are with me."

Her eyes sparkled, bright from the victory over the trader. But before she could respond, she tripped. She fell so fast that I could do nothing to stop her from landing on the ground. Her arms were tight around the small pot of precious purple dye, and thankfully none of it spilled.

Adjusting the handle of the basket over my arm, I helped her to her feet.

"Stay on the ground, *zonah*. It's where you belong" came a woman's voice from nearby.

Kiya's fall was no accident.

"Go back to Egypt" spat another voice, male this time.

"Ignore it," I said, grabbing her hand. "Let's just go on."

She took a deep breath, and then a step, but was pushed back by the shoulder of another woman.

"You don't belong here." An expression of seething hatred was in the woman's eyes, which were lined with thick kohl. An irony—Kiya's were unadorned today.

Kiya stood her ground. "I am just as much a part of this nation as you. I took part in the Covenant."

My heart cheered her, but just as quickly, fear quenched the pride. We were surrounded by people who immediately judged Kiya's character by her heritage and the actions of her ancestors.

"That Covenant is for our people, not yours." The woman pushed her florid face near Kiya's.

I could not keep my mouth closed any longer. "The law given by Mosheh says different. All are welcome. And my *sister*"—I accented the marital relation—"abides by the Torah, just as you." I marveled at the strength of my own voice. "Don't you see that we are one nation here? We are not slaves anymore, squabbling over bits of bread. We must come together, fight *for* each other, not against."

The woman's eyes narrowed to slits. "Your *sister* should have been put to the sword with the rest of the idol worshippers."

I shivered at the threat and the gleam of imminent attack in her eyes. The confident set of Kiya's shoulders seemed to droop, so I moved to stand in front of my friend, praying Yahweh would give my spine the strength of an oak tree. But before I could test whether I had any roots at all, someone else rose to Kiya's defense.

"Let these girls be." A man appeared next to us. Although the shadow of a graying beard covered his chin, the kohl on his eyes, the slope of his nose, and the set of his mouth identified him as Egyptian.

The woman's face betrayed nothing, but she took a tiny step backward. Perhaps the echo of an overseer's voice had flared to life at the Egyptian's words.

"These girls have done nothing to you. Let them pass." His words were so steady that I envied their calm delivery.

A Hebrew man pushed himself ahead of the woman, indignation blazing in his expression. "How dare you speak to my wife like that!"

All around us the crowd quieted, curious faces watching this tense interaction.

The Egyptian tipped his head, clearly aware of our precarious position. "I meant no harm."

"You meant no harm?" the man sneered. "Did your king mean no harm when he shackled our people for two hundred years? Or when he murdered our babies?"

"That is not—"

"How dare you lecture us on how we treat you *gerim*. All you have done is create problems. It is your fault there ever was a golden idol in this camp. And your fault that so many died because of it."

The Egyptian put up a hand and shook his head. "I had

nothing to do with such a thing. I follow Yahweh and I have for many years, even before I knew his name. I married a Hebrew woman long ago. Those who died that day did so because they were involved in the debauchery of their own free will."

Confusion weighted the Hebrew's brow for a moment, until it gave way to a heated glare. "It makes no difference."

"Perhaps not to you," said the Egyptian. "But there are many of us among this multitude who took part in the Covenant. As the young lady said, we are all one now."

"I will never"—spittle formed at the corners of the man's mouth—"be a brother to someone whose people enslaved my own. And that girl"—he pointed at me—"is obviously a traitor."

Fear rushed up my back and spread across my shoulders as a few shouts of agreement volleyed around us. Then, before my mind registered the quick move, the Hebrew had his short-sword pointed at the Egyptian's face.

A few more men had slipped through the crowd, some to stand behind the Hebrew, and others now situated near us. Surprisingly, a few of the men who stood beside us were Hebrews ready to defend the Egyptian. We were at the center of a simmering brawl. Blazing insults, like arrows, threatened to ignite the argument into a battle.

This brand new nation was coming apart at the seams. After hundreds of years of domination and murder by evil kings, our newfound freedom had already become a liability to our survival.

I gripped Kiya's hand even tighter and drew her in close to my side. "Do not let go," I rasped into her ear. Then, taking advantage of the standoff between the men and their swords, I yanked her backward, and we slipped into the crowd.

Although a few elbows were thrown our way as we pushed through, one striking me on the cheekbone, most of the attention was on the loud clash that now included the clang of swords to match the shouts. The two of us managed to escape the crowd and mix with a group of women who were wisely retreating back to camp, away from the shouting. With my hand over my throbbing cheek, I begged Yahweh to protect the Egyptian who had come to our aid.

As we neared our own campsite, a stiff wind kicked up, just as the gray clouds released their burden of snow, sending everyone scurrying toward their warm, dry, goat-hair tents. Had Yahweh sent a rare desert snowstorm to cool the tempers of those back near the traders' wagons?

I feared that the effort would be only temporary. Mistrust had been kindled among the different factions of Israel. A mistrust that would only feed the smoldering hostility that threatened to spark a raging wildfire in our camp.

"Does Mosheh know how divided this camp is?" Kiya said with a protective hand over her belly.

"I wish I knew."

"But you! Shira!" Kiya yanked me to a stop. "You were so brave standing up to that horrid woman!"

"Brave?" I laughed. "Didn't you hear my knees knocking together?"

"Well, of course you were frightened. We could have been killed in that mob. You were brave because you, and your knocking knees, stepped forward. You have such strength, Shira. You just refuse to believe it."

27

Gathered under the shade of a linen canopy outside the Mishkan courtyard, a group of men surrounded my brother, all occupied in various stages of building instruments. One worked with a lyre, half formed, the steam rising like an offering from the wood he was shaping over a small fire. With a rough stone, another man scraped at a hollowed piece, the beginnings of a tall drum. Eben leaned over the young man, demonstrating the strokes with the patience of a father but the enthusiastic hand gestures of a boy. He was doing what he loved best, sawdust sprinkled in his hair, summoning music from the heart of a tree.

With limited use of his hand, Eben was forced instead to be a teacher of such arts, passing on the knowledge of woodcarving, his inheritance from our father. To think that these instruments would grace the Mishkan, the dwelling place of Yahweh himself, was nearly unfathomable.

When my father, all those years ago, had wrangled his wayward son into apprenticing in the music shop of Akensouris, he never would have been able to guess that his own heritage would benefit such a divine purpose. I wished that my father were here to see what a credit his son was to him. I wished that my father were here to give me sage advice.

My fumbling fingers seemed to be more of a hindrance to my mother than a help. She had quietly relegated me to working with only rough tent fabrics and woolen tunics, instead of the linen for the Mishkan, which was expected to be of the finest quality. My hands were not made for creating things, and I missed midwifery so much I could feel the ache of it in my bones. It took every bit of determination not to run for Reva's tent this morning. Kiya's confidence in me had nearly convinced me yesterday, but then Leisha's white face haunted the decision, anchoring my feet.

The mirrored surface of the bronze altar, newly positioned nearby, sparkled in the sunlight, catching my eye. *I thought my hands were made for bringing your creations into the world, Yahweh. Now I have nothing at all to offer you.*

Eben called my name and waved. A flush swept over my face when all of the men turned to see who had intruded on their work. I turned aside, feigning interest in the billowing outer walls of the newly raised courtyard. A metallic smell wafted on the breeze, a product of the goldsmiths and silversmiths working somewhere nearby, molding precious tools for the Mishkan.

My mother had been adamant that I bring Eben a basket of food today. A strange request, but with Kiya resting in the tent with Talia, as she should, it was left to me to tend my brother's stomach.

Shivering, I pulled my mantle tighter around me. A snow-chilled breeze had slipped its fingers beneath the white linen fence, causing one corner to escape its moorings and flap in the breeze like a rebellious child reveling in new freedom. I glimpsed the progress on the main tent through its wayward gap, disappointed that it still seemed to be only a wooden frame. None of the elegant scarlet, blue, and purple fabrics had been lifted into place. I wondered aloud just how long it would take to finish such an intricate structure.

"Not too much longer," said Eben, who had abandoned his students and appeared at my side. "The gold panels for the inside are ready, and all the implements for the sacrifices are nearly finished. Ayal and his group will come back with sea animal hides that will make up the top layer."

To distract myself from the thought of capturing and skinning such creatures, and from my deeply divided thoughts of Ayal, I slipped the basket farther up my arm and reached for Eben's hand to examine the damage.

"Your hand is healing well." I fingered the faint remnants of the sutures, made from the same fine goat-gut strings Eben used to make his lyres. How my mother had found such a skilled healer in the confusion that night, I would never know. But the deep scars that crisscrossed his palm seemed to hold his fingers captive. His hand, while utilitarian, would most likely never have the dexterity and skill it had before. My chest ached at the loss.

Eben slipped his hand away. "Ayal will return in two weeks."

I tightened my grip on the basket, welcoming the sharp rasp of its weave against my palm. "He said as much when he left."

"Did he say anything else to you before he left?" Eben peered at me with a curious look.

"No. He said he wanted to speak with me, but Dvorah was injured so he left without doing so." My response came out a bit more clipped than I'd intended, and surprise flickered in Eben's expression.

He paused so long that I nearly ordered him to say whatever needed to be said. "Ayal needs a wife."

Dvorah is more than willing. "I assumed he would marry

soon." My flat response betrayed none of the envy fermenting in my stomach.

"Yes. There is . . . talk. About the arrangement between you and Ayal, with the children. Ayal's family believes it is best that a betrothal happen a few days after he returns from the sea."

It is time to let go. I nodded, not trusting my voice to remain steady but attempting a halfhearted smile.

"Since he has a household in place, such as it is, there is little need to wait very long. A month perhaps. It is best for the children that you move in as soon as possible."

His words tangled in my mind. "Move in? Won't Dvorah be moving in?"

"No, Dvorah will continue to be paid to wet nurse. Ayal wants to continue helping her and her son."

"I am confused." I shook my head to clear the fog. "Why would I move into Ayal's tent when he and Dvorah are married?"

Eben tilted his head to the side and studied my face. "Sister, it is not Dvorah who will be marrying Ayal. It is you."

A clap of thunder struck my brain, and my ears rang as if a shofar had sounded close by. "Me?" With my tongue twisted in knots and tears in my eyes, I shook my head. "I . . . I cannot marry Ayal." My words rasped like the edge of a blunt knife. Had everything around me begun spinning? I gripped my head to halt the motion.

Confusion was thick on my brother's face. "Are you upset? I thought you would be pleased. You seem to love the children. They certainly adore you."

"I do . . ."

He lowered his dark brows. "Ayal is a good man. He will keep you safe."

"But he—"

Eben interrupted me with a sigh, hands on hips. "I will not

force you, Shira. It is your decision to make. But I truly feel this is what is best for you, and it is my duty to protect you."

The same thing he said the last time he sent me away. A vision of that day rose up in my mind, along with a reverberation of the hollowness that screamed in my chest when Eben left me at the gate of Shefu's villa, destined to be a handmaiden to a cruel mistress—alone, heartbroken, and desperate for my mother's embrace.

"But I am safe with you." My voice sounded like Zayna's, small and pleading.

He lifted his hand, his finger hovering near my bruised cheek. "Not anymore. After what happened yesterday at the traders' wagons."

"We made it back safely."

"You did. But two men were beaten."

I sucked in a gasping breath. "An Egyptian?"

"I don't know. But there have been more than a few altercations. Threats made against the tribe of Levi."

"What kind of threats? From the *gerim*?"

"Not only the foreigners. Many from the other tribes are angry about what happened after the golden-idol incident." His voice was tinged with sadness.

Perhaps a lingering echo of the ancient jealousies between Yaakov's twelve sons had been stirred by the justice meted out that night, and by the honor of priestly duties bestowed on the Levites afterward.

"I had hoped that working together to build the Mishkan would help bind up what was broken between the sons of Yaakov. But although most Hebrews are excited and willing to donate time and goods, too many among the tribes are sowing the seeds of discontent. I fear things will only get worse." He flipped his palm over and stretched his fingers as far as they would go. "I am barely able to protect my own wife with this cursed hand. And now with the baby—" His cheek quirked as he paused.

The unspoken completion of his thought suspended like a clear note in the air. *And now that I have my own child coming, I cannot protect you as well.*

He was right. An unmarried sister was a burden. He had his own family to care for, along with my mother and younger sisters. He was giving me the only gift he could: Ari, Dov, and Talia.

I placed my own palm on his ruined one. "Say nothing more. I understand." Swallowing hard, I pressed my concerns about Ayal into the depths of my stomach and shrugged away the last shadows of desire to return to midwifery. Summoning the courage Kiya insisted I had, I stepped forward and handed Eben the meal basket. "I will do as you say."

My mother gestured for me to follow her into the tent, her face an indecipherable mask. Before my eyes had even adjusted to the dimness, she spoke from the shadows. "Did you speak with Eben?"

I dipped my head. "Yes, he told me I should marry Ayal."

She shifted from foot to foot. "It is a good match. You will be a fine mother to his children."

A stab of pleasure laced with guilt pressed against my ribs. I would be a mother. A mother to children I already loved with all my being. Why was I so hesitant? Ayal's face flickered in my thoughts—a man I could not trust and, therefore, could not love. "I will do what is necessary, for the children's sake."

My mother folded her arms and peered at me. "You do not want to marry Ayal?"

A question that had no clear answer. I shrugged but held my tongue.

"Ayal is young and handsome, and your brother attests to his honor. What more could you ask for?"

I avoided her scrutinizing stare by studying the dark corner behind her. *Eben does not know what a wolf the man is.*

"The boys already love you like a mother, and Talia is anxious when you are away."

Panic pulsed its way through me—how could I be a mother? I loved all three of them, that was true, but to guide them through life? How could I carry such responsibility? And to do so with a man I feared and mistrusted . . . Would he treat me as he had Leisha? Perhaps I was not even the only woman Ayal had lured. Had Leisha known of his wanderings? Was that why there was so much antipathy within the family? Her strange hazel eyes still haunted me as I lay on my pillow at night—would they ever disappear from my mind's eye when my own head lay in her place?

My mother came close, halting the barrage of doubts that assailed me, her eyes narrowed in what could only be described as a look of conspiracy. "You must never tell him."

Wooly confusion filled my head. "Tell him?"

She glanced around as if to ensure no one could see her lips move, even in the empty tent. "That you are barren. Not even your brother knows."

The word struck with a poison-tipped spear. "How could I keep that from him? He deserves to know what he is being bound to."

"He is being bound to a perfect mother for his children." Her chin lifted, and she fluttered a hand over her shoulder. "The rest he can find out on his own. Eben assures me that he is a loyal man. I doubt he would put you aside. Besides, he already has children."

Smothering the reaction that welled up when my mother spoke of Ayal's loyalty, I clasped my hands behind my back and tugged at the end of the braid that hung to my waist. The last time I had defied her, a woman had died. "I will do as you ask, Mother."

She lifted a brow, the reminder of my disastrous choices plain in her dark eyes. "You'd be wise to do so." Her face softened, and she lifted my chin, caressing my bruised cheek with her callused thumb. "It will be all right, daughter. You will have a good husband. A strong and capable man to protect you."

And who will protect me from him?

28

2 ADAR
12TH MONTH OUT FROM EGYPT

Dvorah handed Talia to me and then readjusted her tunic over her shoulder. The baby was already asleep, milky lips pursed in satisfied dreams. The sight of her face stirred the delicious thought—I would be her mother soon. But on its heels, another rushed at me. *This will be Ayal's last child. I am an empty grave for his family line.*

"Marah, Aiyasha, and Yael are waiting for me," said Dvorah, her condescending smile highlighting her friendships with Ayal's sisters-in-law.

I turned away with the pretense of straightening the boys' sleeping mat, trying very hard not to look at Ayal's bed across the tent. This would soon be my home—this place that still harbored whispers of the woman who had died here. Every basket, pot, and blanket at one time had been hers. It was as if I would simply be stepping into her life.

Dvorah interrupted my morose thoughts. "It won't be long now."

"Excuse me?" I said without turning.

"Before Ayal approaches my brother-in-law." Her voice curved upward, as if she was smiling. "You might as well stop looking at that baby like she is yours."

My arms seemed to go slack, and I struggled against losing my grip on Talia. I was hoping that it would not be from my lips that Dvorah heard the news. I could not even make sense of Ayal's decision to myself—how would I explain to her that I had stolen her chance at provision for her child? Turning back around to face her was agonizing. It took everything in me to not flee and hide until someone else dealt the blow.

"Dvorah." I cringed at the sound of my warbling voice. "Ayal has asked my brother . . . he is marrying me."

Dvorah paled. "You lie."

I swallowed the burning coal in my throat. "No. I am sorry. I know you hoped . . ."

"You seduced him."

The barbed accusation stabbed deep, lodging in my core.

"No! I did no such thing, I promise you. It was a complete surprise—"

"I was right, you *did* kill his wife on purpose."

I stifled the cry that sprang to my lips. "How could you think that—?"

She leaned forward, her face dark with fury. "She should have been safe. Hathor was watching over her that day." She pressed a finger into my shoulder. "You did something. I know you did."

"I tried everything I could to save Leisha. Even Reva said so." Was I trying to convince Dvorah, or myself?

She waved a hand of dismissal. "Whether you did or not, you still wanted to steal her husband. Looks like you accomplished your goal." She pushed past me. "I guess I'm not needed anymore."

I snatched her wrist. "Please don't go. Talia needs you. I am sure Ayal will ask you to stay, at least until the baby is old enough. Please don't punish her for this."

She twisted from my grasp, lips flat and nostrils flaring. She looked at Talia with a thoughtful expression and stayed quiet for a long moment. "Fine," she said, her eyes still latched on the baby. "But only because Ayal pays me well."

I sighed. "Thank you."

She smirked, giving a pointed look toward my small bustline. "When you have your own baby, don't come crying to me looking for a wet nurse. You'll have to find someone else."

Her venomous words nicked my heart, but I kept my face composed. *That certainly will be no issue.*

She huffed a tainted laugh. "Although with that tiny set of hips, I doubt you can give birth anyhow."

"My hips have nothing to do with my barrenness." I clapped a hand to my mouth, the breath knocked from my lungs by my careless retort. *What have I done?*

Dvorah's eyes flared and then homed in on me with precision. "You *are* barren? How could you know such a thing when you are not married?"

Of all the people in the world to know my shame, it had to be Dvorah? I refused to humiliate myself more by divulging deeper secrets. I pressed my lips tight, shaking my head.

Her almond-shaped eyes pinned me, and she tilted her head. "Interesting," she drawled, one hand splayed on her hip. "And does Ayal know the reason you are unable to give him any more children?"

My thoughts staggered about. How could I have been so foolish as to hand Dvorah such a weapon? "Please. Please don't tell Ayal. My mother said—"

"So not only did you seduce him, now you are hiding your barrenness from him?"

My blood rushed to my feet. "No. I— You don't understand . . ." I put a hand on my forehead, trying to steady myself. Somehow, Talia lay undisturbed in my arms.

Dvorah's smile crept up slowly, like a serpent through the weeds. "Oh, don't worry. I'll keep your secret." She leaned close. "For now."

⁓

Kiya's long fingers threaded through my hair, fashioning an intricate braid around my crown, soothing away a bit of the sting of Dvorah's words from this morning. But nothing could reel back my own too-revealing ones.

"Tighter please," I said, then winced when her finger caught in a snag.

She tapped me on the shoulder. "Hush now. You said I can braid it how I like."

With my mother off meeting with the other master weavers, Kiya's boredom had compelled her to badger me into being her hairdressing subject.

Somehow, having my long, dark curls unfettered and hanging over my shoulders made me uneasy. How much longer would she take? I tapped my fingers on my knees to distract myself from the discomfort.

"Why do you always keep it cinched so tight? Your curls are so beautiful," she said.

The memory of a dark silhouette against a bright doorway, glimpsed through the bloody, tangled curtain of my hair, stained my vision for a moment. A clot formed in my throat. I cleared it before answering, hoping she would not notice the hitch in my voice as I lied. "If I don't keep it tight, it gets in my face when I work."

She was quiet as she braided. Had I given myself away? Kiya was my closest friend, my sister, but although I had been tempted many times to tell her about the Egyptian, my mouth refused to say the words. I clenched my fists, digging my nails into my palms, the move reminding me of Reva's admonition that I should stretch my scars.

"There!" She patted the top of my head. "Turn around so I can see the front."

I arranged a smile before I complied, then looked up at her. "How do I look?"

She tilted her head, inspecting the work from her chair. "Much better than our mistress ever did."

"Tekurah was bald!"

Kiya laughed. "I meant her braided wigs."

"Remember that one she wore with the tiny bells?" I wiggled my fingers near my ears. "She dinged and dinged all night long. You know that had to have driven her mad."

"It did. I saw her face when no one was looking. But she was so stubborn, she told all her friends how much she adored it," Kiya said. "You probably didn't know this, since you were stuck in the kitchens then, but the next dinner party, all her friends had wigs with bells."

I smothered a giggle. "How did you endure it?"

"I spent the entire night biting my cheek every time I had the urge to laugh. I was still tasting blood the next morning." She arched a black brow as she stood and smoothed her dress over the small mound of her stomach. "She never asked for that wig again."

Little arms slipped around my neck from behind. "Are you finally done, Shira?" Ari said. "Come play."

"I am." I dragged him, giggling, into my lap to tickle him. "And what would you like to play?"

He twisted his lips to the side with a glance up at his twin, no doubt wondering what game could include Dov without aggravating his hands. I was glad that his guilt over Dov's injury had seemed to wane, or least transform into a compulsion to entertain and protect his brother at all times. "We will hide and you will come find us! Cover your eyes!"

I complied, but with a reminder not to stray from our campsite or wake their sister, who was napping in our family tent. Putting aside the basket of wool they were cleaning, Shoshana and Zayna joined the game. My ears followed the giggles of the four children as they searched out hiding places across the campsite.

Announcing loudly that I was now on the hunt, I made a show of searching for them in Eben and Kiya's tent, lifting baskets in the common area, and then throwing my hands in the air and declaring they were all much too clever for me.

Muffled little-boy laughs greeted me as I crept around the back side of their hiding place in my aunt and uncle's tent. Smirking to myself, I carefully moved two of the rocks that anchored the wall to the ground and lifted the fabric to peek beneath. "Got you!" I called.

Ari and Dov both startled and then melted into puddles of laughter. The sounds of their delight lifted my spirits higher than they had been in weeks. *What a pleasure it will be to be their mother.*

After backing out of the tent on hands and knees, I squatted to tack the tent wall back down and then stood and brushed the dust off my clothes and palms. Kiya's braid was in disarray—she would not be pleased with me. Blowing tendrils upward, I spun around, straight into Ayal's chest.

He grabbed my arms to steady me, a teasing smile on his face. "And what are you doing? Robbing your aunt and uncle?"

Flustered by his sudden appearance after two weeks away, I stammered, "No . . . The boys were hiding . . . we were playing a game . . ."

His laughing gaze traveled from my face to my hair. His lips twitched.

Remembering the wildness of my appearance, I flushed and tried to rearrange the chaos.

"I like it," he said with a subtle wink, reminding me of the lamb's birth and the innocence of my attraction to him then. Everything was so muddled now. Leisha. Dvorah. The children. *Betrothed.* The word clanged through the confusion with the clarity of a shofar. *I am to be betrothed to this man!*

I took two steps backward, my attention flitting to Eben, who was standing behind Ayal and looking entertained by our exchange. I raised my brows, knowing Eben would understand my unspoken question. *Have you told him my answer already?* He nodded, confirming he had accepted the proposal on my behalf.

Ari and Dov rescued me from the dilemma of what to say next. With cries of "Abba! Abba! You are home," they collided with their father, voices clambering over each other to announce how much they'd missed him.

Kneeling, he swept them both into his long arms and pulled them close. "And I missed you, my little shepherds. Were you very helpful while I was gone?"

They bobbed their little heads up and down.

"I am glad to hear it. Are you ready for our surprise?"

"Yes! Can we go now?" said Dov.

"Have you kept it a secret?"

"Yes, Abba." His tone was somber. "I did not even tell Ari."

"Then I shared my secret with the right young man," Ayal said.

"What is it, Abba? What is the secret?" pleaded Ari.

Ayal's amber gaze snared me. "Why don't you bring Shira along and I'll show you?"

29

2 ADAR
12TH MONTH OUT FROM EGYPT

ook at me, Shira!" With his small foot, Ari shook the twisted branch below his perch, causing a few almond blossoms to drift onto the blanket below.

Dov laughed with delight as a snowfall of white and pink petals trickled down around him, skimming his bronze curls. "Do it again, Ari!" He giggled, urging his brother to climb higher into the gnarled branches.

Tucked between the hills like an ancient secret, this white-crowned almond grove was Ayal's reward to the boys for their patience until his return. The trees were heavy with blossoms, promising a plentiful harvest in a few months and lending honeyed sweetness to the air. I had sloughed off my mantle to invite the sun's kiss on my eager skin. The afternoon breeze and the gentle hum of wandering bees whispered promises of warmer days ahead.

"Not much farther, son, or you will fall to the rocks and snap your arm like a twig. Then who would help me wrestle the lambs?" Ayal's rich voice startled me with its closeness. I twisted around to find him only two steps behind me, smiling up at Ari.

Anxiety fisted in my stomach as Ari ignored his father's warning and hoisted his body higher into the tree, grimy bare toes dangling near my head.

Ayal looked down at me, a sparkle of delight in his eyes, bringing to mind the day we had worked side by side to bring a lamb into the world. For the briefest of moments, I allowed myself to absorb the golden-hued light in his eyes, imagining that a bit of that brightness was for me.

But the shadow of Ayal's betrayal—of his wife, and of me—quickly doused the flicker of attraction, replacing it with jolting distress for the upcoming celebration and the reminder of Dvorah's threat. I looked away, searching for my mother, Jumo, and the girls among the lush vegetation in the wadi. I was grateful they had come along to search out more plants for dyes. Their presence tempered my unease.

"He is fine, Shira." His tone was low, soothing. He must have interpreted my expression as concern for his son. "The boys are beginning to test their own limits. I don't want my sons to be afraid of a tumble. A scrape or two will teach them just how far they can go on their own."

Acknowledging his wisdom with a nod, I attempted to clear the trepidation from my face.

Ari shimmied out of the tree in a flurry of leaves and blossoms, beckoning Dov to help him search out smooth stones to toss into the stream that meandered through the grove.

Trying to ignore the overwhelming presence of their father at my back, I watched them as they wandered, poking around in the water with sticks, exclaiming loudly when a fat salamander darted from their path, and crouching to examine a black beetle caught up in the current.

A slight sensation, as if Ayal had fingered the end of my braid, caused me to stiffen. Perhaps I had only imagined the touch, but nevertheless, his proximity was suddenly the only thing my mind could register.

"Why won't you look at me?" Ayal's low voice in my ear and his breath on my neck caused a shudder to travel the entire length of my body. I had not been so close to him since that day at the stream and, until Eben's revelation, had never expected to be again. That brief, beautiful moment before he released me and fled surfaced. The memory—soft as one of the white petals that sprinkled down around us—still lingered on my lips.

I leaned a hand against the almond tree to steady myself, the gray bark scraping my palm, doubts whispering in my ear. *You don't deserve this. Leisha died at your hand. How could you do this to Dvorah? What will she say to him? What makes you think Ayal will stay true to you after what he did that day?*

My anxiety spilled out like a waterfall. "You need not go through with this. I will not be offended. I am sure Eben will understand. I—I will make him understand."

His intake of breath shocked me into twisting around. A mistake—he was still too close. My heart lurched.

"Why would I do that?" His voice rasped like flint against my resolve. There was unexpected pain in the sound.

"This is not fair to Dvorah." I rocked back on my heels, anxious to put distance, even if only a few more inches, between us. His nearness clouded my mind. I blinked slowly, willing my long breaths to quiet the thudding of my rebellious heart.

"Dvorah?" Confusion wrinkled Ayal's brow.

"She needs protection just as much as I—perhaps more so." I pulled my arms tighter across my middle. "She has a son."

He searched my face with an intensity that nearly compelled me to take a couple more steps backward—away from the pull of such an enveloping gaze. I did not trust either of us.

"You think I should marry Dvorah?"

My eyelids fluttered and I nodded, but my stomach wobbled, revolting against the lie.

He looked over at the boys, both of them too caught up in their explorations to notice the tense conversation between their father and me. He scratched at his beard. An irrational fear that he was truly reconsidering squeezed in my gut. Why was I so torn? I should not be so drawn to this man. He was not safe.

He sighed and folded his arms across his chest, fists clenched. "And what do *you* want?"

The question reached in to grab my soul, twisting it until I could barely breathe. *I want to be their mother*, my selfish heart whispered. Yet there was no way to do so, other than to marry Ayal and hope that somehow, by Yahweh's mercy, he would be more faithful to me than his first wife.

I dropped my chin. "I will do what my mother and brother ask of me. I know Eben begged you to protect me, and I understand his concern. Forgive me for saying anything."

Silence curled in around us, hemmed us into its disquieting presence. Why had I even said anything? Leaning my body against the tree, I ran a finger along a gash in the trunk. Although deep, the wound had healed over, leaving a ragged scar. I tipped my chin to take in the warm sunlight that filtered through the glorious abundance of white above me, suddenly struck by a memory from yesterday.

Zayna had been examining one of Jumo's masterfully designed vases, painted with blossoms similar to the ones above my head. She'd dropped the vessel, and it had landed with an ominous crack against the ground. Devastated, Zayna bawled, no doubt terrified that Jumo would scold her.

Instead, Kiya's brother had consoled her, showing her how he would glue the pieces back in place with a small amount of bitumen, then transform the fracture into a tree branch with his paints. "The broken pieces will make this vessel even better," he had told her, brushing a kind hand over her dark curls. "I will make it into something new and even more beautiful."

Jumo's vase and the scarred almond tree next to me gave me hope that beauty could triumph over affliction. Perhaps something good *could* come of this painful situation.

Taking solace in the thought, I scrambled for words inside my head and plucked the most honest ones to present as a peace offering. "I do not want to be parted from the children. I love them." Ari and Dov were tossing pebbles at a little pink lizard perched on a rock nearby, missing wildly. Their sweet faces, now alight with mischief, had become my world. "I will do my best to care for them, in honor of their mother."

A caustic laugh from Ayal startled me. "You know nothing of their mother."

Shocked by the flash of malice across his face, I flinched. But he was not looking at me; his eyes were on his sons. Within moments, the grim set of his mouth softened, and my body relaxed in response. He opened his mouth as if to say something.

"Shira!" My mother's bright-eyed interruption came from nearby. "Look at all the madder root we found! Enough to finish that last panel." She, Jumo, and the girls carried baskets filled to overflowing with a jumble of plants. Yellow-headed yarrow and the wispy tails of red roots spilled over the sides. My mother was an expert at ferreting out flowers and roots that yielded the most vivid colors—a skill that served her well in this foreign wilderness.

With a dip of my head, I excused myself from Ayal's presence, unsure whether my last-minute plea had convinced him to sway his decision toward Dvorah or if I had just angered the man upon whose mercy I would soon be totally dependent. Regret for both outcomes stirred in my belly.

30

DVORAH

Matti whimpered in his sleep, pulling the wool blanket farther over his head. I rubbed circles on his back, muttering reassurances to soothe his agitation. How much longer would I have to suffer these drunken fools with their rough conversation, gathered around the fire outside? My boy needed sleep, needed the escape of dreams.

"I won't wait much longer," said a voice in a clipped accent I could not place.

"You'll wait until it's the *right* time." My brother-in-law's arrogant sneer registered in his barbed words.

Sharp responses clashed and tumbled over one another, some cursing Hassam for his slowness in avenging the men killed on the night of the Golden Apis. I agreed with them. The Levites needed to pay their outstanding debt for fighting alongside that daft old man who talked to clouds and bushes. Yet, there were

194

thousands of men in this camp who were loyal to Yahweh, men who had been training daily to fight the vicious Canaanites. How would Hassam get away with such a blatant attack? Surely they would be caught.

Even so, my blood stirred at the thought of my husband's death finally being paid for. Tareq had kept company with men just like the scum outside, but he had saved me back in Egypt, rescued me from the brothel, and hadn't been nearly as abusive as Hassam. I missed the buffer of his presence—especially for Matti's sake.

A small voice whispered in the back of my head. *He went of his own accord that night. Participated willingly in the drunken debauchery. Maybe he deserved it. Maybe you are better off.*

Hassam swore. "We cannot just barrel in, swords flailing about, and win. We must be smart. Know every risk. Weigh every possible outcome. We must know where they are at all times. When they are most vulnerable."

"And who has the most beautiful women!" said another with such a lurid tone that there was no mistaking his interest in the scheme.

My skin crawled at the implication, but I didn't care what, or whom, they took. The Levites had stolen everything from me. And it was not only *gerim* who craved vengeance. The number of Hebrews among Hassam's friends did not surprise me. The preferential treatment for the Levites had become a thorny issue for many of the other tribes. When the whole camp was rearranged, with the honored Levites encircling the newly raised Mishkan, the number of Hassam's acquaintances had multiplied like rats in a grain silo.

"How will we know such things?" The accented voice rose above the others.

I strained to catch Hassam's answer but heard nothing. A shuffle near the tent startled me as the door flipped open.

195

"Dvorah. Get out here." Hassam's slurred demand chilled my bones. My hands went numb.

With a frantic glance to ensure Matti was still asleep, I crawled over Hassam's two wives, who watched me with wide, black-smudged eyes, and slipped out of the relative safety of our tent into a gathering of intoxicated men with the gleam of retribution in their eyes. I shivered as they leered at me. Digging my nails into my palms, I resisted the urge to flee back inside.

I had learned long ago to hem in my emotions with a stone wall. Many men thrilled on fear. Reining in my reactions with a steady hand had been the only defense against the annihilation of what was left of my soul. I scanned the circle, glaring at each man in turn until I no longer felt the churn of terror in my gut.

"This is how we will know." Hassam slipped his arm around my shoulders. His rank breath assaulted my nose, and I stiffened but refused to satisfy him by reacting.

"Dvorah here is my eyes and ears among the Levite camps. And sometimes"—he grabbed my hand and held it up in the air—"my fingers!" He guffawed loudly, and his sycophants echoed his drink-induced humor.

He nuzzled my face with a stubbled cheek. "You'll make sure we know the best time to move forward with our plans, won't you, my lovely sister-in-law?" He snaked his hand inside my dress.

I tasted bile. Hassam had left me alone for the most part since Tareq had died, seeming more interested in his Egyptian wives who lolled around the campsite half-naked. But there were times when interest sparked in Hassam's light eyes and I wondered how much longer I could avoid the growing lust behind them. For that very reason, I kept a small dagger tucked in my belt alongside Isis at all times. Hassam had kept me safe since Tareq died, if only to use me to get what he wanted. But I had no compunction against skewering him if he went too far.

Shrugging away, I locked my arms over my chest but aimed a calculated smile at him. "Of course. You know how much pleasure it gives me to help my husband's brother."

His gaze narrowed for a moment at the iron-tipped reminder of Tareq. Hassam's resolute loyalty to his brother in life was my only hope for safety after his death.

Hassam pursed his lips with a hint of resignation but then lifted one brow in obvious warning. "Good. I am glad to hear it."

He turned away from me with a call for another pot of drink to be passed around the group. I fled into the tent, hoping the alcoholic diversion would veil my retreat. I slid my body down beside Matti under the wool blanket.

His cold hands reached for my face. "*Ima.*" The desperate whisper shattered my composure and I pulled him close, shielding him from the hot tears that spilled into his honey-brown hair.

Time was running short. I had to protect my son, and myself, from Hassam and the retribution he would surely bring down on our heads.

Shira and Ayal were to be bound in betrothal tomorrow evening, but that mattered little. He was a man like any other. A man who, by all accounts, had been without a woman for a long time. I would make sure Ayal married me instead, by using all the weapons in my arsenal.

31

SHIRA

The storm over the mountain rested today, hushed, as if to respect the ceremony taking place within our circle of tents. Usually the Cloud stacked high above its peak, but today it canopied over us, a translucent *chuppah* of light above our heads, with changeable colors swirling like unearthly paint across a wet sheet of fine papyrus.

I stood next to Ayal, with my brother on my right side. Ayal's gray-bearded eldest brother, who barely gave me a cursory glance before the ceremony, stood on his left.

Ayal had offered the customary *mattan*: an alabaster jar of fine perfume, two turquoise and silver necklaces, a copper ring inset with a pale green beryl stone, and a beautiful wooden flute carved with such intricacy that even Eben eyed it with interest. All these gifts were no doubt left over from the bribes the Egyptians had pressed into Hebrew hands when we fled the country, but it surprised me that Ayal would give me so many precious things as bridal gifts.

I wondered fleetingly what he had given Leisha for their betrothal. Regret for the thought immediately washed over me, bringing with it the sight of her bloodless face and her intent words pressing me to protect Talia. What would she think of me standing next to her husband, preparing to make him my own?

Slamming a tight lid over thoughts of Leisha, I focused on the grizzled elder who stood before us, a short, plump man with a long beard that floundered in the breeze like the tail of a horse. As of today, Ayal would be my husband in everything but physical union, and I would begin preparations to enter his tent within a month's time—an unusually short betrothal—to complete the marriage covenant. He would come for me in the night, unannounced, to begin our new life together in his tent. When the elder asked Eben and Ayal's brother for their promises that the agreements between us would be kept and that the wedding would be consummated in a timely manner, sudden panic gripped me in its fists.

Did Ayal know? What had Eben told him of my past before agreeing to this arrangement? What must he think of me? Even many of our neighbors had looked at me askance after the attack, disparaging glances at my midsection trumpeting their opinions about my innocence in the ordeal. The humiliation still vibrated in my soul.

Somehow, the elder's voice penetrated the thick curtain of my musings. With a wide gesture to the shimmering Cloud above us, he declared that we were now joined in covenant, before Yahweh himself, and spoke a blessing over us. As of this moment, the betrothal could be broken only by death or divorce.

Bending down, Ayal graced my veiled cheek with a lingering kiss that made all the witnesses around us melt into a hazy mirage and heat flood from my hairline to my feet.

Although I expected him to move away, he leaned in to whisper in my ear. "It was not Eben who asked me to marry you, my beautiful bride. It was I who begged him."

Before my mind could register the astonishing, perplexing words, he was gone and my mother's arms were around me, dark eyes glistening with rare emotion. After she kissed my forehead, she passed me to Kiya who, although holding Talia in one arm, gripped me to her side and showered me with congratulations. I barely heard any of them over the sound of Ayal's words turning over and over in my mind, like stones tumbling in a stream, polishing away some of the rough edges of my doubts.

However, as I nuzzled the top of Talia's head and inhaled the intoxicating scent of the baby who would soon be my daughter, a needle-sharp reminder pressed in. Although Ayal had kept his word and had not touched me—at least not until today—he kept the same distance with Talia. He provided for her without complaint, but since the day she was born, he had barely even looked at the child, seeming quite content that she live with me. The strange dichotomy of a man who loved his boys with abandon yet rejected his tiny daughter tainted my fresh joy, snatching it like a ripe berry from a tree.

Ari and Dov took up residence beside me on the ground, eager to share choice morsels of gazelle meat with me and exclaiming to everyone who would listen that they had helped prepare the honeyed manna cakes. Sticky-fingered and grinning, they delighted in being allowed to stay up far past moonrise and enjoy the betrothal feast. Ayal sat on the other side of Dov, and more than once, I caught his eyes on me as I interacted with his sons.

Although Marah and the other women had attended the ceremony, they disappeared soon after, with forced excuses of ushering small children to beds. Their husbands, however, remained.

All three of Ayal's brothers sat around the fire, their long bodies stretched out on the ground and easy banter warming the air. Two of the brothers were much older than Ayal and one was close to his age. Neither parent seemed to be present, so I assumed they had passed away back in Egypt and any sisters had been married off to other clans.

"You have not met my brothers yet?" Ayal's low words in my ear intruded on my appraisals of his family. Looking around, I realized Dov was perched on Jumo's lap. Kiya's brother was drawing pictures in the dirt and entertaining him with stories. Ari had migrated to Kiya's side where she sat near her tent, cradling Talia in her arms. There was no bronze-haired buffer between Ayal and me anymore, and although the two of us were seated at the center of a small crowd, made up of both of our families and a few friends, the space between us suddenly felt achingly intimate.

"No. I only saw them shearing the day Ziba had her lamb," I said.

"That one, with the longest beard." He leaned even closer and pointed. "That is Yonah, the eldest of us. He is married to Marah. They have six children." Yonah seemed to laugh the loudest of the men, his rich voice floating above the group.

"On his right is Noam," Ayal said, "the next oldest. He is married to Yael, and they have seven children aged between eight and seventeen." Ayal's lips twitched with amusement. "Noam hates celebrations. Just look at him."

The scowl on Noam's face was visible even in the limited firelight.

"Why does he not return to his tent, then?"

Ayal's arm brushed mine as he closed the gap farther, one brow lifted. "You've met his wife?"

Trying to ignore the zing of awareness from his skin against mine, I nodded. Yael was the loudest woman I had ever met.

The few times I had seen her with her children she bullied and chided them out in the open—not that it did any good. I had never seen any children so out of control in my life. More than once I had been forced to protect Dov or Ari from their rough games. I could imagine Noam's reticence with enduring the lot of them. I stifled a smirk.

"Yes, exactly." Ayal frowned, but humor leaked into his eyes. "I'd wait for that brood to go to sleep before coming home too." Although he tried to hide it, a tiny flicker of something passed through his expression. Anger? Regret? I searched his face, but he deflected with a light laugh.

"That is Tomek." He pointed to the brother closest to us, who was pantomiming some tale, using his whole body for effect. "He is only ten months older than me and, as you can see, already halfway drunk."

Yonah noticed the two of us watching their conversation and nodded acknowledgment to me with a warm smile that reminded me of Ayal. Immediately, I forgave his less-than-enthusiastic stance during the binding ceremony.

"Who is with the sheep?"

"Yonah asked some of our cousins to watch them, along with their flock." Ayal smiled. "He said he would not miss his brother's betrothal celebration for anything."

"Did he not attend last time?" The question popped out of my mouth before I could rein it in. I pressed my lips together, shocked at my brazenness.

Ayal's cheek twitched as he stared into the fire. "There was no celebration last time." The simple statement was laden with meaning yet edged with a subtle hint that he had no interest in discussing it further.

"May I offer my blessings on your betrothal?" Tomek stood over us with a lopsided grin, his cup raised in salute.

"Thank you, brother." Ayal's response sounded guarded.

"She's a pretty one, little brother." Tomek winked. "Prettier than my wife let on. Even if she is a tiny thing."

"Go sit down, Tomek." Ayal's warning was sharp-edged.

"What? I am saying I like her, Ayal." Tomek's laughter had a subtle bite. "Besides, anything is better than Leisha, right?"

Ayal stiffened. "That's enough."

Out of the corner of my eye, Eben's movement caught my attention. He was moving toward us, slowly but with purpose.

Tomek looked down at me, his expression suddenly sober. "You *will* be a good, faithful wife? Won't you, little Shira? Like our brother deserves?" The threat, and the insinuation, behind the words was as clear as the starlit sky.

Eben's hand came down on Tomek's shoulder before I could respond to the strange question. "All right. That's enough for tonight, my friend. Let me walk you back to your camp." His words were friendly, but his tone brooked no argument.

Tomek pressed out his bottom lip and lifted his cup again. "As I said, I wish you much joy." His stance wavered before he turned and strode into the night without waiting for my brother to follow.

Ayal stayed silent, the firelight reflecting in his eyes, highlighting a hint of sadness. It was as if he had suddenly retreated behind a wall. The sudden urge to reach out and touch his face, to skim my fingers down the high plane of his cheek and to implore him to reveal his hurts was so overwhelming that I looked around, desperate for a distraction.

I found one in Ari. Using the black curtain of Kiya's hair to hide behind, Ari was entertaining Talia with a game. Peeking out again and again, he pulled a face. Talia giggled. Encouraged by her mirth, he became more animated each time, eyes wide, tongue lolling, and fingers pressing his nose skyward. Unable to control myself, I laughed.

With a startled look, Ayal turned to me.

"I'm sorry." I placed two fingers on my lips, then pointed at the object of my amusement. "He is so sweet with Talia."

A faint smile tugged at his lips. "That he is."

"Both of them are wonderful brothers to her."

He agreed with a soft hum. His gaze swept over my face, landing on my lips. "And you are—you will be—a wonderful mother."

Although Ayal's kind statement was meant as a compliment, my mother's demand of silence pricked at my conscience. I cleared my throat, turning to watch the pop and spark of the campfire. Someone tossed another log into the flames, and heat flared against my skin. Truth battled submission in my heart until I could no longer sit still. I excused myself on the pretense of putting the boys down to sleep.

I stood, looking around for Dov, who was no longer sitting with Jumo, wondering if he was off playing with Shoshana and Zayna. But instead of the little boy, my searching gaze met with Dvorah waiting just outside the circle of firelight, arms folded across her chest and open malice on her face.

Her eyes flicked between Ayal and me for a brief moment, the corner of her mouth twitching upward. The unspoken reminder of her threat was as loud as if she had screamed it across the campfire. *I'll keep your secret. For now.*

She lifted her chin, smile charged with warning, and vanished into the darkness, having apparently abandoned her original intention to nurse Talia. I cast a panicked glance toward Ayal and nearly groaned with relief when I saw him engaged in conversation with Jumo. My silent interaction with Dvorah had gone unseen.

I feared, however, that the secret she carried would not stay in the shadows for much longer.

32

Marah's cold glare bore through me like an obsidian-tipped spear. "It was you, girl. It could be no one else."

"No, please believe me. I could never do such a thing." My words scraped against one another, leaving my throat raw. I swallowed, but the swell of tears refused to retreat.

She gestured widely to her tent, which was cluttered with many baskets, pots, and rumpled pallets. "There was no one else in here today. Only you."

As if hanging from the edge of a precipice, I clung to the truth. "I have no reason to steal from you. None."

She smirked. "I do not care what your reasons are. Give me back my necklace."

I turned up trembling palms. "I do not have it. You are welcome to search me."

She scoffed. "As if you are not wily enough to hide it while I do. What is the use? Just give it back."

It had been at least half an hour since Marah had trapped me in her tent and accused me of stealing her jewelry. Only one day after she had witnessed my betrothal to her husband's brother, she interrogated me as if I were a stranger. I could do nothing but repeat my answers and continue to affirm my innocence.

"Look at the guilt on her face." Aiyasha jerked her chin at me. "She has it."

Marah pursed her lips, her superior expression reminding me of my Egyptian mistress. "Of course she does. She's no different than that *zonah* Leisha."

Aiyasha leaned forward, her face just inches from mine. "Give. It. Back."

"Please, you must believe me. I would never steal anything from anyone, least of all any of you."

"You aren't married yet." Marah's arched tone was mocking, indicating that I never would be. "He doesn't know that you are a thief." Marah's face mirrored her insides—pinched, weathered, and sallow.

There was nothing I could say to convince them of my innocence. I was glad Yael was missing from this hasty trial; with her loud voice, the whole camp would hear these accusations.

My shoulders dropped. "What do you want of me?"

"Ha! I knew she would confess." Aiyasha's beautiful face contorted into a sneer. Although she was a few years older than I and had given birth to five children, she still looked like a maiden, skin flawless and dark brows swooped high above her blue-green eyes.

"Confess what?" Dvorah slipped in through the tent flap, eyes luminous. She had overheard our conversation.

"This thief stole my necklace. I caught her in here earlier with the sin of it plain on her face." Marah seemed to revel in the retelling of her account of the truth—the version where she left out the design of the necklace, a long, turquoise-beaded chain with a pendant displaying a naked Isis with outstretched wings. I had seen it around her neck before but noticed that Marah only wore it when her husband was nowhere in sight.

It was Aiyasha who had sent me to Marah's tent, indicating Marah had a small pot of medicinal ointment for Dov's scars. If I had not run out of oil this morning and been unable to find Reva, I would never have asked any of these women for help in the first place, but for Dov's healing, I would endure any torture.

"I do not doubt it. She is nothing if not deceitful." Dvorah folded her arms and relaxed into a smug stance.

Aiyasha giggled, curiosity in her lifted brow. "Oh, do tell, Dvorah."

Dvorah smiled, the malicious movement unfurling slowly, as if to lengthen my distress. "I caught her kissing Ayal." She divided a look between the two women. "Well before Leisha died."

She had seen us? On that awful, confusing day? Fighting the instinct to flee from the horror of her revelation, I curled my toes into the sandy floor. My mind reeled back to the stream: my open invitation to Ayal's advances, his lips on mine, the searing touch of his skin against my cheek. All of it had been an enormous mistake, and the woman who hated me had been witness to my greatest sin.

Marah and Aiyasha stood like pillars, slack-jawed and wide-eyed, as if stricken with the loss of speech.

"Obviously, it was her plan from the start to seduce him, and who knows what else?" Dvorah left the insinuation hanging in the air, but by the gasps from the other women, there was no question as to her accusation.

How could I possibly defend myself against such allegations when the hostility in Aiyasha and Marah's eyes proved that they believed every word? I opened my mouth to explain, to refute Dvorah's conjectures, but my tongue refused to comply. Whether or not he had deceived me, I *had* welcomed Ayal's attentions, craved them like honeyed wine. It was my fault. Hot tears trailed a fiery path down my cheeks.

Just like when I was thirteen, my shame was on full display.

"That's right, you have nothing to say. You are, at the very least, a liar and a thief. My husband and his brothers will be told." Marah flicked a hand toward the exit, dismissing me. "Consider this betrothal broken."

⁓

"Where have you been?" Kiya met me at the edge of camp, concern setting her golden eyes ablaze. "I thought you went to fetch ointment for Dov."

Under the shade of a nearby canopy, the boys were taking turns tossing almond shells into a pot—one of the few games Dov could take part in. My shoulders sagged. In the upheaval of Marah's accusation, I had forgotten the oil I set out to retrieve in the first place.

Kiya took hold of my arm when I did not respond. "Shira—sister. What is wrong?" Pulling me close, she engulfed me in a hug.

The natural embrace—from this woman who used to stiffen whenever I touched her—knocked down my last defense. Fear, hurt, and confusion spilled over, watering Kiya's shoulder. She rubbed circles into my back, murmuring encouragement, coaxing me to explain such anguish. Before I could tighten my fraying emotions or braid together my unraveled composure, rambling confessions tumbled over themselves in between sobs: the allegation of theft, Dvorah's accusation, Leisha's death, my involvement with Ayal all those months ago.

When the well of revelations ran dry, Kiya pulled back, compassion and surprise written on the tablet of her face. "You have been keeping secrets, my sweet sister."

A stab of guilt pierced me. "I have, forgive me."

"Why?" She frowned. "Don't you trust me?"

"Of course I do! You know I love you."

"Then why would you hold back what was going on inside your heart?" She placed a gentle hand on my cheek. "You know I would neither accuse nor condemn you."

"I do." I inhaled. "I was afraid."

She furrowed her brow.

"I did not want you to worry, or to say something to Ayal or Eben."

"Eben would have throttled him." Kiya lowered her chin.

"Yes. He would have." I winced. "But it really was—" I stopped and tugged at my braid.

"Was what?" She flattened her lips, waiting for me to finish my thought.

"My fault."

"You think it's your fault that Ayal took advantage of you?" Her tone was incredulous.

"I had been . . . dreaming about him . . . wishing that he were mine." My face flamed. I escaped her searching gaze to stare down at the hands that had clutched Ayal's tunic with such eagerness. "I all but begged for his advances." I flushed again but braved a glance at her. "But I did *not* know about Leisha, or I would never have done such a thing."

"It doesn't matter that you did not know!" She threw her hands in the air. "*He* should have kept his hands to himself, no matter *how* you looked at him!" Kiya's voice spiraled upward, and I shushed her with a finger to my lips, tossing a glance around the campsite. Thankfully, only Dov and Ari were nearby. My mother must have taken Talia and the girls with her as she worked with the other master weavers. She seemed to have already taken to her new role as a grandmother.

"I know that he was wrong," I said. "Very wrong, and he still has not explained himself, which leads me to wonder whether he is even ashamed of it. But he did try . . . I think, once, until Marah interrupted. Even so, I could have walked away. Whether he was married or not, I should not have thrown myself at him like that. And then I let his wife die—"

"Stop!" Kiya's eyes blazed with fervor as my disjointed explanations fizzled out. She gripped both of my shoulders, as if ready to shake me. "Don't you dare blame yourself, Shira. It had nothing to do with you. Nothing. As long as I have known you, you have always taken the blame, even when you did not commit the sin."

Stepping forward and deceiving Tekurah about who had broken her treasured ebony box had been an easy decision, and one I would gladly make again to protect Kiya. Without my acceptance of those consequences, she and I might never have become friends, and therefore Jumo most probably would have died in that last devastating plague in Egypt.

"You should have left me to my punishment, but you took the burden on yourself that day—practically begged Tekurah to flog you. And here you are, blaming yourself for a woman's death you had no control over, and for Ayal's deceitful, lustful behavior. This must stop, Shira. When will you stand up for yourself? And the truth?"

I shuddered, the tail end of my sobs reverberating in my chest.

Kiya pulled me close again, her sweet breath on my forehead and her growing belly pressed between us. *Four more months*, whispered my midwifery training. "You had such courage the day you stood up for me. You did not flinch as you told Tekurah that you had broken that cosmetic box. I was in awe of you—confused"—she breathed a laugh—"but in awe. I could not understand how such a fragile girl could be so strong."

"I do not feel strong. I feel like one stiff gust will snap me in two."

"But you are. You are the most loyal person I know. You will go to any length to protect those you love. You stood against that woman at the traders' wagons. And you even stood up to your own brother when he was hesitant to take in an Egyptian girl, her crippled brother, and her mother the night before we left Egypt." She gripped my arm and squeezed. "Why won't you believe me? You are one of the strongest women I know. Stronger than me, for certain."

"This coming from a woman who sacrificed herself to an Amalekite for *my* freedom?"

She brushed aside my deflection. "Now, are you going to confront him about what he did?" She frowned at me in challenge. "Because if I need to tell Eben, I will."

My heart beat frantically against my ribs. "No, you can't do that—"

"Oh, I can and I will, to protect you." She cut off my argument. "There is nothing I won't do for you, my friend. And if you don't clear this up with Ayal, I will be forced to bring Eben this information."

I searched her face and saw nothing but determination. She had me in a corner. "How would I even begin such a conversation?" I rubbed a thumb into my palm.

"You like him, don't you?" One corner of her full lips tilted. "You said you had been dreaming of a life with him before his wife died."

I shifted backward, startled by the blunt question.

She prodded me with a high arch of her fine brows. "Don't you?"

The truth demanded to be free of its fetters and Kiya was the sister of my heart—I trusted her implicitly. I heaved a sigh. "I do."

"And you want to be his wife? You want to be a mother to Talia and those sweet boys?" She gestured to Dov and Ari who were scraping together mounds of dirt with their toes and then smashing them with loud giggles, blissfully oblivious to our tense conversation.

More than anything. I nodded.

"Then you must talk to him, Shira. Stand up for yourself, lay out your concerns, and ask him to explain himself. I cannot believe you have let it go this long without doing so. I only know of Ayal what Eben has told me, but he has only good things to say about him. Something was very wrong between Ayal and Leisha, although Ayal did not confide the cause. But Eben rarely saw them together. Ayal spent most of his time with the sheep. My husband is not perfect by any means, but he is a fairly good judge of character. Perhaps there is much more to this than we know."

Kiya was right. I had allowed this to drag on too long. I must demand answers—today—and reveal my own secret before Dvorah did it for me. Yet, with the accusation leveled at me this morning, would he even listen?

"But Marah and Aiyasha, they will say—"

"No." She shook her head. "Stop worrying about what they will say. You know the truth. Tell it. Ayal will know." She squeezed my arm again, encouragement in her steady gaze. "He will know."

33

DVORAH

If I had any chance of turning Ayal's head away from Shira, it was now.

Marah's shrill voice echoed around the campsite, informing Ayal of Shira's *theft* after he had returned from the sheep. I slipped my hand inside my belt and whispered a prayer to Isis. What fortune, that Aiyasha had sent Shira into Marah's tent only an hour after I had slipped inside and lifted the necklace from a basket. I had hoped that Marah would not notice for days, but it had worked in my favor—it was Shira they blamed, not me.

This morning I had given Leisha's golden Isis charm to Hassam, which appeased him for the moment, but this beautiful one I kept close to me. I stroked the shimmering turquoise beads and the golden sun-disk crown of my lovely goddess. The Queen of Heaven would ensure that my plan succeeded because I would rely on her arts, one more time.

With his mind full of tales of Shira's treachery, and Marah's strong opinions on his dalliance with the girl before his wife died, Ayal would be off-balance when he returned to this tent, his guard down. I could not fail.

Arranging myself on his sleeping mat, I folded my head into the cradle of my knees and drew upon jagged memories from my childhood. I let myself linger there, just long enough to summon tears to my eyes, but not enough to distract from my singular purpose—protecting my son. The alluring scent of my lotus perfume wafted around me, giving me confidence that my purpose would be realized today. I tugged at the laces of my tunic, ensuring they were loose.

A shuffle of sandals outside announced his presence and my pulse strengthened, thumping out a call to action in my temples. The orange afternoon light had dimmed, and Ayal held no lamp. To my great satisfaction, he did not notice me curled up on the mat as he came inside and dropped the flap behind him. He released a weighted sigh and dug his fingers into his thick hair.

With another quick prayer to Isis, I lifted my head and sniffed.

Ayal started and gasped, his hand at the dagger on his belt.

"It is only me." I swiped at my eyes. "Dvorah."

"Dvorah?" He dropped his defensive stance and shifted back on his heels. "What are you doing here? The baby is with Shira."

"I am so sorry. I did not know where else to go."

"Is something wrong? Should I fetch Marah?"

"No, please, I only want to speak with you for a moment and then"—I sucked in a shuddering breath, playing my role just right—"I will go."

His shoulders dropped a bit, and concern colored his voice. "Has someone hurt you?"

Who hasn't? "No. But my son . . ."

"Someone has hurt your son?" He bristled.

Excellent. I had chosen the correct weapon. Now to twist the knife of truth just enough.

214

"My brother-in-law is tiring of caring for Matti and me. He demands that I give him all of the milk and wool and says that without it he will no longer protect us. And now that Talia is nursing less and less . . . and then with you marrying Shira . . ." My words tumbled out in a well-calculated rush.

"He would turn you and your son out?"

I nodded, making a show of covering my face and letting out a sob.

"Oh . . . now, please don't cry. We will find a solution." Ayal's voice was closer now, he'd swallowed the bait.

I shook my head. "There is not much I can do. Matti is getting older, and Hassam's wives grouse about watching him. Soon I will no longer be able to do midwifery either."

Dropping my hands from my face, I stood. "Forgive me. I don't know why I came here. You have more to deal with than my problems."

His face was a mass of confusion and compassion. "No. I want to help—"

I cut him off. "You have always been so kind to me, and I hoped that . . . well, I don't know what I hoped." I stepped forward. "I'll just go."

He put a hand on my arm, and my hope drew fresh breath. "Please. Dvorah. Let me help you. You came to my assistance after Leisha died, and I am grateful."

"I don't know that there is much you can do . . ."

He scratched at his beard. "I can at least continue paying you to nurse the baby."

"But it won't be much longer . . ."

He pressed his lips together. "Do not worry about that. We have plenty of milk and wool to spare. We will continue to pay you as long as you need, or until you find . . . someone else to care for you and your son."

Ayal truly was a kind man and would be a good father to

Matti. I almost regretted using him, but I could not let this chance slip away. With a quick swallow of ridiculous nerves, I stepped forward and threw my arms around him, placing my head on his chest. "Oh, thank you, Ayal. You don't know how much this means to me." I released a sob against his tunic, although the smell of sheep clung to him like a disease.

He stiffened and patted my back. "Oh . . . well, it is the least I can do . . ."

Slipping my arms tighter around his waist, I pulled him close, hoping that the months without a woman in his bed would be my greatest ally. I melted against him, settling my curves against his body in the way I had been schooled. I slid my hand up his arm, allowing my fingers to meander along his bicep. I licked my lips and, pulling back to look up at him, willed an expression of complete vulnerability as I sniffed against fabricated tears. "You are a good man. I will never forget your kindness."

Ayal's eyes were as wide as those of a gazelle caught in torchlight, but his stance did not soften. What was wrong with him? He'd had little problem tossing aside his fidelity for Shira. *How dare he reject me!*

Urgency nipped at the heels of my anger. Matti was what was important. Not my pride.

Before I could even ask her for assistance, Isis answered my plea, delivering a gift right into my hands. The tent flap parted, only a small way, but enough to catch a glimpse of Shira's stricken face as she took in the sight of her betrothed wrapped in my arms.

As triumph surged in my bones, I slid my hands to his shoulders and kissed him—on the cheek, but close enough to his mouth that from Shira's standpoint it would appear as nothing less than a passionate embrace. I closed my eyes to complete the ruse and let my lips linger a moment.

Strong hands wrapped around my wrists and pulled them down in front of me. "Dvorah."

With a quick glance back to the doorway to ensure that Shira had indeed disappeared, I allowed Ayal to press me gently but firmly away.

"You *know* I am betrothed to Shira." His reminder was as firm as the grip he maintained on my wrists.

"But Marah said she was a thief." I blinked, as though innocent of such dealings.

He shook his head. "I do not believe a word of it."

"She was the only one in the tent. Who else could have done such a thing?"

"I know Shira, and she would never take something that does not belong to her."

She won't take you either. I have ensured that.

"I know you want to believe the best of her, Ayal, but the fact is, she is guilty."

He released my hands. "How can you, too, accuse her when she has been so kind to you?"

Confusion tugged at me. "Kind?"

"Yes, she has nothing but good things to say about you. She even told me once of what a good midwife you were. Of how strong and knowledgeable you were."

Why would Shira say something like that? I had gone out of my way to brush her off whenever we had worked together. She was such a mouse that undermining her had been easy. Whenever I snapped at her, she dropped her eyes to the floor like the obedient slave she was; although, at times, a flare of something like challenge glittered in her eyes. But just as quickly, the spark always disappeared, leaving her at my mercy.

No. I would not let such a stupid little girl steal my last hope. I pushed Ayal's argument out of my mind.

"The fact is, Ayal"—I slid my hand in a slow, suggestive trail from my waist to my neckline, my blood surging as his eyes immediately followed—"Shira can't give you what I can give you." I let my eyelids drop as I wet my lips. "She has no idea how to please a husband."

Ayal stepped back. "Dvorah, I am sorry if you misunderstand me—"

"There is no misunderstanding." I let my false innocence drop, along with the shoulder of my tunic. "I want you. I need you. And you need me too."

"Dvorah. Stop." Although he twisted away, eyes on the far wall, the warning in Ayal's tone startled me. "Put your clothing back on."

"You do not want that." I let seduction lower my voice.

"Yes." He folded his arms across his chest. "I do."

What was wrong with him? I had never seen a man so immune to such open enticements. Stricken with confusion, and not a small bit of embarrassment, I pulled my tunic back up on my shoulder. Shira had no problem tempting him that day by the stream, how could this have failed?

"Am I so repulsive?" I snapped.

"No, Dvorah. You are a beautiful woman." He dragged a hand over his face but still did not look at me.

"Then why would you choose that girl over me?" I lifted my chin. "She is nothing."

He lifted a censuring palm. "I will not let you insult her. She is soon to be my wife."

My blood ran hot. "She can't give you what you need. She can't even give you a child."

Ayal's head whipped around. "What do you mean?"

I lifted a brow. "Oh, you don't know? The perfect woman has not been honest with you? Ha!"

"What are you talking about?"

"She's barren, Ayal."

The statement seemed to knock him backward. "How do you know such a thing?"

I waved a flippant gesture. "Oh, she told me a while ago—and insisted I not tell you, of course."

Hurt played across his face, but I did not care. This was my last chance. I must make him understand that Shira was not a viable choice.

"So you see, I have no problem accusing her of stealing. She is a proven liar. To hide something so important from her own betrothed?" I shook my head and clucked my tongue against my teeth. I stayed quiet a moment to allow my accusations to take root. He scratched at his beard, an annoying habit, but seemed to be contemplating.

"I would never do such a thing, Ayal." I softened my tone and took a step forward. "I can be a good wife to you. I can be everything you want."

He lifted his eyes, and the sincerity in them halted me. "No. You can never be what I want. You cannot be her."

34

SHIRA

My feet refused to walk in a straight line. As blurred as my vision was, I was not sure how I even arrived at my campsite. The image of Ayal embracing Dvorah would not abate, no matter how hard I tried to shove it away. It pulsed in my mind with every step, jeering, mocking my foolishness. What did I expect? Ayal was not a man of his word or, in any stretch of the imagination, faithful. I had known this from the start. And what I had witnessed today was only testament to my instincts.

Perhaps this was all for the best. Dvorah obviously was in love with Ayal, and he with her. Why had he betrothed himself to me in the first place? To provoke her to jealousy? No . . . she had seemed all too willing to accept him before—conspicuously so. None of this made any sense.

I slipped in through the flap of my mother's tent, grateful that Kiya had been too occupied with the boys to notice my return in the dim light. The woolen cocoon enveloped me in a sense of safety, and I forced a deep breath, unsteady though it was. My mother's bright, multicolored, striped rugs beckoned, and I folded my legs to meet them.

I dropped my head and cried but refused to allow any sound to escape my mouth. I could not bear Kiya's sympathy just now.

With the smell of salt in my nostrils and my tunic wet from my anguish, I laid my cheek on the floor in front of me, taking solace in the familiar feel of the wool against my skin. I concentrated on the sensation of the scratchy fabric and the tang of its gamey odor instead of the constant repetition of images in my head. Dvorah's arms around Ayal, the victory in her glance, her lips raising to his . . .

Dov laughed nearby, striking another painful blow. I had lost the boys. I had lost Talia. Dvorah would tuck them under their blankets. Kiss their fears away. Watch their legs lengthen and their faces change moment by moment.

Closing my eyes, I turned my face and pressed my forehead to the floor. I stretched my arms wide and lay there, a broken branch shattered on the ground.

Yahweh. Why do you give and then take away? You give me a glimpse of midwifery and then steal it. You give me the promise of marriage and then snatch it. You give me a taste of motherhood and then rip it from my hands. Am I truly worth so little to you? To anyone?

My name and the flicker of an oil lamp woke me, startling me from the sleep that somehow had followed the outpouring of my heart. I pushed myself up to my knees and scrubbed at my face.

"Here she is." Eben's hand was on the tent flap as he peeked in at me. "I found her."

"May I speak with her?" Ayal's rich voice outside caused

gooseflesh to rise on my arms. My eyes widened as I shook my head vehemently at my brother.

He narrowed his eyes at me. "Yes. Of course."

Why would he do such a thing? "No, Eben. Don't—"

He put his hand up, cutting off my insistent whisper. "You need to hear what he has to say."

Please no, I mouthed at him. But he winked, instructed me to trust him, and disappeared.

"I will be only a few paces away," he said loud enough for me to hear. "So if she calls out, know I will come in and slay you where you stand." His threat was delivered thick with sarcasm.

He is joking with Ayal? Now? After I had been shamed and used by this man who proclaimed to be his friend? And now he would let that man come inside my mother's tent, alone, to speak with me? Fury at my brother jolted me to my feet. What kind of strong fence would let in such a wolf?

Yet as soon as Ayal ducked inside the tent and unfolded himself to his full height, my anger retreated and I stumbled back a few steps. Ayal placed an oil lamp on the overturned pot near the center pole of the tent. The glow from the one wick cast shadows around the space. If only I could melt into the darkness beyond its edges. I stared at the light, worrying the end of my braid.

"Shira. Look at me." Ayal's whisper was tinged with desperation. "Please."

I dragged in a steadying breath before complying.

Ayal was unraveled. His dark hair stuck out in places, like he had been yanking at it in frustration. I had never seen his face so pale, as if he did not spend every day toiling in the sun.

He dug his fingers into his hair again, proving my assumption correct. "You saw us."

I nodded, tears springing up again. I wished I could wipe them away, along with the image of him and Dvorah embracing, but my arms had lost all strength.

"I'd hoped Dvorah was wrong. That I could somehow explain to you before you heard from someone else . . . but then you saw us. . . . As soon as she told me you had been there, I came looking for you. I explained to your brother. But still . . . I'd hoped she was wrong." His words tripped over one another, circling back around as if chained together. His chin dropped and he squeezed his eyes shut, as if simply speaking the words was painful.

"You have nothing to explain. I will make sure that Eben does not hold it against you." I cleared a warble from my throat. "You are free to break the betrothal." *Divorce. Even before our marriage has been made complete.* The shame of it would prevent me from marrying again.

His head snapped up. "No! You must listen to me. Please. Please let me explain."

"What is there to explain? You love Dvorah."

"No! I could never."

"So it was only a dalliance?" I winced. "Like when you . . . like by the stream?"

"No . . . You don't understand." He stood taller. "She threw herself at me, surprised me in my tent."

"Why would she do such a thing?"

"I think she did it to protect her son. She seems desperate to get away from her brother-in-law. She sees me as a way to be safe."

"But I saw you kiss her."

"You saw *her* kiss me."

"But—"

His eyes pleaded with me. "Shira, did you see me return the kiss?"

"No . . ."

"Did you see me push her away? Tell her that I have no interest in her? That it is only you I want to marry?"

A confused rhythm thrummed in my ears, and I shook my head. He took a step closer, and although my instinct was to back away again, I stood fast.

"Hear me, Shira. I don't want her. I want you. I've always wanted you. So much that I dragged you into my own sin that day by the stream."

I snatched a quick breath, startled by his admission and needing air to brace myself against the trembling that had begun deep at my core. I could not fathom his words, could not fit the ragged edges together in my mind. "But it was my fault . . ."

"Your fault?" His eyes went wide. "You think it was your fault that I reached out and took what wasn't mine? You didn't even know that I was married. I could tell by the way you looked at me with such . . . such hope. And, coward and wretch that I am, I coveted your sweetness so much I nearly destroyed it with my actions." He dragged his hands over his face and groaned. "I kept the truth from you so you would keep on looking at me that way."

My courage soared at his admission and I asked the question that had been branded into my heart for months. "Why? Why would you do something like that to Leisha? She was your wife. The mother of your children. How could you wrong her like that?"

He shook his head. "Leisha." The bitter way he said her name shocked me. "Leisha had not been my wife for a very long time."

"What do you mean? You were married until she died, were you not?"

"Leisha did not see it that way."

My knees wobbled. "I am so confused."

He lifted sad eyes. "I know. I have been so wrong to keep all of this from you. I hate myself for not telling you everything from the start. I had hoped to keep you protected from the truth."

"The truth?"

"The baby." He paused. "Talia is not my child."

I felt the blood drain from my face as my suspicions were confirmed. "Whose child is she?"

"I don't know. And from what I gathered from the last time I spoke to her, Leisha did not know either." His tone was flat, as if the idea had no effect on him. "Leisha was never faithful to me. Within a few months of the birth of the boys, she revealed her true nature. Sometimes she disappeared overnight, and sometimes for days. Always she came back, smelling of other men and drink."

"But why didn't you . . . ?" I let the question hang in midair.

"Divorce her?" He scratched his beard. "I considered it, many times. I could have easily thrown her off. My family encouraged it. But whenever I said something, she would come crawling back to me, repentance on her lips, begging me to forgive her. There were stretches of good times, times where she would act like the mother she should have been, and then she would slip into deep valleys, cry for days on end, sometimes rage at me, and then she would disappear again."

He stepped closer. "It was for the boys' sake that I did not toss her out, Shira. If I had done so, she would have few options but to turn to prostitution to survive. And then, when the plagues struck, she was so terrified that she stayed home with us, did not venture out at all. She locked herself in our house and kept the window barred shut. I tried to console her. Promised her I would keep her safe, that Yahweh was coming to deliver us. After all the beasts died in the fields, she was inconsolable. She insisted that we travel from Avaris down to Iunu, to be near her parents. Said it was the only place she felt safe. Her father was Hebrew, but her mother worked in the temple."

"You were in Iunu, my town?"

He nodded. "She fought me that last night we were in Egypt. It took some convincing to get her to leave her parents and to come with us." His shoulders slumped. "To my everlasting shame, there were times I wished she had stayed there and left us alone. Dov and Ari did not deserve the mother they were born to, they deserve so much more."

He held me in a long gaze but then dropped his eyes to the floor. "It was that night that I saw you." He tugged at his ear. "You were so caught up in helping everyone, making sure everyone was comfortable, keeping your sisters calm. You did not even notice me watching you."

I furrowed my brow, trying to piece together the hazy memory. "You were in our house that night?"

He dipped his chin in confirmation.

Realization dawned as I laid my memories of that night alongside his. *The couple with two boys, huddling in the shadowed corner while the twins slept between them.* The vague recollection began to clear, revealing details I had long since forgotten. "Kiya and her family came in soon after yours did. My attention was drawn to her," I whispered.

The oil lamp flickered and danced. "It was when you sang," he said, his words dropping low.

"What do you mean?"

He took a cautious step toward me, as if approaching a skittish doe. "Your voice, Shira. You sang that night to calm all of us, and in the midst of the horrors, the beauty of your voice staved off the fear. I had never heard anything so breathtaking as the music that flows from your lips. May Yahweh forgive me, even in the dark, I was half in love with you before the song ended."

Somehow my legs had turned to wet reeds. I reached out to steady myself with the tent pole.

"There is nothing in my life as lovely as you, Shira. I was wrong. So wrong, to approach you by that stream. I succumbed to my thirst for your kindness, your gentle spirit, your innocence. You are everything Leisha was not." He glanced at the flickering lamp. "She had not spoken to me for months, other than to remind me that the babe who grew in her was not mine and to fling curses at me in the name of foul Egyptian gods." His jaw tightened. "She barely acknowledged the boys. She brought idols into our tent, although I forbade her from doing so, and flaunted her blasphemy whenever she could."

The memory of Dvorah's charm in Leisha's hand paraded through my mind.

"I tried so hard to stay away from you after we delivered the lambs. I made excuses to Eben constantly and stayed in the fields as much as possible to avoid the chance of crossing your path. But my loneliness only fueled desire for you. You appeared in front of me that day at the stream like an apparition from my dreams, and in that moment of weakness, I gave in."

"But why did you not tell me this earlier? Why keep me in the dark?"

He hooked a hand around the back of his neck and closed his eyes. "I have nothing to say in my defense. I wanted you as my wife. My sons need you as their mother. You love them like their own did not. I did not want to risk losing you."

He looked up, his gaze imploring. "Please. Forgive me. I beg of you, extend me mercy. If not for my sake, then for the sake of Dov and Ari. They would be devastated if I ruined this." He closed the gap between us and gripped my hand. "I could never want Dvorah, Shira. It is you I love."

I studied his face and the depths of his amber eyes and found no falseness within them. A surge of exquisite pain spread from the center of my chest. "But I am nothing. I am plain, and small, and fearful. Dvorah has strength. She has beauty that I could never match. She can give you . . . a future that I never can."

Slowly, and with a question in his eyes, he moved his hands to my face. The contact of his work-worn palms on my cheeks turned my insides to melted honey.

"How . . ." he whispered, and the sweetness of his breath enticed me to lean in. "How can you say such things? You are nothing if not brave. You were ready to marry me, although I gave you no cause to trust me. Reva told me how you fought to save Leisha that night. A small, fearful woman would have done no such thing. Eben bragged about how you stood tall against the men at the trading wagons in Kiya's defense. You are brave, and the most beautiful woman in the world to me. You *are* my future."

I could not breathe. Could not answer. Could not keep my thoughts in order.

Ayal's revelations shone a light on my own secrets, and I knew that I could not hold the most important one in any longer. No matter what my mother said. I inhaled, savoring the last breath before I laid everything before him.

"I am barren, Ayal. There will be no children from my body." The words dropped like boulders into the space between us. My head felt feather-light as I braced for his angry response. His accusation of deception. His back to turn.

But instead of pushing me away, he pulled me closer with a sigh, enveloping me in his strong arms. The smell of his work and his skin tempted me to invite the intoxicating mixture deep into my lungs. With his lips against my forehead and compassion in his voice, he spoke the words I could never have anticipated. "Oh, my beautiful songbird . . . I already know."

35

Startled by a call from outside, I yanked myself away from Ayal, although the movement felt like prying open my eyelids in the midst of a delicious dream. Eben stuck his head in the door and looked back and forth between us with teasing suspicion. Heat rushed up my neck to set my face on fire.

"I hate to burst in on this intimate discussion but, Ayal, Tomek is here. Some animal has attacked your flock. We must go."

I stepped forward, palms up. "I want to help." Expecting Ayal to refuse, I steeled myself, preparing to plead. I wasn't yet ready to watch him walk away.

Instead, he offered a pleased smile and his hand. "Come, then."

We hastened through camp, led into the darkness by his sense of direction toward the wadi and the glimmer of blue light from the mountain. Eben and Tomek had gone ahead of us with a torch to light their way. Ayal explained that two of his brothers were watching over the flock tonight, but there had been sightings of a big cat, possibly a leopard, the last few nights.

Strange that an animal would dare approach our vast numbers. But perhaps a wildcat would risk anything if it were hungry enough. And there was plenty of food to be had among us—flocks of sheep, goats, and cattle covered every spare inch in the valley. Some had even spread to the valleys nearby, where scrub brush grew in abundance and bright grasses had sprung up after the recent rains. Mosheh, the shepherd, knew the right place to bring his people.

Surefooted, Ayal picked his way up the wadi toward the bray of sheep echoing against the rose-granite walls. His family had been fortunate to claim this area; although the flock was panicked, they were unable to escape into the night. Without releasing me, Ayal slipped through the flock, pushing a few aside with his hip, but speaking calm reassurances to them as he did so.

With his back to us, Eben held his large torch aloft, illuminating a horrific scene. Yonah and Tomek were at the center of the flock, on their knees, covered in blood. Panic for all three of them spiked through me until my attention was drawn to the source of the blood—two sheep on the ground in front of them, struggling, bleating pitiful cries.

"What happened?" Ayal strode toward them. I tried to slip my hand away, unsure of the affectionate display in front of his brothers, but he only gripped me tighter.

Yonah glanced up, a hint of annoyance curving his brow as he took in the sight of us, but he jerked his chin toward a dark shadow sprawled on the ground nearby. "A leopard. Took them down before we even knew what hit us."

Horror sprang into my throat. These poor sheep. With dreadful silence a wildcat could sneak up on man or beast with swift and disastrous consequences. A tremble made its way through me as I imagined Ayal facing down such a monster in the black night. He squeezed my hand before releasing me. "I need to help, but stay close."

The two sheep were soaked in blood, their sides shredded by the leopard's claws. Would either have a chance at survival?

With sure hands, Ayal examined first one and then the other.

He pointed at the darker brown one. "This one is too far gone, but the other should be all right if we can clean out her wound. I'd hate to lose another pregnant ewe."

Yonah and Tomek lifted the other sheep and moved it to the edge of the flock. I turned my back to avoid the purpose of Tomek's knife glinting in the torchlight. I braced for a cry, a sound that announced the death of the wounded animal, but only the bleats of the agitated flock met my ears.

Ayal knelt by the tawny ewe, holding her neck to the ground with one hand as he doused the wound with a pot of water. The frightened animal thrashed against his ministrations, kicking and trying to get her feet underneath her. One of her hooves slammed into Ayal's leg, and he groaned. So blinded by pain and terror, the ewe could not understand that Ayal was helping her. He placed his knee on her back legs to pin them down, but her front hooves scraped against the rocky ground in a frantic motion.

Desperate to help, I mimicked Ayal's position with a knee on her shoulder and my hands against her neck. With every ounce of strength I had, I pressed down to keep her still. When I felt a slight release of the tension in her neck, I placed one hand on her face, stroking her forehead with firm but gentle strokes. "Calm down, *ima*. Ayal will take good care of you. Calm down." And because the instinct was uncontrollable, I sang under my breath.

Just as Ziba had done, the sheep began to relax, her white-rimmed eye suddenly focusing on me and her panic abating. She stopped trying to escape and allowed me to hold her down.

"You are beyond description, Shira. I may have to bring you to the fields with me every day." Ayal's smile chased away the chill of the breezy night.

"That she is," my brother said with a knowing smirk. "You chose the right woman. Too bad I had to bribe you with five donkeys to get you to take her." He winked.

"Only five donkeys?" I lifted my chin in defiance. "I had to give Kiya eight to persuade her to take you on."

Eben threw back his head and laughed, the echo of it bouncing off the cliffs.

"Oh, now, Ayal, I think you might have a sharp-tongued one here." Tomek came into view, scrubbing at his bloody arms with a dirty rag. Embarrassment flooded through me. What could have possessed me to joke so openly with Eben in front of these men?

Tomek flashed me a grin. "I like her."

Swiping my forehead with the back of my hand, I fought a smile as I looked down at the ewe. After dressing the wound, Ayal sat back on his heels and allowed the sheep to scramble to her feet. Although her coat was stained, the cuts were fairly shallow. The leopard must not have gotten a good hold on her.

"We are fortunate there weren't more losses," Ayal said. "How did you bring that cat down?"

Tomek scratched his chin, bravado in full force. "The thing had one of our rams in its jaws and was dragging it up onto that ledge." He pointed at a low outcropping. "Yonah distracted it just long enough that I was able to shoot it with an arrow before it slipped away."

"You two were lucky it wasn't you in its jaws." Ayal pointed at an overturned wine flask near the flickering campfire with a raised brow.

Tomek waved his hand in the air. "Oh, don't you worry, the scream of that cat sobered me up right away. I'll never forget that sound as long as I live. It yowled like some vicious desert she-devil."

Shaking his head with a sigh, Ayal washed his hands in what was left of the water, dried them on his tunic, and then reached out for my hand. I hadn't realized how much I'd missed the contact until my fingers were braided with his cool ones again.

"Let's go, Shira. And let these fools clean up their mess."
Ayal moved to leave, but Yonah grabbed his arm from behind.

I had never been so close to Ayal's oldest brother. The silver
that threaded his beard surprised me, and I wondered just how
many years separated the two. Yonah looked more like a father
than a brother, in my estimation.

"This young woman did a fine job of helping tonight, Ayal."
Yonah looked down at me and smiled. "I don't know what the
issue was between you and Marah this morning, but you can
be assured, you won't hear of it again."

I dropped my eyes, mortified that he knew of the ordeal with
the necklace. "It was a misunderstanding, I assure you."

"I do not doubt that one bit." Yonah spat into the dirt and
pointed a thumb at the dead cat. "My wife is just like that leopard—on the prowl at times, always looking for her next victim."

He guffawed, and the sound echoed off the walls of the wadi.
"But if you show her as much strength as you showed with that
ewe, she'll retract her claws. You'll see."

Eben led the way out of the wadi with his torch, Ayal and
I trailing behind its glow. Although I had just witnessed the
aftermath of a wild animal attack, Ayal's nearness enveloped
me in a feeling of safety that I had never before experienced.

Just before we reached the edge of camp, Ayal slowed his
steps, then stopped and turned toward me. "Before I take you
back, I must hear you say it."

"Say what?"

He drew me in, his other hand searching out mine. "That
you forgive me."

Purple darkness curled itself around us as Eben and his torch
continued on. My brother must have the utmost trust in Ayal to
leave us with only the stars to keep watch. I swallowed, waiting
for the familiar fear to prickle in the back of my throat. It did not
come. All hesitation was gone, replaced with the patter of my

heart as I reveled in the affection glowing is his amber eyes and the rush of madness in my limbs at the feel of his skin against mine. He had wronged me, he had wronged his wife. But I could not ignore the sincere repentance I saw in his expression.

"I cannot condone what you did to Leisha," I said. "No matter what she did to you, you had no right to stray from your vows."

He stiffened, and I feared he would pull away.

"However—"

"Oh, how I love that word . . ." Relief gushed in his voice.

I stifled a smile and tugged at our joined hands. "However, I believe that you are truly sorry. But please promise me . . ."

"Anything."

I took a minute to gather my thoughts, and my courage, before proceeding. I edged my words with a hint of warning. "Promise me that you will be faithful, whatever comes. No matter how strong Kiya thinks I am, I could not endure such a thing."

He sucked in a breath as if stung by my entreaty, and I began to apologize for my harsh tone.

"No." He lifted a palm to interrupt. "I deserved that." He dropped his hands to his hips and bowed his head, as if contemplating his answer. He lifted sober eyes to mine. "I vow to you, before Yahweh himself"—he gestured to the Cloud above the mountain and then wove his fingers into mine—"that you are the only woman I will ever love, and I pledge my heart and my fidelity to you alone. I vow that I will spend the rest of my life proving your trust in me will not be in vain."

The sweetness of night-blooming jasmine flooded my senses as I leaned into him. "And I vow the same."

He tugged me close. "I have wasted precious time with you. I should have humbled myself months ago, begged your forgiveness, instead of hiding out with my sheep, wallowing in guilt."

"Yes. You should have. And I should have insisted on answers, instead of hiding inside my own heart. But—" I placed a hand on his chest, feeling the steady rise and fall of it, and took strength from the reminder that both of us were given breath by the God who brought us together, in spite of our faults. "You have my forgiveness now."

"I do not deserve such mercy, and I do not deserve you as my wife." His hand swept over my hair and trailed down my back, following the path of my braid. He pulled it over my shoulder and stroked the end of it with his thumb. Leaning down, he put his lips close to my ear. "I cannot wait to undo this braid."

With a shiver, I lifted my face to look into his eyes, searching for confirmation of his earlier declaration of love. I found it in the open delight of his gaze and again in the way he whispered my name, his mouth hovering over mine, his palm sliding under my chin. "Please? May I?"

Yes, my heart sang, and my breath echoed the same, and in a moment his mouth met mine. The tentative and guilt-ridden kiss by the stream could not compare with the overwhelming sensation of melting into him. The taste of his mouth and the ache of longing burned any latent indecision away. His arms wrapped around my waist, lifting me off my feet until they dangled in the air. I slid mine around his neck and pulled him tighter, daring him to let go and delighting in the heady thrill that sang in my blood.

With a smile against my lips, he slowly put me back on my feet. I wavered, leaning against him for support and suddenly realizing just how close we were to the edge of camp. The moment had seemed so thunderous inside my head, the crash of my heartbeat so deafening, that people must be poking their heads out of tents and scanning the sky for flashes of lightning.

"I have to take you back now, as much as I absolutely loathe the thought." He brushed his fingertips across my cheek, the move leaving a trail of tingles in its wake. "But if I don't"—his fingers traveled down my neck and to my collarbone—"I will have more to apologize for."

"I am sure my brother is wondering what happened to us," I whispered, trying to control the tremble of my knees.

His tone was sober. "I cannot be alone with you again until our wedding night, my little bird. I desire you too much." He touched a finger to my lips. "I care about you too much."

"How long? How long until you come for me?" My whisper sounded more desperate than I'd expected.

Leaning forward, he placed his forehead on mine, his nearness teasing me, begging me to reach for him. "Not one minute longer than necessary, I assure you."

36

A long shadow stretched over me as I flipped the last manna round on the cooking stone. "Shalom." Ayal's low greeting set flight to a covey of flutters in my stomach.

A swirl of nerves and pleasure had accompanied every glimpse of him since the night he held me in the dark—a reaction that always gave me away whenever he partook of our family meals. Kiya never failed to tease me about the roses that insisted upon blooming in my cheeks. If only my skin were as golden-toned as hers and more able to disguise my emotions.

"Shalom." I greeted him with as much tranquility as I could summon to mask the pounding of my besotted heart.

"May I ask something of you?" he said.

Anything. I nodded.

"You have heard that all Levites are to be consecrated tomorrow?"

"Yes, Eben said there will be sacrifices offered for the first time in the Mishkan."

237

As he was not yet twenty, my brother was not included in such instructions, but Ayal would be obligated to fulfill his new duties as a priest. Seven days of sacrifices would set apart the men who would serve in the holy place.

"I must shave." He frowned. "My beard, and my head."

My face echoed his expression. Ayal's dark hair fluttered about in the breeze, bringing attention to its imminent demise. He had trimmed it a few weeks ago, but already it curled around his ears again, inviting my touch.

"Will you help me? My brothers' wives are attending them, and I don't trust another man to do it. I could end up with only one ear." He smirked.

I lifted a brow. "I *would* rather have a husband with two ears."

I tossed a shy glance at Kiya across the camp, and she volleyed back with a self-satisfied grin before lifting a bit of milk-sopped bread to Talia's lips. Kiya was delighted that Dvorah had disappeared after her failed seduction of Ayal, and had taken ownership of Talia's nourishment. I gathered the bread and laid it in a basket to cool. My own stomach had lost its earlier bite.

I followed Ayal to the edge of the campsite, where he sat on a three-legged stool made by my brother, one of the last vestiges of our home back in Iunu. Ayal handed me a pouch, and inside I found a pair of shears, a honed copper blade, a linen towel, and a jar of oil that smelled of sandalwood and myrrh.

At a loss for how to begin the task, I stood behind him and surveyed the campsite. The boys were off on an adventure with Jumo, my mother, and the girls, looking for more useful roots and plants. Kiya was busy entertaining Talia in the shade, and my aunt and uncle were resting in their tent. No one was paying any attention to Ayal and me, but I felt self-conscious all the same.

Ayal turned to look at me over his shoulder. "Just start

chopping it off. It grows so fast now, it will only be a few weeks before it's over my ears again."

"Mine does as well." I said, lifting a tentative hand bearing the shears. "I notice that it is even a bit thicker since we left Egypt. I wonder if the manna has some sort of effect . . ."

Since our daily diet had consisted of mainly manna, everyone seemed healthier. Even the elderly who left Iunu on the backs of wagons now seemed to have renewed vigor, and the livestock were healthier now than when they had lush Egyptian fields to graze upon. "Perhaps I should cut mine as well while I am in command of your sheep shears."

Ayal swiveled on the stool. "Don't you dare."

I went wide-eyed, thinking he was serious, but teasing leaked into his expression and I remembered what he'd said about loosening my braid. Warmth revisited my cheeks. With a wink he turned his back, leaving me flustered, grateful that no one could hear our low conversation and very much trying to push away thoughts of my upcoming wedding night. Threading my fingers into Ayal's silky, dark hair did nothing to help.

With a deep breath, I held up a hank of hair and snipped it away, silently reassuring myself that it would grow back. "This reminds me of tending to my mistress back in Egypt." I brushed back a lock from beside his ear. "Although, I had to shave her head so frequently that I rarely had to cut so much."

Ayal cleared his throat, but his voice came out husky. "How long did you serve in her home?"

"Almost four years—until she sent me away after the plague of flies."

"Your mistress sent you away?"

I smiled to myself. "Tekurah was petrified of magic. I think she was convinced that I would put some sort of curse on her, since Hebrews weren't afflicted by the flies and our beasts did not die. I was very surprised that she let me go."

"Why did you not work with your mother as a weaver?"

My hands stilled their motion. And although my heart called out the answer, my mouth refused to follow suit. *He will hate you. He will look at you differently. He won't want you.*

"Shira?"

"My brother," I sputtered. "My brother's master had a friend looking for a handmaid, and Eben wanted me to go, so I did."

Ayal was silent for a moment. Did he suspect my lack of transparency?

"Was your master good to you?" His question was hesitant.

"Oh yes, Shefu was more than kind to me."

Ayal visibly exhaled. He must have been imagining the sorts of incidents that had been played out among many female Hebrew slaves and their masters.

"No, it was Tekurah, Shefu's wife, who was awful." A sardonic laugh escaped my lips. "It was a full year before she stopped slapping me for every offense and was finally satisfied with my work as her handmaid."

Ayal's fists were clenched in his lap, and his back tensed as if he were ready to defend me.

I placed a reassuring hand on his shoulder. "It is all right. She was awful at first, but I survived. After that year, she relied on me so heavily I received no more than an occasional tongue-lashing. She was much harsher with Kiya." I glanced at my friend, who was now sleeping under the awning with Talia tucked by her side. I may have endured Kiya's punishment during that time, but her friendship had been worth the trouble.

Ayal's hand covered mine. "It's a good thing that woman is far away. Or she wouldn't have a head left to shave."

I giggled, fingers to my lips, and he laughed with me. How good it felt to be laughing with Ayal again. The tension that had hovered in the air since Leisha's death had dispelled. I mouthed a word of thanks to Yahweh.

"There now. That is as much as I can do with the shears."
My stomach flipped at the loss.

He ran an exploratory hand over his closely-cropped head.
"Feels so strange."

I poured the oils into my hands and, with a quick inhale,
began rubbing the rich-smelling mixture into his scalp. He released a little groan of pleasure. "Perhaps I should have you
shave my head regularly. That feels wonderful."

With a nervous laugh, I handed him the pot and insisted
that he rub the oil into his beard, afraid that such an intimate
gesture would betray just how much his nearness affected me.
I washed my hands in a nearby pot of water and wiped them
dry, not willing to chance a sharp blade in slippery hands.

Lifting the copper blade from the pouch, I tested its edge and
then began my task. The memory of the monotonous chore
returned, and I lost myself in the strokes. When I finished shaving his head, I moved around in front of Ayal, and my breath
caught at the first sight of him without his hair.

"That bad?" He frowned. "Do you want to break off the
betrothal?"

I pursed my lips, pretending to consider the offer. "Hmm.
Possibly." I squinted. "Perhaps if you wear a turban . . ."

He threw back his head and laughed. "You'd better finish
the job before you make your final decision."

"All right." I pinned him with a look. "But hold still. A turban
will do nothing to hide an ugly scar across that handsome face."

His eyes danced with laughter, and for a moment I found
myself drowning in their fathoms.

Blinking off my daydreams, I lifted the copper blade, pushed
his chin into place with a finger, and then took a long swipe
up his neck. I released my breath, thanking Yahweh for all the
times Tekurah had demanded every single hair be removed from
her body. My hand did not shake.

Ayal watched me from beneath lowered lids. The more I tried to ignore the scrutiny, the more aware I was of my hands on his skin and his knees bracketing mine. I paused to wipe the blade on the linen towel, needing a break from the effort.

"I wish I did not have to do this." Ayal's words seemed pained.

"Shave?"

"No." He waved a hand in the air. "All of this. This consecration. This setting apart of the men in our tribe."

"Is it not an honor? For all of you to serve in the Mishkan?"

He frowned. "It is." He looked away. His jaw worked, as if grinding his teeth against something he wanted to say. He closed his eyes and drew a long breath through his nose. "But I do not feel worthy."

It was the last thing I expected to hear from Ayal's lips, and it shocked me into silence.

He dropped his head into his hands. "I asked for your forgiveness, Shira. But I did not tell you all of my sins."

He paused, and my pulse tripped. What more would he say? Was I not the only one he had approached while still married? Were there more lies to uncover?

Looking down at his hands, he sighed. "Leisha was not a happy woman. As I have told you, she was unfaithful to me. Many times. My family, as you well know, did not like her, and the unfaithfulness became more and more obvious as time went on. But it was not only for that reason."

He lifted sad eyes to mine. "She was with child when I married her. The twins were born only a few months afterward."

"They are not—?"

"They are," he said. "They are mine. At least as far as I know. And they resemble me so much I have little doubt."

They did. Ayal's features were mimicked in so many ways in the two boys. His smile in Ari—his laugher and his light, warm eyes in Dov.

"I wish I could plead youth or ignorance or something else, Shira. But I knew what I was doing. I accompanied my brother on a sale of ewes to her father in Iunu. When she suggested a . . . secret meeting, I did not hesitate."

He ran a hand over his half-shaved face.

"My father never forgave me for bringing such shame to our family. He had already made arrangements to betroth me to the daughter of another Levite. Leisha's mother was Hebrew, but she had been well-known as a prostitute before she married. My father refused to even give the customary bridal gifts or celebrate the marriage in any way." He shook his head. "Although my brothers did not hold it against me, their wives always have. They were merciless with Leisha."

As they are with me.

He dropped his head into his hands again. "Now you know what a wicked man you are bound to. If I had restrained myself, I would not have put her, or myself, through such misery."

I knelt in front of him and waited for him to meet my gaze. When he finally did, I placed my hand on his knee. "Remember when Yahweh spoke from the top of the mountain?"

He nodded, his eyes glassy. "I felt so exposed, as if every horrible thought and deed I ever committed was laid bare for everyone to see."

"I did as well. But after the Voice stopped, didn't you feel clean? As if by dredging all that blackness out of your heart, Yahweh washed it away?"

He sighed and softly brushed his knuckles down my cheek. "I have never felt so free as I did in those hours afterward. I felt brand new."

"Then why are you still carrying this burden of guilt?"

"I have asked myself the same thing again and again. So many nights I lay awake out in the fields, searching the stars for such answers."

Pulling his hand from my face, I turned it over and caressed it with my palm. "It reminds me of something Reva told me. That I have been nurturing my scars instead of speaking truth to myself and allowing them to heal. Like Dov, curling his hand up and refusing to let us rub oil into his wound so it can mend. And look at the beauty that has come, even from the ashes of your sins. Dov. Ari. Talia. It seems to me that Yahweh somehow takes the broken parts of us and builds something better than we could imagine."

It is time to speak truth. To yourself, and to Ayal. The thought came so clearly to my mind that I knew it was not of myself, but something deep in my spirit—an echo from the Voice, commanding me to let go.

"I have not been completely honest with you either, Ayal."

His head snapped up, confusion across his face.

Dropping my hands to my lap, I clutched the copper blade. I scraped my thumb against the edge, procrastinating. After a long, slow breath, I released the truth. "It was not only because Eben found a place in Shefu's home that I went to serve Tekurah. It was for my safety."

He bristled, but his eyes beckoned me to continue.

I sighed, drawing courage from the honesty he had gifted to me. "His name was Akharem. He was an Egyptian overseer. And I believed myself in love with him."

37

I wandered down the cobbled street, bare soles scraping against the uneven stones and daydreaming of the secret smile Akharem had given me as I left the workshop. As the son of the man who owned the linen shop, he was charged with overseeing the weavers. He watched me under the guise of his job, but each covert wink of his kohl-rimmed eye made me desperate for the next. My thirteen-year-old heart knew little of men and saw only the handsomeness of his face, not his heritage.

Dragging my fingertips along the rough wall of a mud-brick house, I turned the corner. Blinded by the bright sun, I stumbled on an errant cobblestone, pitching forward, but hands grabbed me before I could slam into the ground.

Blinking against the brightness, my maladjusted eyes registered only a black silhouette against the blaze of a blue sky.

"Are you hurt?"

I shaded my eyes with a hand, trying to place the familiar

voice. The subject of my meandering thoughts stood next to me. My pulse pounded a feverish rhythm.

"Thank you, my lord, I am fine. Just fetching a basket of food from our home." I took a step, assuming he would release me. Instead, his grip curled tighter around my upper arm, his fingertips pressing into my skin. My stomach lurched as I braced for a rebuke.

He laughed. I startled at the sound, and my bewildered gaze collided with his. Realizing my mistake, I dropped my eyes to my dusty toes.

His grip loosened, but instead of letting go, he slid his hand down to my wrist, a note of humor in his voice. "Don't scuttle away, little mouse. I will walk with you."

A jolt of confusion swept through me, and I once again looked up at him. Instead of anger or censure, there was a pleasant glint of appreciation in his eyes. He reached up and brushed aside the rebellious hank of hair that had drifted into my eyes, skimming my forehead with his finger. I had gathered my unruly curls against the back of my neck with a length of string that morning, but they refused to be contained.

As my mind scrambled to keep up with my pulse, I shrank back. "That is not necessary, my lord. I know my way."

His bottom lip pushed out in displeasure, and he dropped his chin with a chastened look. "You do not wish my company?"

Was Akharem actually interested in me? I understood the disdain Eben felt toward Egyptians after the horrific death of our father, but there were many kind Egyptians—such as my brother's master, the owner of a musical instrument shop.

Besides, Akharem was only a few years older than I was, and a few of my friends were already betrothed—one even expecting her first child. How could I refuse the company of a handsome man who showed interest in me? Especially one who appeared in my dreams every night?

The streets of Iunu were deserted. Eben would never know. Allowing a small smile, I nodded. With a flourish, he gestured for me to continue on.

The Hebrew Quarter was just as deserted as Iunu in the heat of midday. Those not working at the looms or making bricks for various building projects all over the city were taking a respite from the blaze within their homes.

I unlatched the door to our home and stepped across the threshold, telling Akharem I would be but a moment to fetch the basket I had been charged with retrieving. Without a lamp lit in our tiny mud-brick home, it was dark inside; the lone high window had been shuttered against the heat. But the light from the open door trailed directly to the basket of barley cakes and dried fish I had accidentally left behind this morning. It sat on the floor near my sleeping pallet.

As I reached out to grab the handle of the basket, the room went dark. Why had the door closed? My eyes searched the blackness in vain. An arm snaked around me from behind, locking me into a fierce embrace. A hand clamped over my mouth just as I attempted to scream.

"No. No, little mouse. I would not do that," he whispered into my ear as his fingers dug into my cheeks. "I can easily snap your pretty little neck." His other hand moved to my throat with just enough pressure to affirm his threat.

My eyes grasped for something to latch onto, but I could see only outlines and black shadows. My breath went shallow behind his smothering hand, and my pulse pounded in my ears. His iron grip tightened, and his voice rasped as he pulled in a heavy breath. "I have waited long enough."

His lips gazed my neck, and I cringed. *This cannot be happening.* What could I do? He was not very tall, but solid and muscular. I had no chance of escape. My mother and aunt were at the looms, my brother working at the musician's shop, and my sisters being watched by a neighbor. No one would know that I was a captive inside our home.

Why had I insisted to my mother that I would be fine walking alone today? Begged and cajoled to be trusted with a grown-up task? I whimpered, and the sound seemed to come from outside my body, from somewhere in the darkness that engulfed me.

Akharem slithered his hand inside the neck of my tunic. Terror seized me in a grip of paralysis. I tried to call out, but my mouth was dry. Only a choked "please" passed my lips.

"That's right, beg, little one. I know you want me too. " He swiped me off my feet with his leg and pushed me to the ground. I smashed my head against a jar as I tumbled down, but before I could clutch the bleeding wound, Akharem locked both of my wrists in one of his hands.

The Egyptian twice outweighed me and had me pinned to the floor. My mind reeled, trying to devise ways I could slip away, but my limbs would not comply. I was helpless and too terrified to fight back.

His hot mouth came down on mine, and he kissed me fiercely. The sickening thought that this horrid man was the first to ever kiss my lips flitted through my mind, sparking a surge of courage. I did the only thing my disoriented mind could devise.

I bit his lip, hard.

He spat and cursed and slapped me, knocking my head on the hard-packed dirt again. I tasted blood; my head throbbed, and lights flashed behind my eyelids. The tie on my hair had come loose, and my long curls were wild, covering my face and pinned painfully beneath my body.

Was he going to kill me? I was glad I could not see his face through the curtain of my hair. Without seeing the decision in his eyes, I could still hope my life would be spared, even if my heart whispered it would not.

He yanked at my tunic, jerking it above my knees.

"Please. Please don't do this." Useless tears stung my skin and slid into my ears.

"Worthless little Hebrew. I'll do what I want. You've been asking for this for weeks."

⁓

I lifted my eyes, blinking away the all-too-vivid memories of that day, but the shame clung to me like a noxious weed. Ayal's jaw was stone, his nostrils flaring and every muscle taut, as if ready to attack. I flinched, leaning back against my heels. Would he hit me? Push me away and break the betrothal?

"If I could walk back to Egypt this moment, I would find that overseer and . . ." His hands flexed, as if around Akharem's throat. "When Eben told me that an Egyptian had forced himself on you, I had imagined many horrific things, but for that animal to blame you? For what *he* did?"

My hands trembled. "You knew?"

He placed his palms on either side of my face. "Of course. Your brother is an honorable man; he would not keep such a thing from me." His sunlit eyes were pools of compassion. "But, Shira, I want you to know that it changed nothing. I wanted to marry you then, and I want to marry you now."

"You do?"

"Why would such a heinous act mar my opinion of you? No matter what that . . . that devil said, you did nothing to encourage him."

I closed my eyes. "I wanted his attention."

"You were thirteen, my sweet. You were not out to entice him. Any more than you were out to seduce me when I—"

I put my fingers to his lips. "It is not the same. It was wrong, yes. But not the same. And it is forgiven."

He grasped my hand in his, kissed my palm and then the inside of my wrist. The sensation rippled like a cool breeze up the skin of my arm. "Here you want me to let go of the past, stop beating myself up over my sins, and yet you flog yourself over someone else's?"

Was that what I had done? Taken on the weight of Akharem's sins? Telling the story to Ayal had already seemed to lighten that burden. Reva was right, I needed to stretch the scar, even if it hurt, so that it did not hold me captive anymore.

He trailed his thumb across my lips. "Hear me, my sweet songbird. You cannot blame yourself anymore. From this moment on, I want you to see yourself as I see you—your true self. You are no longer powerless, no longer a slave. You are the woman I love."

"And you," I said. "You are no longer who you were before Yahweh brought us out of Egypt. You are not a slave anymore either. What you did before is washed away. I hold none of it against you."

I glanced up at his head, now shaved clean. "You are no less worthy to be consecrated to Yahweh than any other man. He has chosen you. Accept the gift." I sank into the depths of his eyes. "We both need to see ourselves more clearly."

His lips tipped up into a smile. "Perhaps we do. But if I could see myself right now, I would see half a beard."

I shook my head, laughing. "If Eben and Jumo come back and find you like this, they will never let you live it down."

"Then you had better finish shaving me." His brows wiggled with mischief. "Besides, I am quite ready to have your hands all over my face again."

38

A song exploded into being—the voices of thousands of Levite men merged into a joyous anthem of praise toward Yahweh. Every hair on the back of my neck and all up and down my arms prickled at the strange, awe-inspiring sound. Today the Mishkan and the tribe of Levi would begin the process of being consecrated unto Yahweh, both set apart to be used in sacred service for the God who had brought us out of Egypt.

As twilight began to creep over the eastern ridges, I pictured Ayal among the mass, dressed in pristine white, shaved clean by my hand, and his low voice joining with his brethren in worship. Oh! To be beside him and see the polished silver trumpets raised to musicians' lips. Or to sit among the string players—some trained by my own brother—and be enveloped by the music dedicated to the One out of whose own imagination music itself was conceived—what I would not give for such pleasures.

Although our tents were near enough to the center of camp that the top of the completed Mishkan was in full sight, the tall, white fence around it obstructed our view of the proceedings.

Even so, I found myself raising to my tiptoes, gripping my brother's shoulder to boost myself higher in a futile gesture to see something, anything.

Being Ayal's betrothed allowed me the privilege of bringing him meals while he was working in the courtyard over the last few days. Passing by the richly woven gates filled me with extraordinary pride in the part my family had played in their construction. My mother's hands, along with Kiya's, had woven one of the scarlet, blue, and purple panels that spanned one half of the entrance. Even my few hours stirring the red dye-pots had contributed to the effort.

I had been present to see the bronze laver as it was being set into place, marveled over the refraction of sunlight shattering into a thousand colors across its polished surfaces, and watched as many men worked together to unfurl and secure the blood-red inner covering and the rainproof outer layer.

Even before the last strains of that first song had faded, a second began, slower and more pensive. Although I could not hear the words, the dips and swells of the composition seemed familiar. When I found myself humming along and able to anticipate the harmonies, my hand flew to my mouth to stifle a gasp.

My brother's arm slipped around my shoulder, and he pulled me to his side.

Tears of delight flowing, I looked up and saw the same emotion displayed on his face. "Is it—?"

He cleared his throat, and his lips twitched with pride. "Yes. It is the song composed by Abba. I taught it to some of the musicians during our lessons. They must have passed it along to the others."

A song created by my own father when I was a tiny girl was now lifted in praise by hundreds of voices. *Oh, Abba, I wish you were here*. Although Eben's wounded hand prevented him from playing music with the same dexterity, he was still able to pass his knowledge on to others. In doing so, he achieved a greater purpose than if he had nurtured his gift alone. In spite of the pain and heartbreak, Eben had honored his father and Yahweh. Perhaps if he had not been injured Eben would have kept my father's song to himself instead of teaching it to others.

I clasped my hands together in front of my chest and closed my eyes, savoring every note like the most succulent fruit. If only to capture each one in my memory—to taste their sweetness again and again.

Too soon, the echoes of the precious tones faded against the cliffs, only to be replaced by the blast of many silver trumpets. Talia, who was strapped to my back, wailed at the strange sound. With my mother's help, I transferred her to my arms, whispering reassurances into the curl of her ear until she relaxed against me. I rubbed circles into her back until her eyes drifted closed.

A voice floated on the breeze, broken into unintelligible syllables. It was more than likely Aharon, whose translations from Mosheh usually resounded so well off the rocks when he spoke from the ledge above the crowd. However, today his speech from the center of the courtyard was swallowed up by distance and the linen fence.

Looking around at our well-ordered tents, organized by tribe, clan, and family, I marveled at the change in us. A chaotic multitude had limped out of Egypt, broken and bedraggled. Bound in covenant to Yahweh, we now had a code of laws, a priesthood, an army, and a judicial system.

We were no longer a ragged group of slaves, but a nation.

The sun melted into the horizon, and the longer the garbled speech by Aharon dragged on, the more fidgety the children became. More than once my mother was forced to issue stern looks at Zayna, who chattered with Dov and Ari. My sister had appointed herself mother hen over the two boys and was drawing pictures in the dirt to entertain them, a trick she'd learned from Jumo.

Someone behind our tent called out, "Look at the Cloud!"

All heads swiveled away from the Mishkan and toward the mountain. The Cloud was on the move. As darkness descended on the valley, so too did the swirling column of light. It hovered over the congregation and soundlessly moved into position over the Mishkan, then slowly, as if it were an eagle landing in its nest, lowered itself just above the covering, illuminating the landscape around us as if it were the middle of the day.

We all dropped to our knees, compelled there by the nearness of such brilliance and the fearsomeness of the roiling storm contained within the Cloud. Even Zayna and the boys cowered on the ground with their hands over their eyes. Yet the thick veil of smoke obscured its true intensity—the radiance of which, my instincts told me, would probably kill us all in an instant if revealed in its fullness.

Why would Yahweh choose to do such a thing? Bring his glorious *shekinah* presence among us? Especially after the horrors of the Golden Apis we flaunted before him?

An image surged into my mind. A few days ago, Ayal had come to share a meal with us after taking his turn with his brothers among the sheep. After greeting me with a chaste kiss to my cheek and a whisper that bloomed heat into my face, Ayal had folded his long legs onto the ground next to Dov and Ari, asking about their day and participating in a game involving a few stones, two twigs, and an overturned basket—the rules of which I was still at a loss to understand. But he laughed with them, indulged their imaginative play, and they responded by fighting for supremacy over his lap and chattering with the father who showed such an interest in their childish games.

Just as Ayal desired to be with his children and find pleasure in their presence, so Yahweh had come down to the valley floor, exposing his greatness in more detail and showing great mercy in overlooking our fickle hearts. Yahweh wanted to be close to us—just like an abba with his precious children.

39

Ari stood on his toes, peering through cupped hands toward the Mishkan. "The sun is almost gone. Where is Abba?"

"He will be here soon." I mussed his dark curls. "Why don't you and Dov go ask my mother what you can do to help with the meal?"

His small shoulders dropped. "All right, Shira." He turned to go, but then twisted back around, his face puckered in thought. "Are you my *ima* now, Shira?"

I knelt down to look directly into his face. "Do you want me to be?"

He tilted his head. "My other *ima* is gone forever."

A howling fissure split wide open in my chest. "Yes. She is gone. But she asked me to take care of you." A small stretch of truth, but a necessary one.

"Then I am glad you are my *ima*." He leaned forward, pressed a kiss to my lips, and with an impish grin headed off to find his brother. Standing, I watched him trot away completely unaware that his simple gesture had assuaged the razor-edged memories of Leisha's death.

"I really should not be so jealous of a little boy." The husky voice from behind me caused a smile to curl my lips.

I smothered my humor with mock censure before turning to face Ayal. "Then perhaps you, too, should go find my mother and offer your help."

He lifted a teasing brow. "I may do just that." He stepped close and dropped his gaze to my lips. "And then I will be back for a reward."

Inhaling the tantalizing combination of Ayal's masculine scent and the incense from his tunic, I nearly groaned at the effort it took to step backward. *How much longer?* It seemed that this betrothal had lasted a thousand years instead of four weeks.

"I think my mother has enough help." I cast a glance over my shoulder at the giggling boys as they swung the hanging goatskin bag back and forth between them. Sloshing the milk until it fermented into smooth curdled yogurt was a task they eagerly embraced.

"Besides . . ." I swept my gaze over the long, white tunic that had been spotless this morning and now bore the marks of his first full day of priestly service. "I would rather you stay and tell me about the Mishkan."

He smiled. "What would you like to know?"

"Everything."

Kiya emerged from the tent across the way with Talia in her arms and leveled a sly smirk at me before walking off. At times, I practically had to wrestle her, and sometimes my mother, for a turn at holding the baby. She doted on the precious little one. It wouldn't be long before she held her own child; her stomach protruded more every day. I found myself constantly holding back the midwifery questions that bubbled to my lips the closer she came to the fullness of her pregnancy. She even begged me to come with her to visit with Reva, but I refused. The temptation to give in to Reva's repeated efforts to talk me into returning was too torturous.

"I've never seen anything so magnificent, Shira." Ayal looked back at the enormous tent at the center of camp. The Cloud hovered above it, shimmering blue against the backdrop of the purpling twilight. He closed his eyes as if reentering the Mishkan in his mind.

He told me how the gold-plated walls reflected the constant flicker of the enormous golden menorah and the floor-to-ceiling curtains, woven from red, blue, and purple and embroidered with strange beings with outstretched wings. He spoke of the bronze altar, the rich smell of the sacrifices, and the spicy incense that wafted past the curtains.

"Only Mosheh and Aharon are allowed to pass into the *Kodesh Hadashim*," said Ayal with quiet reverence. "If anyone else passes the curtains into that holiest place, they will die. In fact, we have been warned that to take lightly any of the instructions for worship will result in death as well." He turned to me, determination in the planes of his face. "I stood there today, with my Levite brothers around me, worshipping the One True God as his presence hovered nearby—I cannot begin to describe the honor. I love being a shepherd. It is in my blood. But I am *called* to serve Yahweh as a priest."

Hushed, we watched the last of the sunlight relinquish its grasp on the horizon. Contentedness stole over me and I breathed deeply, relishing the quiet strength of the man who would soon be my husband.

"I know that Leisha's death was hard on you, Shira. But why haven't you returned to midwifery?" Ayal's soft question nearly knocked me sideways.

"I don't know that I will. I have plenty to keep me occupied with the children."

He leaned closer. "But it is *your* calling."

"I used to think so too, but I was wrong."

He shook his head. "No, Shira. I was there the day you guided Ziba's lamb, you were absolutely serene. And then, again, when the leopard attacked our flock—I had never seen anyone handle trauma with such clear-headed grace."

"But those were animals, Ayal. When Leisha died in my care—"

"Her death was in no way your fault."

"My head may understand this, but my heart does not agree."

Facing me, he grasped my shoulders and pulled me close. "Sweet songbird. I know you are wounded. Believe me, I understand what it is like for something to cut so deeply that it seems it will never heal. But Shira, you are just like that frightened ewe after the cat attack. Quit fighting the hands that are trying to heal you."

With a sigh, I succumbed to his embrace, not caring who was watching. The linen of his priest's garment was soft against my cheek, and the unique scent of the Mishkan enveloped me in peace.

"That reminds me." I slipped away. "I have something for you."

He followed me to our family tent. Warmer days had convinced us to roll up its sides to invite the fresh air to take up residence. Folded on the end of my sleeping pallet was his gift. I placed it in his outstretched hands with a nervous laugh. "I am in no way a gifted weaver. Even Kiya, who has been weaving for mere months, puts my paltry skills to shame. But I made this for you because of the new *mitzvot*."

He held out the tunic I had woven for him, and it unfurled to his knees. He glanced at me, appreciation in his eyes, then placed it against his body and ran a hand down the multicolor-striped fabric. With his fingers, he explored the embroidered hem and the knotted, fringed *tzitzit*, which served as a constant visual reminder of the Covenant and the laws we had agreed to obey.

"Do not look too closely." I dropped my eyes. "Or you will find all the places where I dropped threads and spoiled the pattern."

"But those are the best parts." Ayal's lips twitched with humor. I furrowed my brow, thinking he was mocking me.

"I am quite serious." He tossed the tunic over his shoulder, then grasped both of my hands. "Those little mistakes will remind me that this was made by these very hands." He turned them over and gently, with his eyes locked on mine, kissed the center of each of my palms. "It is not the perfection that matters, sweet Shira, it is the love of the one who created it."

40

DVORAH

*I*f this woman does not stop shrieking in my ear, I will shake her by the shoulders until that baby comes out.

I bit my tongue against ordering the laboring mother to quiet down—but only because Reva was here. Working with the old midwife made me nervous. I always had the feeling she loomed over me, watching every move I made, trying to trap me into making a mistake—like that terrifying fire-cloud that had hovered over the Mishkan since the ceremony three days ago, not too far from this very tent.

Reva's dark, beady eyes missed nothing, and she was quick to criticize my missteps. More than likely, Reva blamed me for Shira's refusal to return to midwifery.

As if this wasn't her fourth birth, the fool woman screamed again, eyes rolling back in her head, a profanity flying past her lips, followed by an order for Reva to "get the thing out of her."

She gripped my arm as I steadied her on the birthing bricks, digging her fingertips so deep into my skin I nearly cursed along with her.

Reva scowled. "The baby is not coming easily, Dvorah. We need to change Gameliah's position."

I helped Gameliah kneel on her sleeping mat as Reva directed, a position that never failed to remind me of Shira and the night Leisha died. The night Talia was born.

It had been weeks since I had walked away from Ayal's camp, but I could still feel her little hands kneading my skin, hear her coos, see her wide eyes watching me like a hawk as I nursed her—

Gameliah howled, interrupting my fruitless thoughts, as Reva checked the baby's progress. The woman kicked back like a braying donkey, slamming Reva in the shoulder. I grabbed the woman around her waist, using my weight and strength to prevent her from flipping over. Unruffled, Reva continued her examination, obviously used to flailing arms and legs and verbal abuse by crazed mothers.

The midwife was always so calm, her voice strong and steady as she dealt with the women. I envied her ability to keep her emotions in balance, even in the most dire of circumstances. I had been so terrified the night Leisha bled out that my body had gone paralyzed. I could not have helped Shira even if I had wanted to. And although Shira had fled later, her calm reflected Reva's; her hands never trembled.

But I was good at this as well. I never forgot anything Reva taught me, my arms and hands were strong, and each time I assisted with a birth I was more confident, more assured that I would soon be able to midwife on my own. Each delivery was a small victory over Shira, even if I'd never be Reva's pet.

Shortly after dawn, and what seemed like hours of the woman roaring and bellowing and panting like a chariot horse, Reva announced that the baby's head had crowned. Gameliah slumped to her side in exhaustion, moaning and weeping as if she were a little girl and announcing that she would not, could not, do any more.

Right as the next contraction hit, a thunderclap shattered the quiet, so close that it seemed to come from inside the tent itself. My teeth slammed together as the reverberation vibrated deep into my bones. A flash of light illuminated the tent, mimicking the flame of a million torches. Every hair on my body stood straight on end, and I was momentarily blinded by bright colors that floated in front of my sight.

"What was that?" Gameliah shrieked. "A storm?"

Rare storms sometimes slipped across the mountains, surprising us with drenching rains, but not since the day of the Covenant had I heard such violent thunderings. I shuddered at the reminder of that horrible Voice trumpeting in my ear, condemning me with its every terrifying word, reaching into the pit of shame inside me and finding no bottom. I had been glad when so many people begged Mosheh to stop the Voice from speaking to us again. It was far too invasive. I preferred Isis, my quiet goddess with the eternal smile and no voice of judgment.

Reva's face was nearly as pale as the laboring woman's, but her voice was smooth as glass. "Gameliah, I do not know what just happened, but we must deliver this baby. Focus on pushing, or the little one will not survive. Push. Now."

Still reeling from the terrifying light, and ears ringing from the sound that had fractured the stillness of the camp so early in the morning, I followed my duties by rote.

Overlapping noises came from outside—shouts from the direction of the Mishkan, the shrieks of children awakened by the crack of thunder against tiny ears, the bleat of goats and sheep startled by the commotion.

Reva ignored the chaos and delivered the baby, a tiny Levite to follow in his father's footsteps. The rap of jealousy knocked loudly as I watched Gameliah fawn over her son. My son barely remembered his father. The only legacy Tareq had left us was slavery to Hassam and his whims. Who would guide Matti on his journey to manhood? My bloodthirsty, depraved brother-in-law? The thought of my sweet boy imitating Hassam made me ill.

A shofar blew. The call for the elders to meet was a distinct pattern familiar to all of us. What could have happened that the elders had been summoned? A shiver ran up my arms.

Somewhere close by, a mourning wail began. Gameliah startled from her oblivious perusal of the baby. "Did that come from near the Mishkan?" She clutched him closer, panic in her wide eyes. "My husband! Yehuel was helping with the sacrifices this morning."

Although I cared nothing about her man, I welcomed an excuse to get away from the volatile woman and her gushing over the baby, so I offered to go find out what had happened.

There was chaos near the Mishkan—men coming and going from the entrance, faces pale and drawn. I touched the arm of a woman who stood gawking nearby, clutching a satchel to her chest with whitened knuckles. She jerked as if I had poked her with a stick.

I lifted a hand to steady her but caught myself and snatched it back. "What is happening?" I said.

The woman's brown eyes were so big they seemed to consume her face. She shook her head back and forth. "It is awful. So awful." Her lips pressed into a tight frown.

"What? What happened?" For the second time in as many hours, I had the urge to shake a woman by the shoulders.

"Fire struck Aharon's sons. Right from the center of the Holy Place. One of the priests who witnessed the awful moment said it happened so fast that the two men were dead before their charred bodies hit the ground."

I stifled a gasp of disgust. "Why?"

"No one knows." She shrugged her shoulders. "They must have offended Yahweh somehow. One man said he saw them drinking heavily last night."

I had never met Aharon's sons, did not even know their names, but my mind automatically ascribed my husband's face to theirs. I could not scrub away the conjured image of Tareq lying in their place, smoke rising from his fire-stricken flesh, the light snuffed from his eyes. How could Aharon's own sons be killed? Weren't they among the elite of Mosheh's precious Levites?

Disgust churned in my gut as I shivered at the implication. If even direct descendants of Levi received no mercy for missteps, then I—born of a Hebrew *zonah* and some nameless Egyptian customer—could certainly expect nothing better. I would have to protect myself—and my son, whose own Hebrew blood was even thinner than mine—no matter the cost.

There had to be an escape from Hassam's yoke. I was so tired of stealing for him. Tired of being bullied. Tired of seeing Matti wilt when Hassam cursed him for being in his way, or drinking more than his allotment of water, or being too noisy, or whatever other reason Hassam fabricated to scald my boy with his words.

I had thought Ayal was my path to freedom. If he had married me instead of Shira, Hassam would have left me alone. But I was Hassam's direct line to Hebrew tents and the treasures within. He would not let me walk away easily.

I returned to the tent to tell Reva what had happened. Although Gameliah gasped at the news of Aharon's sons, she was relieved that it was not her own husband dead on the ground in front of the altar.

White-faced and silent, Reva went outside to wash her hands. Gameliah, suddenly the picture of sweetness and maternal doting, chattered to me about the baby and how beautiful he was, but my mind was on my escape.

The timing must be just right in order to get away from Hassam while keeping Matti safe. But where could I go? The camp was so organized now that there would be nowhere for me to move without suspicion. Hassam would too easily find me in the outer camps. He must be satisfied that I was under his control and did not have the courage, or the intelligence, to break away. I must continue the ruse that I was little more than a simple-minded, easily manipulated fool.

Realizing that Gameliah had fallen asleep with the baby at her breast, I strained to detect Reva's graveled tones close by—but heard nothing. Perhaps she had wandered off to learn more about Aharon's sons.

After glancing again at Gameliah to ensure she was sleeping, I peeked inside the nearest basket. Clothing. Another trunk nearby held only sandals, a few empty pots, and a foul-smelling goatskin bag. I almost closed the lid. *Wait. Perhaps . . .*

I opened the bag and nearly gasped with joy. A golden armlet sparkled inside the bag, along with two leather cords strung with silver *deben*. I tucked the *deben* inside my leather pouch and lifted the armlet. The gold was clear and smooth and studded with enormous pearls the color of snow. I ran my thumb over one, marveling at its perfect, soft sheen. This would certainly keep Hassam convinced that I had no ideas about running away, that my loyalty was to him.

"What are you doing?"

I dropped the armlet back in the bag, heart galloping at the censure in Reva's voice.

"I was . . . looking for . . . something. Another blanket for the baby."

Reva's pointed glare shot straight to the center of my lie.

"How long have you been stealing?"

I flinched, surprised at how deep the accusation, and the truth, cut me. Reva had been good to me, even if she had ignored me when Shira was around. The explanation pressed against my teeth, its urgency making my eyes smart. *I have no choice. My son is at stake.*

"I should have believed her," she said, her hands on her hips and those gray eyes piercing me as she shook her head. "When she warned me you were up to no good."

Shira. I should have known she was speaking against me. Her cloying sweetness was no more than a mirage, just as I had suspected. She and the rest of the Levites were nothing but murderers and thieves.

"Well?" Reva urged. "Do you have anything to say?"

I set my jaw.

"Nothing? After I have spent the last few months training you? After I took you under my wing even though my every instinct fought against it? You have *no* explanation?"

I stared her down for a moment, wavering between dropping to my knees and begging for mercy, or spitting in her face. What could I say that would alter the condemnation in her expression? My words were worth nothing. I pressed my lips tighter.

"All right, then." She turned away, flipping a dismissive gesture toward the door. "I have no use for a thief. Go."

Gameliah released a moan in her sleep, followed by a sigh of contentment, which caused the baby to stir and smack his little lips. The tiny sound gouged through my thin veneer of control, and I spat a curse to guard against its intrusion. Twice now I had been within reach of the peace that stupid woman had, only to have it ripped away, first by the Levites and then by Shira. Fury pulsed through me as I turned and left the tent. They would both pay.

Thanks be to Isis, Reva had not searched me. The silver *deben* I carried in my pouch would at least be something to offer Hassam and soften the blow before I told him I was no longer a midwife. He would be furious that I had recklessly cut off his supply of jewels and gold.

How long could I avoid admitting the truth? Perhaps I could part with a few small trinkets I had stowed away, to allay any suspicion and postpone the inevitable beating I would receive.

Foolish. I had forced my own hand with my carelessness. Now I must get away. I would not let him take his anger out on Matti. Last week, I had found bruises on my little boy's upper arms in the distinct shape of a man's fingers.

The wails of people mourning Aharon's sons sprang up all around me as I picked up the pace toward my son. A fitting memorial to my hope.

41

SHIRA

8 NISSAN
13TH MONTH OUT FROM EGYPT

My eyes flew open. I jolted upright in my bed, fumbling with the blanket that had wrapped me in a tight cocoon. Ayal called my name again from outside, a repeat of the sublime sound that had reached into my fitful dreams. *My bridegroom has finally come for me.*

I had prepared every evening for a week in anticipation of this moment—washing in the stream, laying out my finely embroidered dress, braiding my rose-oil-scented hair tightly, and taking long, slow breaths to force sleep into my body—but still, the shock of his arrival in the middle of the night left my composure in shards.

My mother must have known that he was coming for me tonight. Cross-legged on the floor, she worked her needle, even in the dim light of one sputtering oil lamp. She looked amused by my flustered state. "Breathe, dear one."

I gulped.

"Let me help you dress." She lit another lamp. The flame sizzled as it burst into being, and my nerves echoed the sentiment. Shoshana and Zayna awakened at the sudden brightness, jumping up from their pallet to fetch my veil. They carried it between them, chattering with excitement, discussing their own weddings someday and the impossible sheerness of the linen my mother had woven.

My mother lifted the gown and slipped it over my head. The double-layered linen rippled down my body like water. Kiya had gifted me one of her mother's lovely dresses and then she and my mother had altered its fit and embroidered a pattern of purple lilies and tiny bluebirds all around the neckline. I trailed my hand across the delicate design, fashioned by love and a small amount of Kiya's hard-won Tyrian dye.

Voices around the tent grew in number. Ayal's late-night arrival had no doubt attracted witnesses. Panic fluttered against my ribs. Would his brothers be with him? Who else was here to gawk as Ayal escorted me to our wedding tent? Hopefully not those awful women who had interrupted Kiya's wedding feast.

Distinct voices distracted me from my worries—Eben's smooth tones and Jumo's low ones, joking and laughing with the bridegroom as he waited for his bride. *For me.* My brother called out my name again with a playful admonition that Ayal had waited long enough.

My mother laughed and placed her cool palm on my face. "That he has. The way that man watches you, I knew it would not be more than a few days before he snatched you away."

With a quick kiss to my suddenly overheated forehead, she covered my embarrassment with the linen veil and guided me to the door of the tent.

The grinning faces of Eben, Jumo, Yonah, and Tomek greeted

me first, before Kiya's lovely one appeared. She slipped a quick hug around my neck and a whisper of blessing into my ear.

The filmy linen over my face could not prevent my gaze from colliding with Ayal's, though I was grateful for its camouflage of the hot flush on my cheeks. His beard was already beginning to fill in along his jaw, and his dark hair, though short, was making a reappearance. A flash of remembrance—of my fingers weaving through his hair as I cut it—made my stomach ache with longing for the silken waves.

Standing tall and silent, Ayal seemed to be drinking in the sight of me as a slow smile lifted into place. He reached out a hand and I gripped it, marveling at the way his long fingers wove perfectly into mine.

With a wink and a tiny jerk of his head to warn me, Ayal turned and fled the campsite, one stride to my every two. Laughter bubbled up inside my chest, but I concentrated on keeping rhythm with his footfalls.

A few teasing comments followed us out of the campsite, but my mind was so hazy with joy and anticipation that I heard little. Our families would be close behind us, torches lighting their way, ready to begin a wedding celebration that would last for days, but it seemed Ayal had little interest in the traditional escort to our marriage tent. I was grateful for it—my heart was in a race with my feet.

Through the shadows and around the outskirts of campfires we moved, like two nightjars on wing. A cool breeze pressed the veil against my face and I longed to rip the fabric away, but I had played out this night in my mind a hundred times, anticipated the image of Ayal's face as he lifted it himself. I refused to relinquish the suspense.

The silhouette of the Mishkan stood black against the star-brushed sky. Although the Cloud had stood over it for days, tonight it perched atop the mountain, its blue-white light illuminating the path to our wedding tent. I glanced at its now-familiar brightness and imagined the Creator looking down at us from the heights and declaring this night *tov*, just as he had upon the union of his first children in the Garden. The thought filled the hollows of my chest with peace, leaving no room for fear or trepidation.

I had not been inside Leisha's dwelling since Dvorah had fled. Though I knew it was to be my new home, the fleeting thought that I would be intruding on someone else's abode gave me pause. Distracted, I stumbled on a stone in my path.

Ayal whipped around to steady me, chest heaving from our flight through camp. "Forgive me, I am going too fast."

"No. I am fine. Just clumsy. It's hard to see in the dark with the veil."

"And a little nervous?" A tease lifted his voice.

"A bit." I chewed my lip for a moment, but truth flowed from my mouth in a desperate rush. "I thought you would never come."

Ayal's rich laughter seemed to seep through my skin, soaking into my blood and raising my body temperature as he tugged my hand and led me to the entrance of the tent. Golden light seeped through the slit.

He turned and pulled me close to him, his anise-sweet breath on my face. "I know. It has been too long. Work on the Mishkan took longer than I'd hoped. I was also preparing your new home for you. I wanted it to be . . . comfortable."

I placed my hand on his chest. "I am sure anything would be lovely, Ayal. I am pleased just to be with you."

"Perhaps. But all the same, the time was necessary." He gestured for me to lead the way.

With a trembling inhale, I pushed aside the flap and stepped inside, bracing with reluctant expectation.

All misgivings floated away like mist. This tent stood in the same place as it had before. From the outside it looked no different, but the inside was completely changed. The simple pallet Talia had been born upon was gone, replaced by a bed fashioned of layers of plush sheepskins, pillows, and linens, nearly calf high.

There was not one familiar item inside. Every basket, every crate, every clay oil lamp was different. I recognized the rugs covering the floor as all made by my mother's hand, their colors vivid even through the filter of my veil. Two of Jumo's painted wall-hangings hung from the woolen walls—one a joyful scene that reminded me of the lush beauty that defined the Egypt of my childhood and the other a brilliant depiction of the Cloud stacked high above the mountain.

Ayal slipped his arms around my waist, his chin resting on the top of my head. "I wanted this place to be your home. To chase the shadows from its corners," he said with a hint of hesitation. Was he unsure that I appreciated his effort? That I understood the significance?

His gesture gave me courage. I twisted my body around and wrapped my arms around him, laying my head against his work-hardened chest. "This is the kindest thing anyone has ever done for me. Thank you."

"I want to see your face," he whispered, his voice thick. The steady thrum of his heartbeat quickened. "I am desperate to see your face."

I took a step back, and he lifted my veil. His expression was even better than my imaginings. I tried to memorize the exquisite beauty of the moment, the curves of delight around his mouth, the way his eyes reflected the flicker of the oil lamp—as if the light instead emanated from their depths.

All too soon, his smile tipped into mischief as he reached for me. "So it *is* you. I worried that Eben might pull a trick like Lavan did with Rachel in the days of old." He smirked at his own joke and shook his head. "Poor Yaakov."

I widened my eyes. "Ah. But you have not yet fulfilled your seven years of labor. Perhaps I should go and find a 'Leah' to take my place." I feigned an attempt to slip from his grasp.

His grip on my wrist turned to soft iron. "Oh no. You are not going anywhere." His voice had dropped into a dangerous tease that made my mouth go dry. "I have waited far too long for this moment." He slipped the veil off my head and dropped it to the floor behind me.

He leaned close and lifted my chin. "You are mine." He brushed his lips along my jawline until I shivered. "You are mine here, alone, for seven beautiful days and seven beautiful nights. And I want to cherish you. Every. Single. Moment."

Although my lips were aching for his touch, he took me by the shoulders and gently turned me around. One hand slid from my shoulder and up the side of my neck, then down the length of my hair. I closed my eyes, savoring the caress against my back.

After a kiss that traveled the length of my neck, that made my toes curl into the woolen rug and my bones turn to sweet wine, Ayal began to undo my braid.

42

14 Nissan
13th Month Out from Egypt

The smoky tang of roasting lamb saturated the air. My sisters, always eager to help, took turns spinning the meat on the spit. Fat slicked off the roast, crackling and spattering into the flames. My stomach howled with expectation.

I was so grateful that Ayal had asked my family to join with his in celebrating this memorial feast. Eben sat across the fire with Kiya leaning back into his chest, his good arm tucked around her middle as if shielding the cocoon of their developing family. Thankfully, the baby in my arms tempered the unbidden envy that reared at times as I watched Kiya's middle expand. She had a little over two months left, if I guessed correctly.

I pulled Talia closer to my chest, a tiny shield against the pointed glares and behind-hand whispers of Aiyasha and Yael. The last week of secluded bliss with Ayal had wrapped me in such contentment that I had nearly forgotten just how much his brothers' wives disliked me. They were cordial to the point of falseness around their husbands, but their laughter had a sharp edge that seemed to slip perfectly between my shoulder blades. Dvorah's disappearance had altered their expressions from suspicious to outright contempt. None of them knew the real reason she had not returned.

The shadowed recesses of our tent called my name. If it were not for the distraction of the baby nestling into me, her wispy hair tickling my skin, I would slide into their depths. I had missed this beauty over the past few days—the heft of her in my arms, her smell, the curve of her fingers around mine, her luminous eyes watching me as I fed her with the spouted milk jar.

I crossed gazes with my husband, and the teasing glint in his eye fanned flames into my cheeks, causing my skin to tingle. Tradition had allowed us to drink deeply of each other for seven full days, while our families celebrated together—but it had not been enough.

With a quick glance at the baby, Ayal attempted a smile that did not reflect in his eyes before shifting his attention back to Jumo beside him. I tensed, instinctively holding Talia tighter, protecting her from the slight. Was I expecting too much of a man who had been betrayed too often? Or would he learn to do more than just tolerate her? *Yahweh, help him to see Talia.*

As she fell into full-bellied sleep in my arms, I relished the feel of her little body, slack against mine, and the rhythmic lift and fall of her tiny chest. *My daughter.* My heart thrilled at the word. She would call me *Ima.* She would come to me with her fears, her worries, her triumphs. Now that I was fully allowed to call her my own, as much as if she were my own flesh and blood, joy welled up like a song—its melody pitched high and sweet, drowning out the dissonance of my husband's indifference toward her.

Yonah called for our attention, standing in the center of our gathering, his tone and posture highlighting his status as head of Ayal's family. "We have been charged by Mosheh to have a memorial feast in remembrance of our last night in Egypt. The night Yahweh liberated us."

My mind traveled over miles of sand and rock, through the depths of the sea, back to Iunu and the broken Egyptian people we left behind.

Yonah gestured to Tomek's youngest boy. "For the sake of the children, who do not remember that dark night exactly one year ago, we will recall it together as we eat."

With a steady tone, Yonah recalled the nine warnings Yahweh gave to Pharaoh and the devastating plagues he unleashed on Egypt. My tongue still remembered the repugnance of the bloody water and the rot of the frog-death. My skin twitched at the memory of the unforgiving burn of the biting lice.

After the third plague, Yahweh had protected us. But the horror of watching the affliction of the Egyptians beneath the heavy hand of judgment—the flies, the boils, the pestilence, the locusts, the hailstorms, the blackness—was still fresh in my mind.

Dov and Ari, barely three years old when we left Egypt and oblivious to the destruction around them, were enthralled all throughout the telling. They had sidled up to sit on either side of me, eyes wide.

Yonah gestured to the lamb on the spit behind him. "As you remember, each family was commanded to select one spotless lamb to bring into our homes. And again, this year, we did the same—brought one innocent animal to live among us in preparation for its sacrifice."

Dov and Ari had been smitten by the brown-faced lamb, taking turns leading it around by the rope. When the time came for the creature to be butchered, they'd hid inside the tent, teary faces pressed into my lap until the deed was done. The lamb's fathomless eyes haunted me as well, its innocence reminding me how precious the blood smeared across our lintels and doorposts had been, to stay the grasping hand of death. Such a heavy price for our redemption from slavery—the lives of Egypt's firstborn sons.

Yonah continued, "After four days of inspecting the lamb for spots or blemishes, we slaughtered the animal and applied its blood around the doors of our houses. This was a signal to Yahweh that we had heeded his warnings and that we would be faithful to this Covenant of Blood."

"What is a covenant, Shira?" Dov asked in a loud whisper. Marah leveled a glare at me, as if assigning me the blame for the interruption.

Before I could respond, Yonah smiled at the boy. "A covenant is a binding agreement, one that requires the shedding of blood. It says that Yahweh is our God and King and that we will listen and obey."

"By why does a lamb have to die?" Dov folded his arms across his chest and lowered his brows. "I liked him. He was nice."

With grandfatherly compassion in his expression, Yonah frowned. "I know. But is it better for a lamb to die or your brother?"

Dov's eyes widened as he gaped at Ari.

"If we had not painted our doors with the lamb's blood that night, Ari, who was born before you, would have died, just like thousands upon thousands of Egyptian boys did. Do you understand?"

Dov hesitated, but then nodded.

"And remember," Yonah said, "way back in the Garden, when HaAdam and Chavah disobeyed Yahweh?"

All the children nodded this time, for the stories of the Garden were told again and again around campfires, their histories entwining so completely with our own memories that it seemed only a few years ago that our first ancestors had walked with Yahweh in the cool of the evening, instead of thousands.

"What did Yahweh do when they ate the forbidden fruit?"

Zayna made the connection and called out, "He killed an animal to make clothes!"

Yonah smiled. "That's right, Zayna. Not only does this lamb we eat tonight remind us of the way that Yahweh rescued us from slavery, it also reminds us of how he took care of our ancestors from the very beginning. Even after they had disobeyed, he killed an animal and fashioned clothes for them. An undeserved kindness, for sure."

He lifted his voice. "So we will partake of the lamb and the bitter herbs just as we did before we left our homeland. We will remember that night when a spotless lamb's blood was traded for our own so that we might be born into a new life as free men."

Weighted silence hung over us as we ate the same meal we did one year before, with our sandals strapped to our feet, ready to flee as the cries of mothers and fathers rent the sky with keening wails for their firstborn sons.

But just as it had that last morning in Egypt, when our faces welcomed the sunrise as free people, the somber mood around the campfire began to wane. Laughter and chatter began to fill the void left by Yonah's strong voice.

Eben pulled out a small lyre and surprised me by playing a song written by Mosheh, a celebration of the watery victory over Pharaoh. Although Eben lacked the same dexterity as before, the beautiful tune inspired me to sing a soft harmony.

As soon as the song ended, Ayal leaned over Ari and brought his lips to my ear. "I wish we were alone." His low whisper tickled my ear and warmed my blood. "And you were singing only for me."

"Shall I recount the glories of war?" My lips twitched at my own jest as Ari slithered from between us to go beg for the privilege of playing one of Jumo's drums.

Ayal slid his long body closer and his arm behind me. "As long as I can listen to your lovely voice, you may sing whatever you like." He brushed back my headscarf to drop a kiss behind my ear.

A giggle kindled in my chest, but the dark look Marah cut toward us extinguished it. Ayal followed my line of sight just as Marah turned away.

"Is she being civil?" he asked, his tone seething. "If those she-wolves so much as bare their teeth at you—"

I placed a soothing hand on his thigh. "I am fine."

"Yonah and Tomek ordered them to treat you with respect."

His statement took me by surprise. "They did?"

"After the way you helped with the sheep? Of course. They understood then why I was so determined to have you as my wife." The deep grooves curved around his smile. "Before that day, the flock witnessed many an argument between us."

The thought of Ayal clashing with his brothers over me was sobering, and I did not miss that he had omitted Noam and Yael from the conversation. "I do not want to be a point of contention between you and your family."

With one finger he turned my chin toward him, forcing me to look into his eyes. "Shira. My songbird. My love. You are my family now. Together, you and I, we are something new."

During our time of solitude together, Ayal had shared more of his life with Leisha and the pain and humiliation of his failed attempts to protect her from herself. I, too, had revealed more of my own hurts—the sting of rejection when my brother sent me away after the attack, the abuse at the hands of Tekurah, the doubts that assailed me every time I considered returning to midwifery. So many broken pieces between us, yet somehow they all seemed to fit together.

In a sudden move that startled me, Ayal leaned forward, craning his neck as if scanning past the circle of firelight and into the dark depths between tents. Concern pinched his brow.

"What is it?" I peered into the void as well but saw only blackness.

"Someone was watching us." He stood and gestured for Jumo to follow him. "Take the children to the tent. I'll be back soon."

Dread snaked around my spine. Ayal had been honest with me about the tensions vibrating within the camps. The run-in Kiya and I had at the traders' wagons had been only one of many incidents, each more violent than the last. Ayal's swift reaction bore evidence to the truth: Although we had all walked through the depths of the sea together, there were enemies within this multitude.

～～～

When Talia was asleep and the boys nestled together like puppies on their pallet, I slipped out of the tent to wash my hands and face in the large, rain-fed pot by the door. A chill swept off the mountain peak, where the remnants of a late snowstorm had laid a white shawl across its shoulders. I shivered as I shook the ice-cold water from my dripping hands. When would Ayal return?

". . . chased Dvorah off . . . she got what she wanted." Marah's whisper rasped from somewhere close by.

She is talking about me. Curious, I tiptoed closer to the conversation but stayed in the shadows.

"Do you really think they were carrying on before she died?" said Aiyasha.

"Oh, I have no doubt. Remember, he didn't restrain himself with Leisha either. That's why he had to marry that crazy *zonah*. Mark my words, a baby will come within the next five or six months." Yael snorted, unapologetic voice lifting. "Probably didn't even wait until her body was cold."

They were slandering me. Slandering my husband. Although Dvorah had disappeared weeks ago, she was still inflicting damage. I turned, meaning to slip back inside my tent and burrow in with the children to soothe the sting of the barbed words, but Marah's final jab stopped me.

"She'll probably toss aside Leisha's brats the minute she pushes out her own."

Too far. Swift resolution braided my spine with iron. I spun around and strode into the middle of their circle, head high. "How dare you say such things! Ayal is a good man, an honorable man. Any mistakes he made are in the past. Forgiven." Shock at my own boldness coursed through my limbs. "Leisha *was* a bitter woman. But what did you do to welcome her? Did you invite her in with open arms? Accept her as one of you? Or even treat her with the hospitality afforded a stranger?" I braced my hands on my hips, driving a look of accusation into each woman's eyes. "No? I did not think so."

Their open-mouthed astonishment barely registered before I continued. "Have you ever considered that she might have been a different woman had you tried? Had you not elbowed her to the side? Cast her to the edges of your family?"

Aiyasha glanced away, the first to soften her stance.

"At the very least, there can be no excuse for treating her children with such antipathy—children who are among the sweetest I have ever known. Children who I would never, never in a thousand years, walk away from. Even if I was not barren."

Satisfying silence followed me back to my tent. I ducked inside, heart pounding, and found my husband with a broad grin across his face.

"Apparently," he said, wicked delight dancing in his amber eyes, "she-wolves are no match for my songbird."

43

I plunged the sheet back into the icy water, scrubbing with vigor against a large rock. My body ached from the strain of squatting with Talia on my back, but this would be the last chance to wash our linens and clothing in the lake before we left the foot of the mountain tomorrow.

In the distance, the men were rolling up the second layer of the Mishkan covering. Ayal had been gone since daybreak, working alongside the other Levites to disassemble the huge tent and its gold-plated wooden walls, pack the sacrificial implements, dismantle the altar and laver, and then load each item on wagons and carts. He and his brothers had already merged their own small herd with the large one that belonged to all of the Levites. When not taking his turn among the other priests, Ayal would be working among the sheep he loved, guarding the lambs that would be offered for sacrifice one day.

"Why must we leave?" Yael muttered, gesturing to the sparkling lake and the abundance of green that had sprung up along its edges. "There is food here, fresh water, and no one has bothered us."

Aiyasha laughed. "Who would, with the Cloud guarding us? The traders won't even come into the camps."

I had been astounded when Aiyasha had come to my tent this morning with an invitation to wash linens with them. It had been over a month since I'd stood up to the three *she-wolves*, as Ayal called them, and although they still ignored me most of the time, I'd noticed the other children had begun including Dov and Ari in games—a victory that thrilled me even more than the begrudging acceptance by the women. Marah had even offered to watch the boys today.

Yael twisted a towel in her hands, squeezing the moisture from its coils, then snapped it in the air as she chatted with Aiyasha about how much she had left to pack, and that Noam refused to help.

A tall Nubian woman with her hands on her hips spun to face Yael, her tiny beaded braids bouncing with the motion. "Watch out! You are spraying me with water!"

"How dare you speak to me like that?" Yael aimed a murderous glare at her.

The Nubian woman pursed her full lips, an incredulous eyebrow arched high. "Forgive me. I did not know I was addressing a queen." She bowed with a flourish, one hand over her heart.

I clenched my lips tight, desperately willing a laugh not to escape. Unaccustomed to anyone lifting their voice at her, and even less with being mocked, Yael narrowed her eyes to tiny slits of fury. "If I *were* a queen, I certainly wouldn't allow *your* kind in this camp."

"My kind?"

"Yes. Your kind." Yael's voice rose, as did the ugly sneer on her face. "You *gerim* who are not part of any tribe but continue to live among us as if you were one of Avraham's children."

Everyone within our vicinity had halted their work, all eyes on the two women. I hoped this altercation would not mirror the one Kiya and I had been snared in, especially not with Talia strapped to my back. A few other foreign women with all varieties of skin tones moved to stand behind the Nubian woman, ready to defend their fellow outcast.

All trace of jest vanished from the Nubian woman's face. "I am just as much a part of Avraham's family as you, dear lady. My husband was circumcised with the rest of the men after the Covenant, and I spoke the same binding words you did. As Mosheh says, our heritage does not matter, only our commitment to Yahweh."

Yael snorted, a distinctly unfeminine sound. "I doubt your *commitment* would be so strong if food did not fall from the sky every morning."

The Nubian woman lifted a basket and placed it on her head. "I will go wherever Yahweh leads—food or no food." She turned and walked away.

The woman's simple statement and abrupt departure silenced Yael. The onlookers melted away, satisfied there would be no more sparks between the two women, and I breathed a prayer of thanks that the brawl at the traders' wagons had not repeated itself.

Aiyasha and Yael returned to scrubbing their laundry and within a few moments were gossiping as if the confrontation had never happened. I, however, could not get the woman's words out of my mind. "*. . . wherever Yahweh leads . . .*"

Where was Yahweh leading us? The land of Canaan may be only a couple weeks' walk from here, but what were we headed into? The rumors of the savage tribes that inhabited the area—barbarous child-sacrificing people—made the blood curdle in my veins. Our men had been strengthened by daily exercises in the hot sun and nourished by manna, and they were healthy and strong, but regardless, they were an untried army of former slaves, not a well-honed machine like Pharaoh's soldiers.

And no matter the organization Mosheh imposed on the tribes, disunity, rebellion, and a lingering refusal to sever Egypt's hold on our hearts seemed to undermine his every effort. We were a fractured people, a vessel made up of disparate pieces with jagged edges. A nation, yes—but one only beginning to find its footing.

A hand touched my elbow, jolting me from my discouraging thoughts. "Shira?" A young girl stood beside me, with long, black hair, a face that seemed vaguely familiar, and a baby on her hip.

"You are Shira, correct?"

"I am. And you are . . . ?"

She blew out a breath of relief. "I thought for sure that was you. Do you remember me? Hadassah?" She smoothed the baby's flyaway brown hair with a proud smile. "This is Eben."

"Oh! Eben! Hadassah!" My memories slipped into order: the first birth I had attended, the fearful young girl, the husband killed by the Levites. I tried to control my sympathetic expression, but her smile wavered, as if she realized that I had connected her joy with her sorrow.

"So you heard, then, about my husband?"

"Reva told me. I am so sorry."

"He was much older than me, you know. We'd only been married a year. He was kind for the most part, but that night . . ." She closed her eyes for a moment. "That awful night was not the first time he strayed."

A bolt of compassion speared me, and I placed a reassuring hand on her shoulder, wishing I had wisdom to offer. "Oh, Hadassah."

"Please don't feel sorry for me." She kissed the baby's forehead. "I may not have been loved by Nadir, but look what

Yahweh gave me. This sweet boy. My little rock. Out of all the ugliness that night and the days that followed, Eben was my little lamp in the dark. And every night I sing that song to him . . . you know . . . the one you sang to me when I was laboring? He loves it! Don't you, Eben?" She nuzzled his cheek. "He won't sleep without the song, even though my voice is nowhere near as lovely as yours."

"Is Nadir's family caring for you?"

"They are for now. Although, since Nadir has no unmarried brothers, we are a burden. I pray Yahweh will bring me a husband who will love both of us."

"And I will pray the same." Talia squirmed on my back, flailing a hand over my shoulder.

"Is this your baby?" Hadassah craned her neck to get a look at her. "I do not remember you being with child."

"No . . . I married a man whose wife passed away. This was her child."

"Ah." Hadassah smiled. "Yahweh gave you a light too."

Eben fussed and bucked backward in her arms. "This heavy little rock is hungry. We will leave you be," she said.

I stroked Eben's downy head to soothe him. "I am so glad to have seen you."

"And I you, Shira. I will never forget what you did for me that night. My mother died before we left Egypt, and Vereda holds no love in her heart for me." She gave me a look that conveyed pure gratitude. "The way you held me up, sang to me, infused me with courage—you are a wonderful midwife."

I resisted the urge to argue with her. "Thank you. I did not know what I was doing. It was my first birth, and I was a shattered mess. I was simply offering you whatever I could."

"It was enough, Shira." She cupped a palm over her son's plump cheek. "It was enough."

As Hadassah walked away, Eben watched me over her shoulder.

The first time I'd seen the boy, his eyes had been cloudy blue and his tiny fingers grasped wildly at the air. Now the boy named after my brother fixed me with a brown-eyed stare, then lifted a chubby hand and waved.

The motion knocked the air from my lungs.

"I will go wherever Yahweh leads . . ."

I was no different than Israel. No different than a newborn babe. Grasping, straining to define my purpose through the haze. This nation had been conceived in spite of our forefathers' sins, woven together in the harsh womb of Egypt, and born of great suffering. But Yahweh was making something new, something unique and beautiful, from all our disparate, jagged pieces. Life from death.

I had been led from slavery and brought through the waters— born into a brand-new life. And yet I refused to let go of my shackles. I had measured my worth only by the broken pieces of my past, instead of Yahweh's beautiful design.

My paltry efforts had been a blessing to Hadassah, and I had saved Talia in spite of my inadequacies. I had snubbed the calling on my life out of fear, and now I must return to what I had been made to do. My hands may not have been created for designing beautiful things, like Jumo's, Eben's, or Kiya's, but they *were* created for guiding Yahweh's masterpieces into the world.

Through my tears, a faraway gleam caught my attention—the bronze altar being lifted onto a wagon, reminding me of the day Eben had told me I should marry Ayal.

I was wrong, Yahweh. I do have something to offer you. Myself. This broken vessel.

Smiling, I lifted my eyes to the peak of the mountain and the center of the Cloud, imagining Yahweh smiling back. *I will go wherever you lead me, and it will be enough.*

44

DVORAH

I led Hassam and his eight ruffians through camp. Their pace leisurely, they joked together with a casual air that would not bring attention to their dark plans. Pulling back inside my veil, I thanked Isis for its camouflage—no one would look twice as I moved through camp. Just another widow with black grief wrapped around her. No one could see the vengeance hidden within its depths.

Throughout my apprenticeship to Reva, I had kept a careful eye on which tents held the most wealth, careful to steal only when there was no chance of being caught but memorizing every glint of gold to return for later.

Although Hassam had ranted at me for my recklessness in losing my place, I reminded him that I had gleaned enough knowledge of the Levite camps to ensure plenty of gain for each of his men. But for me, there was only one tent with treasure worth obtaining.

Although it had taken great effort to convince him, Hassam had agreed that tonight was the best night to strike, while the Levites were dismantling the Mishkan, loading it onto wagons, and preparing for the move tomorrow. The great majority of the men would be away from their tents.

The confusion of the departure would serve to dissuade anyone from seeking justice. For just how would they find Hassam's men in the midst of millions on the move toward Canaan? And of course, since they were dressed as Egyptians, heads shaved and eyes black with kohl, no one would be able to point out any of them with certainty.

My brother-in-law's group of conspirators had dwindled; their numbers had thinned after the Mishkan was raised—perhaps out of sudden tribal pride or some other such attack of loyalty—and the group shrank again after Aharon's sons were destroyed. But I did not care whether Hassam's plan was successful or not. I had my own revenge to exact.

Equal parts pity and disgust had played across Ayal's features as he spurned my advances, destroying my last hope that day. When I foolishly revealed that Shira had caught a glimpse of our encounter, he fled the tent, desperate to go after the stupid girl without a backward glance.

They would both pay for their easy dismissal of me. I would take what I wanted—what should have been mine. I would go somewhere else in the camp, change my name and the story of my heritage, feign recent widowhood, and never have to see Hassam again.

He was not the only one who was grateful for the anonymity the organized chaos tomorrow would provide. I had packed what I needed last night, along with the few trinkets I was able to ferret away under Hassam's nose. It would be simple enough for Matti and me to slip out while Hassam and his filthy wives drank to victory.

But first, to claim my own prize.

I had waited long enough. Isis had finally heard my pleas for justice, for recompense. She would protect me this night, for Matti's sake. She owed me.

Pointing to various tents as we wound through camp, I gave Hassam and his men silent indications as to which tents were the easiest targets, moving toward my own with a practiced air of casual indifference.

Slipping between Ayal's tent and Tomek's, I mouthed another prayer to my goddess that I would be invisible. The night of the memorial celebration Ayal had somehow caught a glimpse of me in the shadows. I had barely slipped away undiscovered, my heart even more bent on repaying the lovers after their disgusting display of affection. *They don't deserve her*, screamed the gaping cavern from deep inside me.

I waited for the span of a few measured breaths, ears straining for male voices nearby. When satisfied only Shira and the children were inside, I arranged a look of desperation on my face and slipped through the door flap.

Shira spun around at my entrance, her face expectant, as if to welcome her bridegroom instead of her enemy. The pleasure in her expression melted into surprise and then, quick on its heels, concern.

"Dvorah! What's wrong?" She reached out with both hands.

A papyrus wall-hanging behind her snagged my attention. Painted in vivid hues and deep shadows, the depiction of our camp around the mountain with the fiery Cloud at the center was extraordinary. A pang of something pinched my chest, but I shook my head, brushing it aside. "You must give me the baby. They are coming." I channeled urgency into my whisper.

"Coming? Who?"

"My brother-in-law and his friends. They are attacking Levite tents—right now. We need to get the baby out of here right away. I have a place we can hide." The half-truth poured like warm honey from my mouth, and I stifled a self-satisfied smile.

Conflict, disbelief, and stark fear swirled in her features, her green eyes dominating her pale face.

"How do you know this?" she asked, moving closer to where Talia sat on the ground, chewing on a rag doll.

How big she had grown since last I held her. Black hair curled around her tiny ears, and a deep dimple pressed into her stubby chin. How old was she now? Six months? Seven? Roughly the same as the other one would be, had she lived past that bloody night—the night the Levites took everything: my husband—the only man who had ever protected me—and the too-small baby who had been born in the aftermath, never to take a breath.

I shoved the fruitless trail of thought aside as my purpose rushed back with clarity. *Get the baby. Run.*

I gestured to Shira. "Hurry. There is no time. We must get her out of here."

As if to prove my point, a shriek rent the stillness. One of Hassam's men must not have been careful and startled a woman. Shira flinched, wide-eyed.

"Do you see? We must go! Hand me the baby. I'll hold her while you ready the boys."

With one last glance at the door flap, Shira nodded and reached for Talia, who gurgled as she was lifted. Shira kissed her cheek with a whisper of assurance and then handed her to me.

Victory sprang up from my core, nearly overtaking my careful demeanor with a shout of glee. I pulled my warm little trophy close to my body and took a couple of covert steps backward as Shira urged the boys to gather their cloaks. She glanced back at me with suspicion, almost as if she had guessed my plan, but I reminded her that we must make haste. As soon as she bent to gather essentials from a basket, I tightened my hold on the baby, spun around to flee, and ran headlong into a man's naked chest.

Hassam stood in the doorway, a bloody sword hanging by his side.

Dropping the door flap behind himself, he stepped forward. The reflection of the oil lamp danced in his black gaze. "And where are you going, *sister*?"

My blood stilled in my veins as he surveyed the child I clung to in a protective hold against my chest. His clean-shaven chin lifted as he reconciled my true intentions with my lies.

"Let me go, Hassam," I said. "There is nothing worth taking here. I've already checked. You got what you wanted anyway, didn't you?" I gestured with my chin at the sword in his hand.

"Hmm." His eyes flicked toward Shira behind me. "Perhaps . . . Perhaps not."

"Dvorah, what is going on?" Shira's question was delivered with more strength than I thought possible.

Hassam peered around me as if just noticing her, his oily tone amiable. "Ah. And who might you be?"

A shiver unfurled up my back. "No, Hassam," I warned.

He glanced at Talia again, false admiration and naked malice somehow perfectly balanced in his expression. "That's a beautiful baby. Best be on your way with her."

Hassam was leaving me no choice. I knew the depths of his depravity, had witnessed it many times. It was Shira or all of us—the baby and boys included.

My stomach squeezed violently as I turned around. Avoiding Shira's terror-stricken stare, I told Dov and Ari to follow me, willing my voice not to shake as fiercely as the rest of my body.

Against my better judgment, I locked gazes with the doomed woman, and her stark, pale expression told me she had already accepted her fate. The dip of her pointed chin gave me permission to remove the children. She looked so small standing in the dim light of the lamp, like a child herself. Deep within me, a carefully assembled wall crumbled to ashes.

Trembling, I ushered Dov and Ari out to hide in the dark shadows between tents, urging them to cover their ears and close their eyes until their father returned. Then, clutching Talia, I fled into the night.

45

SHIRA

The counterfeit Egyptian moved toward me—slow and measured like a wildcat, kohl-darkened eyes locked on his prey. A chill swept down my legs, up my back, and filled my belly with ice.

Although I knew the cosmetics, the shaved head, and the Egyptian garb to be a ruse, the memory of another set of kohl-smudged eyes narrowing in on me reared up like a serpent. Hassam was built larger than Akharem and his skin was much lighter, but the intent in his expression made them identical in my eyes. Was this truly happening again?

This time, it was not solely the act of a depraved man. I had been offered to this monster by Dvorah so she could steal my daughter. The stench of such an evil deed seemed to fill my nostrils, choking me. How could one woman do such a thing to another? Was my life truly worth so little to her?

Hassam stopped within inches of me and grazed the tip of his sword up my leg, lifting the hem of my tunic. My nails bit into my palms. He lifted his hand, and I flinched, but he laid the back of it against my cheek and dragged it down my face, making the hair on my arms and neck prickle with horror.

"It'll be over soon, little Hebrew." He licked his lips slowly, as if in no hurry to destroy me. He seemed to revel in prolonging my terror. My heartbeat launched into a violent throb that pulsed all the way to the soles of my feet.

Would he even stop at murdering me? Would he go after the boys next? Through a slit in the tent, I had seen Dvorah hide them in the shadows. My sweet boys were out there, unprotected, and witnesses to the face of the man who threatened me now. Resolve and resignation bound together in a tangled knot in my stomach. *I need to keep his attention on me as long as possible.*

Hassam outweighed Akharem by a large measure and towered over me like one of the giants I had heard lived in Canaan. The glint of lust and murder in his eyes was unmistakable, and the blood on his sword attested that I was not his first victim tonight. My fractured thoughts wavered between two choices: submit and pray he would spare my life, or attempt to fight and lose it.

If I shouted for the boys to run and find help, perhaps they would be safe, but if I called attention to them, Hassam may turn on them first. I had no choice but to beg like a slave under the lash of Pharaoh's whip.

My shoulders dropped as my will crashed to the floor. Echoes of my strangled pleas to Akharem sprang to my lips. "Please. Please. Don't do this."

"Don't bother fighting." Sharp warning edged the words, but then he shrugged, his lips carved into a grotesque smile. "Whether you live or die matters little. You Hebrew slaves are worth nothing."

The gleam of triumph sparked in his eyes as I wilted. He

pressed his hand against my chest, pushing me backward until my heels pressed against the soft lambskin of my bed. The image of Ayal's face burst into my mind, and mourning wailed inside my chest. My husband. My love. Would he ever look at me the same way again? His wife—whom he had defined as brave—proved again she was no more than a coward, crumbling into a thousand pieces, imprisoned in shackles of fear.

You are no longer powerless, no longer a slave. Unbidden, the words Ayal had spoken suddenly formed in my head, reverberating again and again, growing stronger with surprising speed. My pulse seemed to lengthen, and the muscles in my arms and legs contracted.

Ayal's words had planted seeds of truth that day, and the realization that I believed them suddenly bloomed. A defiant shout poured out of my mouth in a powerful rush. "No! No! Yahweh, save me!"

Hassam took a surprised step backward, but then he whipped his sword to my neck with a growl. "Quiet, or I'll slit your throat."

Energy surged into my limbs, along with a calm that defied all reason. "Go right ahead," I said through gritted teeth. "I'll fight you with every last bit of my strength." I lifted my chin, defiance curling my lips. "And my husband will finish you off after I am dead. Blood for blood."

Hassam's eyes went wide, as if somehow a warrior stood in front of him and not a tiny woman, but he recovered just as quickly. Rearing back, he slammed the flat of his sword against my temple and then knocked me back onto the bed with his foot while spewing vile curses against me, against the Hebrews, and against the Levites. He dropped his body on top of me, crushing me beneath his weight. I gulped for air and bucked hard against him, attempting to twist out from underneath.

"Give in," he snarled, his breath as putrid as an open grave.

Do not, a Voice commanded inside my head. *Fight. Yell. I am here.*

Hassam tried to bring his lips down on mine, but I yanked my head to the side. Although my ears still rang from the blow to my head, I kicked and flailed and bit his hand as he tried to cover my mouth and wrestle me into submission. He jammed his forearm against my throat, cutting off my air supply and my voice, as he tried to control my leg with his other hand.

Realizing that he had dropped the sword, I slapped my left hand with surprising force against his ear and slammed my right palm up into his nose. Blinking and face bloodied, he spat out a curse in the name of a god I'd never heard of, then pressed his forearm harder against my throat and groped for his sword on the floor.

"Get your hands off Shira." The command came from somewhere behind Hassam. I strained to see, but dark shadows gathered in front of my eyes, distorting faces and whispering defeat in my ears.

Hassam cursed as the shimmer of a sword slid along his throat. Three blurred figures stood above us. I squinted, my air-starved mind conjuring the faces of Marah, Yael, and Aiyasha.

No! They could not be here! Hassam would kill them too. Lights danced behind my eyes as my head began to swim. I squirmed against the force of his arm on my neck. *Run! Run away!* my mind cried to my phantom rescuers.

"What are you going to do, *zonah*?" Hassam's challenge seemed to come from far away as my brain fought against the blackness that was consuming me. Was Marah truly here, threatening Hassam with his own sword?

I blinked, my sight clearing just as she sneered and slid the sword across Hassam's throat in a swift motion. Blood gushed from the shallow wound as Hassam roared and cursed her, threatening to do worse to her than he'd done to me. He lunged, releasing me, but Marah jammed the sword into his shoulder. Air whooshed into my lungs and I gulped, hands at my throat. Never had a mouthful of air tasted so beautiful.

Hassam had fallen to the ground, screaming in agony as Marah dug the sword into his side. With unbound hair flying, Yael and Aiyasha joined the fight, both of them pounding with their fists, kicking him, and grunting at the exertion. Marah slammed the butt of Hassam's sword down again and again on his head. I curled up on the bed, violent tremors overtaking my body as I watched these women, once my enemies, fight for me with dogged ferocity.

46

"What is happening here?" My husband filled the doorway, his face shadowed by the dimming light of the oil lamp and his eyes locked on the bloody, unconscious man on the floor, whom Marah and Yael had bound with papyrus ropes.

From her protective stance in front of me, Aiyasha practically snarled, "This man attacked Shira."

"What?" The roar of his deep voice reverberated through me. On impulse, my body curved farther inward.

"Dvorah led him here." Aiyasha glanced back at me, as if she were reluctant to repeat the truth. "She took Talia."

Where has she taken her? My precious girl. Is she frightened? Hungry?

Rage transformed Ayal's features, hardening his jaw to granite and narrowing his eyes to dark slits. With his sword swiftly drawn, he moved to stand over Hassam. "What—What did he do to my wife?"

"He tried to—"

"I am fine." I interrupted Aiyasha with a croak, trying to

lift myself. My voice rasped against the residual burn of Hassam's chokehold.

Ayal's eyes swept over my face and my ripped clothing. He clenched the hilt of his sword with such force that his knuckles went white. Abruptly, and with a rare curse, Ayal bellowed to his brothers. Confusion swirled around us as Tomek and Yonah's wide shoulders filled the tent. Shivering, I cowered as the three men dragged Hassam by the arms. Awakened by the rough handling, Hassam swore and bucked against them.

I closed my eyes, pressing my hands to my ears, and allowed the fury of my rushing pulse to drown out his screams. Aiyasha sat next to me, rubbing circles into my back as the man's howling curses faded away. Pressing my cheek against the linen of my marriage bed, I inhaled, willing my husband's lingering scent to calm me in his absence. *Come back! Stay with me!*

As if he had heard my silent plea, suddenly Ayal's hands were on my face, stroking my skin with feather-light touches. "Shira. Shira, my sweet wife."

I clung to him, burying my face in his chest to muffle the sobs I could not restrain. He smoothed my hair, and his lips pressed against the crown of my head. Shame burned hot down my cheeks. Would he send me away like Eben had done? Pushing away the thought to focus on the most important one, I struggled to release myself from his grasp. "We need to find Talia. I need to try to—"

"No. You are not going anywhere." He tightened his hold and pulled me closer.

Could he not even look at me? He labored to breathe. I could only imagine what vile visions might be going through his mind. I saw them too. Fractured and laced with patches of blackness, they swirled around inside my head, causing bile to rise again in my throat.

"He did not—" I choked on the word. "He did not . . . succeed."

300

Ayal expelled a breath that sounded more like a sob. He kissed my forehead, my eyelids, my chin, my lips. "My sweet wife, my little bird."

"You should have seen her, Ayal." Aiyasha sounded like a hen clucking over her chick. "She fought that monster with everything in her. Like a tiny warrior. She was barely conscious but kept kicking and ordering him to stop."

I remembered only the remnants of blackness, the swirling memory of the women's faces as they pummeled Hassam, and Dvorah's pale one as she fled into the night with my daughter.

"I told you that you were strong." Ayal caressed my cheek with his thumb. I braced against the pain that radiated from the bruise beneath my skin, but the ache inside my chest, the hollow place Talia had left behind, hurt much worse.

"She's gone, Ayal. My little girl. How could Dvorah . . . ?" I choked on my whisper, tears coursing down my face again.

Aiyasha leaned down and brushed my hair away from my face with a look of tender compassion. "I will go take the boys to your mother, Shira. Merit, our neighbor, has been watching them since they ran to us."

"No!" I pushed Ayal away and sat up, my plea bleeding desperation. "Please. Bring them here. I want them to know I am safe."

"Are you sure?" Her brows lifted in disbelief.

I had lost my daughter this night. I wanted—no, I *needed* to see my sons' faces. "Please—" My voice cracked as I reached out to her. "I must hold them."

"I think you are right, they need to see their *ima*." With a squeeze of my hand and a rueful smile, she exited the tent, leaving me stunned at her change in attitude. Ayal and I exchanged a glance of bewilderment.

Anticipating the boys' arrival, I smoothed my disheveled braid and straightened my clothes, hoping all evidence of Hassam was gone. With horror, I realized that the rugs next to the bed were soaked in blood.

"Ayal!" I gestured to the mess. "Please! Before they come in."

With speed that belied his lanky form, he rolled them up and tucked them into a corner, just as two dirty, tear-stained faces poked inside the tent flap.

"*Ima?*" Ari's voice trembled.

Arranging what I hoped was a look of calm reassurance on my face, I waved them over to me. "It's all right. I am safe."

With cries of relief and more tears, they ran to me, wrapping skinny arms around my neck and pressing sweaty bodies into mine.

"We wanted to fight that man," Ari said with ferocity, his brow furrowed. "He was hurting you."

"We heard you yell, and then someone told us what to do," said Dov, scratching his nose.

The reminder that the boys were so close to what almost happened sent a chill through my body. "What do you mean? Who told you?"

Ari shrugged his shoulders. "A man said, in a big voice, '*Dov and Ari, run, go get* Doda *Marah.*'" He poked out his lower lip. "So we did."

I looked to Ayal, who seemed just as incredulous. "Was there another man out there?"

He shook his head. "The two guards were killed before the attack. Tomek and Yonah were with me at the Mishkan, Noam is in the fields with Jumo, and Eben is with Kiya. There was no one close by but women and children."

"Then who . . . ?" I searched the boys' faces for signs of jest or deception, but their expressions were sincere.

"You heard this too?" Ayal asked Dov.

"Yes, Abba. It came from over there." He pointed in the direction of the Cloud that hovered over the mountain again. The

302

glow illuminated the side of our tent, soaking the wall in soft blue, giving the illusion that it stood directly next to us.

A shiver of realization swept through me. Had Yahweh actually spoken to these boys, as he did with Mosheh? Out of the millions of people in this camp, he chose to protect *me*?

But why, if he cared, did he not stop Talia from being taken? I had promised to follow where he led, but must it be into the center of yet another tempest? My roots could not possibly be strong enough to withstand such agony.

47

I saw them everywhere—Dvorah behind every veiled form and Talia in every bundle on a back or clutched against a woman's chest. Every baby's cry was my daughter calling, "*Ima.*" Helpless against the urge, I searched the face of each woman who bathed in the stream around us now, snapping to attention whenever a bubble of childish laughter lifted into the air.

One, two, three days had melted into six weeks without her. What had I missed? How many precious smiles had Dvorah stolen? How many laughs? Had Talia forgotten the shape of my face already?

The hole inside my chest throbbed with longing to hold her silken cheek to my own. My instinct to run back to the mountain was tempered only by the knowledge that Dvorah could not survive on her own in the wilderness. She must be here, among the oblivious multitude following the Cloud northward toward Canaan and the fulfillment of Avraham's promise.

Ayal, Jumo, and Eben had searched relentlessly that night,

but Dvorah had been shrewd, timing her horrific crime in tandem with the turmoil of leaving the valley. Between the dust of wagons and feet and the swirl of people and animals that surrounded us, searching for Talia was like looking for a grain of sand in the ever-moving tides.

Each time the Cloud halted, the men resumed their search, but they were met with more than their fair share of animosity and uncooperative stares from both the *gerim* and the other tribes. Even those with sympathy could do little more than shrug their shoulders. Dvorah had vanished.

"Rinse, please." Kiya leaned over the stream as I poured a jug over her head and scrubbed away the last of the natron cleansing powder. Her hair glimmered, streaming in a glorious black waterfall before she tossed it back in a spray of water and laughter. Her rounded belly pressed against the seams of her crimson tunic, drawing a timeline of her delivery in my head. Within the next few days.

Although the valley where we now camped boasted a shallow stream, there had been something about the water at the foot of the mountain—a distinct sweetness, born either of the depth of its origins or perhaps an ancient blessing from its Creator in preparation for our arrival. I missed the valley where the cascade from the mountain and the outflow from the rock had watered dormant seeds, causing the desert to bloom like a rose. I missed my sweet Talia.

If only I had said something to Reva all those months ago, when I saw Dvorah give Leisha that idol. If only I'd had more courage to speak truth, Dvorah would have been dismissed from midwifery, and our paths would have diverged long ago. If only . . .

I dumped the pitcher over my own head, reveling in the coolness against my overheated skin and the momentary distraction from the scourge of ever-cycling regrets.

"I will be glad to hold my baby soon, but I will be almost as excited to wash my own head and tie my own sandals." Kiya squeezed the water from her hair, reminding me of the first conversation we'd ever had, held by the side of the Nile, just before it turned to blood. Our friendship had been carefully braided together since that day, the product of slavery, circumstance, and the draw of Yahweh. Now it was forged by the iron bonds of covenant and sisterhood.

A splash soaked my backside. I spun around in the water to find Dov and Ari, each with a hand plastered to their mouths and eyes wide with anticipation of a tongue-lashing. Did they really think I would punish them for such mischief?

Squatting down in the stream, I wove my fingers together and pushed a wall of water at the surprised little boys, drenching them along with Zayna and Shoshana. Rainbows danced in the interplay of the mist and afternoon sunlight.

Kiya joined in and splashed them as well, her playful taunts uniting with mine as the children fought back with feeble sprinkles from tiny hands.

My mother and my aunt watched the ruckus from nearby, mouths pursed and arms folded, but it was nearly impossible to ignore the abandon of four-year-old laughter, and soon even the two of them joined in with a couple of halfhearted splashes.

Guilt for my frivolity slipped insidious claws under my ribs as the echo of Talia's laughter fluttered through my heart. Was I already forgetting the loss? I cleared my throat, pushing back the tears that threatened, and used my jug to slosh another stream of water at the boys. Ari and Dov had lost their mother, and now their sister. Their short lives were coated with grief. They needed—we all needed—a little levity.

A shofar ripped through our game, an insistent blast that chilled me in spite of the blazing heat. It was a call to arms and eerily reminiscent of the night the Levites were summoned to be the hands of justice.

After gathering up the boys, who fussed about the abrupt end to their respite from the heat, we hurried toward the encampment. My worry grew with every step. Jumo, who had been waiting for us nearby, met us with deep concern on his face but knew nothing more than we did. After the attack by Hassam, and with the recent threats against the Levites, the men never let us walk anywhere alone.

The center of the camp was roiling with commotion. A large crowd had gathered near Mosheh and Aharon's tents, screaming and shouting, fists and daggers in the air punctuating their loud cries. Something had knocked down the fragile wall of civility. And my husband was at the very center of the uproar, carrying out his duty to guard the wagon that held the golden menorah. Would he be killed defending it?

A few men ran by, blue and white *tzitzit* streaming from the corners of their garments, swords drawn. Jumo's thoughts must have mirrored mine, for he issued an urgent command to hurry, his tone laced with panic.

Kiya shuffled along next to me, her hands against her back and feet splayed wide to accommodate her girth. Just before we stepped into the campsite, she bent double with a gasp. The wet spot on the sand below told me what her tightly pressed lips could not. Her time had come.

With instinct slamming into me full force, I shook my hand free of Ari's grasp and slipped my arm around Kiya's waist to steady her.

"Is this the first pain?" Covertly, I felt her belly, which was as hard as granite.

She shook her head.

"How long have the pains been coming?"

Instead of answering, she put her finger to her lips, eyes wide. "Shh. Listen."

We all went quiet, straining to hear.

"I hear nothing," my mother whispered.

"Thunder," Kiya said. "I felt it rumble through the ground."

Zayna whimpered and darted to my mother's side. My youngest sister had always been terrified of storms, to the point of hysterics. *Ima* pulled her close. "Perhaps it was only a drum—"

The dark eastern horizon contradicted her reassurances. A black storm was hurtling toward us with as much ferocity as Pharaoh's army had on the other side of the sea.

"Jumo, my mother and I will get Kiya inside and comfortable. Can you take the children to Aiyasha?"

He nodded and then kissed his sister. "And I will send Tomek to find Eben."

The melee at the center of camp seemed to be growing instead of abating. Somehow I doubted that my brother would see his wife before she delivered. Thunder rumbled a prolonged cadence, and lightning flashed with such brilliance that the south wall of the tent lit like a torch.

Kiya groaned, low and long, as my mother and I guided her to the bed. She laid back, the mound of her stomach lifting and lowering with the quick pace of her breathing.

"Someone must find Reva," I said.

My mother looked at me, her gaze searching. "You can do this."

I felt the blood drain from my face. "No, I cannot."

"Yes." She patted my shoulder. "I will go fetch Reva. I know where her tent is." She leaned in close. "But you must examine her, Shira."

"Reva will be here soon."

"If I can find her."

I tugged on my braid. "I can't do this alone, not after . . . I cannot hurt my sister. Reva should be here."

"Listen to me." My mother put steadying hands on my face. "You love Kiya. You will not hurt her. You did not hurt that other woman either. Reva said you saved Talia's life that night. From the stories I have heard, you are the best apprentice Reva has ever had. You must do this. Now."

Her words swam around in my mind as if underwater, muted and distorted. I tried to pull away, shaking my head. Thunder rumbled again, and lightning flashed nearby. I felt its proximity in the spiked response of the hair on my arms and neck.

"I trust you, Shira," said Kiya from her place on the bed. "Who better than this baby's *doda* to bring the little one into the world?"

I twisted away. "But you cannot—"

My mother would not let go of me, she forced me to look at her again. "You know, much better than I do, what Kiya needs at this moment."

I drew a breath that entered my body in convulsive gulps. Could I possibly do this?

A silent whisper reached through my panic. *Lay your broken pieces on the altar. It will be enough*. The promise somehow spread inexplicable peace through my body.

"All right." I bobbed my head and pushed aside the vision of Leisha's white face. "Be careful, and hurry back."

I closed my eyes, gritting my teeth against the words I had to say. But there was no time to hesitate. This labor was going fast—too fast—and a cursory examination had given life to my greatest fear: Kiya's baby was in trouble.

Where was Reva? Where was my mother? How could I do this? Alone?

"Kiya." I gripped her knee to prevent her from jerking against the pain. "My friend, I need you to turn over now."

"What is wrong?" Her words tangled with a groan, becoming a terrified plea.

"The cord is coming out first. We must take the pressure off of it right away."

Another sustained roll of thunder shook the ground. The ghostly look she gave me ran a chill down my back.

"Jumo," she breathed. "That is what happened to my brother when he was born."

I had guessed as much from what Kiya had told me, that when Jumo was born something had gone wrong and crippled him, affecting his speech and his limbs in a drastic way, the affliction he had lived with until healed by Yahweh.

"Flip over now," I commanded. I would not let Kiya's baby suffer what Jumo had, if I could help it. Without a miracle, Kiya or the baby, or both, could die.

With my assistance, Kiya knelt on hands and knees. I instructed her to try not to push and allow me to try to change the infant's position. *Please, Yahweh, make the baby shift beneath the pressure of my hand.*

Kiya panted and moaned, her black hair swinging free with every jerky motion. As had been my habit from when I had apprenticed with Reva and a mother panicked, a song began to move past my lips. A song of hope and promise. A song of Yahweh's love for his people. Kiya's breathing began to slow, and in response the baby shifted, just enough to move the cord aside and ensure it was not around its neck.

"There!" I said with a release of all the tension in my lungs. "It is out of the way."

"What is out of the way?" My mother's voice came from over my shoulder. Lightning flashed behind her as she entered, and thunder grumbled a quick reply.

"Where is Reva?"

My mother shook her head. "She cannot come. You must do this on your own, daughter."

"But I—"

"There is no one to help. The other midwives refuse to come."

"What do you mean?"

She pursed her lips and, with a glance at Kiya, gave a tiny shake of her head.

Why would the midwives refuse? What reason could they have for leaving a woman to suffer? Reva would never stand for such a thing. Where was Reva? How could I possibly do this without her?

The barrage of questions was swept away by a hiss of pain from Kiya. Exhaling, I blinked to clear my head. "The cord is out of the way now, but we must get the baby out fast. Help me lift her, and then let her squat against you. Hold her up as she pushes."

My mother obeyed my instructions, keeping her dark eyes trained on me as I reassured Kiya through each building contraction—"All will be well," and "Your baby is safe," and "Yahweh is with us."

With a final, agonizing scream from Kiya, a tiny body entered the world. A baby girl with a dark crown of hair and a sloped nose like her mother's—a baby girl who lay perfectly still in my hands. Panic formed in my belly, then flashed through my body with the force of the lightning that continued to shatter the sky.

I had killed Kiya's baby.

48

First Leisha, and now Kiya's daughter. Yet even as grief swept over me, Reva's words whispered in my ear. *Only the giver of life has sovereignty over death.*

Ignoring Kiya's and my mother's demands as to why the infant was not moving, I swept the tiny girl into a clean linen towel and began to rub her lifeless body with sure, gentle strokes, just as Ziba had done with her lamb.

"Hear now, precious little one," I said, reining in my fear with a bright, hopeful tone. "Your *ima* is waiting to hold you. We all want to know what color your pretty eyes are."

Please, Yahweh. This sweet girl is yours. She is in your hands more than mine. Please. Breathe life into her nostrils as you did HaAdam in the Garden. My desperate plea brought an idea to mind, something I'd seen Reva do before.

I placed my mouth over her tiny nose and mouth and, with the smallest of breaths, blew into her body, willing the spark of life to flare. Her chest rose and fell. Two more of my breaths became hers.

Was it my imagination? Did her body move?

A little gasp. A twitch of her leg. Then a lusty cry announced

Kiya's daughter was very much alive. Every nerve in my body echoed the sentiment. The passion, the fervor I had felt the first time I helped deliver a baby rushed back with such force that it nearly knocked me over. I wobbled in relief and exhilarated exhaustion.

My face was doused in sweet tears as I laid the infant across Kiya's chest with a triumphant grin. "Here is your daughter, sister of my heart."

With her black hair bristling out every which way and her tiny bud of a mouth searching, the little one nuzzled into Kiya.

"She is—" Kiya's voice broke. "She is beautiful. The most perfect baby I have ever seen."

I smiled, more than happy to agree. "She will be as extraordinary as her mother and her grandmother."

Tears trailed down Kiya's face, dripping onto the blanket beneath her. "I wish she were here," she whispered. "I will name my daughter Nailah in her honor."

"She would be thrilled, I am certain." I kissed Kiya's cheek, and then Nailah's tiny one. "And so proud of you."

If only Reva had been here as well, to see me push through my fears and renew my passion for midwifery. I turned to my mother. "Where is Reva?"

She smoothed the blankets around Kiya's feet and then gestured for me to follow her to the other side of the tent. She shifted from foot to foot as she watched Kiya nuzzle the baby. "Reva went to help a woman among the *gerim*."

"Someone in labor?"

"Yes, in fact, it sounds as though there are quite a few women in need of midwives."

"Then I must go."

"No!" She gripped my arm like a vise. "You don't understand. Reva left right before the storm began. No one knows where she is, or even if she is alive."

"Did no one go with her?"

She flattened her lips. "No. Just as they refused to help Kiya because she is Egyptian, they refused to set foot in the *gerim* camps."

"Reva is alone? With no one to help her?"

"Shira. No. This storm . . . it is too danger—"

"Mother." I twisted my arm away. "I know you are trying to protect me, just as you always have done." I gestured to Kiya and her new daughter. "But this is what I am supposed to do. I did not believe it before. I was afraid to believe, afraid to face the pain. It is for Yahweh alone to command this storm. Regardless of the cost, I will use the gifts he has given me to save lives."

Leaving my mother with her mouth agape, I stepped out of the tent. Lightning split the sky with a thousand forked tongues, and violent thunder shook the ground. Blinded for a moment, I blinked my eyes, remembering the terrifying storm that had plagued Egypt, with huge shards of ice and swirling clouds that obliterated entire villages. I almost expected hail to pelt down, but the air was dry. It crackled across my skin, lifting the hairs on my arms. I scrubbed at the unnatural sensation. Another strike hit behind me, and then to my left. Above me the sky was dark, eerie in its stillness. It was as if a great ring of fire encircled us, licking only at the far reaches of camp.

Two men emerged from the shadows. I shuffled backward, thoughts skidding back to Hassam's attack, but it was Ayal and Eben who approached.

Relief squeezed the breath from my body as I ran to Ayal, slid my arms around his waist, and buried my face in the safety of his chest. "Thank Yahweh you are safe."

He ran a hand down my tousled braid and drew me closer. "How is Kiya?"

"Oh!" I pulled back and spoke to my brother. "You have a daughter—one that might well rival your wife for beauty."

Eben's euphoric expression was highlighted by another flash of lightning. "And Kiya?"

"She is doing well. Anxious to see her husband."

After pressing a kiss to my cheek that spoke of elated gratitude, Eben disappeared into their tent.

"What is happening, Ayal? This storm . . . it's so strange." A crash of thunder punctuated my query.

His silence was deafening, his grip on my shoulders too tight.

"Ayal. Tell me."

"The outer camps are burning."

Dvorah. Talia!

I yanked away from his hold with a jerk. "We have to go! We must find her!"

"Shira. We have searched this camp. Dvorah has blended in somewhere. There is no possible way you will find them tonight."

"But my daughter. My baby . . ." Tears burned my cheeks.

Ayal cleared his throat. "Our daughter."

With a start, I looked up at him. "Our?"

He lifted my chin and kissed my lips. "I was so angry . . . and so wrong. That sweet baby is not to blame for what Leisha did. With Yahweh's help, we will find her. I will not rest until we do."

I closed my eyes, drawing a shuddering breath. *She's in your hands more than mine.*

"Let's get you inside." He twined his fingers into mine and turned toward our own camp. "Are the boys with Aiyasha?"

"Oh. Yes, they are . . ." I planted my feet and tugged him to a stop. "But I must go find Reva."

"Is something wrong with Kiya?"

"No. There are women in need of midwives. I must help."

His brows scraped the sky. "You are returning to midwifery?"

"There is no one else to help Reva. The other midwives refuse to help the *gerim*."

He scratched at his beard, his eyes drawn to the south. "You are not going anywhere near those outer camps, Shira. This is no natural storm."

"What do you mean?"

"The *gerim* were on the verge of rioting tonight. That's why the shofarim sounded. They were demanding we return to the mountain, where we were safe and our thirst quenched by the rock. Some went even further, threatening to take back the gold they'd offered for the Mishkan and flee back to Egypt, where food and water are plenty. This storm is from Yahweh. A judgment for rebellion."

After all the stories of Canaan—oaks, sycamores, and cedars stretching to the sky, rolling hills embracing valleys replete with nuts, dates, wheat, fruits of every kind—they were fighting to stay in this barren land? Accepting the paltry offerings of the wilderness when Yahweh had promised us so much more?

Yahweh, will we never be satisfied? Will we forever be grasping and squalling like infants? I prayed this storm would burn out the last of Egypt from the hearts of the *gerim*, and the tribes, before Yahweh turned his favor from us.

Lightning scrolled across the sky again, outlining an orange haze to the south. How many tents were burning? How many people lost?

Not one more, if I could prevent it.

Renewing my silent plea for Yahweh to protect Talia, I lifted my head to meet my husband's gaze. "I have already had this conversation once tonight. I am going. Reva needs me. There are babies and mothers who might die without help. I refuse to have that burden on my soul."

Ayal studied my determined expression and then, with a

half-grin that smacked of satisfaction and not a small amount of pride, held out his hand to me. "Lead the way, my love."

Five women congregated beneath the large canopy outside Reva's tent, taking refuge from the sudden downpour of rain. I scanned their drawn faces—midwives, all of whom I had crossed paths with a time or two while working with Reva. Why were they not out looking for her?

Dripping wet, we approached the group. Ayal had to duck to fit beneath the black wool covering. Rain sheeted off the fabric like a waterfall.

"Has anyone yet found Reva?" I wiped my face with the back of my hand.

Tuya, a tall woman clothed in rich Egyptian fabrics and kohl thick on her lids, eyed me and then Ayal with naked suspicion. "Not yet."

Next to Tuya stood Sanai, round-faced and with springs of coiled hair escaping her head covering. She crossed her arms over her body, as if holding herself together. "She hasn't been seen since the first lightning strike." Fear flitted across her brow as another booming clap of thunder sounded. "It hit right where she was headed." She pointed southwest of camp.

"Come then, let's find her." I lifted my hands, imploring. "She needs us."

The two women glanced at each other.

Pursing her lips, Tuya lifted her chin. "We are not going into that storm. Or near the outer camps."

Sanai peered up at Tuya. Although her body leaned toward me, she seemed to be seeking permission from her friend. "There *are* many that need our help, Tuya."

Tuya winced and turned her face toward the flickering common fire. The other three midwives refused to meet my curious gaze.

With another pleading glance toward Tuya, Sanai braved an answer, but her voice was low. "There have been a few *gerim* here, asking us to assist with the wounded. And there are at least three foreign women in labor and two who have had miscarriages—"

"We are not going anywhere near those *gerim*, Sanai. They deserve the punishment they have received."

I stood in mute horror, gripping Ayal's hand as I gathered a response. His presence filled me with courage, his silence proving confidence in my ability to stand strong. "So you would condemn the women, their babies, and possibly Reva to death by not even lifting a finger?"

Unaffected, Tuya lifted a shoulder. "They did not have to follow us into the desert. All they have done is complain and incite riots. Even influenced Hebrews to stand against Mosheh." Her upper lip curled in disgust. "The repulsive things that go on among them . . . no wonder there are so many babies being born."

"Perhaps so." I released my hold on Ayal and dropped my fists to my hips. "But what of the babies? Do they deserve your indifference as well?" Somehow not intimidated by Tuya's towering height, I stepped closer. "And Reva? She trained me to be a midwife, as I am sure she trained you. Are none of you willing to find our teacher and help her bring these children into the world?" My voice strengthened, as if the roots of newfound confidence had found sustenance in hidden depths. "Are we not one nation? Are we not one people here?"

None of their expressions hinted at wavering. *Yahweh, what can I say to sway them?* In answer, a glint of gold at Tuya's neckline caught my eye.

"Besides," I said, "there are a few of you who have used amulets of Isis, Tawaret, and Hathor in your work." I aimed a slow, deliberate look at each midwife's face. Tuya flinched and looked away. "How is their rebellion any worse than your sins? Or mine? It seems to me that all of us are in this camp only by the grace of Yahweh. None of us deserve to be in his presence. We should all be struck down, like Aharon's sons."

Indignation lifted my voice, lending it fresh strength. I gestured to the sky, where the black clouds had scattered, leaving a vast sky of sparkling stars in their place. "The storm is over. Yahweh must have sent the rain to put out the fires. None of us are guiltless here, we have all grumbled a time or two, questioned Mosheh's wisdom and therefore Yahweh's will. He is showing us mercy, or the whole camp would burn. And I, for one, will show mercy to those people. I will walk the length and breadth of this camp to find Reva and work alongside her to bring precious babies into this world. And that is what they are, no matter where they came from. Each child—each life—is precious. And you—" I leveled another scorching gaze at all of them. "You of all people should know that."

"She is right."

I turned toward the familiar voice, nerves sparking to life. *Miryam.*

Stepping beneath the canopy as she pushed back a sodden mantle from her head, the wizened face of Mosheh's older sister was blank, but her eyes shimmered and I glimpsed pride in the set of her pursed lips.

"Why are you all standing around? There are women in need. Babes to birth. It does not matter where they came from, how they were conceived, or what the *gerim* have done. We are midwives; we serve other women. How will we ever be one people if we do not break down the walls between us?"

She squinted one eye and pointed a gnarled finger at me. "This young apprentice has offered you a chance to remove some of those bricks, to reach across the divide. And who better to start with than mothers and babes?"

Chastened, or perhaps intimidated by her authority, all five midwives, including Tuya, gathered their healing bags and slipped out from under the canopy. My heart swelled at the direction of their feet—toward the edges of camp.

"Reva was right," said Miryam, her watchful eyes trained on me.

"She was?"

Miryam nodded. "You are the one she has chosen to follow in her footsteps. To train up the next generation of midwives."

My jaw dropped. "Me? Why?"

"You know Reva, she keeps things to herself." She cocked her head. "But, yes, I can see it too. You remind me of the woman who trained me so many years ago. She, too, found her courage among the ashes, and strength when waves of doubt threatened to drown her. She learned to stand tall, even against a vicious Pharaoh."

"Shifrah?" Reva had told me months ago that Miryam had been taught by the famous midwife who, alongside Puah, had disobeyed Pharaoh's orders and saved so many Hebrew baby boys—including Mosheh himself. I laid a hand on my heart. "The comparison honors me."

"Oh, she would have liked you. I am sure of it." She sighed. "I wish she were here to see this." Miryam lifted her eyes, looking at the sea of tents that surrounded us. "To see her legacy in the faces of so many families that would not exist without her courage."

Miryam placed her hands on my shoulders and leaned in close. "You will see the same, Shira." The woman's voice rang with the authority of a prophetess. "The lives you usher into the world will give birth to the first generation in the Land of Promise, and like Shifrah and Puah, your family will be blessed through your obedience to Yahweh." She squeezed my shoulders, the warmth of her hands soaking through my tunic and into my bones. "Do you believe this?"

Snatching a quick breath of rain-freshened air, I looked up at my husband, whose wide smile and pride-filled eyes encouraged me to embrace the promise. "I do," I said, without looking away from the man I loved.

"Good." Miryam patted me. "Now go, you two, and find Reva. She needs your help."

49

Smoke rose all around us, remnants of the fiery discipline meted from the center of the storm. The caustic odor of its spiraling wisps clung to my skin, choking my breath as surely as if it had its fingers about my throat.

The rain had done its work, but more than a few tents still smoldered in the dark. The reek of charred and sodden goat's hair overwhelmed my senses. Moving toward the place Sanai had indicated that Reva went right before the outbreak of the storm, Ayal led me through the maze of overturned wagons, blackened animal carcasses, and people sitting in the dust and mud wailing, using the ashes of their destruction to cover their heads in mourning.

A group of men, carrying a shrouded body between them, blocked our path.

Ayal pulled me close to his side. "Have any of you seen a midwife, an older Levite woman?"

"Couldn't say." A Nubian man, his dark face smothered in ash, jerked a chin over his shoulder. "We've been gathering the wounded in the meeting area. There have been some women there, tending injuries." He grimaced. "It's a grisly sight, though, for your little wife there."

Ayal glanced at me. "She is more than capable." His sincere confidence in me undergirded my own.

As we stepped into the wide meeting area, a shudder of horror vibrated in my chest, and my throat flamed with unshed grief. It was worse than I had anticipated. Bodies sprawled on the ground, some moving, some still. The moans and cries of the wounded grated against my ears. I was grateful for the shroud of night—daylight would reveal too much.

"You here to help? Or looking for someone?" A woman rose to her feet. Her dark skin and closely-cropped hair glimmered with sweat from her ministrations to the wounded. Was she a healer?

Ayal responded first. "Both. My wife is a midwife. We are looking for a friend, another midwife who came here right before the storm to deliver a baby."

The woman cocked her head, studying me. Wooden bracelets clanked on her wrist as she rubbed her own pregnant belly. She was tall, her bearing almost regal, with a wisdom in her gaze that reminded me of Reva, although she was not too much older than I. Wrapped around her long neck was a linen scarf edged in silver beads that twinkled in the firelight, a strange thing to wear in such circumstances. "You are a midwife?" she asked.

"An apprentice still, but yes."

"Can you deliver an infant on your own?"

I nodded, an image of Kiya's daughter flitting through my mind, strengthening my belief in my own capabilities. "My friend Kiya just gave birth tonight. I delivered little Nailah myself."

A little gasp slipped past her full lips. "Kiya?"

"Yes. Kiya. She is married to my brother."

"She is Egyptian?"

"Yes. We served in the same household in Iunu."

The woman's eyes grew large. "Her mother's name is Nailah? Her father's name is Jofare?"

"You know her?"

"She was my mistress."

I whispered the name I had heard many times from Kiya's mouth. "Salima?"

She nodded, luminous tears forming in the corners of her dark eyes.

I reached out to grasp Salima's hand. "She speaks so highly of you."

"I never thought I'd see her again." Her other hand traveled to the beautiful scarf that encircled her neck. It must be the same one Kiya had given her the day she had been sold into slavery. "She is here? With the Hebrews?"

"She is. Her mother is gone, sadly. But Jumo, her brother, travels with us as well."

Salima clutched her fist to her chest. "An answer to my prayers."

I smiled, feeling instant kinship with this stranger through the shared love of our friend. "And mine."

She released a loud breath. "You must take me to her tomorrow, but right now, we must go. A woman had just begun labor pains, but I was forced to leave and tend some of the wounded. I was heading back to check on her."

Salima's long legs led me through the maze of tents—some burnt, some unscathed, some flattened in the mud.

"Are you a midwife, Salima?"

"No, although I have delivered a few babies when needed. Some would call me a healer," she said over her shoulder. "But it was my mother who taught me the correct herbs to use when I was a girl. I only apply what I learned from her and others. And I pray. Yahweh is the true healer."

That he was. Jumo was evidence of that, a boy born with twisted limbs and garbled words, now strong and healthy—

healed by only a word from Yahweh's mouth. Salima would be astounded when she saw Jumo again, without a doubt. I was tempted to say something, but anticipation of her reaction to the miracle kept me silent.

Leaving Ayal outside, I followed Salima into an undamaged tent, the familiar sounds of a woman in labor quickening my steps. Lying on a bedroll in the center of the room, a young girl sprawled, panting and sweating. Her waters were broken and, although her mother and two aunts were at her side, they were all grateful for my presence. Salima ducked out of the tent with a promise to return soon.

With the same rush of memory that had accompanied Nailah's birth, I slipped easily into my role as a midwife. By the time the slippery infant landed in my arms, I realized I had not once worried that I was on my own. After the babe was clean, swaddled, and full-bellied in his mother's arms, I kissed his little cheek and stepped into the night.

The sky was clear, as if there had never been a violent storm marring its expanse. The Cloud had returned to its unearthly form as a column of light off to the north of camp. A few tenacious stars glinted in the silvering dawn.

Ayal reached for me, his long arms snaking around my body. "You amaze me."

"Oh?"

He kissed my forehead. "I was listening."

I threw a glance back at the tent. "I hope that poor woman doesn't know that."

"It's nothing I haven't dealt with in the fields."

I giggled. "A ewe and a woman are not the same, Ayal."

He laughed under his breath, his lips traveling up my cheek. "This is true. A sheep is much calmer giving birth."

I smirked. Although it had been her third child, the woman had shrieked like a wildcat.

A thin, piteous cry reached my ears.

"Do you hear that?" I pushed away from Ayal, straining my ears and standing on tiptoe.

The sun had just begun to rise, its first tentative rays sneaking across the horizon. Had I conjured the sound in my mind? So many times over the past weeks I had imagined the phantom of Talia's cry—

"*Ima!*" The second plaintive call sounded so much like Ari's voice that I moved toward it without conscious decision. Grateful for the growing light, I stepped over mangled tents, blackened baskets, and smashed pots in my singular determination to reach the child.

My heart lodged in my throat when I saw a tiny boy, smaller than Ari and Dov, crouched in the dirt as if he had abandoned hope of anyone coming to his aid. His face and hair were covered in sooty ash and mud, tears streaking through the mess. "*Ima,*" he said, gesturing to the collapsed tent behind him.

Half of the tent was burned. A wagon had toppled over the other half, crates and baskets spilling from its carcass. Someone must have tried to escape with their belongings at the height of the storm but then broken an axle, toppling the tent in the process.

I knelt and opened my arms to the boy. Without hesitation he walked into them, leaning his head against my shoulder.

"*Ima,*" he repeated. "Under there." There was no movement in the flattened tent. A sick feeling churned in my gut. Had his mother burned? Or been crushed under the weight of the wagon and its contents?

Poor, sweet boy. How long had he waited here, alone and terrified? I swept a hand over his face, trying to remove some of the tear-stained soot from his skin, then brushed my fingers through his hair to dislodge the ash and mud. The color of his hair was highlighted by the first rays of dawn. It was golden. Lighter than any hair I had ever seen before.

I implored my husband with a look. "I think his mother is inside."

"I don't think she could . . ." He swept a hand over his face.

"We must try. Even if there is only a chance." With a soft command to the boy to stay put, I grabbed the corner of the closest crate and yanked. It refused to yield.

Ayal joined me, and together we tugged at the soggy fallen tent. The charred fabric gave way but led only to more soot-stained baskets and pots. We moved aside a few of the smaller crates but found only singed rugs and blankets, smashed pots, and sand.

Ayal worked to move two large wine amphorae, fractured but still leaking their sweet contents into a bloody puddle in the sand. Another large crate, smashed and revealing a cache of weapons and fine Egyptian armor, lay in my path. My foot touched something soft and yielding. A body?

Energy surged into my bones as I pressed my hand onto the spot. "Ayal! Here!" I tore at the fabric, which revealed a bare and bloodied leg, encircled with a silver beaded anklet. A silver chain, lined with tiny bells, that I had seen many times—on the ankle of the woman who had stolen my child. My heartbeat thundered in my ears. "Dvorah? Dvorah! Can you hear me?"

Hot tears dripped down my face as I tore at the splintered crate that anchored the wagon to the ground and held Dvorah captive beneath its weight. Bracing myself, I wedged my bloodied fingers beneath the corner of the bed and pulled with all my might. Large hands pushed me aside. Ayal groaned as he strained to lift the wagon.

"Careful! Talia may be under here too!" I dug my fingers into my hair, which floated about, unbound, in the ash-laden morning breeze.

Desperation on his face, Ayal heaved again with a loud grunt. The wagon gave way and the crate slid off to the side, toppling onto the sand and spilling the rest of its golden spoils. He whipped a dagger from his belt, sawed a hole in the wet fabric, and tore it open. A woman, curled on her side, became visible.

"Is it her?"

With the utmost care, Ayal rolled the woman onto her back. It was Dvorah, the side of her face blistered and hair singed.

I covered my mouth against the instinct to cry out. "Is she . . . ?"

Ayal leaned over her, placed a hand on her chest. His eyes widened. "No. She is alive." He brushed a hand across the un-burned half of her face. "The wagon must have struck her on the head. She is unconscious."

My knees wobbled.

"Oh, no." Ayal sucked in a sharp-edged breath, then lifted tormented eyes to mine. "Shira—"

A small, still bundle lay on the ground, half hidden by the remnants of the tent and protected in the curve of Dvorah's body. A little foot poked from the bundle.

Ayal uncovered my daughter, whose face, although covered in soot, was untouched by flames. He lifted Talia and cradled her close to his chest. "Please. Please, Yahweh. Forgive me," he whispered.

A tiny flutter of her long, dark eyelashes was all it took to knock the breath from my body. My legs gave way, and I sagged to the ground in relief.

50

DVORAH

My skin is on fire!
I lifted my hand to stop the flames from eating me alive, but someone pushed it away, preventing me from assuaging the pain. I cursed the interruption, cursed the person who caused it. Why would someone want me to keep burning? Who would be so hateful?

I struggled against the blackness behind my eyelids, forcing them to open, knowing that I would see fire and smoke, but instead I saw a billowing tent ceiling, one that was not alive with fire, not toppling in on me and drowning me in smoky constriction.

Where is Matti? I attempted to echo my screaming thoughts out loud, but a thousand needles clawed the side of my face, sparking the burn to life again. I moaned his name, and my throat flamed as if I had swallowed coals.

A gentle hand brushed against my hair, and a soothing whisper urged me to calm down, reassuring me that Matti was safe. My body relaxed as the voice hummed a wordless tune. *My son. My boy is safe.*

Slowly, the blurred scenes of memory linked together—flashes of lightning cracking the sky in constant succession, so bright it seemed like the middle of the day; the slam of heat and light jolting the ground nearby, fire chewing a hole in the tent wall; and then something plowing into the tent, bringing it down on my head and trapping me beneath its weight. I had struggled against the sucking blackness that threatened to pull me under, but I couldn't see Matti and I could not move. I called to him as smoke clogged my lungs. The baby was still in my arms, I felt her warmth against my chest even as the flames crept closer to us.

Another wave of unconsciousness tugged at me, calling me to let go and rest. *Just a moment . . .* I curled my body around the baby . . . *just a moment of peace.*

"Dvorah?" A voice called to me from beyond the veil. "Can you hear me?"

A flicker of light beckoned me to open my eyes. An indistinct form hovered over me, silhouetted by the light of an oil lamp.

"Dvorah?" Familiarity screeched into my mind. Shira's voice. Shira's face close to mine.

I shrank back against the soft bed and flicked my gaze around the tent in which I was held captive. It looked familiar. A wall-hanging decorated with bright greens and blues hung nearby, the same one I had noticed the last time I had been here—this was Shira's tent.

Alarm circulated through my body. I struggled against the heaviness in my limbs and the raging pain that speared my left leg. Shira put a hand on my chest, pressing me back onto the bed. Her bed. The bed on which I left her to be . . .

"You are safe here. But you must not move."

Why was she speaking in such gentle tones? As if I were a laboring mother she was attempting to calm with soothing words. I opened my mouth to speak, but my cheek flash-burned again and I could not prevent tears from trickling down my face.

She smoothed the hair off my forehead with incomprehensible tenderness. "There now. Matti is just fine. Your cheek is badly blistered, and you must have inhaled smoke. It may take some time for you to speak without pain."

My pulse raced, and my breath came in short gasps. I begged the gods for an escape, and my eyes wheeled around, searching for the door.

"I'm so sorry that your lovely hair was burned." A pinch formed between her green eyes. "We will have to cut the other side to match. But it will grow."

She was worried about my hair? I wanted to scream at her. *What kind of foolish woman are you? I left you to be destroyed by Hassam! I endangered Ari and Dov! I stole your baby!*

Talia! With desperation, I turned my head to the side, searching for her on the bedroll in the corner. Shira's gaze trailed mine.

"Are you looking for the baby?"

I blinked confirmation.

"She is with Ayal." Her haunted look revealed little, so I questioned her with a painful lift of my brows. *Is she alive?*

With a shuddering sigh, she nodded. "Yes. Talia is alive. She inhaled smoke as well and is still struggling to breathe with ease. But I believe she will recover." Shira squeezed her eyes shut. "For a moment there, however, I thought she was gone. I thought I had lost my daughter all over again."

Her eyes fluttered open, and she gripped the loose braid that hung over her shoulder. Suddenly, she stood and backed away from the bed. "Why?" She echoed my own thoughts. "I have scoured every inch of my mind to understand your actions. You left me here to be ravaged by your husband's brother—" She drew a breath through her nose. "Thanks be to Yahweh for rescuing me in time."

I furrowed my brow, but even that tiny movement stung like a scorpion's lash against my cheek.

"I will tell you the story later." She answered my unasked question with a hint of uncharacteristic smugness in her expression. "Hassam was taken to the elders. I was not the only woman attacked that night. Two other women were murdered on their sleeping mats, as well as a number of men who were standing guard. He was sentenced to immediate death by stoning."

I breathed a sigh of relief without a whisper of guilt. I had spent these last several weeks looking over my shoulder, startling at every male voice, seeing Hassam in every shadow.

She watched my reaction, and her face softened. "You are glad he is gone?"

I dipped my chin slowly.

"Did you mean for me to be violated and killed that night?"

Deciding it was worth the agony, I shook my head.

Tears shimmered in her eyes. "I could not believe that you did. No matter how much you hated me, it was hard to believe that a woman would offer up another to such evil."

My mother's hardened features flashed across my memory. *"You'll do what the master tells you. Just like I did when I was your age. Just like I am doing now. Survival is what matters, little Dvorah."* I blinked against the remembrance of her callous words when she'd offered up her daughter to be sold in the brothel that had mangled her own soul.

"I forgive you."

The words that cut into my bitter memories were clear, their meaning plain, but disbelief screwed my face into a painful scowl. What was she trying to do? Manipulate me? Make herself look righteous before sending me to the elders to be condemned like Hassam?

She leaned down until she was a handspan from my face. "I have had two days to think. Two days to weigh what I would say when you awakened. And here it is—I forgive you."

As she watched my silent astonishment, she smiled, a hint of tease lifting her thin brows. "You don't believe me, do you?"

I pursed my lips. Of course I didn't believe her.

"Dvorah, since the day we met, you've manipulated me, humiliated me, and undermined me." She folded her arms and cocked her head to one side, her braid slipping over her shoulder. "You did not know anything about me. You did not know the wounds I carried. I think perhaps you thought I considered myself better than you in some way, or that I was out to take what you wanted."

You do think you are better than me.

She sighed, resignation in the sound. "But I did not know you either. All I saw was someone out to destroy me, not another woman whose heart was hurting too."

She placed a soft hand on mine. "I have a feeling you and I are more alike than you know. From some of the things you said, and from your actions with Ayal, I sense that you . . . well . . ." Her eyes radiated grief. "Let us just say that Hassam was not the first man to attack me. But he was the one who did not succeed."

A few scattered hints laced together in my head. Her skittishness around Ayal and men in general, the inexplicable drive to please everyone around her. I doubted she could fathom the horrors of my own past, but yes, we had something in common.

She nodded slowly, confirmation in her expression. "But here is the difference between you and me, Dvorah. I tried to protect myself by pretending that it never happened, which only caused me more misery, because I blamed myself for what that Egyptian did. I let him win by lying to myself about who I really was. But I am learning to stop defining myself by my past and by the evil inflicted on me by others. I refuse to allow bitterness to hold me in bondage. So, I forgive you." She fussed with the linen sheets that covered me, gently tucking them under my chin. "I don't know what you have been through, Dvorah. But there has to be a reason you took Talia—and it was not only jealousy, was it?"

I closed my eyes against her scrutiny. I had thought having Talia, feeling her little body next to me day and night, would blunt the pain of the baby I miscarried after the Levites killed Tareq. But every time I looked at Talia's sweet face, every time she laid her head against my chest and slept, Shira's agony played across my vision.

There was nothing that could alleviate the anguish of seeing my precious infant daughter—so tiny, so still—lying on the bed after my body had betrayed me. I had blamed the Levites and their murder of my husband, but something had not felt right for days beforehand, and I was only five months into my pregnancy. Stealing Talia had not stitched up the gaping wound in my heart, it had only sharpened the edges—and hurt Shira.

Realization flooded through me. *I regret hurting Shira.* She was correct that I did not know her. I had judged her harshly and assumed she had done the same to me. I tried to steal her husband, led a monster to her tent, and kidnapped her child, yet here she sat, forgiveness on her lips and compassion in her touch. Tears spilled over, the salt of regret stinging my wounds anew. I welcomed the torture as atonement for my actions.

"You must rest now," she said. "Matti is with Kiya and my mother, playing with the boys. Other than a few scratches, he was unharmed. In fact, he wriggled out of that tent and saved you with his loud cries. Yahweh led me right to him. You and I have much to discuss, but for now, let me say this—I am a terrible weaver, Dvorah." A rueful laugh slipped past her lips. "The pieces that I make tend to have quite a few dropped threads. But I refuse to let those black spots have control over the pattern. I will let *Yahweh* determine the design. He is a much better artist than I."

I wrinkled my brow. What was this crazy woman talking about?

She leaned down to cup my untouched cheek in a gentle palm, her green-gray eyes full of tenderness. "I don't know what happened to you. I hope that someday you will trust me enough to tell me. But I do know you have been holding on to bitterness that nearly destroyed you. It nearly destroyed me. Release it, Dvorah. Let it fade into a memory. Lay your broken pieces down before Yahweh and let him make you into something new."

How could such a thing be possible? Just let it go? The drive to survive, and to take back what was mine, had been the only thing keeping me from splitting in two these past months. Why would Yahweh care anything for me, anyhow?

"You have a beautiful son, Dvorah. Matti is so sweet, so gentle—in spite of the things I suspect he has endured." Her voice grew stronger, laced with unrelenting conviction. "But if you continue to cling to those black threads from your past, you will destroy him too."

The change in her was striking. When had timid, self-effacing Shira become this outspoken, courageous woman? I had seen glimpses of her resilience as we delivered babies, but now the extent of it awed me. What kind of strength did it take to forgive someone like me?

"Sleep now. I'll be back in the morning to change your bandages." She turned to leave.

With sudden desperation, I wanted to speak, to explain my

actions, but even swallowing was agony. I snapped my fingers to catch her attention.

She spun around, baffling concern for me evident in her expression.

I am sorry, I mouthed.

"I know." She brushed a tear from her cheek. Before she slipped out the door, she stopped and looked over her shoulder. "Oh, and Dvorah? Thank you."

Startled, I lifted my brows.

"Without your body shielding her, Talia would have been crushed. Thank you for saving my daughter's life."

51

SHIRA

A northern wind, mingled with the satisfying scent of incense from the Mishkan, washed across my face as I emerged from my tent into the still, rose-tinted morning.

The hills around this valley were painted white by the brush of manna on their slopes, but even that could not disguise the vibrant green of date palms and velvet hills dotted with sheep and goats.

After a lingering kiss that had sparked memories of our wedding night, Ayal had gone ahead to gather manna, leading Talia by the hand. Since discovering the use of her chubby legs, she refused to be carried. She squatted in the long grass to explore, and Ayal mirrored her motion, highlighting his tendency to cater to her whims. She giggled and swished a hand through the drifting grains, enchanted by the swirl of white in the breeze.

Since the moment he had lifted her from the ashes and pleaded for her life, he had loved her as his own. The storm had burned away more than just rebellion that day; it had washed away the blame Ayal had assigned an innocent child for her mother's sins.

A shriek of delight slid from her lips as he swung her onto his shepherd-strong shoulders, causing sweet tears to blur my vision for a moment. The boys slipped past me to catch up to their father, Ari in the lead. Dov returned to slip his arm about my waist and urge me to "hurry, *Ima*" before bounding after his brother and challenging him to a race. Dov was reveling in his new freedom from the bandages on his scarred hands.

A brief image of Ari and Dov with broad shoulders and wide chests flitted through my mind. These sweet boys would never know the humiliation of slavery, never feel the lash of Pharaoh's whip against their backs. They would walk as free men on the ground promised to our forefathers, raise their families in the towns promised to the Levites, and serve in the Mishkan like Ayal.

Even now, twelve spies, one from each tribe, were making their way through the heart of Canaan to bring back firsthand reports of its resources and the obstacles that lay before us.

But Yahweh had brought us this far, hadn't he? Preserved our people for hundreds of years? Rescued us from Pharaoh and led us through the depths of the sea? Mosheh continued to assure us that Yahweh had already prepared the way before us, and I, for one, believed it was true.

This lush valley, with its winding river, numerous fresh streams, and trees heavy with fruit, had cradled a large village. But the houses were empty and the fields overgrown, as if the entire population had heard we were coming, loaded up their belongings, and disappeared.

Would that be what the spies would encounter in the Land?

Empty villages, homes ready to be reinhabited? Crops ripening for the harvest in a few months? My hopeful imagination ascribed a bit of the former glory of fertile Egypt to this unknown land: swaying palms, vibrant flowers of every hue, crystal waters, and verdant fields.

What would it be like? To plant my roots deep in the soil of my new home and watch my children branch into their own families? To help birth the first generation in our own land—the first of a thousand promised to our people? This new nation was still struggling to embrace its identity, and that of the *gerim* adopted into the seed of Avraham—but there was beauty in the union.

Dvorah emerged from my mother's tent, limping, manna basket in hand. I smiled to hide the instinctive urge to wince at the permanent damage to her beautiful face. The screaming red scars were still angry after all these weeks, and her thick hair was trimmed just below her ears—but she was alive.

"Shalom! Coming with us to gather?"

She scowled, the move accentuating her disfigurement.

"I am!" Jumo jogged past with a playful pat to my head and a smirk over his shoulder.

I mimicked Dvorah's glare, and he responded with a ridiculous expression that rivaled those devised by my four-year-old sons. But who could be annoyed by Jumo? His sweetness was, as Kiya had said, like honey to a swarm of bees. No one could resist.

"Does he never act like a grown man?" Dvorah's breathy comment was tinged with condescension.

My hackles rose at her criticism of the friend I considered a brother. "Jumo has endured more than you can ever imagine, Dvorah. He is enjoying a freedom now that he never knew as a child. As if he were born all over again."

Curiosity rose in her expression as her dark eyes followed

Jumo toward my family, but she quickly cleared her face of the emotion and gave a disinterested shrug.

It would be slow, this building of trust between Dvorah and me. But since my mother had offered her and Matti a place to live, she had little choice but to endure my efforts at friendship. I had won Kiya over, had I not? If Yahweh had not yet given up on this unruly multitude, and on this fractured vessel, how could I give up on Dvorah?

"Ladies, your manna-gathering will have to wait."

Dvorah and I turned to find Reva with her hands on her hips and bead-like eyes trained on us.

"There is a woman in labor, an Ethiopian woman named Salima. She is asking for you, Shira. Says she is a friend of Kiya's."

Without hesitation, I followed.

A Note from the Author

As Kiya's story began with a question (Who were the mixed multitude that went into the wilderness with the Hebrews?), so Shira's story began with a question: What did the Hebrews do at the foot of Mount Sinai for over a year? Newly granted freedom by Yahweh and unaccustomed to life outside of Egypt, I wondered how the people, both Hebrews and foreigners (or *gerim*) adjusted to their new reality. As most students of the Bible will remember, the twelve sons of Jacob very rarely lived in unity and from their earliest days nurtured jealousy and strife within the family. Even after the Hebrews settled in the Promised Land, there are many instances of the tribes raising swords against each other and the old enmity between the brothers flaring to life hundreds of years later.

How then did these people who had lived all over the country of Egypt, many who had assimilated into its culture and religion, live together in peace at the foot of the Mountain? My guess is that they did not. We have been conditioned by Hollywood to see the Hebrews as one unified body of people, but there were so many divisions between them—divisions amplified by hundreds of years of slavery, confusion about the nature of the God of their fathers, and a tendency to turn back to the religious practices they had known in Egypt. It must have been a monumental task to organize such a mob, to convey clear directions, to explain Moses' motivations, to counteract false religious notions, and to calm the fears of the people who had lived in bondage their whole life and, like Shira, had endured horrific things in Egypt that scarred their hearts.

Besides, anytime there is a group of people living in close quarters with not much to do, there will be contention. Poor Moses was so busy dealing with all the whining and bickering going on in the camp that his father-in-law had to force him to delegate the duties. Add in anger over the slaughter of three thousand after the worship of the Golden Calf and the special position that Levites were granted, and I have no doubt there was some grumbling going on in those tents (Psalm 106:25) against the Levites, against Moses, and perhaps against the mixed multitude who camped on the edges—hangers-on who hadn't assimilated with any tribe, or who weren't yet accepted, or who were there for less-than-honorable reasons.

During this time, one of the most unique building projects of all time was undertaken. Yahweh could certainly have miraculously provided a complete and perfect Tabernacle (*Mishkan*, which means "dwelling place"). But instead he invited Israel to be a part of the work, to come together in their first act of unity as a nation and build it together. They responded by donating so many goods that Moses told them to stop giving! Much of Pharaoh's gold and silver was put to good use out there in the wilderness.

And yet, after working together to build a beautiful portable sanctuary in which the Dwelling Presence of the Most High would reside among them, as soon as they left the mountain, the whining, fussing, and rebellion kicked up again, resulting in fiery anger singeing the edges of camp (Numbers 11), a reminder that the God of Grace is also the God of Justice, and that it was he who placed Moses and Aaron in leadership before them, a divine act of protection for the people he loved. Unfortunately, the lesson was not well learned, and the people of Israel continued to balk God's direction, protective laws, and the men he had placed in authority over them all throughout the forty years of wandering.

Turning my attention from Egypt to the Wilderness was a challenging task, as there is very little physical evidence of the Exodus between Egypt's boundaries and Israel's. There were no temples, no cities, no grand obelisks—just a horde of nomadic people, and their livestock, living in tents. And just like the timing of the Exodus, the route they took is obscured by time and arguments between scholars. There are tantalizing clues within the pages of the Word for those who are interested in searching them out, as I would encourage every reader to do; but just as I think Yahweh hid the name of the Pharaoh for his purposes, I have a suspicion the real location of the Mountain was obscured to discourage veneration of the created instead of the Creator, just as Yeshua did at the transfiguration (Matthew 17). Instead of building shrines and making pilgrimages to a mountain, we should be worshipping the One who created that mountain and graciously spoke his laws to his people from its summit (Deuteronomy 4:11-14) even if it terrified them.

Young Miryam shows up in Exodus 2, keeping watch over her brother's floating basket, and then again as an old woman, a prophetess, and an influential woman whose strong opinions later lead to undesirable consequences (Numbers 12). We have little clue as to the rest of her life. Some rabbinic sources insist that the venerable midwives who stood against Pharaoh, Shifrah and Puah, were none other than Yocheved and Miryam, and although I do not subscribe to that conjecture, the thought did spark my imagination—which is why I chose to make Miryam an apprentice to them instead, perhaps inspired by watching her mother protect her brother all those years ago and convinced, as Shira is, that every life is precious.

I am still astounded that this journey began with just me (and my laptop) wandering into the wilderness and has grown into an army of people marching alongside me, supporting me, refreshing me, sustaining me, and encouraging me to not give in when the way seems daunting.

My husband, Chad, my partner for nineteen years, leads the way with loving sacrifice for his wife and kids and indulges my extreme right-brain tendencies to the best of his extreme left-brain ability. You love me, sweetheart.

Mom and Dad supported and encouraged me all along, raised me with a love of learning and books, encouraged my independent and (quietly) curious mind, and allowed me to pursue my passions. I am eternally grateful they were chosen to be my parents.

My precious children, Collin and Corrianna, are so patient with their introvert mama and force me out of my writing closet and into the sunshine, and tell everyone, including random strangers, to buy my books.

Tammy Gray, the best of writing partners, has invaluable honesty and talents. She challenges me, encourages me, and inspires me to stretch myself beyond my self-imposed boundaries. Shira's story would not be the same without her insight.

The rest of my fabulous Iron Quills ladies bless my life and stories every Monday night. Lori Bates Wright, whose generous heart, sparkling dialogue, and story of courage and sacrifice is an inspiration. Dana Red, whose depth and wisdom and love of language is invaluable to our group. Laurie Westlake, whose encouragement to step forward and accept God's calling has given me new confidence to walk a path I had been reluctant to embrace.

Nicole Deese is my accomplice in nightly after-hours writing shenanigans. Her encouragement, advice, and keen eye for character development has become essential to my writing process. We critique, we laugh, we color youth flowers.

Juli Williams always knows the right questions to ask, the right words to say, and how to round up the troops. She's the E to my I. I'm so grateful we are kindred spirits.

Laura McClellan offered her beautiful home as a retreat one weekend so I could immerse myself in Shira's world and read the entire book out loud to myself without interruption or onlookers questioning my sanity.

All these experts have lent me their wisdom: Camellia May, whose willingness to critique my midwife scenes was invaluable for this woman who has never given birth, nor assisted with such. Dr. Terrence Espinoza, who patiently answers my questions about biblical history and the Hebrew language. Dr. Valerie Gorman, who played along with my hypothetical ancient medicine procedure questions and willingly shared her knowledge. Any mistakes regarding the arts of midwifery, biblical history, the Hebrew language, and medicine are purely my own.

Eugene and Heather Johnson allowed me to spend some time with their sheep and answered my questions about birthing and herd behavior. Heather Hardin shared her shepherding knowledge and the sweetness of the ewe/lamb connection from her experience assisting with deliveries.

Thanks to all the beautiful Desert Wanderers who enthusiastically support the OUT FROM EGYPT series, with special thanks to Amanda Geaney for being such a champion for biblical fiction and the fabulous team that made my first launch party the best launch party that ever was: Ashley, Anni, Sam, Elisabeth, Julie, Shelley, Gretchen, Karla, Shanya, Trina, Juli, Cassi, Jessica, Luci, and Graci.

Beta readers Karla Marroquin, Kristen Roberts, and Ashley

Espinoza gave me honest feedback and shared their appreciation for Shira's story.

Tamela Hancock Murray, the best agent an author could be blessed with, is so encouraging and supportive. Raela Schoenherr, Charlene Patterson, and Jen Veilleux offered their talent and editing expertise to ensure that Shira's story is the best it could be. Jennifer Parker's breathtaking cover designs are second to none. Noelle Buss, Amy Green, Brittany Higdon, and the entire team at Bethany House have supported and encouraged me through this new adventure with such warmth and expertise. I am still pinching myself that I am allowed to call myself a Bethany House author.

And finally, to all the readers who took a chance on reading a debut author and shared your thoughts, e-mails, and hearts with me, I am honored that my work is in your hands.

This army of supporters just keeps growing—there are so many that I cannot name them all, but each is valuable and I am grateful to my Father for every single one.

QUESTIONS FOR CONVERSATION

1. Shira struggles through indecision about the calling on her life and allows doubts, fears, and her past to affect her choices. What things have you felt "created" or "called" to do? How have you experienced doubt in that calling? What joys have you experienced by embracing your calling?

2. After hundreds of years in Egypt, the Hebrews were only beginning to learn about who Yahweh was and how they were expected to behave as his people. What new insights did you gain about Yahweh? About the Hebrews? About yourself?

3. Shira discovers that Dvorah and some of the other midwives were using charms and amulets as they delivered babies, a holdover from their years in Egypt where these tokens were considered imperative during childbirth to protect mothers and babies. Throughout the early history of Israel, the people continued to run back to use such things, refusing to trust fully in the God who brought them out of Egypt. When have you been temped to trust in something (or someone) other than God?

4. Reva tells Shira that although "you may not have any children of your own body . . . every baby guided to birth by your hands will be a child of your heart." When have you experienced loving someone not "of your flesh" but "of your heart" through adoption, friendship, or other means? How does this reflect God's heart?

5. Shira, Ayal, and Dvorah are all dealing with the wounds of their pasts in different ways. When have you held onto pain instead of surrendering it to the Lord? How did it affect your relationships with others?

6. When they were frightened that Mosheh had died at the top of the mountain, the people of Israel coerced Aharon to build a golden idol, most probably a statue of Apis or Hathor, venerated mediators to the gods in Egypt. When have you rebelled against God? What did his correction look like in that instance? How did you see God's grace when you repented?

7. Shira endures false accusations from Dvorah and from Ayal's sisters. When have you experienced wounding at the hands of other women? Did you have a Kiya to encourage and comfort you? How can you work to build other women up in your circle of influence?

8. Have you ever had a person like Reva who speaks truth into your life? If so, how did he or she impact you? If not, what difference might it have made during a trying circumstance?

9. Shira discovers that she was allowing trauma from her past to define her and was blaming herself for things that were not her doing. When have you held onto "black threads"

from your own past that affected your behavior and relationships? What steps did you take to be free from self-condemnation? What lies about yourself have you had to replace with truth?

10. Ayal had a tendency to hide out from his problems instead of dealing with them head-on. When have you avoided confrontation? What consequences did it have?

11. The word for the congregation at Mount Sinai in Greek is *ekklesia* (meaning "assembly" or "called out ones"), which is the same word used for the church in the New Testament. What similarities do you see between the ancient Hebrews and the modern church? What does being "called out" mean to you?

12. Although Kiya is now part of Israel through the Covenant and through marriage, she is still regarded as an outsider. When have you felt like an outsider? Who reached out to you or defended you, like Shira does for Kiya in that situation?

13. Shira has difficulty seeing herself for who she really is and accepting her worth and strength even when the people around her assure her of her talents and positive attributes. When have you been blind to your own strengths? How did you learn to see yourself more clearly?

14. The next book in the OUT FROM EGYPT series takes place forty years in the future, at the end of the Wilderness Wandering. The Bible is fairly silent on these years in the desert. What do you think happened during that time? What differences do you think you will see in the Hebrews in the next book? How do you think Shira and Kiya will have changed?

When she is not homeschooling her two sweet kids (with a full pot of coffee at hand), **Connilyn Cossette** is scribbling notes on spare paper, mumbling about her imaginary friends, and reading obscure, out-of-print history books. There is nothing she likes better than digging into the rich, ancient world of the Bible and uncovering buried gems of grace that point toward Jesus. Her novel *Counted With the Stars* won the 2013 Frasier Contest and was a semifinalist in the 2013 ACFW Genesis Contest. Although a Pacific Northwest native, she now lives near Dallas, Texas. Connect with her at www.connilyncossette.com.

More Biblical Fiction

Egyptian slave Kiya leads a miserable life. When terrifying plagues strike Egypt, she chooses to flee with the Hebrews. Soon she finds herself reliant on a strange God and falling for a man who despises her people. Will she turn back toward Egypt or find a new place to belong?

Counted With the Stars by Connilyn Cossette
OUT FROM EGYPT #1
connilyncossette.com

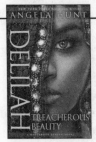

Abandoned and forced to beg for food to survive, Delilah vows to one day defeat the men who have taken advantage of her. When she meets Samson, she knows he is the key to her victory. To become a woman of prominence, she must win, seduce, and betray the hero of the Hebrews.

Delilah: Treacherous Beauty by Angela Hunt
A DANGEROUS BEAUTY NOVEL
angelahuntbooks.com

Only two men were brave enough to tell the truth about what awaited the Hebrews in Canaan: Caleb and Joshua. This is their thrilling story, from the toil of slavery in Egypt through the trials of the wilderness to the epic battles for the Promised Land.

Shadow of the Mountain: Exodus by Cliff Graham
SHADOW OF THE MOUNTAIN #1
cliffgraham.com

You May Also Enjoy . . .

Roman Tribune Clavius is assigned by Pilate to keep the radical followers of the recently executed Yeshua from stealing the body and inciting revolution. When the body goes missing despite his precautions, Clavius sets out on a quest for the truth that will shake not only his life but echo throughout all of history.

Risen: The Novelization of the Major Motion Picture by Angela Hunt
angelahuntbooks.com

This powerful series brings the books of Ezra and Nehemiah to vivid life, capturing the incredible faith of these men and their families as they returned to God after the Babylonian exile. This story of faith and doubt, love and loss, encompasses the Jews' return to Jerusalem and their efforts to rebuild both God's temple and the city wall amid constant threat.

THE RESTORATION CHRONICLES: *Return to Me, Keepers of the Covenant, On This Foundation* by Lynn Austin
lynnaustin.org

⬧ BETHANYHOUSE